Red-Hot Revenge

*Revenge is a dish best served red-hot
with passion!*

Three passionate novels!

In October 2006 Mills & Boon bring
back two of their classic collections,
each featuring three favourite
romances by our bestselling authors...

RED-HOT REVENGE

The Greek Tycoon's Revenge
by Jacqueline Baird
The Millionaire's Revenge
by Cathy Williams
Ryan's Revenge by Lee Wilkinson

MORE THAN A MISTRESS

His Virgin Mistress by Anne Mather
Claiming His Mistress by Emma Darcy
Mistress on His Terms
by Catherine Spencer

Red-Hot Revenge

THE GREEK TYCOON'S REVENGE
by
Jacqueline Baird

THE MILLIONAIRE'S REVENGE
by
Cathy Williams

RYAN'S REVENGE
by
Lee Wilkinson

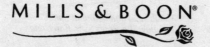

MILLS & BOON®

MILLS & BOON and MILLS & BOON with the Rose Device
are registered trademarks of the publisher.
Harlequin Mills & Boon Limited,
Eton House, 18-24 Paradise Road, Richmond, Surrey, TW9 1SR

RED-HOT REVENGE © by Harlequin Enterprises II B.V., 2006

The Greek Tycoon's Revenge, The Millionaire's Revenge and
Ryan's Revenge were first published in Great Britain by Harlequin
Mills & Boon Limited in separate, single volumes.

The Greek Tycoon's Revenge © Jacqueline Baird 2002
The Millionaire's Revenge © Cathy Williams 2002
Ryan's Revenge © Lee Wilkinson 2002

ISBN 10: 0 263 84970 8
ISBN 13: 978 0 263 84970 7

05-1006

*Printed and bound in Spain
by Litografía Rosés S.A., Barcelona*

THE GREEK TYCOON'S REVENGE

by

Jacqueline Baird

Jacqueline Baird began writing as a hobby when her family objected to the smell of her oil painting, and immediately became hooked on the romantic genre. She loves travelling and worked her way around the world from Europe to the Americas and Australia, returning to marry her teenage sweetheart. She lives in Ponteland, Northumbria, the county of her birth, and has two teenage sons. She enjoys playing badminton, and spends most weekends with husband Jim, sailing their Gp.14 around Derwent Reservoir.

CHAPTER ONE

'I'M NOT even going to get to first base, am I, honey?'

Eloise's luscious lips parted over even white teeth in a stunning smile, her green eyes sparkling with amusement. 'No, Ted. You're not.' She shook her head, her red-gold hair swaying gently around her slender shoulders, and not being able to stop herself, she laughed out loud at the exaggerated woebegone expression on her companion's face.

'I knew it. When your luck is out, it's out,' Ted Charlton stated in his deep American drawl. 'But what the hell? Eloise you're a great companion, and we can still talk—more than I could ever do with my ex-wife, that's for sure.'

Ted had told her over the meal that he was in the process of getting divorced for the third time as his wife had run off with a younger man, and Eloise felt sorry for him. Probably about fifty, he was no Adonis, but his personality and wit more than made up for his homely appearance.

'*You* certainly can,' Eloise teased him. 'I think I know your life story from high school.'

'Heaven forbid—I am boring you.'

Bravely she reached out and placed her hand on his arm. 'No truly, you've led such a fascinating life. I hope I have even half as much fun.'

'A beautiful talented girl like you, the world is your oyster. It gives the old ego a boost simply to be seen out with you, and if I can help you in any way I can, I will.'

It wasn't a cast-iron contract to invest in KHE, the jewellery design company she shared with her two friends,

Katy and her husband Harry, but it was almost as good as, Eloise thought happily.

'That's very kind of you.' She beamed at her companion. She had never dined with a prospective investor in her life, and she would not have been doing it now, except Katy—who was seven and a half months pregnant—had not been feeling well. Harry, who looked after the business side of things, wanted to stay at home with his wife, but had arranged a dinner with Ted Charlton, and so Eloise had been railroaded into taking his place.

'Not kind; it's just common sense. You and your friends really have something; in a few years I can see KHE jewellery boutiques in every capital in the world.'

Eloise laughed out loud. 'Now you're exaggerating.' She was glad she had taken Harry's place; the evening was a success and the relief was enormous, both business-wise and personally…

She hadn't wanted to come. Dinner dates and dancing were not her scene. The flimsy top she was wearing was not hers, but Katy's. Eloise's preference was for casual trousers and baggy shirts, but surprisingly Ted Charlton had somehow put her at her ease, and she was amazed to realise she was actually enjoying herself.

'Maybe,' Ted said, rising to his feet. 'But how about you to take a chance on my old bones and dance with me? We can leave the business details until tomorrow, with your astute Harry around to dot the i's and cross the t's.'

For a split second she hesitated; then, rising to her feet, Eloise took his outstretched hand. 'Sure thing, Ted,' she said in an appalling attempt at an American accent and they were both laughing as they moved around the small dance floor in each other's arms.

*   *   *

Marcus Kouvaris leant back against the bar, a glass of whisky in his hand, and slid his other hand into the pocket of his trousers. The stunningly attractive blonde at his side immediately slipped her arm through his, allowing her small breasts to press against him. He flicked her a knowing, sensuous smile. They both knew where the evening would end—in bed... Nadine was a top model and a more experienced sexual athlete he had yet to meet: and he needed the relief. Marcus took a sip of his whisky and frowned.

He'd spent a great deal of the past twelve months at his villa on the Greek island of Rykos, keeping a protective eye on his Aunt Christine, his late mother's sister, and her daughter Stella, who had their permanent home there. He'd been trying to give them the comfort and support they needed after the tragic death of their husband and father, Theo Toumbis, in a car crash. Unfortunately it had seriously curtailed his sex life, and celibacy was not his style.

He was in London for a few days on private business. But he intended to bed the very willing Nadine every night, though he was far too wary a male to let her know that. Marcus took another swallow of the amber nectar, glanced idly around the room, and stilled.

It could have been a couple of frozen peas rubbing against his arm for all the effect Nadine's breasts had on him. His teeth clenched and his dark eyes narrowed in angry recognition on the couple seated at the table on the other side of the dance floor. The man he dismissed with a fleeting glance. But the female...the female was Eloise...innocent, virginal Eloise, who blushed when a man so much as looked at her!

As Marcus watched, he saw the girl lean forward and place a hand on the much older man's arm, and smile up at her companion.

Marcus's firm lips curved in a hard cynical smile; it

confirmed what his informant had told him. Eloise was certainly her *mother's* daughter…the mother who had conned his Uncle Theo out of a great deal of money with Eloise's assistance. The reason Marcus was in London was to gain recompense for his aunt and cousin.

The money was not important to him with his wealth; supporting his aunt and cousin didn't even dent his finances. But it was a matter of principle. Nobody stole from him or his family and walked away free.

On a more personal level he harboured a nagging doubt that Eloise had played him for a sucker with her professed virginity. He'd respected her innocence and restrained himself to some light kisses the last time they met, only to have her disappear without a word. Nobody made a fool of Marcus Kouvaris and got away with it…

His dark eyes narrowed on the object of his thoughts. Eloise, if anything, was even more beautiful than she had been at nineteen, and when she rose to her feet his dark eyes trailed over her in a blatant male appreciation. Her upper body was clad in a gold camisole that revealed the creamy mounds of her breasts, before slipping into the waistband of a long black crepe skirt, demure in its slightly flared style until she moved. Then an enticing length of leg was exposed by the subtle slit in one side. A gold belt heightened the whole elegant effect, emphasising her tiny waist, and three-inch gold sandals completed the picture.

He felt an instant stirring in his groin and it had nothing to do with the woman he was with. His dark eyes narrowed angrily. Dammit! But Eloise was some woman. The epitome of femininity, she moved with an instinctive grace, and when she smiled her incredible green eyes glowed, and further highlighted the pale, almost translucent skin that contrasted so stunningly with the fiery red hair.

Five years! Instinctively the hand in his pocket curved

into a fist, his fingers tingling. He could remember as if it were yesterday the silken softness of her skin, the feel of her in his arms, and his body hardened further. He tore his gaze away from Eloise and looked at her companion. He recognised the man from the financial papers. Ted Charlton, a wealthy American entrepreneur who had recently parted from his wife.

A thunderous frown creased his smooth brow. Marcus had intended giving Eloise the benefit of the doubt; she had been very young and probably under her mother's influence. The report lying on the desk in his penthouse suite stated that KHE was a small but successful jewellery design company with a lot of potential. Reading it, Marcus had no doubt KHE was the same company his Uncle Theo had thought he was investing in, Eloise by Design. It was the same business plan and one of the same partners that had signed the contract with Theo five years ago. Eloise Baker! Even so, Marcus had been prepared to negotiate the repayment of Theo's investment from profits in a businesslike manner. But seeing Eloise dancing and laughing with the older man filled him with such fury, he changed his mind.

Marcus Kouvaris had never suffered from jealousy in his life and consequently did not recognise the emotion. But suddenly he was wishing he hadn't dismissed the investigator he had hired to find Eloise quite so finally over the telephone. The man had called him in Greece a couple of weeks ago, and said he had found Eloise, who turned out not to be Chloe's sister, but her daughter. He'd given Eloise's address in London and the name of her company. Marcus had asked if Eloise was guilty of any other frauds, and the detective had drawled she was as pure as the driven snow, with a rather nasty laugh at the end of it.

When the detective had asked if he should forward the

personal file he had on Eloise, Marcus had told him to bin it. He only needed Eloise's address. He couldn't admit even to himself, he didn't like the idea of reading a list of her lovers.

Now he decided it was time to do some investigation of his own into the elegant Eloise, and he smiled with malice as he watched the pair.

Held comfortably in the arms of her companion, Eloise glanced around. The supper club, in the heart of London's Mayfair, was the latest in place to dine. The food and service were superb, the lighting discreet, the women beautiful, and the men wealthy. She gave a contented sigh as Ted led her expertly around the small dance floor. She had conquered a personal fear, and unless she was very much mistaken Ted Charlton was going to invest in their company.

'Don't look now,' Ted said softly, close to her ear. 'But there's a man standing by the bar who's been watching you like a hawk for the past few minutes, and is now looking daggers at me.'

Of course Eloise did look. Immediately her green eyes clashed across the crowded room with narrowed black. For a long moment she was incapable of looking away. Her heart made a crazy leap in her chest. 'Oh,' she gasped, and stumbled.

Marcus tilted his arrogant head back, and arched one perfectly formed brow apparently in query, then slowly allowed his gaze to roam over her slender body with studied masculine appraisal, before returning to her face, his eyes widening in supposedly surprised recognition. His expressive features relaxed; a slow sensual smile parted his firm lips as he lifted his glass towards Eloise in acknowledgement of her presence.

Ted's arm tightened protectively around her waist, just as the music stopped. 'You know him?' he asked as he turned her away from the stranger and led her back to the table.

'You could say that.' Eloise picked up her champagne glass, with a hand that shook, and drained it before replacing it on the table. She tried to smile but her composure had taken a heck of a jolt. 'I met him in Greece on holiday years ago, but I haven't seen him since.'

'A holiday romance?' Ted prompted.

'Yes.' She sighed. 'I suppose it was.' She hadn't thought so at the time. She'd thought he was the love of her life. He was the first man Eloise had ever had a crush on—the only man, she silently admitted. They had met thrice, and then he had to leave suddenly to visit his ailing father, and she'd returned to England, and had never heard from him again. Perhaps it was just as well, as when her mother had explained Marcus Kouvaris was a financial wizard who had made a fortune from the technology boom and, unlike some, had hung on to it, and made more, Eloise knew he was well out of her reach.

'Eloise. It is Eloise Baker?' The deep, slightly accented voice was instantly recognisable, and slowly she lifted her head.

Eloise could feel the colour rise in her cheeks as involuntarily her green eyes flickered over his tall, broad-shouldered frame. Older, but he was still as incredibly attractive as ever. Thick black hair, olive-toned skin, with perfectly symmetrical features, a firm jaw and a smile guaranteed to make any woman melt...

'Eloise, yes,' she confirmed with a tentative smile. 'But Smith, not Baker,' she corrected him without thinking. At least he had remembered her first name, if not her second;

that was some consolation given he was notorious for the number of women he dated.

'Smith, of course, but it has been a long time,' Marcus said smoothly. Without realising it Eloise had admitted she'd lied. His gaze swept over her, her eyes were the green of the finest emeralds. Her cheeks were streaked with a becoming shade of pink, innocence personified.

Marcus's belly knotted. He couldn't recall ever being this angry with anyone in his life, and it took all his formidable willpower to stop himself dragging her by the glorious red hair from her seat and throttling her with it. But instead, using all his considerable charm, he added, 'Though you don't look a day older, and if it is possible even more beautiful than you were at nineteen.'

Eloise could feel her face burning even brighter at his open flattery. 'Thank-you,' she mumbled and, tearing her gaze away from his dark compelling eyes, she finally noticed the blonde hanging on his arm.

'Allow me to introduce my friend,' Marcus said coolly, catching the direction of her gaze. 'Nadine, this is Eloise, an old friend of mine, and her companion...' Marcus turned his attention to the older man watching the exchange with astute blue eyes. 'Ted Charlton, I believe. We haven't been introduced but—' and he mentioned some financial article, and the two men shook hands.

Eloise took the slender limp hand Nadine offered her, and wasn't surprised at the other woman's cold smile. If Eloise had been on a date with Marcus, she would not have wanted company either. She could still remember how he had affected her five years ago and how heartbroken she had been when her mother insisted they had to leave the villa on Rykos before Marcus had returned to the island.

Eloise had left a note with her address in England for

Marcus with the maid. She had lived in hope for over a year that he would contact her again, but then circumstances changed her attitude and she stopped wondering and waiting for him; she had bigger things to worry about.

'Join us for a drink.' Ted made the conventional offer.

'Some other time, perhaps,' Nadine cut in before Marcus could speak and, linking her arm firmly through the tall Greek's, she smiled. 'Your friends have already eaten, Marcus, and I am starving. You did promise me dinner.' She pouted, her long red fingernails stroking down the sleeve of his jacket. 'For starters,' she purred.

Eloise suppressed a grimace of distaste at Nadine's obvious seduction technique.

'Nadine, darling, I'm sure you can wait a while.' He smiled at his girlfriend, but the tone of his voice warned her not to argue.

Seats were pulled out and another bottle of champagne ordered.

'To old friends.' Marcus raised his glass and looked directly at Eloise. Her eyes met and fused with his and for a moment she was transported back in time to a Greek island, and her heart raced again as it had then, the first time they'd met.

'And hopefully new ones,' Marcus continued, addressing Ted.

They all touched glasses, and Eloise took a hasty swallow of the sparkling liquid. She was shocked at the rush of awareness simply being in Marcus's company had aroused in her. She had thought herself over him long ago, and she was grateful for Nadine's timely contribution to the sudden silence.

'Marcus and I have known each other for almost two years and he has never mentioned you. So when did you meet him?' Nadine demanded, her gimlet eyes fixed on Eloise.

'I was on holiday with my m…sister, Chloe,' she stammered, feeling the colour rise in her face. 'We had rented a villa on the island of Rykos in Greece. Chloe was a friend of Marcus's Uncle Theo, who was the developer and had built the villa along with five others. When we held a pool party Theo brought Marcus along to the party and we…'

Marcus almost snorted in disgust. 'How is your sister?' he cut in abruptly. The detective he had hired had taken almost a year to unravel Chloe Baker's various names, before discovering the woman had never had a sister but a daughter with the name of Smith. Probably the most common surname in the English language…

Eloise glanced across the table at Marcus. Hooded dark eyes hard as steel stared back at her. Did he know she'd lied all those years ago? But her mother had insisted she called her Chloe, and pretend to be sisters. At thirty-six, Chloe was not going to admit to having a grown-up daughter, and Eloise had agreed. Or was he frightened she would tell his girlfriend all the details of their brief romance? He must really care for Nadine.

'My sister died over three years ago,' Eloise mumbled. She hated lying, and suddenly realised there was no need to any more—her mother was dead. But now was not the time or the place.

'I am sorry.' Marcus mouthed the polite response but there was a singularly lack of sympathy in his expression. 'Chloe was a quite remarkable woman.'

She was, Eloise thought sadly, and if it had not been for her mother, she would never have been able to set up in business herself, but she had never really got to know her mother well. Pregnant at seventeen by a sailor, Tom

Smith, Chloe had married him, and divorced him three months after Eloise was born. Then she had left Eloise with her grandparents to be brought up in the small Northumberland coastal town of Alnmouth and disappeared. Four years later she returned with a different name after another failed marriage, loaded down with presents for her little girl, and apparently had become a very successful businesswoman. From then on she popped in every year or so...

For Eloise her mother had been a fairytale figure, beautiful and elegant in designer clothes, bringing gifts. It was only after the death of her grandparents, when she had completed her first year in art college, that her mother had actually spent some time with her. Chloe had taken a real interest in what Eloise was doing and declared herself fascinated by her daughter's skilful designs, and even suggested they go on holiday to Greece and so they had taken their first and last holiday together on Rykos.

'Sorry, I have brought back sad memories.' Marcus rose from the table and held out his hand to Eloise. 'Come dance with me and blow away the cobwebs of the past.'

'But—' Nadine said sharply.

'Then, Nadine, we will eat, I promise.' He shot his girlfriend a brilliant smile, and a brief glance at Ted. 'With your permission, of course, old man?' he asked while clasping Eloise's hand and urging her to her feet, not waiting for an answer.

'Nadine is going to die of hunger if you don't feed her soon,' Eloise tried to joke, as Marcus slipped an arm around her waist and pulled her firmly against the long powerful length of his body.

He was taller than she remembered; she had to tilt her head back to look up at him, but that was a mistake. The years had been kind to him, and close up he was even more staggeringly handsome than she remembered. An aggressively virile, sophisticated male, he exuded an aura of raw sexuality that the formal tailored dinner suit and white silk shirt did nothing to hide, and it terrified her.

'Nadine's hunger is never for food,' he returned, a mockingly sensual smile curving his wide mouth. 'She is a model; she doesn't eat enough to feed a bird. You, on the other hand, are every man's fantasy of the female form.' His hand at her back slowly stroked up her spine and just as slowly down to settle rather low on her bottom, while his other hand clasped hers and held it firmly against his broad chest.

'Are you implying I'm fat?' she said with mock horror, fighting to appear the sophisticated woman when inside she was quaking.

Marcus let his gaze drop to the firm thrust of her obviously braless breasts against the gold fabric, and then back to her face. 'God forbid! You have the perfect figure. Full and fat are not the same thing.' And the hand he had held firm against his chest somehow contrived to be held against hers, his knuckles brushing against the soft upper swell of her breast.

She should have been horrified. She had never been this close to a man in four years, never wanted to be. But now, to her utter amazement, she felt her nipples harden against the fine silk of her top, and she had to drop her eyes to his chest to mask the sudden flare of desire that heated her face. A tiny pulse at the base of her throat was racing, and she was appalled yet secretly thrilled by her helpless response to his innately sensual masculinity.

'I do believe you are blushing, Eloise,' Marcus teased as he moved her expertly around the floor to the sexy soft tones of a well-known Barry White recording.

'It's hot in here.' She made herself look up at him.

Marcus's perceptive black eyes ran over her now scarlet face, and deliberately he tightened his arm around her, bringing her into impossibly close contact with his long, lean length. He felt the tremor in her body, and he fought to mask the cynical smile of masculine satisfaction that threatened his oh, so caring features, even as he fought to mask his own body's instant arousal. He dipped his head and whispered softly in her ear, 'And getting hotter by the minute.'

He was flirting with her, Eloise knew, and she should have been angry, but the reverse was true. The slender fingers of her hand flexed, curved into his broad shoulder, and clung. His warm breath, his hard body, the softly murmured words all conspired to turn Eloise's bones to mush; her legs felt wobbly, and her heart felt as if it would burst. It was as if the trauma of the past had been swept away and once again she was the adolescent teenager, totally besotted by the sophisticated overpowering charm of Marcus Kouvaris.

'Your girlfriend,' Eloise got out. What was Marcus trying to do to her? And in the middle of the dance floor with Nadine watching. 'Nadine,' she choked.

'Forget Nadine. I did, the moment I saw you again,' Marcus declared throatily, and observed the deepening colour in her cheeks with a cynical cool. God! The woman could blush on demand, but nothing of his thoughts showed on his chiselled features as his gaze roamed over the perfect oval of her face. 'Why did you leave me without a word, Eloise?' he asked softly, his dark eyes looking soulfully down into hers.

'But I thought you left me.' In shock at her own reactions, she answered honestly. 'I waited ten days for you to contact me. Then we had to leave.' She hadn't wanted to, but her mother had insisted. 'But I left you a note with my address and telephone number with the maid.'

'My father died from the heart attack, and by the time the funeral was over it was two weeks before I could return to the villa. It was empty, no sign of a maid or a letter.'

'I'm sorry about your father.' Eloise's green eyes shaded with compassion.

'Yes, well, it was a few years ago now.' He shrugged his broad shoulders. 'But I definitely never received a note from you, Eloise, believe me.'

With his hand stroking her back, and his expression sincere, she believed him. 'I do. These things happen,' she mumbled.

'I guess the time wasn't right for us then.' He squeezed her gently and her pulse rate went into overdrive. 'But the past is past and I am delighted to have met you again. I often wondered what happened to you,' he said smoothly.

Wondered? Some understatement; a bitter smile tightened Marcus's mouth. When he'd returned to the island and found her gone, he'd ruefully conceded she was the one that got away and tried to dismiss her from his mind. He didn't chase after women, they chased after him, but she had haunted his dreams for years. It was only after Theo's death and he was left with settling the man's affairs that he had hired someone to find her *sister* Chloe, and only recently he had discovered Eloise Smith was the daughter, not the sister, of the devious late Chloe Baker. Seeing her with Ted had finally cured him of the romantic picture he'd carried in his head of an innocent young girl forced by her wicked mother into fraud! The gods must be laughing, he thought irreverently. But he allowed none of his thoughts to show. He eased her slightly away from him.

'I would love to see you again and catch up with what

you are doing.' He gazed down into her beautiful face. 'Have dinner with me tomorrow night?' He held her closer, one long leg easing between hers, as he moved her skilfully in a turn. 'Please.' He watched the green eyes widen with a mixture of fear and excitement, and almost laughed out loud. She had good reason to fear him, the devious little witch—but her sort could never resist a challenge, he knew; he'd met enough in his time.

'Will your girlfriend mind?' The friction of his hard thigh against hers, even through the thickness of their clothes, was enough to send every nerve in her body haywire and Eloise said the first thing that entered her bemused brain.

'Not at all. Nadine and I understand each other; we are casual friends, nothing more.' And, easing her slightly away from him, he added, 'But I'm forgetting your boyfriend, Ted.' This time, Marcus could not keep the hard edge of cynicism out of his tone. 'Will he object to you dating another man?'

Eased from the close contact with his lithe body, Eloise did not know whether to be relieved or aggrieved. He aroused a host of sensations she had never thought she would experience again and she wasn't sure she wanted to. Relief won.

'You're kidding.' She chuckled. 'Ted is a charming man but he isn't my boyfriend. Tonight is a business dinner, nothing more.' That Marcus could imagine even for a moment that she would go out with a man old enough to be her father was ludicrous, and consequently she told him the truth.

'In that case, give me your telephone number.' His eyes narrowed on her laughing face and his large body tensed as he let her go. Was she up to her late mother's tricks, and so sure of success that she had readily admitted her involvement with Ted Charlton was simply business? Marcus needed to know more, but this wasn't the right time to question her, with Nadine waiting at the table for him and Ted watching Eloise like a drooling fool.

Eloise felt the sudden tension in his body, just before his arm fell from her waist; her puzzled gaze shot to his but his expression was bland. Then she realised it was because the music had stopped.

'Your number, Eloise?' Marcus murmured as, with one hand lightly in the centre of her back, he urged her towards the table.

Still in a state of shock at the unexpected meeting and her own response to Marcus, Eloise reeled off her number. 'You will never remember it,' and added, 'but our company, KHE, designer jewellery, is in the directory.'

She did not see his strong handsome face harden into disgust at the mention of designer jewellery, or the flare of white-hot fury in his dark eyes, as he stood behind her and pulled out her chair. By the time she was seated and she had recovered some slight control over her racing pulse and scattered nerves enough to join in the general conversation, and finally look at Marcus, he was all urbane charm and about to leave with Nadine.

'A very impressive man,' Ted said as Eloise watched Marcus and Nadine stroll off to where their table awaited them. The maître d' stood hovering around the pair like a mother hen. But then, a man of Marcus Kouvaris's power and wealth commanded that kind of attention wherever he went, Eloise thought wryly.

'Yes, Ted.' She sighed and turned her attention back to Ted. 'Nadine is a lucky woman.'

'No, you're wrong there, Eloise. She hasn't a hope in hell of catching Kouvaris. But you—you watch out. Take it from a man who knows his own sex. I saw the way

Kouvaris looked, and danced with you. But I have heard rumours about his womanising, and you are far too nice a lady for a man of his reputation.'

'I'll take that as a compliment,' Eloise said softly. 'But I don't think you need worry.' And, with a swift glance at the other couple, the black head touching the blonde, she grinned ruefully back at Ted. 'You're right, he's way out of my league.'

They finished off their dinner with coffee, and Ted persuaded Eloise to make a night of it, so they stayed to watch the late-night cabaret, and dance. It was a fun evening, and Eloise was yawning widely by the time Ted took her home in a taxi.

At the door of the town house where Eloise lived and worked, Ted smiled teasingly down at her. 'I won't come in, before you ask, but thank you for a lovely evening, Eloise, and you can tell your partners they have nothing to worry about. I will invest. I'll be in touch with Harry in the morning to do the deal. Okay?' Planting a brief kiss on her cheek, he said, 'Good night.'

Letting herself into the elegant entrance hall, Eloise ran lightly up the staircase, and stopped at the first floor. She glanced at her wristwatch, and grimaced. Three a.m. It was far too late to call on Katy and Harry now and tell them the good news and she turned to mount the next flight of stairs.

Strictly speaking, the house was Eloise's, but it was also the biggest asset of the company. The basement was the work room, the ground floor the showroom and offices, the first floor was Katy and Harry's apartment, the second floor Eloise's, and the attic apartment was rented by a gay couple.

Julian and Jeff were two beautiful young men. Julian earned his living as a freelance photographer and had made up a fantastic catalogue for KHE jewellery, and also talked quite a few models into wearing it, and that had been instrumental in getting the firm noticed and into several of the glossy magazines. Jeff worked in the showroom of KHE and was great at selling. The female customers adored him, and the male customers, while taking his advice, were not threatened by his beauty. For Eloise it was the ideal set-up; she loved the house and felt perfectly safe.

'Is that you, Eloise?' A stage whisper broke into Eloise's thoughts and, swinging around, she ran lightly back down the stairs and straight into the arms of Harry.

'Break out the champagne, folks. Ted is going to come in with us,' she said as Harry swung her around and into the open door of their apartment where Katy was waiting looking, thankfully, very well, if rather round.

'You're sure?' Katy grasped her arm and pulled her into the sitting room. 'Tell all.'

Half an hour later her two friends had the whole story.

'So…' Katy looked mischievous but beautiful with her black curly hair and big brown eyes; she fixed Eloise with a speculative glance. 'We can take it the business will expand, much like my waistline. But what about this Mr Kouvaris? Wasn't that the name of the chap you met, and then left you on that holiday with your mother?'

Immediately on the defensive, Eloise said, 'Marcus didn't leave me—he was called away because his father was ill, and apparently the old man died.' It was strange to be saying his name out loud after five years of trying to forget it, and stupidly she could feel herself blushing. 'It was no big deal and look, it's four o'clock in the morning. We'll talk tomorrow.'

She was still trying to convince herself of the fact ages

later lying in her queen-sized bed, unable to sleep. She did not want to take a sleeping tablet the doctor had prescribed. She hadn't used them in years, and simply seeing Marcus Kouvaris again was not going to drive her into taking one.

CHAPTER TWO

INSTEAD she practised her relaxation exercises, turned on her back, and let her mind roam freely back to her holiday in Greece.

Eloise had been carrying a tray of drinks out on to the terrace when she had first seen Marcus. He was standing next to her mother and Theo Toumbis by the edge of the swimming pool, laughing at something her mother had said. Eloise had nearly dropped the tray, such was the instant effect of his sheer male beauty on her teenage heart. Dressed casually in white shorts, and a shirt open down the front revealing his muscular chest with a sprinkling of black body hair, and long legs glazed in gold by the afternoon sun, the man looked like the reincarnation of a Greek god to Eloise's naïve eyes and she had stood transfixed simply staring at him.

'Stop loitering, *sis*, we are dying of thirst here.' Her mother's command had the ten or so people around the pool turning to look at her, including Marcus.

Eloise blushed scarlet, and for a second Marcus's eyes met hers, before she dropped her head and stepped forward.

Miraculously he appeared at her side. 'Here, let me take that. A beautiful young girl like you should be waited on, not the other way around.' And that was how it had started...

He'd introduced himself as Theo's nephew and had encouraged her to strip off the long cotton shift that concealed her white skinned, bikini-clad body, and join him in the pool. Marcus in his swimming trunks was enough to make any woman weak at the knees, and Eloise had been no exception. He had talked and teased and flirted with her and by the end of the evening he knew she was an unattached nineteen-year-old student on holiday abroad for the first time in her life with her sister Chloe who had rented the villa.

Eloise had hated lying to him, but her mother had insisted no one should know they were mother and daughter, and it had seemed a small price to pay to spend time with her mother. Eloise knew her mother loved her in her own way; she had proved it when after the funeral of her parents Chloe had not even minded that they had left all they owned to Eloise, including the house. Eloise had felt terrible, and it had taken all her powers of persuasion to get her mum to at least take the money from the sale of the house. Even so her mum suggested she set up a joint account and they could share the proceeds. Eloise happily agreed, but never touched the account until after her mother's death.

Stirring restlessly on the bed, Eloise ran the tip of her tongue over her full lips; it seemed like only yesterday she had felt the touch of Marcus's lips on hers for the first time. Sighing, she rolled over on her stomach and buried her head in the pillow, the memories coming thick and fast.

Before Marcus had finally left, well after midnight, he'd gathered Eloise gently into his arms and kissed her, and from that moment she knew she was in love.

At ten the next morning Marcus had turned up in an open-topped sports car, and whisked her away to the other side of the island.

'Come on, sweetheart.' Marcus stopped the car only a few feet away from the edge of a cliff, stepped out and was holding open the passenger door with one hand and a picnic basket in the other with a blanket over his arm. 'We're going to have a picnic.'

'Here?' Eloise glanced around the rocky outcrop not more that a yard square.

'Trust me.' Marcus grinned, and she did.

The steps were cut deep into an almost vertical cliff, with an old rope strung along the cliff face as a handrail. It was the scariest walk Eloise had ever experienced in her young life, and when she finally stepped onto the smooth sand at the base of the cliff her legs were trembling. Marcus dropped the hamper and the blanket on the white sand and gathered her into his arms.

'All right?'

Fighting to steady her erratic breathing, whether it was from the descent or the sensation of being enfolded against his hard, lean, scantily-clad body, she did not know, Eloise looked around and then up into his grinning face. 'It's perfect.' It was a totally secluded horseshoe shape of sand that led down to sparkling blue sea.

After a swim, they shared a meal of cold meat, chicken, salad, and fresh crusty bread, washed down with champagne.

'You're spoiling me.' Eloise sighed, lying back on the blanket, replete and perfectly happy.

Propped up on one elbow, Marcus's dark eyes sparkled with amusement and something more as they met hers. Suddenly the clear summer air shimmered with tension. 'This is nothing to what I would like to do for you,' he murmured huskily, the index finger of one hand gently outlining her lips. 'For your mouth,' he husked; the finger trailed down her throat, and lingered for a moment on the pulse beating madly there. 'For your elegant neck,' and then lower to the valley between her breasts. 'For your luscious breasts.' His voice thickened.

Eloise felt as though she was touched by fire, every nerve-end in her body tingling with vibrant life. She linked her hands around his neck, her fingers tangling in the silky black hair of his head. Marcus raised his head and moved so he was straddling her trembling body, and then gently brought his mouth down on hers, the tip of his tongue outlining her lips and, as her mouth opened, plunging deep into the moist sweet depths. Electric excitement thrilled through her, the rub of his thighs against the outside of her hips incredibly erotic, and as his mouth followed the path his finger had so recently taken, her excitement built higher and higher.

He buried his head in the valley between her breasts, and somehow her bikini top was no more. She trembled violently as he murmured something huskily in Greek, before his tongue licked across the crown of her breast, and very gently suckled the rosy tip in his mouth.

A lightning flare of response struck her without warning, and her body arched up against his hard, lean frame, brushing his groin in helpless response.

Marcus lifted his head, and gazed down into her dazed green eyes. 'You like that,' he husked. With one hand he stroked down from her breast to the tiny waist to lay flat on her belly. 'Tell me what more you like, my Eloise?' he demanded throatily, while his mouth found her other breast and repeated the sensual assault.

Eloise had never experienced anything like it before, yet somehow it all seemed natural—Marcus, the kiss, his touch. Tremor after tremor coursed through her veins as his other hand swept down the length of her body, from hips to thigh to calf and back up. His touch scorched her sensitive skin like a brand, and her breasts ached with a pleasure that she did not know existed, creating a need for more and more of the miraculous sensations.

His long fingers effortlessly slipped under the last scrap of material covering her nakedness, and suddenly Eloise tensed in innocent fear of where her wild emotions were leading. Her hands fell to push against his chest. 'No, no.' He was going too far, too fast...

Marcus jerked his head back, and her hands dropped to her sides. 'No. You say "No," but you want me.' His keen gaze raked the full length of her near-naked body, the pointed tips of her breasts, and then back to her eyes.

She stared up at him, her lips parted to speak. She did want him, but... Her green eyes huge, she glanced past him to the sea.

'You're not a tease, I hope?' his deep voice demanded hardily and she glanced back at him. 'I abhor women who lead a man on, lie with their body.'

'No. No.' Eloise could not bear him to look at her so cynically. 'It's just, I... Well, I haven't.' She could feel her skin getting even hotter but it was not with excitement, it was with embarrassment. He was a twenty-nine-year-old sophisticated man of the world; how could she tell him...? 'I've never, I haven't—' She lowered her lashes over her too revealing eyes, and swallowed hard. 'I'm a virgin.'

'A virgin?' he exclaimed. 'You're not protected.' His black eyes widened in stunned amazement, and then narrowed at her guileless face, the blush that suffused her skin, and a slow smile parted his sensual mouth. 'Ah,' he murmured and from that moment on his whole attitude changed.

Marcus was transformed from a sophisticated sensual male on the make, into a tender, caring companion. The rest of the day he treated her like some rare species of the female sex, though he could not stop touching her. But his touch was light on her silken skin, the few kisses they shared undemanding. When they parted later that night with a promise to meet again the next day, the kiss he pressed on her soft lips started as a gentle good night and quickly developed into a passionate embrace. But with iron self-control he ended it with a curse in Greek and a softly mouthed promise. 'I am going to make everything perfect for you, Eloise.'

Eloise went to bed that night with a head full of dreams of love and marriage, and the next morning Marcus arrived and told her his father was ill, he had to leave, she had been sad, but not unduly worried, as he'd promised to return.

Yawning wildly, Eloise rolled over onto her side and burrowing deeper under the duvet. March in England was cold. Not like Greece, she thought wryly. But then her Greek dream had ended long ago and she would do better to forget the memories, and get on with her life today. She would go out to dinner with Marcus for old times' sake, but that was all it would be, all it could be, now…

'We've done it, girls.' Harry came dashing into the basement workroom, with Jeff hot on his heels, waving a bottle of champagne, and a grinning Ted Charlton bringing up the rear.

Eloise looked up from her drawing board and Katy put the soldering tool down carefully on the workbench and slowly stood up, her eyes flicking from Harry to the older man.

'You're sure, Mr Charlton? Aren't you supposed to be looking after the showroom, Jeff?' she said sternly, but her brown eyes were alight with excitement.

'I'm sure, lady.' Ted chuckled. 'So sure I have persuaded your husband and Jeff here to close the showroom and let me take everyone out to lunch to celebrate.'

Eloise said nothing but the grin on her face said it all.

Five minutes later, the bottle of champagne was opened and the five all raised their glasses. 'To KHE, Paris. Thanks to you, Ted.' Harry made the toast.

Over lunch the deal was discussed. The money Ted was investing would be used for the creation of a KHE boutique in Paris. Better still, Ted actually knew of a property for lease on the Rue St Honoré, one of the most fashionable streets in Paris, and he reckoned if Harry got in quick it could be theirs. Harry had already made the booking for his flight to France the next day and a meeting with the owners, and he had the cheque for the first instalment of Ted's financing in his pocket.

The entry phone rang, and Eloise cast a last hasty look at her reflection in the mirrored door of the wardrobe. She grimaced slightly. She had tried for the sophisticated look, and had swept up her hair in a French pleat, and apart from the black skirt she had worn last night, she was wearing the only thing she possessed that was not casual: the suit she had bought for Katy's wedding. A fine wool jade green suit in a classic style, the jacket short and with a matching camisole underneath, the straight skirt ending an inch above her knees, and kitten-heeled black pumps on her feet. Conservative, she told herself, except for the intricately set silver and amber pendant around her neck and the matching amber earrings, both her own designs.

Katy had been right last night when she'd made Eloise borrow the gold camisole. It was way past time Eloise updated her wardrobe. But, working behind the scenes in the jewellery business designing and manufacturing, her wardrobe consisted of jeans and sweaters, and a few voluminous Indian cotton caftans, for when the weather was hot. But it was too late to worry about the state of her wardrobe now and, snatching up her purse, she dashed from the bedroom through to the sitting room to the door of her apartment, just as someone knocked on the door.

Surprised for a second, she hesitated and the knock sounded again, and she opened the door.

Marcus was leaning negligently against the doorframe, wearing a superbly elegant dark blue suit, and looking every inch the incredibly attractive, sophisticated male of her dreams.

Heat prickled her skin. 'How did you get in?' she demanded. It was not the opening she had planned, it sounded rather aggressive even to her own ears.

'Hello to you, too.' A sardonic brow arched. 'Shall I go out and start again.'

'N-no, of course not.' Eloise stammered, badly shaken by her instant response to his powerful presence.

'Relax, Eloise, your friend Harry downstairs opened the front door.' He smiled.

His smile dazzled her and, with his hand at her elbow supporting her, Eloise felt vaguely protected and actually did manage to relax slightly. 'Harry and Katy are my business partners,' she offered.

'He sounded more like your guardian.' Marcus remarked with a wry twist of his lips. 'He managed, in the space of less than a minute, to ask me who I was, where I was taking you, and what time I intended bringing you back.'

'That sounds like Harry,' Eloise confirmed with a chuckle, as they exited the outer door to the street. 'Katy and I met him when we were at art college and looking for somewhere to live. He managed the estate agents, and he took one look at Katy and fell in love. He found us an apartment, and was never away from the door until Katy agreed to go out with him, and now they are married.'

'A determined man; I like that,' Marcus offered, as he opened the passenger door of a sleek black car and ushered Eloise inside.

Starting the engine and driving off, Marcus shot her a brief sidelong glance and said, 'I intended taking you to a rather nice French restaurant, but I'm expecting a call from the west coast of America some time this evening so I've arranged for us to dine at my hotel. I hope you don't mind.'

Stilling a panicked shiver, Eloise cast a glance at his perfectly chiselled profile, Marcus wasn't a stranger and it wasn't their first date, so why was she hesitating?

'Eloise.' He flicked her a quizzical smile. 'It was either the hotel, or cancelling our dinner date.' It wasn't a lie—he was expecting a call—but also he wanted her on her own when he challenged her to explain her part in the scam her mother had pulled on his uncle.

'Yes, yes. That's perfectly all right.' She burst into speech. She was being stupid; she was twenty-four, not fourteen, and with a man who was no stranger to her, for heaven's sake, she told herself firmly.

The hotel was one of the best in London, and walking across the vast foyer with Marcus at her side, his hand gently at her elbow guiding her, she was glad she had taken time with her appearance. She was congratulating herself on her ability to mingle with the best, when Marcus stopped in front of a bank of elevators.

'Are we eating in the rooftop restaurant?' she asked, excitement bubbling in her veins. Walking into the elevator, she turned her sparkling green gaze up to his face adding, 'I've heard of it; the view is supposed to be marvellous.'

Intent dark eyes watched her apparently simple delight. 'Not exactly; we are dining in the penthouse suite,' Marcus drawled. 'But the view is equally as good. I know because I own the hotel.'

Involuntarily her jaw dropped. 'You own…your suite,' she stammered. The hotel dining room was one thing, but to be alone with Marcus in his suite was inviting intimacy… Eloise blushed scarlet at where her thoughts were leading, and her slim hands closed nervously together. But she could hardly object now, without looking like a fool.

Black-lashed ebony eyes skimmed over her tense figure, and finally settled on her burning cheeks. 'The call I am expecting is confidential,' Marcus murmured dryly. 'And your body language is very expressive,' he opined. 'I invited you to dinner, and you look like you expect to be the main course,' he chuckled.

Somehow his laughter eased her tension, and she walked into the elegant room, feeling much more confident. It was a vast room with a dining area. A table was already set with the finest linen and silverware. A few steps led down to the seating area where two large sofas flanked a low occasional table, and a massive glass wall looked out over the city.

'The bathroom is through there if you need it.' Marcus indicated with a wave of his hand to a large double door set in the rear wall. 'Have a seat while I order.'

She looked at the low sofas but opted to sit at the dining table.

In a matter of minutes Marcus had ordered the meal and a bottle of the best champagne and, after the wine waiter had filled their glasses and left, Marcus lifted his glass to Eloise. 'To the renewal of our friendship, and may I add you look enchanting.'

'Thank you.' Eloise blushed, her eyes meeting his across

the small table. His incredible eyes darkened for a second, and surprisingly she shivered.

'Cold?' Marcus asked.

'No, someone walked over my grave. I'm fine, really; it is the first day of spring.'

'Some spring in England!' Marcus teased. 'You must come to Greece for Easter. Now that *is* spring.' And he went into a description of the wild flowers on Rykos.

Over a meal of asparagus soup, followed by sea bass cooked in herbs and spices, the conversation flowed easily. Marcus was a witty and educated man, and Eloise gradually felt all her inhibitions disappear as she relaxed and fell deeper under his spell.

She refused a dessert but quite happily accepted yet another refill of champagne. When the dessert Marcus had ordered arrived, an incredible concoction of various ice creams, chocolate, nuts, and fruit, Eloise laughed out loud.

'You are never going to eat all that,' she prompted, grinning at the sheepish expression on his handsome face. 'It looks like a psychedelic leaning tower of Pisa.'

'Now you know my secret vice.' Marcus dipped the spoon into the glass, and lifted it out loaded with ice cream. 'I have a weakness for sweet things.' His dark eyes captured her amused green and, lifting the spoon to his mouth, he swallowed, then licked his lips with his tongue.

Suddenly the humour was gone, and heat curled in the pit of Eloise's stomach as she saw the muscle in the strong column of his throat move as he ate. There was something so very sensual about watching his obvious enjoyment, the tip of his tongue licking his firm lips.

'Want some?' Her green eyes widened and she saw the spoon he held out to her mouth. 'Go on, you will love it,' Marcus encouraged softly. 'It's good.'

There was nothing good about the gleam in the eyes

that held hers, but an explicit sexual promise. Involuntarily she moved slightly forward like a puppet on a string, and parted her lips. The ice cream tasted cool on her tongue, but her body heat shot up another notch.

Swallowing she jerked back and suddenly the air was filled with an electric tension. 'Very nice,' she mumbled.

'I told you so. Now have some more champagne.' He filled her glass yet again.

Eloise took another sip of the wine. Was she the only one who felt the simmering tension in the air? she wondered. And, desperate to get the conversation away from anything sexual, she asked. 'By the way, how is your Uncle Theo?'

Marcus stiffened. 'He died over twelve months ago in a car accident, leaving a wife and child.' He placed his glass back on the table.

Well, she had certainly succeeded in breaking the tension, Eloise thought ruefully, Marcus's face was like stone. 'Oh, I am sorry,' she mouthed her condolences.

'Why should you be? He was nothing to you; it was your sister, Chloe, who was his friend,' he said bluntly.

Scarlet colour burnt her cheeks, and whether it was the wine or nerves that made her do it she did not know. 'About Chloe…she wasn't my sister, she was my mother,' Eloise admitted, equally as blunt.

'Your mother? You do surprise me. Chloe didn't look old enough,' Marcus conceded, shooting her a veiled glance. It was a parody of innocence, he knew that. He had caught her by surprise last night and she had admitted her surname was different from her *sister's*. Obviously, rerunning yesterday's conversation in her mind, she had realised she had made a mistake, and her blushing revelation was damage limitation on her part. But, watching her, he wasn't so sure; her embarrassment looked genuine.

Relieved he had apparently taken her confession so well, a reflective smile curved Eloise's full lips. 'You're right. Chloe was only seventeen when she gave birth to me. That's why, when we hired the villa for a month, she insisted I pretend to be her sister.'

'But wasn't that hard for you? You were very young to have to lie all the time.' Marcus sympathised with an edge of irony in his tone and, reaching across the table, he took her hand in his in a comforting gesture.

'No, not really,' Eloise found herself admitting. 'I didn't know my mother very well. She divorced my father three months after marrying him, he disappeared and she married again quite quickly. My grandparents brought me up, while Chloe pursued a very successful career around the globe.'

His hand tightened on hers. 'So it was from your mother you got the desire to do well in business.'

'Yes, I suppose you could say that.' She hadn't thought of it that way, but he might be right. 'In fact, Chloe was very proud of my going to college, and if it hadn't been for her, Katy, Harry and I could never have made such a good start as we did.'

'How's that?'

'Well, with the money Chloe left me, we were able to set up business.'

So that was her story! Very plausible. Chloe's death lent weight to her words. God, but she was good, Marcus thought cynically. If he had not seen her name on the contract, he would have believed her himself.

'That must have helped to ease the pain of your mother's passing,' he said in a voice tinged with sarcasm.

'Yes and no.' She smiled a little sadly, and continued. 'But Harry said it was important, if you want to appeal to the top end of the market, to be in the right place, and he found the property in Mayfair and I made the downpayment on the Georgian house where we live and work.' She never realised what she was revealing as Marcus encouraged her to talk. She told him their dream of expanding the business throughout Europe, possibly the world.

'With your enthusiasm, I'm sure you will be very successful.' Marcus let go of her hand and, picking up the champagne bottle, refilled their glasses. Black lashes dropping down over his brilliant eyes, he added, 'A toast to your success and may you get everything you deserve.'

Eloise picked her glass up, and watched his strong brown fingers curl around the stem of his glass. He had wonderful hands, large but lean and powerful, and for a moment she had a vivid mental image of lying on a beach, and those same fingers tracing over her naked breasts. Her face suffused with heat as Marcus's voice broke into her erotic thoughts.

'And to a friendship rekindled.' Marcus touched his glass to hers, his gaze unwaveringly direct on her scarlet face.

'To success and friendship.' She smiled tentatively up at him, her green eyes wide and guileless. But it was a toast and a threat if she had but known it.

Marcus raised his glass and drained it. He could almost be fooled by her naïve innocence, her pleasure in the meal and the champagne. Damn it! She confused him like no other female. Once he made a decision he usually stuck by it, and yet he had changed his mind last night about Eloise and he was in danger of doing it again. Either the woman deserved an Oscar for her acting, or she really was unaware of her mother's trade. But then he recalled the elegant house she owned and, watching her sitting opposite him, she appeared to be modesty personified in a tailored suit that covered her and yet skilfully revealed between the edges of the jacket a glimpse of satin and an amber jewel lying enticingly in the shadow of a cleavage. She blushed like a teenager, while happily discussing expanding her business worldwide, and all these paradoxes made him want to shake her and demand that the real Eloise stand up.

A smile of wry self-mockery curved his firm mouth. Who was he kidding? First he would strip her naked and bury himself in her luscious body over and over again. The memory of her in his arms, the lush promise of her body that he had denied himself, had been a thorn in his side for far too long, and abruptly shoving back his chair he stood up.

Last night he had left a very angry, frustrated Nadine at her door, the picture of Eloise filling his mind. He had a damn good idea he was in for another night of frustration if he called Eloise a crook to her face, and the thought did not appeal.

CHAPTER THREE

ELOISE glanced up in surprise. What had she said wrong? He was towering over her, dark and vaguely dangerous, and she gave an inward sigh of relief when she saw a slow smile quirk the corners of his beautiful mouth. The evening had been magical so far and she wanted nothing to spoil it.

'There is only so long a man of my size can sit on a tiny gilt chair,' Marcus said ruefully, and casually he removed his jacket and loosened his shirt and tie, before adding, 'I need to stretch my legs and relax.'

Eloise swallowed hard. The white silk shirt fitted taut across his broad shoulders; the slightest tracing of dark body hair was visible beneath the fine fabric. His pants fitted snug on his hips and involuntarily her gaze strayed to his long legs. She could feel her temperature rising and it had nothing to do with the warmth of the room.

Luckily a knock on the door heralded the arrival of the waiter with the coffee and it gave Eloise a chance to get her breathing back to normal.

Marcus walked the few steps down to the lounging area, and indicated the low table to the waiter. 'Here, please, and you can take the rest away; we are finished.

'Come and join me, Eloise,' Marcus commanded softly.

Her hesitation was barely perceptible and, telling herself not to be so silly, she rose to her feet and walked down the few steps to join him.

'Let me take your jacket and make yourself comfortable.

I'll be mum—is that not an English saying?' he asked, one dark brow arching in enquiry.

She glanced up at him. 'Yes,' and she tried for a smile. She felt his hands curve around the front of her jacket and she gave a tiny compulsive shudder, suddenly intensely aware of the intimacy of their surroundings, the rising tension in the air around them.

'Allow me.' And slowly he parted the jacket across her body, the back of his hand brushing *accidentally* across her breasts.

Her reaction was instant, her breasts swelling beneath the fine fabric, and she gasped, shocked by her own response.

The jacket fell to the floor. Marcus felt her tremble and he saw the shadowing of arousal in her wide green eyes, and he did what he'd wanted to do from the moment he had seen her again.

He curved an arm around her tiny waist, his dark head dipped and he captured her mouth with his in a kiss of hungry possession. He felt her sudden tension, felt her lips clamp together in instinctive rejection, and deliberately he made his mouth gentle against hers. Using all his considerable sexual expertise, he slipped his other hand around the back of her head and, deftly unpinning her hair, he tangled it in the silken mass, keeping her head firm while his mouth brushed gently against hers, kissing and licking in a tantalising seduction.

Pressed into the hard heat of his body Eloise was vitally aware of every last lean muscular inch of him, and quivers of sexual tension shot through her body. She felt an insidious weakness stealing through her limbs. She should stop this, a tiny little voice in her head cried. But the fierce pounding of her heart and the sweet touch of his mouth on hers drowned the cry out.

Marcus sensed the instant she relaxed in his arms; she made a whimper of sound and he seized the moment to slip his tongue between her lips. She rose towards him, her arms closed around his neck, and slowly, almost tentatively, she returned his kiss.

The silken softness of her, the scent of her—something light and heady—rose to his nostrils and his body hardened. Reluctantly Marcus finally lifted his head, his breathing erratic, but the smile that curved his sensual mouth as his night-black eyes captured hers held an edge of triumph. He had discovered what he needed to know. Eloise still wanted him. She was his for the taking.

Eloise gazed helplessly up into his darkly attractive face, not knowing what had hit her. She ran the tip of her tongue over her swollen lips and swallowed convulsively. Marcus had kissed her, and she had responded—it was unbelievable, amazing!

'Do you want coffee or…?' he breathed against her cheek.

The invitation in the dark eyes that sought hers was explicit. Eloise blinked, her heart thundering in her chest. Dear heaven, she was tempted, very tempted, but something held her back. 'N-no, yes, n-no,' she stammered, and nervously jerked back from his restraining arm. The feelings, the reawakening of sexual urges long suppressed, were all too new and she needed time.

With a husky chuckle, Marcus pulled her back into his arms. 'If you can't decide, then let me help you.' He looked into her eyes. She wanted him, and he wanted her, wanted her with an ache, a hunger that blotted every sensible thought from his brain. So what if she was a liar and a cheat? At that moment he did not give a damn, and he brought his lips to hers again.

Slowly, warmth coursed through her veins again, until

her whole body was on fire for him. Somewhere in the darkest reaches of her brain she remembered she should be wary, but instead she marvelled at her own response as his mouth moved gently against hers in several nibbling little kisses that threatened to draw the breath from her body.

'You are so beautiful,' he murmured, burying his face in her hair. 'You're the most perfect woman I have ever seen.'

'No,' Eloise murmured but her voice was shaky, and when Marcus brushed the hair away from her neck, and began kissing his way down her neck, lingering on the pulse that beat madly beneath her pale skin, she moaned.

'Yes,' Marcus whispered, and kissed her again.

Involuntarily her lips parted to accept the persuasive invasion of his tongue. She trembled, both hands clutching desperately at his broad shoulders, her feminine form reaching out, reacting to the lure of his potent sensuality.

Her breasts were swollen, her nipples tight aching buds, and she writhed against the hard male body, painfully aware of the restriction of the two fine layers of fabric preventing the flesh-on-flesh contact she craved.

His tongue delved deeper in her mouth, and he kissed with a fierce sexual passion that made every cell in her body pulsate in one tumultuous flood of feeling. If he had not been holding her, she would have collapsed.

A sharp whimper of need escaped her as he lifted his dark head; his eyes, black as jet, stared down into hers, and then he deliberately moved against her, letting her feel the hard evidence of his arousal. 'The bedroom, Eloise.' One hand slipped round to cup her breast. 'Say yes,' he husked, as his thumb stoked the rigid tip through the soft silk covering.

She heard the words and she knew what he was asking;

and in a flash of blinding clarity she knew this was her one chance for love. Her one chance to know a man—and not just any man, but Marcus. The only man she had ever loved.

She leant into the hard heat of him, and twined her arms around his neck. 'Yes,' she breathed unsteadily, as he swept her off her feet and carried her into the bedroom.

The room was in semi-darkness; only a bedside lamp shed a small pool of light over a large king-sized bed. The bed penetrated her haze of passion and fear flickered in her eyes but, before she could mouth the words of protest that trembled on her tongue, Marcus laid her down on the bed, stripping her skirt and top from her heated body in between kisses with a deftness that left her breathless.

She started to get up and stopped as, with stunning speed, Marcus shed his clothes. Half fascinated, half fearful, she could not tear her gaze away from his naked form. Shaking, she rested on her elbows. He was so perfect, so magnificently male, a tanned, hard, muscular chest with a light dusting of black hair that tapered down over a flat stomach, and lower... She gulped and swallowed hard, her green eyes flying back to his face as he joined her on the bed.

He loomed over her, his handsome face above hers taut, his dark eyes black and gleaming with a passion, a fire that reminded her of the past.

She was nineteen again and reached up for him, and then his mouth was hot, demanding everything with such hungry intensity she knew she should be frightened. But she did not have time to be afraid as caressing fingers curved around her breasts, and then hot hard kisses trailed down her throat, and a hungry male mouth fastened over the peak of one perfectly formed breast. Her back arched and she groaned out loud as he rendered the same treatment to her other breast.

'You like that,' Marcus rasped.

Eloise whispered his name as she wound her arms tightly around his neck. Her hands stroked his silken hair, and down over his powerful shoulders. Then he captured her mouth again in a long drugging kiss. When he broke the kiss and reared back, her slender arms fell from his shoulders and she felt bereft. Instinctively, she reached out to rest her hands on his chest. Her need to touch him was uncontrollable.

Breathing heavily, Marcus quickly removed the last barrier of delicate lacy briefs and stared down at her. She was so exquisite, so beautiful, her high round breasts with perfect deep rose peaks that begged for a man's mouth, the smooth curve of her waist, the feminine flare of her hips, and the red curling crest that he had ached for so long to discover. He wanted her, he wanted to touch, to taste every inch of her, to bury himself deep in the hot moist centre of her, until she cried out his name in ecstasy and she was truly his.

He closed his hands over hers and lifted them above her head, as he slowly lowered his head and kissed her mouth until it opened to his. He rubbed his chest against her breasts, glorying in the friction, and triumphant at her shuddering response. He cupped her breasts in his hands and rolled each taut nipple between his fingers. His black eyes sought hers, and he murmured, 'Perfect.'

Eloise had never imagined such pleasure existed, and she moved blindly against him. His hand slipped down to her belly and lower to her thighs, and she tensed.

Marcus sensed some resistance beneath Eloise's headlong response, and he vowed he would wait even if it killed him. He had once promised her it would be perfect and he intended to fulfil the promise. He bent his head towards her and tongued each rigid-tipped breast, and then drew her flesh in his mouth.

Eloise gasped his name, 'Marcus,' as his fingers gently stroked between her thighs, slowly, lightly. She felt electric shock-waves of sensation jolting through her body; she wanted him, and she wanted to cry out, but instead she pressed her mouth to his throat and bit down in a fever of frustration.

Marcus stifled a groan and the swift kiss he pressed on her love-swollen lips turned into a savage duelling of tongues, as his long fingers parted the petals of her womanhood and found the hot, damp, velvet flesh throbbing, waiting for him…

He touched her gently, softly, fast then slow, until her hips arched towards him, and her hands dug into his shoulders and she was calling out his name.

Eloise shook violently, a fierce tension she had never experienced before jerking her every nerve and muscle tight, driving every single thought from her head, and leaving only a fiery need that was almost pain. 'Please,' she moaned, her head thrashing from side to side. His hands slipped under her hips and lifted her clear of the bed. She felt the velvet tip of his hard male flesh stroke and then with one thrust he was there, where she wanted him to be.

Eloise felt the briefest of pains, and then it happened. Marcus's great body stilled for a second in disbelief.

She moaned his name and he moved deep and hard, filling her, stretching her, and taking her on a wild journey of almost mystical proportion. She felt the mighty strength of him thrusting, driving her on, until she cried out as her slender body convulsed in a paroxysm of sensation, and he joined with her until she had lost all sense of self, and the two of them became one perfect whole.

Afterwards she lay in his arms and felt the light caress of his fingertips against her sweat-damped flesh, soothing and caressing; he was murmuring husky words in Greek she did not understand. She sighed her delight, then tensed as his fingers found the ridge of flesh forming a scar on her inner thigh.

'What is this?' Marcus asked lazily, leaning over her and, by the dim light, let his slumberous eyes sweep over her beautiful naked body to where his fingers had found a small ridge of flesh. One long shapely leg had a scar about four inches long almost at the top.

'Nothing.' Eloise tried to cross her legs suddenly embarrassed. 'Just a scar. I'm sorry if it upsets you.'

'Oh, no, sweetheart,' Marcus exclaimed and smiled down at her. 'It does not upset me; in fact it is rather endearing. A tiny blemish in such perfection makes you seem more human,' he opined, and brushed her lips with his. 'But how did it happen? You did not have it when you were nineteen.'

'No... well...' She hesitated, and swallowed hard. 'I was locked out of my apartment and I broke a window to get in, and cut my leg—nothing serious.'

'Nothing serious,' he murmured, moving down her naked body; he let his fingers trace the scar, feeling anger for her accident, and fiercely protective. As his woman there would be no more accidents, he vowed, and his lips followed the path of his fingers. This time the loving was slow and tender, but the end was the same, one perfect unity.

Eloise curled up close and wrapped her arms around his neck. She did not want to think about the past. She did not want to think about anything except how much she loved this man. Tonight had been a revelation and, for the first time in her life, she knew what it was to be a woman, and it was all because of Marcus. She hugged him, finally admitting to herself she had never got over him. She had loved him as a teenager, and she loved him now and probably always would, and a contented sigh escaped her.

'Sighing. I didn't think I was that bad,' Marcus prompted and tilted her chin with a finger, his dark eyes gleaming down into hers.

'That was a happy sigh,' she speedily corrected him and, lifting a finger, she placed it over his lips. 'And you know it, Buster. I can see smug male triumph in your eyes,' she teased back.

'Cheeky.' He grinned broadly. 'But I...' Whatever he was going to say was cut off by the loud ringing of the telephone.

Hauling himself off the bed, Marcus picked up the phone from the bedside table, and as Eloise watched the laughing teasing lover vanished and the hard-headed businessman took his place. He was talking in Greek, and when he finally put the phone down he turned to Eloise. 'Sorry about that.'

'You really were expecting a call.' She had had her doubts, and it was nice to know he had not tricked her into his suite, and bed.

'O, ye of little faith,' he mocked with a grin. 'Actually, I have to make another one and, much as I would love to spend the night with you, I'd better get you back before your friends wonder what has happened to you.'

She wrinkled her nose at him. 'I am a grown woman.'

He planted a kiss on the tip of her nose, 'And if I stay here much longer I will be a grown man,' he drawled sexily. Eloise blushed at his innuendo, and Marcus laughed out loud. 'For a sophisticated lady, you blush delightfully.'

'It's the bane of my life,' she admitted with a grin. 'The penalty for being a redhead, I suppose.'

Marcus sent her a flashing smile of pure male satisfaction. 'A natural one, as I now know, but if I don't make this call my penalty is going to be the loss of a rather large deal.'

'Heaven forbid, business first.'

He gave her a playful shove. 'And you can have the bathroom first, and if you're lucky I might join you.'

Eloise shot him a startled glance and, swinging her legs over the side of the bed, she grasped the sheet and pulled it around her. She caught Marcus's husky chuckle, but she wasn't brave enough to parade in front of him naked—yet. She walked across to the bathroom door and turned. Her green eyes sparkling, she drawled, 'Promises, promises,' with a shake of her beautiful head. She could joke because she felt so great. He hadn't said he loved her, but she was sure he did, and they had all the time in the world to get to know each other.

But in that she was wrong.

Five minutes later she walked back into the bedroom, and there was no sign of Marcus. Quickly she slipped back into her rather crumpled clothes, and wandered through into the sitting room.

Almost dressed, he was shrugging his broad shoulders into the jacket of his suit. He looked heartbreakingly handsome, and Eloise wanted to fling herself into his arms. Instead she picked up her own jacket and slipped it on, suddenly shy.

'Sorry, Eloise.' He strode towards her. 'But the call was a bit more complicated than I had envisaged.' He slid a comforting arm around her shoulder. 'I'd better get you home.' His dark eyes rueful, he looked down at her. 'I need to get on to the computer.'

'Oh.'

Marcus noted the crestfallen expression on her lovely

face. 'I'll call you tomorrow. I promise.' And as he said it he knew it was true. He wanted this woman far more than any other woman he had ever met, and he did not want the relationship compromised by what to him was a paltry sum of money.

He was Greek, and honour and pride meant a lot. He had been very close to his Uncle Theo, who had been taken for a fool by Chloe Baker, and, sure Eloise had benefited from her mother's scam—in fact all the evidence suggested she was in on the scam with Chloe. But it did not follow that she would do the same on her own. He had made some calls today and, as far as he could ascertain, Eloise worked hard at a successful business and, unlike her mother, she was not known for granting sexual favours to men, while conning them out of money.

Why spoil what promised to be a great affair by seeking monetary revenge? Everyone was entitled to one mistake in life, and she had been very young. His mind made up, he gathered Eloise into his arms, and kissed her. 'Forgive me,' he murmured against her cheek.

Staring up at him, Eloise was astonished to see a flicker of vulnerability in his lustrous black eyes, and her heart swelled with love. He was actually worried about leaving her, proof that he really cared. 'Of course, Marcus, always.' She lifted a finger to his lips. 'Don't worry. You forget I have a business to run myself—I understand.'

If only he could... 'Yes, I know,' Marcus said shortly, his arm dropping from her shoulder to curve round her elbow and lead her to the door.

Sensing the tension in his huge frame, she tried hard to reassure him as they went down in the elevator. 'Actually, I am going to be very busy myself. We are expanding and opening a branch in Paris.'

'Isn't that rather sudden?' Marcus queried, urging her out of the elevator and into the hotel foyer.

Eloise's glance flew up to meet dark enigmatic eyes. 'Not really. After dinner last night, Ted and I stayed on to watch the show, and had a real fun evening. We danced and joked and Ted agreed to invest the money to expand KHE in principle.' She grinned up at Marcus. 'It was great, but it was three before I got home, and then we talked over the possibilities of opening in Paris. Ted actually knows of some great premises that are available.'

By *we* Eloise meant Katy and Harry, but Marcus drew a totally different conclusion. His dark eyes blazed with savage violence that Eloise was totally unaware of; she had no idea of the effect her rambling explanation was having on the man at her side.

'It was so exciting, it was after five before I finally got to sleep, then this morning we signed the deal, and went out for lunch to celebrate.' The enthusiasm in her tone was unmistakable. This had been one of the best days of her life—success in business, and in love.

A muscle knotted in Marcus's jaw. *Home at three and finally asleep at five!* It did not take Einstein to work out what she had been doing, and yet he could have sworn he was her first lover, more fool him... He'd been wrong about Eloise—and he'd been taken in by her beguiling act. Just like Ted had.

'You've planned everything out pretty carefully, I see. Good for you,' he grated, lashing himself into a fury at her deceit, made all the more powerful by the fact that an hour ago he'd been willing to forgive the damn woman anything.

Yet by her own admission she'd spent the night with Ted Charlton, persuaded him into parting with the money she wanted and rounded the date off with lunch. Eloise was exactly like her mother. Her sexy body had addled his brain, but no more... This time she was going to pay...

'Get in the car,' he said between gritted, even white teeth.

Eloise never noticed the icy anger in his eyes as he leant over her and fastened her seat belt. She simply wallowed in the heavenly scent of his magnificent male body, and finally realised what animal magnetism was really all about.

The car stopped before the entrance of her home, and she turned to Marcus but he was already out and walking around the front of the car. He opened the passenger door and held out his hand. Trustingly Eloise curled her fingers around the firm warmth of his palm, as she straightened and they walked to the door.

'You have your key?'

'Yes.' Reluctantly, she let go of his hand while she extracted the key from her purse and inserted it in the lock. She glanced up at him uncertainly. 'Do you want to come in?'

'No, I have to dash.'

He was a tall, broad silhouette outlined by the streetlight, his features in shadow, and for a moment she wondered what lay behind the dark mask of his face. And what was the protocol when you had slept with a man? Suddenly she was nervous for no reason. 'Well, thank you for a lovely evening,' she said softly, and stupidly offered her hand.

'I think we are past the handshaking stage, Eloise, way past,' Marcus drawled mockingly, making no attempt to take her hand. 'I'll be in touch. But I think I might have to go to America for a while.'

Her heart sank. She might not see him again for weeks.

'Promise,' she demanded urgently; there was something about the cool remote look in his eyes that worried her.

One dark brow arched sardonically. 'Oh, I promise, Eloise.' With a speed that left her breathless, he hauled her into his arms, and kissed her with a savagery that left her reeling. He spun on his heel and was opening the car door before she could say good night.

CHAPTER FOUR

'SO WHAT do you think?' Eloise did a pirouette, showing off the black strapless cocktail dress with a skirt that ended a good three inches above her knees, clinging to every curve of her body in between. 'The new me.' Her green eyes laughing, she sought the opinion of Katy, who was sitting on Eloise's sofa a bit like a beached whale, her eyes wide as saucers.

It was Saturday evening and Eloise had spent the whole day shopping for a complete new wardrobe, and for the past hour she had modelled them all for Katy.

'I'm stunned. They are all gorgeous—quite a metamorphosis from the perennial student to an elegant woman, and not before time.'

'I know.' Eloise sat down beside Katy on the sofa. 'I never really felt the need, what with working and living here, plus I don't feel so guilty spending money on myself, now I know Ted Charlton is backing us thanks to you and Harry.'

'Don't thank us,' Katy said, staggering to her feet. 'In my opinion, your new dress sense has little to do with the business expanding, and more to do with a dark-eyed Greek, and I'm glad for you. But be careful.'

Eloise felt the colour rise in her cheeks. Katy was right, but since her dinner date with Marcus her whole attitude had changed. It was four days since she had dined with him, made love with him, and she was missing him quite dreadfully. She only had to think of the kisses they'd shared to be able to taste him on her lips, and when she thought of the rest, her body burned. She could hardly believe the transformation from celibate female to the hungry, needy woman she had become, but she liked it. She felt like a teenager again, and jumped every time the telephone rang.

'Did you hear what I said?' Katy chuckled at the dreamy expression on her partner's face. 'Be careful.'

'I don't know what you're talking about; I only had dinner once with the man.' She had not told Katy everything! 'As for being careful—' Eloise got to her feet '—aren't I always?' she murmured dryly. 'Come on, I'll help you back down stairs. Harry should be back soon.'

The door slamming and a voice yelling 'Katy' made the two women smile.

'Speak of the devil.' Eloise laughed as she helped Katy down to her apartment.

Half an hour later, Eloise walked back up to her own place. Harry had returned from Paris, having completed the deal on the property to expand the business. Everything was going great, and all it needed to make Eloise's life perfect was for Marcus to return.

Relaxing by the telephone on Sunday evening, if one could call it relaxing, as she lived in hope Marcus would call, Eloise idly leafed through the morning paper. Her hand stilled, and her happy state of anticipation, took a nosedive. Her stomach turned in a nauseous roll, her eyes fixed on the glossy photograph in the celebrity section. Marcus Kouvaris with his beautiful companion Nadine snapped at a charity ball in London on Thursday evening. The night after he had taken Eloise out…

Eloise stared at the image of a devastatingly attractive Marcus in a black dinner suit, smiling at the tall blonde hanging on to his arm, and wanted to weep. What a fool she was. Floating on cloud nine, imagining a relationship with Marcus Kouvaris, dreaming impossible dreams of love, and even marriage, rushing out and buying a whole new wardrobe on the strength of *'I'll call you'*... She ground her teeth together in angry frustration at her own lunatic behaviour.

Slowly, like an old woman, she got to her feet, the paper dropping unnoticed to the floor, and made her way to the bedroom. Her eyes filled with moisture. She flopped down on the bed and let the tears fall. She had vowed at nineteen never to cry over another man again. Strictly speaking, she had not broken her vow, she thought between sobs as she was crying over the same man. But didn't that make her an even bigger idiot?

She rolled over onto her stomach, buried her face in the pillow and sobbed her heart out. Her slender body shook with the force of her grief.

Finally, all cried out, she turned over onto her back, and with sightless eyes gazed at the ceiling. She could remember every touch, every kiss, the awe, the wonder she'd felt when he'd finally possessed her. But what for her had been a miracle, for Marcus had obviously been simply another roll in the hay. When she finally slept a tall dark man haunted her dreams, and she cried out in her sleep.

Work was Eloise's salvation, but even that did not occupy her every waking hour, and she found herself making excuses for the man. Perhaps his date with Nadine was innocent, perhaps he would still ring her—and she despised herself for her weakness.

But as March gave way to April, and then May, and Marcus never contacted her again, finally Eloise accepted it was history repeating itself. Marcus had forgotten all about her. She and Katy worked flat out to build up a whole new range for the Paris branch and work stopped her brooding over Marcus.

Katy gave birth to a fine baby boy, Benjamin, and Eloise found herself more involved in the business side than ever. But designing was her strong point so they decided to employ two more staff—a young man, Peter, fresh out of college, to help with the actual making of the pieces, and then there was Floe Brown, a woman in her fifties who wanted to get back into work after being out of the job market for years, who was an absolute gem. When not helping Harry in the office she quite happily looked after the baby and let Katy work; it was a brilliant arrangement.

Eloise had reason to be grateful for her new clothes, even if she had bought them with one particular man in mind. Surprisingly she discovered they gave her a growing confidence in herself. Because of Katy's involvement with her new baby, Eloise, who had left the publicity aspect of the business to Katy and Harry, now found she was more involved with the setting up of the Paris boutique, doing interviews, and socialising with the ultra-chic French. A welcome spin-off was she actually developed a veneer of sophistication that effectively masked her naturally very private nature.

It was a warm June afternoon, and just two hours to the grand opening of KHE of Paris. Eloise glanced around the elegant shop with a professional eye. The jewellery on display was some of their best work and, fingers crossed, she prayed the new outlet would be a success. They had spent an awful lot of money and taken on quite a debt, but according to Harry it was manageable. It had better be, she thought dryly, or they might all end up out on the street, instead of in the plush hotel where they had spent the last two days getting everything ready.

'Right, Jeff. I'm leaving you in charge; don't touch any-thing, and don't start on the champagne. Katy, Harry and I will be back by five-thirty, ready to open the doors for the preview at six. Okay?'

'Stop fussing; go and make yourself beautiful. Julian is determined to get some really stunning photographs to-night for the glossy mags. If even half the people invited turn up it will be a great success, so stop worrying.'

Standing in front of the bathroom mirror in her hotel an hour later, Eloise could not help worrying. Outlining her full lips with one last coat of lip-gloss, she patted them with a tissue, and stepped back. Her red hair was piled high on the top of her head in a coronet of curls. Her make-up was subtle, a touch of eye-shadow and eyeliner accen-tuated her wide green eyes, her thick lashes held the light-est trace of mascara, and a light moisturiser was all she needed. Around her throat she wore a glittering jade and jet choker that draped down her breastbone in a waterfall of intricately cut beads, one of her own designs, and dis-played perfectly against her pale skin. Matching earrings and a wide bracelet around her slender wrist completed the set.

Eloise ran her hands down her hips, smoothing the fab-ric of the simple black strapless sheath dress she was wear-ing over her thighs, to where it ended some way above her knees.

Yes, Katy had been right, it was the perfect foil for the jewellery, Eloise thought musingly and, leaving the bath-room, she picked up her purse and headed for Katy's hotel room.

'At last,' Harry blurted as he opened the door at Eloise's knock. 'We're going to be late for our own opening.'

'Don't panic.' Eloise looked at his frazzled expression, and wanted to laugh. 'I'm sure everything will be fine.'

And it was, Eloise thought some three hours later looking around the crowded room. The two French staff they had employed were being kept busy. Julian was happily taking shots of at least four supermodels, and a handful of the top French designers were present, plus a lot of their very wealthy clients.

The jewellery had been admired and sold, plus they had taken a highly satisfactory number of orders and one elderly lady had even tried to buy the set Eloise was wearing. The champagne and canapés seemed to be holding out, and she allowed herself a small sigh of pleasure as she took a sip of champagne. The first drink she'd had, as she'd wanted to keep a clear head.

'I told you, Eloise—' Ted Charlton appeared at her side '—you have a winner, no doubt about it.'

'I hope so, for your sake as well as ours.' She smiled at the burly American.

'Oh, I'm not bothered,' Ted said, and in abrupt change of subject added, 'how well do you know Marcus Kouvaris?'

She stiffened. 'I had dinner with him a while ago. I suppose you could say we are friends.' The fact she had hoped they could be a lot more still had the power to hurt her, and with a dismissive shrug of her slender shoulders she made herself add lightly. 'Or perhaps acquaintances would be a better word.'

'Good, good, that's what I thought.' The obvious relief in his tone was plain.

'Why do you ask?' she demanded.

Ted took a glass of champagne from a passing waiter, and gulped it down, before turning his attention back to Eloise. 'I'm taking you out to dinner later. We'll talk then, okay?'

She liked the older man and she didn't want to make

an issue out of a casual question, especially not about Marcus. 'Okay, Ted.' She grinned.

'Great,' and, patting her shoulder, he moved off into the crowd.

Eloise shook her head, Ted was half drunk already and, draining her own glass, she turned and placed it on the table behind her.

'Hello, Ted, great to see you again.'

Eloise recognised the deep, slightly accented voice above the hum of the crowd, and shock froze her to the spot. It was Marcus Kouvaris. What was he doing here? She certainly hadn't invited him. Though she might have done if he'd ever bothered to keep in touch, her own innate honesty forced her to admit, as she fought to control her pounding heart.

How long she stood with her back to the crowd, she had no idea, but finally schooling her features into a polite social mask she turned around, head high, and let her glance roam apparently idly over the room. Then she saw him. His dark head was bent towards one of the models, apparently listening to what the woman was saying.

He was easily the tallest man present and, with his dark good looks, and wearing an immaculately tailored light-weight beige suit, he stood out from the crowd. Eloise could not take her eyes off him; animal magnetism didn't cover it, she thought helplessly. Whatever *it* was, Marcus had it in spades.

Suddenly he lifted his head and night-black eyes clashed with hers and just as suddenly Eloise had the totally un-ladylike desire to yell at him? 'Where the hell have you been for the past three months?' Of course she didn't, but instead she managed a stiff smile, before tearing her gaze from his.

She feigned interest in the elderly lady who was once

again admiring her necklace, but without hearing a word the poor dear was saying.

A large hand lightly brushed her forearm, to attract her attention; her head jerked up. It was Marcus at her side. Keep it cool, you're a sophisticated businesswoman, she told herself firmly. So what if she had a one-night stand with the man? She wasn't the first and she certainly would not be the last where a sexual predator like Marcus Kouvaris was concerned. She had no illusions on that score, and though he didn't know it he'd done her a favour...

'Marcus, what a surprise. I thought you would be far too busy to attend this sort of thing,' she opined lightly.

'Ah, Eloise, would I miss your opening?' he prompted his dark eyes holding a glint of wicked humour. 'I'm only sorry I didn't get in touch sooner.' His smile was disarming. 'But pressure of work.' He gave a shrug of his broad shoulders. 'That's how it goes sometimes.'

'Yes, of course.' Eloise couldn't say anything else under the circumstances. She had no claim on the man. So he had taken her to bed and taken her virginity? What did that matter to a devil like Marcus?

'I knew you would understand.' His eyes captured hers, faintly mocking beneath hooded lids, and the breath caught in her throat.

'Yes, well, I'm an understanding kind of girl,' she managed in a weak attempt at humour.

'You are also a very beautiful one.' Marcus moved slightly, the sleeve of his jacket brushing her arm. 'You look fantastic.' With casual ease, he reached out and lifted the waterfall of beads at her throat, and let them trail through his long fingers. 'Your design?'

He was much too close. The heady masculine scent of him, the touch of his fingers on her flesh, sent heat flooding through every vein in her body. She swallowed hard, and stepped back. 'Yes.'

'Exquisite.' His hand fell from her throat. 'Congratulations, Eloise. It looks like your latest venture will be a great success.'

With a bit of space between them, Eloise felt slightly more in control. 'Thank you. We hope so,' she responded with a baring of her teeth that she hoped would pass for a smile, and glimpsed a flash of mockery in the dark eyes that held her own.

'Can there be a doubt? After all, Eloise, your mother was highly successful, and you obviously have her talent.' A talent for squeezing money out of men, Marcus thought grimly. But she had other talents, he recognised, as he looked down at her. She was one gorgeous, sexy lady, as he knew only too well, but she was also a liar and a devious little thief. Yet even now if he saw just one genuine smile from her luscious lips, he would probably forgive her everything, and he despised himself for it.

'You think so?'

'Oh, I know so,' he said with the arch of one perfect ebony brow. 'But let's cut out the niceties and get down to what really interests me.' The gleam in his eyes, as he surveyed her slender figure from the top of her head to her toes, left her in no doubt as to what he meant.

Eloise fought down the blush that threatened and said, 'Actually, I'm surprised to see you here. I don't remember inviting you.'

'You didn't. Ted Charlton did.'

Eloise stared up at him, her green eyes puzzled. 'I didn't realise you knew him that well.'

A smile touched his hard mouth. 'You'd be surprised. But let's not talk about Ted; let's talk about you. I suppose it's too much to hope you are still unattached. There must be lots of men in Paris all vying for your attention.'

'I don't think that's any business of yours.' She hid a wry smile, thinking of the twenty-hour days she had worked to get the Paris shop started.

'I thought we were friends.' His gaze was unwaveringly direct 'More than friends.' His deep voice dropped seductively. 'After this is over, let me take you out to dinner and show you.'

For sheer arrogant conceit, he took the biscuit, Eloise thought furiously. He had slept with her, dropped her like a hot potato, and casually walked back into her life, uninvited, months later, and thought he could seduce her all over again. What kind of fool did he take he for? He might be incredibly handsome, and incredibly rich, but he was also a womanising bastard, as she knew to her cost.

'Thank you for the invite, but no, thanks. I already have a dinner date.'

One black brow lifted sardonically. 'Shame. Perhaps some other time, as I remember the last time we dined together you seemed to enjoy my company, and I know I enjoyed you.'

Hot colour stained her cheeks. How dared he remind her of that? She wanted to knock the cynical smile off his rotten face. Her hands curled into tight fists at her sides, and she was rigid with anger... But, remembering where she was, with the greatest difficulty she controlled herself.

'Eloise, isn't it marvellous?' Katy was Eloise's salvation.

Turning her back on Marcus, her gaze flew to her friend's face. Katy looked amused and excited, whereas she felt embarrassed. 'Yes, great.'

'For heaven's sake, lighten up, Eloise. We're a success. Enjoy it, and introduce me to this marvellous man.'

Eloise almost groaned out loud. Marcus had positioned himself at her side, and was standing there, oozing charm... The snake! But she had no choice but to make the introductions. She watched cynically as Marcus, with a few well-chosen words that flattered Katy's beauty and business sense, charmed her friend completely.

'You've met Harry, I believe,' Eloise said as Harry joined the group.

'Yes, the first time guarding the door in London, and I can't say I blame you, Harry, with two such stunningly attractive woman to look after.'

'Your chauvinism is showing,' Katy quipped, and they all laughed.

'Then let me apologise by taking you all to dinner.'

'No, no.' Ted appeared. 'Tonight is my treat. Eloise has already agreed but, hey, why don't you all come—and you too, Marcus? It will save time.'

'Eloise?' Katy deferred, and the decision was hers.

Save time for what? Eloise briefly wondered but, pinning a smile on her face, she said, 'Yes, the more, the merrier.' But inside she was fuming. And what did Marcus mean by *'the first time he had met Harry'*? To her knowledge he had only met Harry once. Was Marcus having a sly dig at her? Her paranoia was showing. Marcus Kouvaris was not worth thinking about.

'Come on, then,' Harry cried. 'Let's thank and say goodbye to our guests. Jeff and Julian can close up. We have already overrun half an hour, and I am not used to eating late; my stomach feels as if my throat is cut.'

General laughter followed, and an hour later saw the five of them seated at a table next to the small dance floor in a nightclub in the Latin Quarter, enjoying a jovial meal.

'I'm stuffed,' Katy groaned, eyeing the last remnants of a huge cream concoction. 'And if I don't get back to the hotel soon, our son will be screaming for his feed, and Floe will be pulling her hair out.'

'Before you decide to leave,' Ted cut in, 'I have something to tell you.'

The meal had been torture for Eloise, who'd been trying to behave cool and unconcerned by Marcus's presence. Forced to watch him win over Katy with his wit and easy charm, when she wanted to yell he was a rat... She gave an inward sigh of relief when Katy proposed leaving—her ordeal was almost over. But she was wrong. It was just beginning...

'Katy, Eloise, I have an announcement to make,' Ted declared.

Glancing at Ted, Eloise, saw the almost conspiratorial look he exchanged with Harry and Marcus, and Marcus's head dipped slightly in a nod of assent. She looked from one to the other, an uneasy suspicion she was not going to like Ted's revelation making her stiffen in her seat.

'I have sold my share in KHE to Marcus here.' Ted gestured expansively with the wave of his brandy glass. 'He made me an offer I couldn't refuse and, before you girls start worrying, let me assure you Marcus is committed to investing double the amount I gave you. Expansion into New York, if you like.' He beamed around the table. 'A great deal all round, isn't it, Harry?'

The announcement hit Eloise like a punch in the stomach. It turned her to stone. She could feel the blood slowly draining from her face, and the panicked increase in her heartbeat. Marcus as a partner—not the kind she had once dreamed, a marriage partner, but a business partner. She glanced at him, and he returned her look without a flicker of emotion showing on his hard features. She searched his hooded dark eyes, but found nothing other than an arched eyebrow at her scrutiny. Why? Why on earth would Marcus buy into their business?

'You knew about this?' Eloise heard Katy demand of Harry, and glanced across the table at her two friends.

'Yes, but I didn't want to worry you with business when you had our baby to look after and all the extra work Eloise had to do. Plus the deal was only finalised three days ago, and we wanted no hint of changing partners so near to the Paris opening. You know what the press are like—the least hint of instability and the rumours would fly.'

Marcus took charge in his indomitable manner. 'Your husband is right, Katy. I have no intention of interfering in any way with your work. You and Eloise will have complete artistic freedom.' Turning his attention from Katy to Eloise, his black lashed glittering eyes trailed over her tense figure, lingering on the curve of her breasts and finally slowly back up to her pale face to trap her angry green eyes. 'I promise,' he vowed softly, 'I will simply be a sleeping partner, a sleeping partner who provides the money, when and where it is needed.' He smiled, a brief curl of his lips.

Eloise's slender hands closed convulsively together on her lap. He sat there, cool, calm, and immensely self-assured, and only she could see the smile never reached his eyes, but contempt and a glint of sexual menace glimmered in the black depths.

'It will be fine, Eloise,' Harry piped up.

'You should have discussed it. I mean, Ted is, was...' Eloise floundered wildly for a moment with a glance at the now thoroughly drunk Ted. He was no help, she realised with a sinking feeling in the pit of her stomach. One look at Katy talking animatedly on the side to Marcus, and she knew Katy had already accepted the deal. Her friend would never go against her husband in any case.

'Are you all right with this new arrangement, Eloise?' Katy finally asked, her brown eyes sparkling. 'Personally, I think it's an incredible opportunity.'

An opportunity for whom? Eloise wondered. And did they have a choice?

'Yes. You're probably right,' she conceded. A steel band of tension was now throbbing across her head, and she took very little part in the ensuing conversation, her thoughts and emotions in chaos.

It didn't make sense. If Marcus had cared for her, she could perhaps understand him investing in KHE. But he hadn't contacted her in over three months. So why? The question went around and around in her brain.

Another bottle of champagne and another round of toasts were drunk to the new partnership, and everyone congratulated everyone else. While Eloise had to battle to keep a smile on her face, her lips were numb with the effort.

'I know I said I would not interfere in the running of the business.' Marcus's comment made Eloise sit up and take notice.

'But KHE is a bit of an obscure title for designer jewellery. No disrespect to you, Katy and Harry, but did you never consider something like, ''Eloise by Design''? It has a much more sophisticated ring to it.' Marcus dropped the original name invented by Chloe and Eloise into the conversation, and watched with narrowed eyes as all the colour faded from Eloise's face. She looked as guilty as sin, exactly as he'd expected. Though he hadn't expected the overlong tense pause, and he turned his attention to Katy. She was staring at Eloise with a mixture of horror and *sympathy*! There was something between them Marcus did not understand...

'We did consider it,' Katy answered. 'But decided we preferred the more enigmatic KHE. We thought it sounds like "key," and the key to a well-dressed woman is the jewellery she wears.'

Eloise gave an inward sigh of relief when Marcus appeared to accept the explanation and asked Katy to dance. At least it would get him away from the table, and give her a chance to try and get her thoughts into some kind of order and make sense of the evening's proceedings.

'No, sorry, Marcus. Harry and I are responsible parents now. It's time we called a taxi and got back to our son. And, by the look of Ted, we'd better take him with us. He doesn't look capable of making his own way back to the hotel.'

'What about you, Eloise?' Marcus queried, turning his head to glance down at her by his side. 'The night is still young. Shall we dance?' His dark eyes lit with amusement and something else she did not want to acknowledge dared her to agree. 'Or are you going to desert me as well?'

Eloise felt the colour surge in her cheeks, and prayed no one noticed. She had been supremely conscious of Marcus all through the meal. The occasional brush of his thigh against hers beneath the table, the apparently friendly gesture when he placed his hand on her arm when making a point, the rub of his shoulder against her when he leant forward to fill Katy's wine glass. He hadn't singled her out particularly, but he'd managed to arouse her to a state of tension without even trying. It was only the presence of her friends that had allowed her to retain a modicum of self-control. Until Ted had dropped his bombshell—and she was still trying to get her head around the fact that Marcus had bought into the company. Dancing with the man was the last thing she wanted. 'No…' She began to make her excuse.

'Of course she will,' Katy cut in, rising to her feet along with Harry and Ted. 'Eloise has been working like a slave for months; she deserves some fun.' Katy answered before Eloise could mouth her refusal. 'She is staying here for a couple of days to sort out any teething troubles, so a late night won't kill her.'

'Do you mind?' Eloise finally found her voice. 'I can speak for myself,' she shot back.

'I know, Eloise,' Katy responded, suddenly serious. 'I'm sorry.'

Marcus glanced back from one woman to the other and for the second time that evening thought there was something going on between them, but dismissed the notion when Eloise spoke.

'Don't apologise.' Lifting defiant green eyes to Marcus, she added, 'Yes, I'd like to dance.' She had vowed never to be afraid of any man again, and she was damned if she would allow Marcus to intimidate her.

The others left, and Eloise found herself held in Marcus's arms, moving around the dance floor to blues music in a state of nervous tension.

Marcus glanced down at her stiffly held head. The thick red coronet of curls had sprouted a few tendrils around her face. He could feel the tension in her and he deliberately tightened his hold, moving more heavily against her.

She shivered in response, but fought the emotion and won, by dint of squaring her shoulders and tilting back her head to stare up into his face. 'Are you going to tell me why, after three months of ignoring me, you've suddenly bought into our company?'

A satiric smile curved his expressive mouth. 'Perhaps I

saw a good deal, and took it,' he said smoothly. 'But you and I both know the real reason.'

'I have no idea,' she muttered, her eyes wide and puzzled, searched his hard features. Perhaps he wanted to make up to her for ignoring her past three months. The amazing thought popped into her head. It was an extravagant gesture, but maybe—just maybe—it was true, and for a while she allowed herself the luxury of believing it.

'No doubt you will enlighten me when you want to,' she said with the first genuine smile she had given him all evening. She was too confused and too tired to argue and, some of the tension easing out of her, she relaxed in his arms.

She knew damn well what he meant. Why else would she relax in his arms and smile? A ploy as old as Eve, but it was too little too late as far as Marcus was concerned. He knew it was a mockery of innocent surrender, but knowing that didn't lessen the impact of her sexy body against his. Marcus almost groaned out loud. Her softness seemed to accommodate the hard planes and angles of him as if made to measure. She was so beautiful, so sweet and receptive. *Christos!* Where had that come from? She was about as sweet as a wasp!

Reining in his raging libido, Marcus stopped and pushed her lightly away from him. He saw the surprise in her eyes, but ignored it. 'I think you and I need to talk, but not here, somewhere private.' Dropping a hand to her waist, he surveyed her beneath heavily hooded lids. 'My apartment or your hotel—take your pick.'

CHAPTER FIVE

SHE had been in danger in falling for his formidable charms all over again, Eloise thought with dismay. He only had to take her in his arms and every sensible thought flew her brain. *'Your place or mine.'* If he thought she was falling for that corny line, he was mistaken.

'Really, Marcus, surely you can come up with something better than that?' She gave a light laugh, casting him a glance from beneath the thick fringe of her lashes. 'I've heard better chat-up lines from a teenager.'

'I'm sure you have, and acted on them,' Marcus said, with dark emphasis. 'But, unlike Ted Charlton, I want a lot more from you than a one-night stand.'

'You think... Ted and me...?' Her sophistication slipped, and shock had her spluttering incoherently. 'Why, you...you...'

Grasping her by the elbow, he led her towards the table, his long fingers biting into the flesh of her arm as his dark head bent intimately towards her, giving the impression to anyone watching they were a close and loving couple, while mouthing harshly, 'You stole from my family.'

She was badly shaken by his assumption she had slept with Ted, and the instant racing of her pulse as his warm breath caressed her ear didn't help. She could barely take in what he was saying, until he concluded with sibilant softness, 'And I want you back in my bed until I consider the debt is paid.'

Involuntarily her jaw dropped. At the same time his hand fell from her arm and Eloise tilted her head to stare at him like a stranded trout, her mouth working and no sound coming out. Feeling the edge of a chair at the back of her knees, she collapsed down on the seat, and cast a panicked glance around the room. She was still in the nightclub, but she felt like Alice in Wonderland falling down the rabbit hole.

Come to think of it, the whole evening had been a bit like the Mad Hatter's tea party. And Marcus could certainly double as the Knave of Hearts, accusing *her* of sleeping with Ted Charlton, while he cut a swathe through women, she thought bitterly. She regarded him with wide angry eyes. And *stole* from him? As far she knew, he'd only been in business with them one day. Was he mad, or what?

'You're crazy,' she declared, finally finding her voice. 'You've completely lost your marbles.'

'No.' Marcus looked at her with cold contempt that made her skin crawl. 'I have the proof, Eloise. This time, you're not escaping the consequences of your actions. I'm going to make sure you don't.'

He was towering over like some great avenging angel— or devil was more apt, she corrected in her head. 'I have never stolen anything in my life. I have no idea what you are talking about,' she said, conviction in every syllable. 'I really don't.'

'Liar.' Marcus's cold eyes raked her with derision. 'You fell into my bed the last time we met, all wild and willing, simply to soften me up—and I nearly fell for it.'

She flinched as though she'd been struck. If only he knew the courage, the great leap of faith in his integrity it had taken for her to make love with him. If he'd continued their relationship, she might have confided in him by now, but she wasn't about to reveal her innermost fears to a man who had used her as a one-night stand.

And yet she could not explain to herself why it should hurt so much when Marcus looked at her with derision. She owed the man nothing.

Eloise opened her mouth, about to tell him so, but fear closed her throat as she recalled his other threat to have her back in his bed. Disgusted with herself, not Marcus, because for one heart-stopping moment she was tempted.

She had to get out of here! Picking up her purse, she tried to stand, but his hand on her shoulder forced her back down.

'Sit,' he ordered.

Eloise couldn't think straight, paralysed by shock as he pulled up a chair and sat beside her at the table, angling his seat so he could watch her every move. She felt sick inside, as with dawning horror she realised he actually believed what he was saying.

'You do well to remain silent.' Contemptuous amusement glittered in his dark eyes as he noted her bewilderment, the scarlet colour in her cheeks. 'Under that aura of innocence you wear so well beats the heart of a con-artist. A very talented, beautiful woman, but a thief nevertheless. I know what you are…' His glittering gaze rested on her with a blatant sexual intensity. 'And yet I want to possess that body, and until such time as I consider you have paid the debt you and your mother owe my family, you will stay with me.'

He had as good as called her a whore, but that paled into insignificance at the mention of her mother. A growing sense of dread seeped into Eloise's mind. 'What has my mother got to do with this?' she asked shakily.

'Oh, please!' Marcus mocked her supposed ignorance, but when she still stared at him with wary eyes, he gestured with his palms up. 'Okay, Eloise have it your way,' and he clarified with impatience, 'Chloe rented one of my uncle's villas, seduced the man, and then persuaded Theo to give her half a million to invest in her jewellery business—with your collusion, Eloise—and the pair of you vanished as soon as the cheque cleared.'

Appalled at the scenario Marcus presented, Eloise felt tension tighten her every muscle. Because, deep down, she had a horrible feeling there might be some truth in his words. Her mother had been close to Theo Toumbis when they'd stayed on Rykos. They'd departed in a hurry. Maybe Chloe had borrowed money from the man. Eloise had not known her mother well enough to say yes or no. But her mother was dead, and in deference to her memory at least deserved her support, Eloise staunchly reminded herself.

'You expect me to agree to be your, your mi—mistress.' She stammered over the word. 'Until I pay off some mythical debt I am supposed to owe you.' Eloise tried for a laugh. 'Dream on, Buster.' Pushing back her chair, she stood up again.

A chilling smile formed on his lips as he also rose to his feet 'Think about it. You agree to my terms, or I pull out of the deal with your firm.' His black eyes, gleaming with an unholy light of triumph, captured hers. 'Tonight's celebration, Eloise, will be looked on as a wake. Without the capital to maintain the Paris branch, you will have to close with a mountain of new debt, and within a very short space of time your London base will go bankrupt. I will make sure of it.'

'You can't do that!' Eloise gasped, amazed at the change in the man from sophisticated charmer into a ruthless, remote figure. She saw the implacable determination in his hard gaze, and she shook with fear and outrage. Rage won...

Well, he was not getting away with it. How dared he

threaten her like this? Who the hell did he think he was? 'I won't let you,' she snapped.

'You can't stop me,' Marcus said without a flicker of emotion. 'Speak to Harry—he will confirm what I say. I'll give you until tomorrow to decide. But think of the effect on Katy and Harry and their baby, their livelihood, before you make up your mind.' Dropping a bundle of notes on the table, he took her arm and urged her forward. 'This is too public.' His dark impervious gaze swept the room. 'Come on, I'll get you a cab,' he added smoothly, viewing her with dark threatening eyes.

'I don't need to think,' she spat, her fury rising to eclipse her earlier fear completely. 'The answer is no—and, as for Kate and Harry, they are my friends. They'll stand by me and ignore your ridiculous accusations.' Eloise took half a dozen enraged steps at his side without realising, then stopped suddenly, yanking her arm free.

'And I'll get my own cab,' she hissed. 'I want nothing from you, and this so-called business partnership will be dissolved tomorrow. I don't know how you talked Ted and Harry into it, but we are getting out.' She stepped out into the foyer.

'As you please.' Marcus's voice followed her, low and lethal. 'Then I will see you in court.'

The heated colour drained from her face. She stilled. The exit to the street and freedom was barely a step away, but for Eloise it might as well have been a million miles. Once she had given evidence in a court case, and it had been the worst experience of her life. No way could she face doing it again. Taking deep steadying breaths, she fought down the panic that threatened to choke her, and slowly turned to face Marcus. 'Court? What do you mean by court?' she demanded starkly.

'Unless we come to a private agreement, I shall of

course present the evidence of your deception to a court of law.' A shrug of his broad shoulders, and Marcus's mouth curled in a cynical smile, apparently registering a supreme masculine indifference either way that made her blood run cold. 'The decision is yours, but you no longer have until tomorrow. I want your answer tonight.'

Eloise swallowed hard, smoothed the fine fabric of her dress down over her hips with damp palms, and wondered what had happened to the Marcus she had first met. The Marcus who had valued her innocence, and then later the lover who had made her initiation into womanhood a magical experience. Was she really such a dim-wit that, for a few short hours, a few kind words and sweet caresses, she forgot what life had taught her? Men could be swine, and worse...

She would never make the same mistake again. Imperceptibly her shoulders straightened, and the ability to disguise her inner thoughts, developed with years of practice, slid back into place in her mind, like a steel trap door closing. She had vowed once never to trust another man as long as she lived, and for a brief space of time she had forgotten, but never again.

'What's it to be, Eloise?'

'First I want to see the so-called proof,' she demanded quietly and shivered at the cold implacability in his saturnine features.

'The evidence is at my apartment, ten minutes' drive away.' His arm closed firmly around her shoulders. 'We can continue this conversation better there, I'm sure you will agree.'

He had an apartment in Paris? Why not? A hysterical laugh fluttered in her throat. The man had everything. Marcus was a powerful, ruthless operator, a legend in the financial markets. Where lesser men made the occasional loss, what he had he kept, be it money, women or property. His nature was obviously possessive; he was a taker, not a giver.

But, held close to him, she could smell the faint musky masculine scent of him, and her traitorous skin heated where he touched. Dear heaven, if he did but know it, he could have had her and everything she was and owned for the asking three months ago—but not any more, she thought with the glimmer of an ironic smile as she agreed. She, more than most, did not appreciate being manipulated by a man—any man…

The apartment was small, more a pied-à-terre, tucked away at the top of one of the classic Napoleon-styled buildings overlooking the Seine. It was clearly designed with a bachelor in mind. A living room that was elegantly furnished and with what looked like a selection of original cartoons displayed on one wall, probably worth more than the apartment. A tiny kitchen area, obviously not meant to be used for anything other than making coffee or heating up a croissant for breakfast. A closed door led to what Marcus indicated was the bedroom, with an en-suite shower and toilet.

Eloise walked over to the ornate dormer window, and looked at the glittering lights reflected with the moonlight on the dark waters of the Seine, and wondered by what trick of fate she had ended up in this mess.

'Would you like a drink?' Marcus asked, standing much too close.

Eloise spun around. 'No. I want your so-called proof and an explanation fast,' she flashed back, disturbed by the intimacy of the place. 'It's not every day one is accused of being a thief.'

'So be it.' She watched as Marcus crossed to a desk in one corner. He opened a drawer, took out a folder, and placed it on the desk, and then laid a document on top. Switching on a desk lamp, he straightened up. 'Feel free to peruse them at your leisure,' he drawled mockingly. 'I need a drink.'

Eloise marched across to the desk, and picked up the document and read the first line. She raked a shaking hand through her hair forgetting her elaborate coronet of curls, in the process. It appeared to be a contract between Chloe Baker, her late mother, and Theo Toumbis, selling Theo a half share in Chloe's latest business venture in designer jewellery for five hundred thousand pounds—''Eloise By Design,'' to be situated in London.

Slowly, with mounting horror, she read on and there at the foot of the page were the three signatures to the contract: Chloe Baker, Theo Toumbis, and last Eloise Baker.

Eloise stared, transfixed. It was an excellent copy of her handwriting, but in fact it wasn't even her real surname.

'I never signed this.' She cast a wild look over her shoulder at Marcus. 'You must believe me, I have never seen it before. My name is *Smith*,' she cried.

'So, five years ago you were not masquerading as Chloe's sister, you were not on Rykos, and you know nothing about the contract?' he drawled sardonically. 'Please spare me the lies. I was *there*, remember?'

'No, yes—no.' Eloise glanced back down at the paper in her hand. 'Chloe must have forged my signature,' she murmured in stricken disbelief at her mother's deceit, and her heart sank as she realised the futility of trying to explain.

Marcus was right; she had been acting as Chloe's sister on the island. A good lawyer would make mincemeat of her claim to be innocent of any knowledge of the affair. She let the document flutter from her hand to the desk and in the process saw the blue folder.

'Oh, no!' she exclaimed, wide eyed with horror she stared at the folder. She knew exactly what it contained before she even opened it. But she made herself open it. She had to have her worst fear confirmed.

'Oh, yes, Eloise.' Marcus appeared at her side, and handed her a crystal glass. 'I think you might need this now,' he said with a grim smile.

She took the glass and took a hasty swallow. Brandy or whisky, she wasn't sure—but, coughing violently, she brushed past Marcus and slid down onto the sofa in a movement singularly lacking in grace. The glass clasped in her hand, every vestige of colour drained from her face, and not even the alcohol could replace it. How could her own mother have done that to her?

Not only had Chloe forged her signature on the contract, the folder contained a copy of the project Eloise had completed for college. The only difference was Chloe had named herself as architect of the plan instead of Eloise. It was a complex business plan including the costings and all the design work, publicity etc, in setting up Eloise By Design, aimed at the top end of the market. It had been Eloise's ambition and dream career. She had received top marks for the assignment.

Later, when Chloe had appeared and Eloise had rather shyly shown her prize-winning project to her mother, she'd been thrilled when for the first time in her life Chloe had taken an interest in what she was studying. Chloe had told her she was very talented, very clever, and she was very proud of her. Naturally, when her mother asked if she could keep it as a memento, Eloise had said yes.

She took another mouthful of the fiery spirit; she needed it. Never in a million years would it have crossed Eloise's mind that her mother would use her assignment as a means to get money out of a man. But, from the little she had seen, that appeared to be exactly what her mother had done. Reeling with shock and the cringing sense of shame and humiliation she felt at her mother's actions, she drained the glass in her hand.

The alcohol kicking in, Eloise leant back against the high-backed sofa, and closed her eyes for a second, the enormity of her mother's deception almost impossible to bear. Slowly she opened her eyes, and cast a covert look at Marcus beneath the shadow of her long lashes. He had shed his jacket and tie, and his shirt lay open at his tanned throat. He was leaning negligently against the fireplace, twirling a glass of whisky in one hand, as though he had not a care in the world.

Well, bully for him, she thought bitterly, aggression taking over from humiliation. Marcus was not getting away with blaming her. 'So my mother apparently conned your uncle into investing in a mythical company. Big deal! That was his mistake.' And she offered a grudging explanation, though she did not think the arrogant jerk deserved it. 'As for the business plan she used, yes, it was mine. My end of year's assignment at art college, nothing more. My mother kept it as a memento. But KHE is not the same company, and your uncle's problem has nothing to do with me,' Eloise declared defiantly and, picking up her purse, she stood up. 'And given they are both dead I very much doubt the dead can sue anyone,' she ended caustically.

He must take her for a prize fool. It hurt her deeply that her mother had used her idea, but that did not make Eloise responsible, and she'd never seen any of the money. Marcus had no case. She was calling his bluff…

'You should stick to designing, Eloise; your grasp of law is negligible. I am the executor of Theo's estate and as such can sue on behalf of his family,' Marcus informed her curtly, a dark gleam simmering like the threat of a lightning storm in the back of his fierce gaze. 'The name you were using at the time is on the contract. Eloise By Design or KHE, the intention and setting up of the company was the same. I also happen to know Theo's money ended up in a joint bank account between you and your mother. I also know you emptied the account to buy the London property you use for business.'

Eloise froze, her hand tightening in a death grip on her purse, her knuckles gleaming white with the strain. 'Oh, my God!' she gasped. She had forgotten all about the joint account. The account her mother had insisted on setting up supposedly to keep the money from the sale of the family home between them. The money Eloise had wanted to give her outright. The account Eloise had never touched until after her mother's death. She had been amazed at the amount of money her mother had left her. But, as her mother's lawyer had pointed out at the time, Chloe had been a very successful business woman.

But what kind of business—thieving? She had even stolen from her own daughter! There could be no doubt about it, Chloe had actually used Eloise's college project to con Theo Toumbis into thinking he was investing in a new company, and forged Eloise's signature…

Sadly Eloise realised she had never really known her mother at all. She had carried an idealised version of a brilliantly successful, elegant woman in her heart and mind for so long, the realisation it was all a myth was a brutal blow and her disillusionment was total.

'Waiting for divine intervention is not going to help you.' Marcus's mocking voice split the lengthening silence. 'You have two choices, my deal or the courts. So what is it to be?'

Little did he know Eloise thought bitterly, that there was no choice at all! She could not go to court…not after what had happened. She risked a glance at his rock-hard profile, the innate ruthlessness in every chiselled line, and any thought of pleading with him died a death. Not that she would have done that anyway, she immediately corrected. She had fought too long and hard for her pride and self-esteem to throw it away on a pig like Marcus.

Drawing on all her considerable will power, she slowly sat back down on the sofa. 'Why are you doing this?' She lifted glacial green eyes to his face. 'Why invest in a company you want to ruin?'

'Admittedly, that wasn't my first plan. Theo was a fool; he gave money to your mother at a time when he was expanding his holiday development on Rykos. It was money he could not afford, and for the next four years he struggled with a cash flow problem, but was too proud to ask for my help. He only mentioned the matter to me a week before he died when his company was going bankrupt.'

'Bankrupt.' Eloise almost groaned out loud; it was getting worse by the second.

'Obviously, as executor of his estate, it is my responsibility to make sure his wife and daughter do not suffer from his stupidity. Revenge is a totally human emotion, and, I admit, I went seeking it from your mother. It took some time for the detective agency I hired to track her down, only to discover she was dead, and there was no *sister*, only a daughter—it took a while longer to track you down,' Marcus declared harshly.

'But in memory of the innocent girl I once knew, I intended to give you the benefit of the doubt. I told myself you were young and probably influenced by your crooked mother. I checked you and KHE out and saw it was a quite profitable company with potential, and I was prepared to simply ask for Theo's investment back over time.'

He had remembered her, and he had been prepared to believe her. That went a long way to improving Eloise's view of him. 'That's a good idea,' she agreed, a glimmer of hope lighting her eyes for a moment. 'I'm sure we can come to some arrangement...'

'Oh, no, Eloise, that option has gone.' In two lithe strides he was standing over her. 'I was prepared to compromise my own convictions because I wanted you in my bed, to finish what we started five years ago. But not any more,' Marcus responded with silken softness. 'Not when I discovered after sharing my bed you quite happily admitted to having shared Ted Charlton's not twenty-four hours earlier, simply to get his money for your business,' he reminded her, his black eyes raking over her in utter contempt. 'You were obviously up to your old tricks again.'

'That's a lie,' Eloise gasped, so horrified by his unjust and ridiculous accusation she could only stare up at him.

'And I am supposed to believe you?' One dark brow arched sardonically. He watched every last scrap of colour slide from her cheeks. God, but she was good, he thought cynically, before adding, 'No way.'

Eloise leapt to her feet. 'You're wrong—I never slept with Ted! And you have a damn cheek insinuating I did,' she flung back at him, her temper simmering.

'Ted told me otherwise. He called me in New York and offered me his share in KHE. Apparently his ex-wife's lawyers had taken him to the cleaners, and he needed the money. It was an intriguing prospect and I helped Ted out of his problem, and acquired part of what should have been my uncle's anyway.'

'You did it to help Ted; how altruistic of you,' Eloise sneered, squashing the wayward thought that perhaps he had done it to help Ted out of a jam. Telling herself

Marcus was rich enough to buy a hundred companies without batting an eye.

'I thought so at the time, until we had a night out to celebrate clinching the deal, and Ted got quite drunk. Ted quite openly admitted to sleeping with you.'

'No, Ted wouldn't do that,' she cried.

'Yes, he did, and I was using sleep as an euphemism.' Marcus drawled sardonically 'We both know what you do in bed.'

Eloise reddened furiously. She had defended her honour once in front of a judge, and the experience had almost destroyed her. Never again.

'You bastard.' Her hand flung wildly and cracked against his olive skinned cheek. 'I have had enough of you,' she screamed, totally losing it. He had dragged up old memories—as if it wasn't enough to know her mother had betrayed her, but so had Ted and Marcus. She was distraught, fed-up and furious. Catching her wildly swinging hand, Marcus yanked her into his arms. She struggled desperately against his hard body. 'Let go of me,' she seethed.

'No.' Marcus lifted her off her feet with frightening ease and, landing on the sofa, he pinned her back against the cushioned arm. 'I am not letting you go,' and his mouth crashed down on hers.

He kissed her with a raw passion; a sexuality that was as savage as it was exciting. Eloise felt his hungry need through every cell in her body, and for a timeless moment she responded with a hot mindless urgency, until he lifted his head and reality kicked in.

Stretched out beside her, Marcus stared down at her, noting the flush of passion on her expressive face, his lustrous dark eyes gleaming with pure male satisfaction. 'The chemistry hasn't changed—you want me,' he challenged in a deep dark voice. 'And, even knowing what kind of woman you are, I still want you,' he admitted with a chilling smile slanting his sensuous lips. 'I bought out Ted because I don't want him around you. I don't want any man near you except me.'

'But why?' she cried. He didn't love her—it was just sex—and she tried to struggle, kicking out at him, but only succeeded in entwining her leg around one of his.

'I thought I made myself abundantly clear, but if you insist.' His upper torso loomed half over her, an imprisoning hand tightened around her waist, lifting, reinforcing the physical contact she was trying to avoid, while his other hand tangled in her hair, tipping her head up to his.

'I know you, sweetheart,' Marcus drawled sardonically. 'Let you out of my sight and you will sweet-talk some wealthy old man into giving you the money you need to pay off your debt. Ted's offer was opportune. I own a large chunk of your company and I can prevent that happening.' Her heart was pounding, her eyes wide open and trained on his darkly handsome face which was taut with anger and something else she could not fail to recognise. 'And no woman makes a fool of me twice,' he concluded curtly.

Winded by the ruthless speed with which he had subdued her, breathless and forced into an intimate awareness of his hard muscled body, all the fight went out of her. But she did try to deny his last assumption. 'No. I didn't…' But he didn't give her the chance.

'No more lies,' Marcus rasped, and he kissed her again.

He wasn't going to listen to her and, even if he did, he would never believe her, not with the proof overwhelmingly against her. His tongue hungrily probed the moist intimacy of her mouth. She wanted to resist, she really did… But a hoarse moan of capitulation was forced from her throat, and her taut body melted against him. She reached for his shoulders and kissed him back with help-less abandon.

The why and wherefore no longer mattered. Time had no meaning; all that existed was the miraculous world of delicious sensations, which only Marcus could provide. His hand at her back urged her up and the strapless bodice of her dress was somehow pushed down. His dark head lowered, burying his head in the soft swell of her breasts until his mouth found a taut nipple to suckle with fierce pleasure.

Three long months, and suddenly physical feelings that she had tried so desperately to suppress exploded in a fe-verish response. The blood flowed thick and hot through her veins. Her fingers spread up and out to bury in the silken depths of his black hair and hold him to her, never wanting the excitement to end.

Marcus lifted his head and looked down at her pale skin hectically flushed with the heat of arousal. 'You're mine,' Marcus grated roughly. 'For as long as I want you.' His glittering dark eyes clashed with her dazed green, and he smiled a predatory twist of his sensuous lips and, rearing back, shrugged off his shirt his hands going to the waist-band of his trousers.

Cool air washed over her aching breasts and a tiny voice of sanity echoed in her head. Her mouth ran suddenly dry, and she tensed in rejection at what she was inviting.

'No,' Eloise groaned. Whether she was decrying his abandonment of their lovemaking or denying him, she didn't actually know herself.

Marcus swore viciously under his breath. His dark eyes, leaping with anger, flashed to hers. 'No. You say no?' His hands stilled at his waist.

'Yes.' Suddenly she was afraid of the half-naked man looming over her.

He almost threw her away from him, her head bouncing on the arm of the sofa as he stood up, and stared down at her with icy eyes.

'You're a very sensual woman. Your whole body trembles when I touch you, your eyes flash emerald sparks, you want me—but obviously your stock in trade is to tease. Well, forget it with me… I've never forced a woman in my life, and I'm not about to start with you. I can't abide a tease.'

CHAPTER SIX

MARCUS could not have hurt her more if he had tried for a lifetime!

A flashback of another time—another man, equally as hard—calling her the same, and the eyes of every one in the courtroom fixed on her. She blinked rapidly and snapped out of her sensual daze. Sick with horror, Eloise stared at Marcus. He thought she was a tease, along with a thief and a whore, so why did her traitorous body react so excitedly with this one man, when he obviously despised her?

Suddenly she was plunged into complete turmoil between her thoughts and emotions. She was deeply ashamed of the fact that she could not withstand Marcus's particular brand of blatant sexuality, even though she knew he had no respect, no love for her at all.

Ashen-faced, she struggled into a sitting position, and pulled her dress up over her tight, aching breasts. Head bent, her hair cascaded either side of her face, hopefully masking the humiliation and desperation she felt from his too astute eyes. She clasped her hands in her lap, her fingers entwining nervously. Her heart raced and she fought for breath—panic or passion, she didn't know.

Marcus saw the pallor of her face before she hid it from him. He noted the defeated droop of her shoulders covered by the mass of her glorious red hair. She looked like some fragile, broken tiger lily sitting there.

Where the hell had that maudlin thought come from? He frowned and shoved his hands into the pocket of his trousers, willing his aroused flesh to subside. She was a man-eating tiger all right. The fragile flower act was a ploy to catch her prey, and he would do well to remember that. His frown deepened. 'What's it to be, Eloise?' A private arrangement or the courts?'

He might as well have said a private affair, because that was what he was demanding from her. She lifted her head. He was standing a foot away, his black hair ruffled where she had run her fingers through it, naked from the waist up. His bronzed torso glistened in the dim light, the muscles clearly defined. She thought of how he had kissed, of how it had felt to have his mouth at her breast, and wished he would put his shirt back on.

'Not the court,' she said a little unsteadily, lowering her eyes. Marcus couldn't possibly know and she couldn't tell him, but it had coloured her life for years.

It had been a sunny June evening, and a game of tennis on the public courts in the park with a student friend. Eloise at twenty had thought nothing of walking back across the park to the flat she shared with Katy. Until she was grabbed from behind, a horrible dirty hand squeezing her breast, and she was dragged into some bushes. Her attacker had had a knife, but she had screamed anyway and struggled like mad, lashing out with her tennis racket. Her top was ripped from her body, and the short tennis skirt was no barrier to the man's marauding hand. The knife was at her throat and she was giving up hope of escape when a dog pounced on her attacker. He lashed out with the knife and slashed her leg before running off. The man was caught, but as horrific as the attack had been the court case that followed was worse.

Eloise would never forget facing her attacker in court, nor could she forget the defence lawyer. He raped her with words. Her perfectly conventional tennis outfit became clothing designed to tease, a deliberate provocation. It was her fault she had long legs, long hair; she shared a flat with a man, the fact it was Katy's boyfriend ignored. The lawyer made her feel dirty and ashamed. The case took two days, and by the end of it when a guilty verdict was returned Eloise was too emotionally shattered to care. And she vowed she would never set foot in a court again.

Lifting her head, she stared at Marcus with cold green eyes. 'Definitely not the court.'

A cynical smile twisted Marcus's hard mouth. 'No court.' Why did that not surprise him? It simply confirmed she was guilty and she knew it. Still, what did he care for her morals or lack of them? He wanted her sinfully sexy body in his bed, until he sated himself, and she obviously knew the score, so there would be no messy break-up when he tired of her. His conscience clear, reaching out, he grasped her upper arms and hauled her to her feet.

'Instead, you agree to be my mistress for one year, *exclusively* mine,' he emphasised, his dark deep-set eyes burning into Eloise's. 'I don't share, understand?'

She understood, all right. One year in his bed: it was blackmail, pure and simple. Well, maybe not so pure…

'At the end of that time I will give you the evidence of the fraud and cancel your debt.'

'I would prefer to pay back the money my *mother* stole.' Eloise accented the word. 'Not me,' she added forcibly; she was not admitting a guilt she did not feel.

'That isn't an option.' But Marcus had to give her points for trying; she looked so defiant, her green eyes blazing, and infinitely desirable. He wondered if he should have said two, or maybe three years.

Realistically, she knew if she lived as poor as a church mouse it would take her years to pay back the money, unless she sold the house, and that would ruin her relationship with her friends, never mind what it would do to the business. It was a catch twenty-two situation. She looked into his hard dark eyes, and she knew he would carry out his threat of court action.

A tiny shiver slivered down her spine, and suddenly she was fiercely aware of his long fingers on the flesh of her upper arms, the sensual heat emanating from his hard body. She thought of his lovemaking; the experience had been an earth-shattering, life-changing experience for her. But how did she know what it had been for him? Not love, that was for sure, but good enough sex as he wanted more, she realised grimly. As for what she wanted, her body had already answered for her, her nipples tight against the bodice of her dress.

'All right,' Eloise said lowering her eyes from his to intense gaze, afraid he would see more than she wanted him to know. 'I agree, one year from today and we go our separate ways.'

'I knew you would be sensible, after all what have you got to lose?' he husked, his hands stroking up over the soft curve of her shoulders.

Eloise didn't answer for a long moment. *I knew you would be sensible.* His arrogant assumption stiffened her spine, as nothing else could have done, a slow-growing, icy anger invading every cell in her body. Marcus did not know her at all, and never would…

For four years she had had no faith in her own femininity and had repressed all her sexual urges, until three months ago when Marcus had shown her in one memorable night what it was to be a woman. For a while she had confused lust with love. But by not contacting her again Marcus had effectively disabused her of the notion, and his actions tonight simply underlined the point.

For the first time in her life she faced up to the fact she

was a mature woman, a sensual being with needs and desires of her own and she had no need to be ashamed of them... Ironically, Marcus had taught her that tonight as well. If sex was all he wanted, *what had she got to lose?* His words! They had already been lovers, and she did want him; she had a sneaky suspicion he might be the only man she wanted. But she owed him no loyalty, nothing, and she could walk away when the time came with her business and life intact.

She let her gaze slide over him, sizing him up, tall powerful, authority stamped in every line, a pure alpha male. She didn't doubt he would take her to court. She lifted her eyes to his face—strikingly handsome, with a strong jaw that was beginning to show a dark shadow, and a wickedly sensuous mouth—and she had made her decision. Why not use him as he intended using her?

'Nothing. Nothing at all,' she finally answered. Eloise saw the blaze of triumph in the glittering depths of his eyes, and his satisfied smile. She felt his hand tighten on her shoulder. She knew he was going to kiss her and she waited until his dark head bent towards her before tilting up her chin determinedly and meeting his smile with a cold one of her own.

'But first we will have to work out the technicalities,' she said brusquely, and saw his head lift and the flicker of surprise chase across his handsome features. 'I will not have Katy or Harry involved in any way in our private arrangement.'

Marcus couldn't read the expression in the depths of her huge emerald eyes. But he guessed she was thinking there was really no way out for her. And this was her way of gaining some kind of control.

'I agree, strictly personal between you and I.' He could be magnanimous in victory, and let her think she had won a point. He drew her closer, he had more pressing needs right at this moment. 'After all it isn't Katy or Harry I want to sleep with,' Marcus drawled in a deep husky tone, his breath fanning her cheek.

She had agreed to be his for one year. He should have felt elated but he couldn't help wondering what her eyes would look like if they were shining with joy for the man she loved, instead of the man she had agreed to sleep with for money, because the bottom line was, that was what she'd just done.

For a second his fingers dug almost angrily into the tender flesh of her shoulder, refusing to admit he was disappointed, telling himself revenge was sweet.

'Marcus…' Eloise planted her hands on his chest with the intention of holding him away. Immediately she knew it was a mistake; the hot heat of his skin beneath her palms was an enticement to stroke, to linger, to explore the muscular contours.

'I love the way you say my name,' he declared throatily. His dark head lowered and his carnal mouth found her parted lips.

The instant their mouths met, Eloise sank beneath a hot hungry surge of passion. It shouldn't be like this, but it was what she'd just agreed their arrangement should be, and her treacherous body felt otherwise. She surrendered instantly to the drugging pleasure of his sensuous mouth and the heated caress of his hands, and within seconds constructive thought became impossible.

His hands wrenched down the top of her strapless dress again, and with a groan Marcus lifted her and suckled an erect rosy nipple. It was a torment, a sweet torment that sent quivering need lancing through her body, and a shocked cry escaped her convulsed throat.

Somehow she was on her back on the sofa, with Marcus

on top of her. He skated a hand over her burgeoning breast, his dark eyes blazing down at her, as his long fingers toyed with her sensitised flesh until she was utterly possessed by the power of sensation. Her hands clasped his broad, tanned shoulders, her fingers trailed with tactile delight over the satin-smooth skin to tangle in the soft curling chest hair, scratching a hard male nipple.

With a low groan Marcus's dark head dipped, and his mouth was on her breast again, but this time his tongue and teeth sent her shuddering into spasm after spasm of mindless pleasure. She twisted urgently beneath him, possessed by a need, a hunger so intense she was lost to all else.

Sinking back on his knees, Marcus grated, 'I want you now,' and a large hand skimmed the fabric of her gown down over her hips and legs, and tossed it to the ground. 'Damn it, I can't wait!' His eyes black pools of desire in the taut planes of his face, he stared down at her. His long elegant fingers grasped the tiny black lace briefs, her only covering, and drew them from her body.

Naked beneath him, Eloise didn't care. He was hot and hard and very male, and she was amazed at her own pleasure in simply looking. But looking was not enough; she wanted him naked as herself. Involuntarily, she reached out her hand and fumbled with the fastening of his trousers. He did it for her...

With a low laugh, a husky sound of primitive pleasure, Marcus covered her mouth with rough drugging kisses, as he dispensed with the remainder of his clothes.

He reared over her, naked, and without warning, in an explosion of renewed passion, he kissed his way down her sensitised body, mouth, breasts, stomach, and finally settled at the juncture of her thighs.

She arched off the sofa like an arrow from a bow, shuddering uncontrollably; never had she experienced such intimacy. She tangled her fingers in the night-black hair of his head, and urged him back up to her.

'You drive me mad.' Marcus growled when he drew level with her passion-glazed face.

He took her swollen mouth with a raw, savage hunger that sent her over the edge into a wild writhing wanton in his arms. She rubbed her aching breasts against his chest. Her arms wrapped around his neck, her fingers digging into his flesh. His hands swept down her body in one long, heated caress and then he lifted her, curling her legs around his lean waist, and surged into her in one mighty thrust.

Stilling for a moment, he shuddered against her, his molten black eyes almost angry burning into hers. 'You do this to me,' he rasped, and thrust again.

Eloise felt him move with every pore and cell in her body, smooth and slow, then fast and rough, driving her ever higher until she was consumed by the mighty primeval rhythm of his huge body, the explosive force of his virility urging her to the ultimate peak of excitement. She sank her teeth into his shoulder, as she soared over the edge into a clenching quivering climax at the same time as he did.

Pinned beneath him, and shivering in the aftermath of passion, Eloise tried to get her tumultuous emotions under some kind of control. But all she could think of was the blessed weight of his hot, damp body, his heartbeat thumping against her breast, the heavy sound of his laboured breathing, a symphony to her ears. Her hands stroked down his broad back, loving the sensation of sweat-slicked skin beneath her fingers, loving him… No… She must not confuse great sex with anything else, ever again. She meant nothing to him, and when he abruptly rolled off her and stood up, she told herself she was glad, burying the memory of the afterglow of pleasure they had shared the first time they had made love in the deepest recess of her mind. She wanted nothing from Marcus, no emotional involvement of any kind, she ruled in her head.

She glanced up at Marcus and was suddenly extremely conscious of her naked state, but it was obvious he didn't feel as awkward as she did. With casual ease he picked up his trousers and stepped into them, zipped the fly, and just as casually bent and picked up her dress and dropped it on her.

'Cover yourself. You don't want to catch cold.'

Catch cold? He had to be joking! She had burned for him, and even now simply looking at him brought warmth to her face she could not hide.

But he wasn't joking. His dark eyes raked over her in analytical scrutiny, and he concluded. 'You're incredibly beautiful, incredibly sexy, but with no morals. Still, two out of three isn't bad,' he offered with a husky laugh. 'There is a bed next door.' A smile curved his sexy mouth, his dark eyes gleaming with renewed desire. 'Let's use it.'

'Let's not.' Eloise pulled her dress over her head and stood up, smoothing the fabric over her slender hips. His amusement and obvious contempt for her as an individual was enough to re-enforce her *no emotional involvement* rule. Marcus hated her, and yet she had fallen into his arms like a ripe plum, and loved every second, she admitted honestly. But she had no intention of following his every command like some concubine; her pride would not let her.

Why, why Marcus? How was it Marcus could turn her into a weak, needy woman, when other men, even men she knew well and respected, left her cold? It had to be her own traumatic past. Plus, she dryly admitted, his undoubted sexual expertise had made her a victim to her own body's uncontrollable desire for the man, and she didn't want to be. She was no man's victim.

With that thought uppermost in her mind, she raked her hands through the tumbled mass of her hair and, discovering a couple of hair pins, she twisted her hair into a knot at her nape, fixed with the pins. Making a determined effort to appear sophisticated, she straightened up and directed a cool glance at Marcus.

'I have to leave. I have a breakfast meeting with Katy and Harry and, as we agreed, it's better they know nothing about...' Was it an affair? Business. She struggled with the wording, the colour rising in her cheeks. 'Our arrangement,' she finally settled on.

'Our arrangement,' Marcus drawled with a sardonic arch of one dark brow. She was doing it again, blushing... The little witch actually thought he was going to sneak around like some illicit lover. Well, she was in for a rude awakening.

'I think the word you are looking for is *affair*, Eloise, and as for keeping it a secret—' he gave her a chilling half-smile '—forget it. You and I are partners in every way, and I will attend the breakfast meeting with you.'

The horrible part was, Eloise knew she could not stop him. Her gaze slid over his half naked body, igniting a familiar flare of heat deep inside her, and she tried to dampen it down. 'With your investment in KHE, that is your prerogative.' She endeavoured to keep the conversation impersonal. But how could her voice sound so matter-of-fact, when inside she was a mass of confusing emotions? she wondered.

'Yes, and don't you forget it.' Black eyes glittered over her taut figure. 'We are going to have a very public affair, Eloise. As I told you before, I'm not taking the chance of you finding some other wealthy fool to bail you out.'

Eloise looked at him, incredulous and inexplicably hurt. 'You imagine I would do that?'

'I know so.' He gave a sardonic laugh. 'And I see no reason to take an unnecessary risk. You will be publicly labelled Kouvaris's woman.' Broad shoulders lifted in a casual shrug. 'I have yet to meet a man brave enough to cross me.' His firm lips curved at the corners in a cynical smile. 'Or foolish enough.'

It was the supreme arrogance that got to Eloise. Her palm itched and she longed to smack the grin off his face, but warring emotions stayed her hand. She did not dare, if she hoped to persuade him to at least try and be discreet. Her stomach churned over at the thought of being branded Marcus's woman. She cherished her privacy above everything.

She looked at him, her green eyes colliding with hard black, and it took every ounce of will power she possessed to hold his gaze. 'Katy knows me well. She will never believe we are an item, not so fast,' she said softly.

Marcus threw his head back and laughed out loud and, taking a step forward, his hands settled on her shoulders. 'Eloise.' He shook his dark head, his eyes lit with amusement roamed over her. 'But we were sweethearts on our first dinner date,' he declared with shattering logic. 'I bet the last three months you waited for my call, wondered where I was and with whom. And tonight, as soon as you saw me, your gorgeous eyes dilated, and that sexy body of yours sent off signals like the firing of a rocket on the launch pad.'

Mortified, Eloise swallowed hard. 'That's not true,' she muttered.

'Katy might know your mind, but your body is all mine. Do you want me to prove it to you again?' Marcus said softly into the suddenly tension-filled atmosphere.

'No.' Her green eyes pleaded with him. 'But please will you be discreet in front of Katy and Harry, at least until they leave Paris? I'll think of something to tell Katy when I get home.' Her lips thinned. 'Obviously not the truth.'

'Yes, okay.' Marcus was prepared to set her mind at rest for the moment.

'Thank you,' Eloise managed to say and, taking a step back, she added, 'You can call me that cab now.' And, while she waited for the taxi, she told him the name of the hotel and the time of the breakfast meeting, plus some of her latest ideas.

Marcus looked at Eloise. She had backed away from him, as far as the door, as if she could not get away fast enough. She was rambling on, and he was pretty sure, she had no idea what she was talking about. As he watched, he realised she actually was incredibly nervous, if not frightened.

His gut tightened, and for a second he wondered if she really was afraid of him, but then he saw the tip of her tongue lick over her bottom lip, swollen from the passion of their kisses. Hell, no, she had wanted him every bit as he wanted her. He was falling into the same old trap of assigning finer feelings to the woman, when he knew for a fact she did not have any. It was more likely she did not want her friend Katy to discover the dubious deal she and her mother had got up to, and realise that Eloise was not quite the honest, straightforward girl she appeared to be.

Picking up his shirt, he slipped it on, a smug smile curving his mouth as Eloise was silenced for a moment, her green eyes watching his every move with a fascination she had great difficulty disguising. He stepped towards her.

The entry phone pealed. The cab had arrived.

Marcus took her down to the street. The soft light of the street lamp turned her glorious red hair into a fiery halo, and he couldn't help himself. He clasped her face between his hands and looked deep into her emerald eyes, then bent his head and kissed her gently on her softly swollen lips. He felt the sudden tremor sweep through her and her sudden tension as she tried to prevent her reaction.

Her resistance was a challenge and he was about to deepen the kiss, show her the futility of trying to deny the devastating physical desire between them. But for some inexplicable reason he didn't. 'I'll see you back to your hotel,' he offered softly, running an elegant finger down the soft curve of her cheek, before setting her free. 'If you like.' He gave her the choice.

'No. No, thanks. We will meet at breakfast in a few hours.'

Once inside her hotel room, Eloise headed straight for the shower. She stood under the powerful spray, scrubbing at her slender body, trying to remove the scent of Marcus from her skin. But it was a futile exercise. She only had to think of him to taste him on her tongue, feel him on her skin, and after five minutes she gave up. Drying herself down with a large fluffy towel, she walked back into the bedroom and, picking up the white cotton tee-shirt she favoured for sleeping in, slipped between the sheets on the wide bed and closed her eyes.

But sleep was a long time in coming. She could have spent the night lying in Marcus's arms. A tear trickled from the corner of her eyes to flow smoothly down her cheek. No matter how she tried to pretend, she knew in her heart she could easily fall in love with Marcus all over again. In his arms she felt safe and loved, which in reality was stupid, she knew. There was no denying the power of the sexual chemistry between them, but it could not negate the fact that they didn't even like each other. He thought she was a thief and worse. Her innate honesty forced her to admit he had good reason to think so. But did that justify his treatment of her? She had tried to explain but he was incapable of listening, or only heard what he wanted to hear.

She had met a lawyer like that in the criminal court at the tender age of twenty, and it had taken her years to recover from the verbal mauling. Consequently, she was not prepared to justify herself to any man ever again.

No, she would play his game, act the worldly woman he imagined she was until his desire for revenge on her ran out. Dear heaven, she'd had plenty of practice at hiding her true emotions. As a child she'd pretended to her grandparents and everyone else she didn't mind her parents never being around. How hard could it be to act the successful, sophisticated mistress of a man like Marcus for one solitary year? A vivid mental image of his glorious naked body filled her mind. Not hard at all when the fringe benefits were spectacular sex, she thought, her temperature rising. She rolled over onto her stomach, muffling a groan of frustration in the pillow, and finally fell asleep.

CHAPTER SEVEN

AT SEVEN-THIRTY the next morning Eloise walked into the dining room of the hotel. She had dressed with care in slim-fitting stone linen trousers, with a matching jacket and mint-green silk top beneath. With the careful use of cosmetics, she hoped she had disguised the ravages of the emotional turmoil and sleepless night from her friends' view. She needn't have worried! A glimmer of a smile curved her full lips as she saw Katy and Harry already seated at a table, by a window overlooking the river. Katy was wearing sunglasses.

Eloise walked over and joined them. 'Hangover, Katy?' she prompted, pulling out a chair and slipping off her jacket. She placed it around the back and sat down opposite her friends.

'And good morning to you, too,' Katy mocked, and Harry laughed.

'Got it in one, Eloise. My wife's first big night out since becoming a mum, and she has overdone it somewhat. Poor Floe got up with the baby during the night, and she's busy packing for all of us. Help yourself to coffee, and you and I can run over what needs to be done. We'll save the big discussion until you return to England.' He cast a loving look to his wife. 'Katy is in no state to have any valid opinion on anything, this morning.'

Eloise poured herself a cup of coffee from the pot provided. The table was set for three and Harry had already ordered continental breakfast. She knew they were leaving for the airport by eight-thirty, and she felt a tiny stab of guilt because she had told Marcus the meeting was at eight-forty-five—but then, as she reminded herself, she didn't owe him any loyalty.

Katy groaned. 'You're right. Keep it light.' Removing her sunglasses, she winced. 'My God, never again!' And, raising bleary eyes to Eloise, she added, 'Trust you to look good. So come on, tell me what you and our new partner Marcus got up to last night after we left?'

'We had a dance and I got a cab home.' Eloise took a long swallow of her coffee, successfully fighting back the blush that threatened. She had a vital question of her own she wanted answered. She had realised in the early hours before dawn when she had time to think straight, Marcus couldn't have blackmailed her half as effectively if he had not now owned a chunk of their company.

Eloise was no fool. She'd realised if it had been a simple question of repaying the money her mother stole, she could probably have arranged a loan on the property that housed the company. It was in her name but was rented at a pep-percorn rent to KHE. Unfortunately, with Marcus now having taken over Ted Charlton's investment in KHE and added a considerable amount to it, he was in a position to ruin them. She didn't trust him an inch, and the more she thought about it the more she did not believe Marcus had bought Ted's share in KHE simply to help the man out. It would not surprise her at all to discover it was the other way around. Marcus had sought Ted out to get a bigger hold over Eloise. He obviously had a healthy appetite for revenge.

'I want to talk to you about Marcus.' Her determined green eyes fixed on Harry. 'How exactly did he become involved with our business? I do think you should have discussed it with me first.' She didn't want to fall out with

Harry, but she could not allow the unorthodox way Harry had behaved go unchallenged.

For the next few minutes Harry explained and, by the time he'd finished, even Eloise could see there was nothing much else he could have done. Apparently Ted Charlton had informed Harry a few weeks ago his divorce settlement had cost more than he thought, and he was going to have to pull out of the deal. But Ted had called back a few days later and told him not to worry, he had lined up another backer, Mr Kouvaris, and he was prepared to invest twice as much as originally agreed. Harry hadn't wanted to worry Katy and Eloise, so he'd decided to keep it to himself until it was finalised and the Paris boutique opened.

Eloise could not argue with his reasoning. Harry had confirmed what Marcus had told her, that Ted had actually offered him the shares. Her sinister reading of the situation was wrong; her paranoia was showing again, she thought grimly.

Marcus had told her the truth, and it made her feel slightly better. But if she ever saw Ted Charlton again she had a few very pointed questions to ask him. Not least why he had told Marcus she had slept with him?

For the next half-hour they discussed the opening and various other matters, and it was suggested Eloise should stay in Paris for a week, rather than the couple of days first arranged, just to make sure everything was going smoothly.

'Okay.' Eloise agreed, draining her coffee after eating the last crumb of a particularly delicious chocolate croissant. 'But hadn't you two better collect Benjamin and Floe? You don't want to miss your flight.' She wanted them long gone before Marcus turned up.

Her stomach was churning and her palms were damp

just at the thought of Marcus's impending arrival. Eloise had little faith in her ability to pretend normality with Marcus in front of Katy. Her friend knew her too well, and she breathed an inward sigh of relief as Katy and Harry got to their feet. Shoving back her chair, she slipped her jacket off the back and stood up.

But her relief was short-lived.

'Well, good morning,' Katy exclaimed.

Eloise felt the hairs on the back of her neck stand on end and saw the smile on Katy's face, just before a strong male arm wrapped around her waist and drew her back into disturbing proximity with every elegant line of a large muscular body. Marcus was early!

'Good morning Katy, Harry,' Marcus intoned brightly.

Eloise stiffened, and shot him a startled glance. He looked vibrantly masculine, dressed casually in cream cotton pants and a matching polo shirt, his dark features relaxed in a broad smile—while tension knotted every muscle in her body, as she fought the tingling awareness his touch always invoked.

Feeling manipulated, but unable to do anything about it, she watched, as with a swift scrutiny of the remains of breakfast on the table Marcus remarked, 'I appear to be rather late.' His glittering gaze switched to her, and without warning his dark head swooped down, his firm lips brushing hers in a brief kiss. 'Eloise, darling, I thought you said eight forty-five. But I forgive you. It is such a delight to see you looking so beautiful and fresh after our late night.' With arrogant aggression his dark eyes lingered on her now scarlet face, challenging her to object to the intimacy.

The swine was doing it deliberately, Eloise thought furiously. So much for being discreet. She cast a glance at her friend and saw the look of astonishment on Katy's face. 'I must have made a mistake,' she muttered, trying to wriggle free from his restraining arm, but his fingers simply dug deeper into her waist.

'What late night, Eloise? You said you had a dance and caught a cab,' Katy demanded, but her eyes were smiling.

Marcus answered for her. 'She did…eventually. But only after we had visited a local place,' Marcus positively purred, as he surveyed Eloise with dark slumberous eyes, making no attempt to disguise the gleaming awareness in their depths. 'It was great, wasn't it, Eloise?' and he smiled.

She cast him a withering glance, and saw the wicked amusement in his smile. His apartment, local place—my eye! Eloise simmered with anger but, with her two friends watching, she could do nothing but agree. 'Yes.'

'Well, sorry you missed breakfast, Marcus,' Harry cut in. 'But we do have to dash. Not to worry, though, Eloise is staying the rest of the week, and she can fill you in on anything you need to know.'

'I'm sure she can,' Marcus drawled, with a long lingering look at Eloise.

Katy's gaze flicked between Eloise and the man holding her, a frown pleating her brow. 'It's okay, Harry, you stay and have a coffee with Marcus. Eloise can come upstairs and help me. I know she wants to say goodbye to her favourite godson,' she informed. 'We will meet you down here in twenty minutes.'

Marcus had to let Eloise go. But not before he had deliberately dropped another kiss on the top of her head with a murmured, 'Don't be long.'

'Right! What is going on?' Katy demanded as soon as they got in the elevator. 'Marcus is all over you like a rash, and I've never seen you so flustered.' She appraised Eloise with sharp eyes. 'Three months ago you had a dinner date with him and told me it was nothing, a meeting between old friends. Now the man is our partner and he can't keep his hands off you.'

Thankful for her escape from the blasted man for a while, Eloise looked into the slightly worried eyes of Katy. Her friend knew her past history far too well to be fooled into thinking Eloise would indulge in a casual affair, and she knew what she had to do.

'I think I'm in love.' She saw Katy's mouth fall open in shock. 'And I think Marcus feels the same.' Katy knew her too well to believe anything less. She had been Eloise's rock and support after the savage attack she'd suffered, and all through the horror of the court case and publicity that followed. She knew Eloise had never looked at a man since. But Katy was a romantic and Eloise knew nothing less than true love would do for Katy to believe her.

'And have you two, last night…well, I mean, did you?'

'Yes and it was fine,' Eloise said telling the truth at least partially, with a scarlet face.

'Oh, Eloise, I am so happy for you.' And suddenly Eloise was wrapped in Katy's arms. 'I knew one day everything would work out for you.'

Watching the happy family group bundle into the waiting cab, and drive away, all the energy drained out of Eloise. She had done it. She'd smiled and convinced Katy she was happy in her new relationship with Marcus. She'd listened while Katy had fantasised of course Marcus must have loved her all along, and that was why he'd invested in their small company. He'd done it for Eloise.

Eloise did not disillusion her, though it did cross her mind for one mad moment to tell Katy the truth, as they were all leaving and she was struck with the most horrendous feeling of being deserted. The safe, successful world she had built for herself was never going to be the same again. But hugging baby Benjamin to her breast and kissing him goodbye had convinced her she couldn't. There was no way on earth she would jeopardise Katy's happy family unit.

Pale and strained, she threw a bitterly resentful glance at Marcus. 'You certainly didn't waste any time publicising our sordid affair.' He'd turned and was walking back towards the bank of elevators on one wall, his hand apparently glued to her waist, urging her along. 'If you think your behaviour this morning was being discreet, then God help me.'

'Smile,' Marcus suggested silkily, his dark eyes absorbing the tense pallor of her beautiful face. 'Or people might think we're fighting.'

'Since when did you care what other people think?' she flung back, her nostrils flaring at the disturbingly familiar scent of him as he ushered her into the elevator and wrapped his arms around her. Stiff as a board, she glared up at him. 'You promised we would keep it private until they had left Paris.'

'So I lied. A man will promise anything to a woman to get her into bed. You are not that naïve, Eloise,' he opined sardonically. 'You've done the same yourself countless times, I have no doubt.' He shrugged his broad shoulders. 'After all, you lied to me about the time of the breakfast meeting.'

She went from red to as white as death. Being caught out in a lie was embarrassing, but realising he thought her capable of using her body to get what she wanted and it didn't actually bother him told her how little he truly thought of her. Anger and humiliation turned her stomach and she tore herself free from his restraining hold just as the elevator stopped.

'You slimy snake, why don't you take a hike?' she spat and, marching straight to her room, she slid the card in the lock and pushed the door. Nothing happened!

A flash of anger stayed Marcus's step for a moment. He was not in the habit of taking insults from a lady, and certainly not one he had thoroughly bedded only hours earlier. But then, she was no lady, he reminded himself. A liar—yes, and a very sexy one at that, and not worth getting angry over. But with a great rear, he thought as he followed her down the hallway. He wanted her in his bed, nothing more he told himself.

Marcus watched her futile attempt to open the door. Her face was pink, she was angry; no, angry didn't cut it. From the set of her jaw and the tension in every inch of her luscious body, he realised she was nervous, her small hand shaking.

'Allow me.' Marcus took the card from her trembling fingers, and opened the door and followed her inside.

'I told you to go.' Eloise turned on him.

Marcus reached out and held her by the shoulders. 'Is that really what you want?' His brown eyes darkened as they skimmed over her, lingering on the swift rise and fall of her breasts, clearly discernible beneath the fine silk blouse she wore, before returning to her face. He caught a brief glimpse of something very much like fear in her gorgeous green eyes, and inexplicably he felt a twinge of guilt.

He'd accused her of being a thief, and with all the subtlety of a tank he'd told her he wanted her in his bed. Then, while she was still trying to come to terms with the passion they'd shared last night, he'd strolled in on her this morning. Angry at her lie about the time, he'd deliberately embarrassed her in front of her friends, making it plain they were an item.

'Why don't we both take a hike, as you so eloquently put it?' Marcus prompted with a wry smile. 'We could spend the day sight-seeing, having fun.' He looked into her eyes, saw the angry puzzlement there, and felt a pang of conscience, but not enough to stop him drawing her against him and covering her mouth with his own.

'Stop it,' Eloise gasped. She fought him at first, twisting her head from side to side. But he was so persistent and oddly tender; his mouth moved gently against hers, not stopping until, with a little moan, she surrendered and kissed him back.

Marcus broke the kiss, put his hand under her chin, and tilted her head back. 'Spend the day with me.' Amused dark eyes rested assessingly on her beautiful if flushed face. 'You know you want to.'

She did... But catching the hint of mockery in his expression was enough to bring her back to reality with a bump.

'I have to go to work.' Jerkily, Eloise pulled away from him. 'That's why I am here.' And, crossing to the bed, she picked up her purse from the bedside cabinet. Once out of his reach, she took a few deep steadying breaths, managed to get her racing pulse under control and recovered some of her formidable strength of will. Turning, she tossed her head, her red hair flying around her lovely face, determination in every taut line of her slender body.

'After all, you do have an interest now in KHE, and the harder I work the more profit for you,' she said curtly.

Marcus gave a sardonic laugh. 'I'm glad you realise that,' he mocked. 'But, as I'm the boss in this affair, I decide which tasks you perform first.' He cast a provocative glance at the bed before his dark gaze returned to her shocked green.

The implication in his hooded eyes as she took a step

in the direction of the door filled her with disgust and, to her shame, a secret thrill. Her heartbeat leapt at the thickening of the atmosphere; fingers clutching her purse, she stepped hurriedly past him. 'I have to go… I have an appointment with the new sales assistant.'

'I'll come with you.'

Sharply disconcerted, she swung back around, and collided with gleaming black eyes. 'You, but…'

'As you so succinctly pointed out, I have a vested interest in the business.'

Two hours later, Eloise walked out of their new shop, silently fuming. She'd thought she was doing quite well with her schoolgirl French, explaining to the new manageress—a very elegant French lady—and a younger female assistant what was expected of them. Then Marcus had cut in and introduced himself as a partner and wouldn't you just know it? Eloise thought, simmering with resentment. The man spoke fluent French, and charmed the two women so completely Eloise might as well not have been there, for all the notice they took of her.

'Did you have to be so damned interfering?' Eloise snapped, as they stood on the pavement in the summer sunshine. 'I'm perfectly capable of instructing the staff. You didn't have to fawn all over the women.'

Marcus caught the anger in her emerald eyes. A hectic flush coloured her cheeks, and he let his eyes wander with sensual intensity over her, lingering deliberately on the proud thrust of her breasts against the silk shirt. His sensuous mouth quirked at the corners in a knowing grin and he chuckled.

She felt her nipples tighten, and his chuckle simply enraged her further. 'What's so funny?' she snarled.

Throwing an arm around her stiff shoulders, he drew her into his side. 'You're jealous, Eloise.'

It wasn't what Eloise had expected, and she spluttered, 'I am not, you egotistical baboon!'

After a second's pause Marcus threw his dark head back and laughed out loud. 'Well, I suppose a baboon is a step up from a snake. But you are jealous?' His amusement lingered in the narrowed eyes that studied her face. He brushed back a stray tendril of red hair curving her cheekbone. 'Why not admit the truth, Eloise?' he demanded huskily. 'It's the same for me.'

Marcus knew as soon as he said it, he had made a mistake. The man he had been five years ago when they first met, and he had thought her innocent, might have admitted to jealousy. But not the man he was today, with the evidence of her perfidiousness always at the back of his mind. He prided himself on being a sophisticated lover who delighted in women, and always brought them pleasure, but never, ever lost control or revealed his own emotions. Somehow Eloise had the damnable ability to make him forget what she really was, and he didn't like it.

What the hell? he told himself. For one day he was going to forget everything and just enjoy…

Eloise's heart skipped a beat. Marcus, jealous? The notion was balm to her battered pride and she was wretchedly aware of how much she wanted to believe him.

His dark head bent and he kissed her briefly on her lips. His arm dropped from her shoulders and he waved his hand in an expansive arc.

'Look around you, Eloise. The sun is shining, we are in Paris, a city designed for lovers and, whatever else is between us, we are lovers. Indulge me and let me show you around.'

She looked at him. The dark vitality of his masculinity was a potent temptation to any woman, and she was no exception. Why he wanted her didn't seem that important all of a sudden. The sun gilded his black hair in golden highlights. Eloise's admiring emerald eyes clashed with smouldering black, and his starkly handsome features darkened, a slow sensual smile curving his beautiful mouth. Her heart missed a beat and resumed at a faster pace.

He extended an elegant tanned hand towards her. 'Go with the flow, Eloise. Isn't that your English expression?' His accent thickened in his husky-voiced question and she allowed him to tuck her slender hand in his.

'Yes.' His glittering gaze mesmerised her. 'Yes, it is,' she agreed, and felt the flow of electricity from his touch through every nerve in her body.

'I thought the Eiffel Tower first. You agree.'

'Do I have a choice?' she prompted with a wry smile, seeing the determination in his expression. He really did mean to do the whole tourist bit, and somehow she found it rather endearing.

'For a beautiful lady, you ask far too many questions,' Marcus remarked and tugged her along the pavement.

They rode the elevator to the top of the Eiffel Tower. Eloise took one look at the panoramic view, and immediately her legs shook and her head spun. She saw Marcus gesture to something in the distance and vaguely heard his voice extolling the virtues of some building, but she felt dizzy. Reaching out, she gripped his arm, and clung. Heights were not her thing.

'Eloise.' His narrowed gaze swept her pale features, instantly recognising the problem, and pulled her into his arms. 'You should have told me you were afraid of heights. We're going back down.' And he held her firmly in his protective embrace, only releasing her as they stepped back onto firm ground.

Eloise glanced back up at the towering iron structure,

and still felt slightly dizzy. She leant against one of the mighty iron supports for a moment, marvelling that she'd actually had the nerve to go to the top. 'I did it.' She flashed Marcus a shaky smile.

'Yes.' He smiled back. 'But I think Les Invalides, and Napoleon's tomb next; it is underground and safe for you. Unless you are afraid of going underground as well,' he queried seriously.

She was elated that at last she had finally seen the view from the top of the world-famous tower. She had never dared do it by herself, even though she had been to Paris quite a few times in the past months—and, surprised by Marcus's apparent concern, her luscious lips parted in a beaming grin. 'Marcus, you're fussing like an old woman,' she giggled.

An arrested expression flickered across his handsome face, and he closed the space between them. He braced his hands on the iron beam either side of her, and covered her mouth with his. And there at the foot of the Eiffel Tower, in broad daylight, with hundreds of people watching, he kissed her with a hunger, a fiery brand of ownership that sent a wave of scorching heat racing through her veins.

'Marcus.' She gasped his name as he released her swollen lips. 'People are looking.'

'So? You're my woman,' he declared on a ragged breath. 'But you're right, I am not usually in the habit of kissing in public. But you drive me crazy.' He looked around distractedly, 'Let's go.'

Marcus could have been one of Napoleon's generals Eloise thought with secret amusement, as he proceeded to lead her to Les Invalides, then across the river to the Arc de Triomphe, and the tomb of the unknown soldier. He pointed out the matching arch over a mile away, marvelling at the skill of the architect.

They sat at a pavement café of the Champs Elysée, and

there with the local Parisians, and the obvious tourists from all over the world, they shared a bottle of wine, and a meal of light fluffy omelettes with salad. Whether it was the wine or the company, Eloise realised she really was enjoying herself. Marcus was a good conversationalist and very knowledgeable about Paris, and as if by common consent they avoided talking about anything personal. Relaxed, Eloise drained her glass and replaced it on the table. She glanced across at Marcus; he was withdrawing some money from his wallet.

'Are we leaving already?' she demanded. 'I quite like watching the world go by.'

And he loved watching her, Marcus realised, but didn't say it. 'Yes,' he confirmed. The jade silk shirt was sleeveless, and the top button was unfastened, revealing a shadowy cleavage. Intellectually, he knew she was a liar and a cheat, but it didn't stop his body responding in a most inconvenient manner.

'I plan we visit the Louvre next for approximately two hours, and then visit the Pompidou centre,' he ground out, shoving one hand in his pocket and rising to his feet.

'Very organised,' Eloise teased him but took the hand he held out to her, and let him lead her down towards the Louvre.

The queue to enter was huge…

Eloise turned laughing eyes up to Marcus, and saw the frustration in the set of his hard features. 'Finally defeated, *mon generale*,' she mocked. 'You have to wait like everyone else.'

'No, I think I have waited long enough.' He tightened his grip on her hand and surveyed her with blatant male intensity.

Suddenly tension simmered in the air between them. The crowd around them vanished and Eloise was drowning in the darkening depths of his deep brown eyes. His thumb stroked the palm of her hand and then he tugged her very gently against the hard heat of his body.

'Why wait to see an ancient work of art, when I have a perfect work of art in my grasp?' he said with blunt urgency. 'My apartment is not far.'

She wanted to lash out at him for looking at her with such arrogant possession. Yesterday she might have done but, after last night, all she could think of was his sensual mouth on hers, his large, strong, naked body possessing her.

He pulled her along the road and into the shadowed entrance hall of a large building. She could feel her heart hammering in her chest, and she could sense the powerful sexual tension that gripped his great frame. At the foot of the stairs, he glanced down at her and, as if compelled, he backed her against the wall and covered her mouth with his own in a ravishing kiss that left her boneless when he finally lifted his dark head.

'Hell! Why did I choose the top floor?' he grated and dragged her up the stairs, finally turning around and sweeping her up in his arms, for the final two flights.

He opened the door, and she was back where she had been last night. This time, Marcus didn't hesitate but marched straight into the bedroom.

Eloise didn't have time to survey her surroundings as he lowered her down the lean length of his superbly fit body. She could feel the tension in his every muscle, the faint musky scent all male and all Marcus, and she quivered, inside heat surging in her lower body.

His hands dispensed with the buttons down the front of her blouse with a speed that smacked of vast experience, but Eloise didn't care; she grasped his lean waist and hung on as he slipped her blouse from her shoulder and flicked her bra open and off.

With a groan Marcus dropped his head and suckled at

an erect dusky nipple, and her hands clenched fiercely in his waist, an involuntary groan of pleasure torn from her throat. Her head fell back, and then her whole body as Marcus eased her down on the bed and, with hands that shook slightly, divested her of her trousers and briefs.

His own clothes were shrugged off in a second and he was over her, large, lean and magnificently aroused. She was awed by his spectacular male beauty and helpless in his grasp as his strong hands swept the whole length of her slender frame. One hand swept upwards over the curve of her thigh, and with his other he caught her throat, and his mouth crashed down on her already parted lips.

His long fingers explored the silken red curls at the juncture of her thighs with devastating effect, even as his mouth trailed down her throat and back to her aching breasts. He lingered there, teasing her sensitive flesh until every nerve in her body tautened to breaking point, in fiery anticipation.

'I have to have you now,' Marcus muttered thickly.

He bit down on a distended nipple, then soothed with his tongue and she writhed beneath him, consumed by a hunger, a need so intense she cried out his name.

The sound of his name from her lush lips drove him to the edge and Marcus arched back and, cupping her bottom, he thrust deep into her hot, tight, silken sheath.

Eloise dug her fingers into the night-black hair of his head, and gave herself up in wild, wanton delight to the primitive joining. She was inflamed to fever pitch, and when he took her mouth again in a savage admission of need she returned the kiss, her tongue duelling with his. His great body stilled, fighting to retain control.

Eloise slid her hand down the indent of his spine, felt him shudder, and clenched his buttocks, needing him to move, to ease the intolerable tension, but he stayed fast.

Lifting his dark head, black eyes burning down into

hers. 'You make me…' but whatever he had been going to say was lost as Eloise involuntarily clenched and tightened her legs around him.

He moved hard and fast and Eloise naturally, wantonly picked up the furious rhythm and was spun into a world of pure sensation that exploded in a shattering conflagration like a star going nova. She clung to him, whimpering cries escaping from her.

Marcus, his breathing audible, stared down into her dazed green eyes, and slowly eased from her allowing her limp body to sink back on the bed. His dilated black eyes still fixed to her, he rolled off her and, brushing her lips with his, he leant on one elbow and stared down at her in silence for a long moment, his large hand stroking down her still-quivering body with a tactile delight.

'Exquisite,' Marcus murmured softly. 'I have never seen you totally naked in the light of day,' and he dropped another kiss on her brow.

Only then did Eloise realise it couldn't be more than three in the afternoon, the summer sun was shinning though the window, lighting every corner of the bedroom, and she was stark naked with a man who was her enemy. 'Oh.' Instinctively, she crossed her arms over her breasts.

Marcus's narrowed gaze swept her hectically flushed face, and lower to her defensive arms over her chest, and then he burst out laughing.

'What's the joke?' she demanded, and with a speaking glance Marcus led his gaze linger on her folded arms, and lower to where his long leg lay over her lower body, then back to her face.

'A bit late to be bashful, darling.' Marcus fought to restrain his laughter. 'After what we've just done.'

Eloise saw the humour in her defensive action, and chuckled. 'Yes, well, I am shy.'

'You can certainly act shy,' Marcus drawled and, lifting

a finger, he traced the smiling curve of her mouth. 'But, thankfully—' he surveyed her with delighted masculine satisfaction '—in bed you are the most wonderfully passionate, sexy woman. I can't get enough of you.'

Eloise almost laughed again, but it was with sick humour. If only he knew since the age of twenty she had never looked at a man. Before that, Marcus himself had been the only male she had allowed to touch her and he still was....

Marcus scanned her naked body spread out before him, and let his finger trail from her mouth to circle the areolae of her breasts; he felt her tremor and, lifting his dark head, he scrutinised her with a reawakening of desire. A tiny muscle pulsed at the corner of his mouth. 'I doubt I will ever have enough of you,' he breathed.

Held by his darkening eyes, she was shaken by his unconcealed passion, and tore her gaze away to look somewhere over his shoulder. To believe him would be the road to hell, she knew. She could not let her guard down, but as he once more took her mouth in a hot hungry surge of passion Eloise caved in. Her hands gripped his smooth shoulders, and skimmed over the tautness of the muscles flexing in his back and, closing her eyes, she bowed to the inevitable.

'You are so hot, so tight,' Marcus rasped as once more he drove her to the heights and, groaning her name, he thrust deeply into her one last time, felt her come and then jerked violently with the force of his own release.

CHAPTER EIGHT

MARCUS flopped over onto his back carrying her with him, folding her in his arms so tenderly, for a second Eloise felt as she had the very first time they made love. But not quite... Then she had felt as though they were one single identity bound by love. Now she knew better...

Her mouth pressed a brief caress against his bronzed chest, breathing in the hot, moist scent of him. Then she lifted her head and collided with slumberous dark eyes. 'I need the bathroom,' she said prosaically and wriggled from his hold.

Standing in the shower cubicle, the warm spray beating down on her, Eloise tried to come to terms with what she had done, but before she could get her chaotic emotions in any kind of order, the door of the shower stall opened and Marcus appeared. Very tall and broad but without an inch of fat on his muscular frame, his black hair and eyes gleaming, he was magnificently male and incredibly gorgeous.

'Allow me,' he chuckled, knowing exactly what she was thinking, and took the soap from her numb fingers.

What followed was a lesson in sensuality that left Eloise weak as a kitten, and clinging limply to his wide shoulders as he carried her to the bed and tucked her in.

She groaned and rolled over on the wide bed, fighting the demons in her mind, and suddenly opened her eyes. It was dark, and for a moment she did not know where she was; then she remembered. She glanced across the bed. She was alone.

Five minutes later, dressed and with her hair combed back in a ponytail, she nervously made her way into the sitting room. Marcus was at the desk, a laptop computer open in front of him, obviously working.

What did one say after spending all afternoon in bed with a man? she thought despairingly. 'I think I'd better be going now,' was the best she could come up with.

Marcus spun around in his seat. 'Eloise, you're awake,' and, getting to his feet, in two lithe strides he was beside her. 'And you're not going anywhere. I've cancelled your hotel room.' With a wave of his hand, he indicated a suitcase on the floor. 'And arranged for your clothes to be sent here. It makes more sense to stay here while we are in Paris.' As he bent his head she knew he was going to kiss her.

Evading his mouth, she stiffened angrily. 'You…you have…my hotel room.' She could not get the words out, she was so mad at his high-handedness. 'How dare you?' she finally snapped. 'You had no right.'

Marcus stilled and studied her beneath hooded dark eyes. 'I have every right, Eloise. You gave me the right yesterday when you accepted my terms to keep you out of court.'

Reminded with such brutal candour of their deal, Eloise paled. 'I see.' And she did—he held all the cards and he was the sort of man that always won. 'But what will I tell Katy?' she murmured under her breath, but he heard her.

'I'll take care of Katy and Harry,' he said arrogantly.

With the same speed and cunning as he had taken over her life, no doubt. Pride alone made her square her shoulders and face him. 'I suppose it will be more convenient for the brief time I am in Paris,' she agreed, and, with a burning desire to hit back at him, she added with mock sweetness, 'after all, why should I spend my money on a hotel bill when I am a wealthy man's mistress? In fact I could do with some new clothes. I didn't bring much with me, because I thought I was only staying a couple of nights.'

Marcus had the gall to laugh. 'That's what I like about you, Eloise. Even when you're down you're never out.'

'Pig,' she snapped. 'I'm going to unpack.' She brushed past him to get to her suitcase.

But later that evening, once more in the wide bed, with Marcus, pig was not the word that sprang to mind. Eloise had to clench her teeth to hold back the words of love that hovered on her tongue, and repeat over and over in her head *no emotional involvement*.

When she finally had the breath to speak and her emotions under control she asked casually, 'How long have you had this place?'

A husky chuckle greeted her enquiry, and held firm against the side of his mighty body, she glanced sideways up at him. 'What's so funny?'

'You, Eloise. Together, we have just experienced mind-blowing sex.' Amused dark eyes rested quizzically on her lovely face. 'And you come out with a mundane question like that.'

Her lips compressed. 'Sorry. I didn't realise conversation was forbidden between bouts of sex.'

'Bouts of sex.' Marcus's expressive mouth curved into a sardonic smile. 'Crude, Eloise.'

'But then you are?' she snapped back.

She felt his body tense, and his fingers bit tightly into her side, and she saw the swift flare of anger in his deep brown eyes. Then the corners of his sensuous mouth quirked in a cynical smile.

'If you really think that, Eloise, then your sex education has not been as extensive as I thought. Perhaps I should show you the difference.' And, flipping her onto her back he hovered over her. Catching her hands in one of his, he pinned them above her head and kissed her.

She felt the latent passion in his kiss, but he went on kissing her, and pinned to the bed she was unable to resist. With hand and mouth he tormented her until she was drowning in something so incredibly erotic that she groaned out loud, and she was incapable of offering any protest as he roughly positioned himself between her thighs.

Her body cried out for him, and in that moment it hit her like a bolt of lightning. She loved him, always had and probably always would. It didn't matter that he was ruthless and arrogant and felt nothing for her but lust. She knew he was the only man she would ever allow to touch her, and a single emotional tear squeezed from her eye.

Marcus looked down at her and stilled. Hell what was he doing? He knew he could have her, here and now, the act primitive and yet satisfying, and it took all his will power to pull back, his body rock-hard and aching.

Eloise glanced up, her green eyes slowly focusing on Marcus, and wondered why he had stopped.

'What we share is not crude, Eloise.' He smiled a rue-fully slightly humorous grin, accurately reading her mind. 'And I intend to keep it that way.'

Marcus watched the fleeting emotions of surprise, regret and finally relief chase across her exquisite features, and accurately read every one of them, amazed at his own re-straint and slightly worried. He had never felt protective of his usual lady friends but for some inexplicable reason with Eloise it was different.

He paused and cleared his throat. 'Now, what was it you wanted to know? How long have I had this place?' Rolling over on his back and curving her unresisting body in the crook of his arm, he proceeded to tell her.

'My father bought this apartment for me when I spent a year here studying French. My father was of the old-fashioned school, who thought if one wanted to be a player in the world-wide business market, then it was essential to speak the two languages of diplomacy, English and French.'

Realising she loved him made her feel incredibly vulnerable but, somehow comforted by the warmth of his body and the deep melodious tone of his voice, she slowly relaxed. 'Ah, so that's why you are so fluent in French,' she murmured. 'And the London hotel—don't tell me he bought that for you as well?' Such conspicuous wealth was unimaginable to Eloise.

Marcus chuckled. 'No, I bought the hotel myself a few years later. When I was a student in London I stayed in a hall of residence. It was single-sex and very correct.'

She looked up beneath the thick fringe of her lashes. The sensual curve of his mouth brought vividly to mind how it felt on her own, and her stomach flipped. She didn't want to like him, didn't want to admit she loved him, and certainly did not want Marcus to discover how she felt, and she hid the disturbing thought with humour.

'Why is it I have difficulty associating you with correct and sex?' she posed. 'Unless, of course, you're a secret S and M freak?' she concluded with a grin.

A husky chuckle greeted her comment. 'Wishful thinking, darling.' And, leaning over her, he added, 'S and M is not my thing, but I will be perfectly happy to oblige if your fantasy is to be bound to my bed.'

'No, certainly not,' Eloise shot back, horrified at where her attempt at humour had led.

'Pity,' Marcus observed with a grin, his dark eyes laugh-

ing down at her, and wondered if she was aware she had
the most expressive eyes; every flicker of emotion was
recorded in the swirling emerald depths. 'Still, I think I
can survive on straight sex, as long as it is with you.'

'Straight sex, with a crooked lady friend.' She said the
first thing that came into her head, and then wished she
hadn't as she saw the swift flare of anger in the depths of
the black eyes that held hers. Then a muscle in his jaw
twitched, a slow smile tilted the corners of his lips again,
and he lifted a finger to trace the contours of her slightly
parted lips.

'Forget the crooked part, and be my lady, and I will do
the same,' Marcus offered lazily. 'The deal we made need
not affect our relationship, unless we let it.' He shrugged
a smooth, tanned shoulder. 'A truce, if you like.'

Pretend the deal never existed. It would be very foolish,
Eloise told herself, but with Marcus's hand slipping from
her lips to her throat and lower, she felt like taking the
chance. His words had given her the first crumb of hope
for the future. 'All right,' she agreed rather breathlessly.

'That design looks really promising.' Katy stood behind
Eloise surveying the drawing board over her shoulder. 'In-
spired, in fact. It just goes to show what the love of a good
man can do,' Katy teased happily.

Eloise grimaced! If only that were true, she thought
longingly. But Marcus's intentions were far less honourable. A lustful revenge was more what he had in mind.

'And where is he?' Katy demanded as Eloise turned in
her seat to look at her friend. 'We haven't seen him for
nearly a week.'

'Marcus *does* work,' Eloise drawled mockingly. 'He has
an office on Wall Street, and he keeps apartments in
London and Paris, but his home base is in Greece. And

hopefully, if we all work a bit harder, we might end up with three or four outlets as well.' She diverted Katy from any more personal questions by asking how the latest designs were selling.

It was over a month since she had returned from Paris. The week in Paris had been a revelation to Eloise, and she blushed at the thought. She'd spent most of it in Marcus's wide bed. They'd eaten out occasionally, and he'd insisted on taking her shopping and spending a fortune on clothes for her. She'd tried to stop him, pointing out she had only been joking when she suggested he buy her clothes, and in any case she was only going to be with him for one year.

His short reply was to remind her of their truce.

On returning to London, he'd insisted on accompanying her to her apartment. She hadn't wanted him in her own home, and she certainly hadn't wanted him to make love to her there, but he did. She couldn't sleep in her own bed at night without thinking of him sharing it with her.

The next evening he had called, supposedly to take her out to dinner; instead, she had landed up in the king-sized bed in his London penthouse, and dinner was a cheese sandwich before, at her insistence, she returned to her own home.

In the ensuing weeks, he had behaved as far as Katy and Harry were concerned as the perfect suitor for their friend, handsome, sexy but more than that—he was caring and concerned, and his input in the business had been invaluable. He had a wonderful sense of humour. Eloise had watched him joking and laughing with Jeff and Julian, and Katy and Harry; they had all dined frequently together, and according to all of them Marcus was wonderful.

He was the same with everyone; even baby Benjamin gurgled when Marcus appeared. Eloise kept reminding herself, he was a master manipulator and a devious swine—but, God help her, even as she hated him for what he was doing to her, she was finding it harder and harder to retain a semblance of distance from the man. Every night that she spent in his bed, when he made love to her with a passion, tenderness, or simply a ravishing hunger, it became more difficult to hold back the words of love she ached to say.

True to his word, their affair was high profile. He'd insisted on taking her to the premiere of a film, where they'd been photographed, and appeared in the gossip column of a national daily the following day. Eloise cringed at the publicity, and lived in fear of anyone making the connection with her past. She had tried to argue with Marcus and, to give him his due, after that one event, he'd bowed to her wishes, and intimate restaurants, and an occasional trip to the cinema had followed.

Surprisingly, as the weeks passed, Eloise found herself actually thinking of Marcus as a normal boyfriend. He did nothing to dispel the notion and remarkably the truce they'd struck in Paris was holding up. Neither ever mentioned the real reason for their togetherness. They talked, they laughed, they made love, and the few times he couldn't see her, he sent her flowers, and phoned every day.

'Daydreaming won't get the work done.' Katy's voice cut into her troubled thoughts. 'Mind you, I don't blame you. Much as I love Harry, I can see what a wonderful catch Marcus is. If you play your cards right, you could keep him—wedding bells, the lot, I'm sure.'

Eloise gave a sharp laugh. 'No, I don't think so.' But in her heart of hearts she wished it were true. It was becoming harder and harder to maintain the invisible barrier she had erected in her mind that kept her from declaring her love to Marcus. And lying to Katy didn't help. She longed to confide the truth to her friend, but she could imagine Katy's angry reaction if she did. *Marcus is not my boyfriend, he simply blackmailed me into being his mistress for a year and in return he won't wreck our business.* Katy would probably kill him…

'And, to answer your first question, he's in New York and likely to stay there for a while. And, knowing Marcus, I doubt if he'll be missing me for long. There are too many beautiful women in the world ready to accommodate him.'

'Your trouble is, you don't realise how lovely you are, both inside and out. But Marcus knows, I'm sure.'

'Thanks for the compliment, Katy, and I hope you're right.' Eloise forced a grin and, turning back to her drawing board, she added, 'But in the meantime I suggest you and I get back to work,' and resumed sketching.

Freedom was a funny thing Eloise mused, as she strolled down Kensington High Street on the second Friday of Marcus's absence. Retail therapy, Katy had said as she'd told Eloise to take off for the afternoon.

Eloise had told herself she was glad to be on her own again, free to spend her time as she chose, but the reality was she missed Marcus's lovemaking—even if it was just sex—and yes, she missed his company. She missed him…

Marcus had stipulated one year as his mistress, and to her horror last night she had actually caught herself working out how many weeks she had left, and resenting his time away from her. He was stunningly attractive, and she had heard New York was full of bright, beautiful women. Alone with her thoughts, she was eaten up with jealousy and finally realised Marcus might not even stay a year with her…

She knew he wasn't actually bothered about the money

she was supposed to be paying in kind. How could he be, when he spent a fortune on clothes and presents for her? She comforted herself with the thought perhaps he had got over his original anger, and genuinely enjoyed her company.

More and more over the past weeks Eloise had the growing conviction Marcus was truly beginning to care for her on a deeper level. He showed it in so many ways— flowers, an exquisite antique emerald and diamond necklace with matching earrings. She'd tried to refuse, but he wouldn't let her, telling her it was a memento of their time in Paris, and had actually belonged to some duchess who was beheaded in the French revolution.

Sometimes the present was small, a single rose, and sometimes ridiculous, like when he left for New York and he presented her with a tiny ugly troll, and demanded, 'Promise me this is the only male you will look at while I am away.' Giggling, she'd promised and they'd made wonderful love. He telephoned her first thing in the morning British time, from his bed as it was about two in the morning in New York, and he liked to talk to her before going to sleep. She found it endearing, and it fed the hope that was growing in her heart that her love for him had a chance.

He was coming back next Tuesday and her spirit lifted at the thought, and she walked into Harrods with a smile on her face. A negligée to knock Marcus's eyes out, she decided. Stopping by the perfume counter, she picked up a tester, and was about to spray some ruinously expensive scent on her wrist when a familiar voice called her name.

'Eloise. How are you?'

She dropped the bottle back on the counter and turned around.

'Ted. Ted Charlton, I have a bone to pick with you,'

she said bluntly, but she could not help smiling at his sheepish expression.

'Guilty,' he held up his hand. 'I know what you're going to say, but let me take you out for an early dinner, and I'll explain.'

It was a warm summer evening and a long, lonely week-end stretched before her. She had nothing planned for to-night other than returning home and watching television. Why not? she thought.

'Yes, okay.' She waited while he bought a bottle of perfume.

'I have a hot date Saturday night,' he explained with a chuckle. 'Let's find somewhere to get a drink and then we'll eat, and I'll confess all my sins.'

Ted found them a great French restaurant and ordered a couple of Martinis, a bottle of good wine and the food.

'I saw the pictures of you and Marcus in the press, and I can guess why you want to talk to me.' Ted's comment came over the aperitif.

Eloise took a moment to find her voice. 'Marcus appears to be under the impression you and I…' She cleared her throat, suddenly embarrassed.

'I know what you're trying to say.' Ted helped her out. 'And I'm sorry, I shouldn't have lied. But try and under-stand from my point of view, Eloise.'

'I'm listening,' she said quietly.

'Marcus Kouvaris is a lot younger than me—very hand-some, very successful, very clever.' Ted lifted his glass and drained it, looking rather wry.

One delicate brow arched quizzically. 'So?' she prompted.

'Well, it doesn't show me in a very favourable light.'

'Ted, forget the light—just tell me what happened,' Eloise said bluntly.

'It was really my ex-wife's fault. Her lawyer did me for

millions, and I had a very sweet deal, almost completed. No disrespect to KHE, but it was worth a lot more than your small business, I was short of cash, and I needed the money quick. I knew Marcus Kouvaris was in town, and I remembered the way he'd looked at you.'

'The way he looked at me? What on earth has that to do with your business dealings?' she asked, totally confused.

'I'm a man; I know how the male psyche works. So I approached Kouvaris to take my share of KHE off my hands. I knew he could easily afford it, and it would earn him Brownie points with you. I wasn't wrong; he agreed immediately.'

'You mean, you think Marcus bought in to KHE to please me?' The enormity of what Ted was suggesting boggled her mind, until she remembered the blackmail. But, even so, Ted's suggestion made her think... Marcus had not gone deliberately seeking shares in KHE, so that must mean something.

'Of course, Eloise, you are a stunningly beautiful woman and a talented artist as well. There isn't a man alive who wouldn't fancy you, believe me.'

'Flattery, Ted, won't get you off the hook. I want to know why you lied to Marcus about you and me.'

'You can put it down to an old man's pride or sour grapes. I invited Marcus to have dinner at my hotel to celebrate the deal, and then at my insistence we retired to the bar. What can I say?' He shrugged his broad shoulders. 'I had too much to drink and this exquisite blonde I had been trying to impress for the past few days made it very obvious she wasn't interested in me—but that she fancied Marcus instead. He made it obvious he wasn't interested, and when she finally gave up and left, after giving me the cold shoulder, I was feeling pretty miserable. So when

Marcus asked exactly how well I knew you—' He hesitated, his face turning a dull shade of red.

At least he had the grace to blush, Eloise thought, holding Ted's blue eyes with her own. 'Go on.'

'I lied and said we'd spent the night together. It was male ego, and plain old-fashioned jealousy. First my ex-wife rejected me, and then the girl in the hotel who'd been quite happy to drink with me the night before only had eyes for Kouvaris. There's only so much rejection one man can take. I admit I was drunk and I didn't see why Marcus should get away worry-free, and if my stupid lie has hurt you in any way I'm sorry.'

Eloise shook her head. 'It doesn't matter, Ted.' The fact Marcus had turned down the other woman made her feel generous. 'I forgive you.'

'You love the guy.'

'Something like that,' she said with a smile. Marcus was not quite the devil she tried to paint him, she knew, and a tiny seed of hope rooted in her brain. Maybe her love for Marcus was not completely futile…

The food arrived and was excellent. It was nice to sit and chat with the ease of old friends; Ted was one of the few men she was comfortable with. Later, when Ted got her a cab to go home and insisted on accompanying her, she made no objection. She even asked him in for coffee…

Marcus swung out of the taxi, and leapt up the few steps to the entrance door of the Georgian building. He lifted a finger to press the bell for Eloise's apartment and realised the door was open. Careless, but it suited his purpose. He wanted to surprise Eloise, and the tingling sense of anticipation at the thought of seeing her again lent speed to his long legs, as he ran up the two flights of stairs without catching his breath.

He'd spoken to her on the telephone late last night and

told her he wouldn't be back until next week. But after putting the phone down, having heard the husky sound of her voice ringing in his ears, he'd wanted her so badly he'd cancelled some meetings and crammed the rest into a couple of hours in the morning, and taken the next flight out of New York.

Marcus moved towards the door at the end of the hallway. He could hear the sound of voices. Good: she was home, and obviously watching the television. His hand grasped the door handle; it yielded to the pressure and he strode across the tiny inner hall, and into the sitting room.

'Eloise, darling.' She spun around in surprise at the entrance to the hall that led to the bedroom, and the breath caught in his throat.

Marcus's gaze flew over her. Her red hair framed a startled but incredibly beautiful face and fell in a tumbling mass of curls over her creamy shoulders. Her body was encased in a wisp of blue silk, tiny straps supporting the slip-styled dress that ended a few inches above her knees. There was no mistaking the firm thrust of her breasts or the tightening of her nipples as she stared at him, and what held him transfixed was not the shock that widened her brilliant emerald eyes, but the sheer wonder of her smile that followed.

'Marcus, you're back!' Eloise cried in delight. 'I wasn't expecting you until next week.' She blinked; it really was Marcus, looking staggeringly handsome in a perfectly tailored silver-grey business suit. But it was the glittering warmth in his dark eyes, especially for her, that made her breath catch.

He started slowly towards her. 'I cancelled the rest of my business meetings,' he declared throatily. 'I wanted to surprise you.'

CHAPTER NINE

IT TOOK every bit of will power she possessed to stop herself running to him and throwing her arms around him. 'Marcus.' She licked her lips nervously. 'I'm…' *Glad to see you*, was what she had been going to say. What a cop-out! He was her lover, and she loved him, and courageously she decided to try honesty. 'I've missed you.' After all, he had returned early; that had to mean something.

He stopped when he was inches away from her. 'Eloise,' he husked. His dark eyes, blazing with desire, scanned her and, reaching out, he folded her in his arms and covered her mouth with his own.

His mouth was hot and searching with a hungry intensity that she met and matched. Eloise whispered his name as his tongue parted her lips. She arched against him and wound her arms around his neck, her hands stroking the silken hair at the nape, before sweeping lovingly across his powerful shoulders.

'So long,' Marcus groaned and pressed her body to his. 'Too long.' He could feel the rounded fullness of her breasts crushed against his chest. This was what he had come back for…

She was all woman; the scent of her, the soft curves and long shapely legs, promised and beguiled. He moulded her buttocks and lifted her, the seductive tilt of her pelvis fitting into the cradle of his hips, as he ground his rock-hard length against her in raw need.

'Ooops, sorry.'

Marcus jerked his head back, his black gaze clashing with the blue of Ted Charlton. The man had obviously just strolled into the room from the direction of the bedroom. Marcus felt the breath leave his body as though he had been punched in the gut, and for a second a red haze of rage blinded him. He swore violently in Greek, and abruptly thrust Eloise away from him. 'You bitch.'

Eloise stumbled back, her eyes widening in horror as she realised what it must look like. 'No. It's not like…' She looked up at Marcus and ground to a halt. The change in him was devastating. Incredulous rage clenched his hard dark features, a muscle jerking uncontrollably in his taut cheek.

'Then what is he doing here?' Marcus's eyes burnt into hers. 'Or shall I guess?' he drawled with cynical contempt. 'A week without sex and you're anyone's.' His gaze sliced back to Ted, apparently unable to believe what he was seeing.

Eloise was shaking, terrified by the cold deadly look in Marcus's eyes; but beneath the terror she had a hysterical desire to laugh at his contemptuous conclusion she could not live without sex for more than a week. If only he knew…

She grabbed his arm. 'No, Marcus, listen to me. I bumped into Ted in a department store; he was shopping for perfume for his girlfriend, and I challenged him to explain what he meant by telling you I had slept with him.'

'I just bet you did. Persuaded him to lie for you?'

'Damn it, *no*.' Eloise cut him off. 'Ted lied to you; he told me the truth over dinner.' She tightened her grip on his jacket as he would have pulled away. 'All about your celebration dinner and getting drunk and the girl in the bar. He told you he slept with me because he was jealous of you. Surely you can see that…?' she prompted desperately.

'All I see is a conniving lying bitch,' he snarled, his black eyes blazing, 'who would sell her body for the price of a dinner,' and she knew he hadn't believed a word she'd said.

The Marcus she loved didn't exist, she realised with blinding clarity. He was a figment of a nineteen-year-old's imagination. She didn't recognise the man towering over her, dark and dangerous, but for Ted's sake she tried once more to defuse the situation.

'I shared dinner with Ted because he wanted to explain and apologise to me for lying about me to you, nothing more—and if you're too pig-headed to see that, tough.'

Marcus took a step towards her and he lifted her hand off his sleeve, then he stopped. Her green eyes clashed with his; she saw the fury and contempt and thought, What was the point?

All that linked her and Marcus was sex. A shameful passion on her side she was helpless to control, and a virile man's lust powered by revenge on his. Marcus did not love her, and never would, and that was the greatest pain of all. She took a deep shuddering breath and suddenly Ted was pushing Eloise to one side and facing Marcus.

'If you want to lash out at anyone, Kouvaris, try me.'

Marcus's hand shot out and he grabbed Ted by the collar and slammed him back against the wall. 'Don't tempt me,' he snarled. He wanted to smash the man's face to a pulp and he didn't question the reason.

'You're a fool, Kouvaris,' Ted grated in a high-pitched voice, nearly choking and clutching at Marcus's hands.

'I can beat the hell out of you, any day, in any way,' Marcus raged, his violence controlled by a thread.

'I know,' Ted shot back. 'That's why I lied and said I'd

slept with Eloise. I saw the way you looked at Eloise the first time I met you,' he stated cynically. 'And I saw the way the girl in the bar looked at you, when the night before she had been all over me. I was drunk, I was jealous and I lied. Rejected by a wife and a bar-girl, I was damned if I was going to make it easy for you to get Eloise. Lousy, I know, but that's the truth.'

The two men stared at each other. Ted's face red and Marcus's grey beneath his tan, only his eyes blazing black with rage.

For a long moment Eloise simply stared at the scene before, all her energy concentrated on fighting the awful pain she was trying to hide. But as she watched the pain dissolved into a quite different emotion.

They were like two stags at bay, both ruthless powerful men, leaders of the pack. She recognised the angry acknowledgement between them—the old giving way to the young, but not without a fight—and a slow-burning anger ignited in her breast.

This was her home, her life. Pride stiffened her spine. She didn't have to justify her actions to any man, certainly not the two egotistical male chauvinists before her, who were scrapping like two dogs over a bone. And in her living room!

'Right, that's it! Cut it out,' she yelled. 'And both of you can get out.'

Marcus shot her a look of outraged incredulity. She was ordering him out… He was the injured party in this debacle.

She met his gaze, her green eyes sparking fire, and she might have laughed if she hadn't been so angry, Marcus looked so put out! 'Let him go,' she snapped.

Slowly, Marcus released his iron grip on Ted's collar and some of the rage faded from his eyes. She was standing tall and proud, her luscious body bristling with tension. She was beautiful when she was angry. She was beautiful any time, and lost in passion beneath him she was paradise. Whether she and Ted were telling the truth or not, was he prepared to give up all that simmering sexuality? The tightening in his groin answered for him. Hell, no—not yet.

Marcus glanced back at Ted. 'I think it's time you left,' he grated through his teeth. 'Eloise is mine.' His narrowed eyes fixed on Ted, his great body tense and towering threateningly over his rival. 'You understand?'

'Do you?' Ted murmured dryly, shaking his head. He walked past Marcus. And, for sheer devilment, stopped and dropped a light kiss on Eloise's cheek. 'So long and good luck, and if you ever need me get in touch.'

'You're pushing your luck,' Marcus growled, taking a step towards him.

'No.' Ted grinned back and, picking up the gift-wrapped bottle of perfume from the table where he had placed it earlier, he waved it in front of Marcus's face. 'I never trust to luck. I have a hot date tomorrow night, and I know how to treat a lady, unlike some.' Laughing, he strolled out of the apartment.

Her legs trembling, Eloise sat down on the nearest sofa. 'I think you'd better leave.' Marcus had claimed her as his, as though she was an inanimate object, instead of an intelligent woman with thoughts and feelings. Well, he could go to hell, for all she cared. She had had enough.

'No,' Marcus bit out, crossing the space between them in one lithe stride. 'I cancelled my plans for the next few days to see you, and I haven't changed my mind.'

He looked down at Eloise. Maybe she was innocent where Ted was concerned. Ted had been very drunk in New York, and bitching at losing his wife and a ton of money. He vaguely remembered Ted introducing him to the blonde bimbo, and then she had been all over Marcus like a rash, so much so he had been quite rude to get rid of her.

As for the rest—his dark eyes roamed over Eloise. She was watching him, her green eyes cool, her luscious mouth held in a grim line. The red-gold tumble of her hair falling over her silky-smooth shoulders, so proud, so brave, and he was yelling at her like a loony.

If he was honest, he doubted she'd ever been involved with her mother's scam. He'd seen the company books, and discovered the company had been set up nine months after Chloe's death. Harry had told him the initial finance was from Eloise's inheritance from her late mother's estate. Eloise had bought the premises. Realistically, Eloise should be the major shareholder, and yet according to the records they were three equal partners, all drawing the same salary. If Eloise was a gold-digger, as he had thought, then she had a very funny way of going about it. Katy and Harry would not have a business if it were not for Eloise.

She was probably innocent of all he had accused her of, and incredibly generous to those she considered friends. Marcus suddenly realised he wanted to be in that company, to bask in Eloise's approval. He'd known a lot of women in his life, some almost as beautiful and with the same luscious curves as Eloise—well, no, not quite as perfect, but some a lot more sexually aggressive in bed. But he also knew with absolute certainty none had come close to affecting him the way she did.

If he'd ever caught any other woman he was involved with alone with another man, he would have walked out the door and out of the woman's life without a second thought. It scared the hell out of him that he couldn't do that with Eloise.

Since the day he'd first met her as a young girl, she'd never really left his mind and, after the last weeks together, the happiest in all his thirty-four years, she had become an obsession. An obsession that had made him act out of character, and dash back early from the USA, his business incomplete, simply to see her. She was a fever in his blood, and he intended to keep her until the fever burnt out. A secret obsession Eloise need never be aware of, but he would have to watch her more carefully in the future. Innocent or not, there would be no more Teds... He would take her home tomorrow, he concluded arrogantly.

Marcus was still here and he still wanted her. Eloise did not know whether to laugh or cry. She could hear her heart thudding in shock, an erratic rhythm against her breastbone. Marcus must be able to hear it in the tense silence, but she dared not look at him; instead, she asked the one vital question.

'So, now do you believe I never had an affair with Ted?' Her eyes focused on the floor. It suddenly seemed imperative to her that Marcus showed some tiny bit of faith in her.

'It's not important. Forget it; I have.'

Her head came back at that, her eyes fixing on his in bitter resentment. She loved him but right at this moment she hated him. He didn't trust her an inch and never would, but still she decided to give him one last chance. The final test, she told herself.

'You saw the perfume Ted had bought. I told you we met by accident,' she said through tight lips. 'I told you Ted had lied and he confirmed it.'

One ebony brow arched in sardonic amusement. 'So you did,' he mused as he sank down on the sofa beside her. He was too close and her pulse leapt at his nearness.

'Will anything convince you?' she asked flatly. 'Spelling it out in blood, maybe?'

Marcus ran a comprehensive eye over her and, reaching out, he let his long fingers tangle in her silky red hair. 'If you want to convince me—' his voice deepened '—feel free to try.'

She had her answer. Sex was all Marcus wanted from her. She tried to pull her head away but he wouldn't let her escape. Her stormy eyes clashed with mocking black and his long fingers in her hair tightened their grip. 'It should be fun,' he teased.

'That's all I am to you, a sex game, you egotistical bastard,' Eloise shot back, her fury edged with fear as his dark head descended. She tensed, eyes wide and glinting with defiance. She was damned if she was going to roll over again beneath his sensual onslaught. That was all she had done since they met in Paris and it had to stop, she told herself.

But her traitorous pulse raced into overdrive as Marcus covered her lips with his own in an explosive kiss. His dark head blocked out the light and his hand curved around her waist, hard and restraining, while he plundered her mouth at will.

Her pulse raced, and she gripped his arms in a last-ditch attempt to break free. But he wouldn't let her go. He simply flattened her to the sofa. His hard, hot body sprawled on top of her, and his mouth continued to ravage her own, rough and then tender as one long hand swept down her body, and back to cup her breast.

She fought for control. 'No,' she moaned against his lips, struggling to breathe, denying the sensations he was forcing her to feel. Her nipples tautened into tight buds, and she trembled, unable to control her treacherous body's reaction. But by a supreme effort of will she lashed out at him with fist and knee.

He reared back, and she caught a brief glimpse of his stunned expression as she flung herself over the arm of the sofa and landed on her feet.

'What the hell was that for?' Marcus sat back against the sofa, rubbing a hand across his cheek.

'Figure it out for yourself.' Her chest heaving, she stood a few feet away, staring down at him with angry green eyes. How it was possible one man could be so infinitely desirable, a great lover, and yet be completely lacking in the emotional department Eloise did not know.

Marcus's eyes were dark and glinting with suppressed anger, and with an impatient gesture he got to his feet and moved towards her. 'You're mad because I chased Ted.'

Eloise swallowed unevenly. 'No, not that you chased him,' she said quietly. 'But that you never believed him and, more importantly, me.'

His dark eyes pinned hers, shrewd and penetrating. 'You want me to believe you; it bothers you that I don't. Why is that, I wonder? Perhaps you care for me rather more than your sharp tongue will admit.'

Any minute his clever mind would work out how she really felt about him, and she couldn't let that happen. 'No, but I object to being treated like a whore, a woman who will sleep with a man one minute and quite happily sleep with another an hour later, and by your actions that's how you see me.'

'Ah, Eloise.' Marcus's expression was grim. He looked at her standing there, so young and looking so incredibly sexy and yet innocent at the same time, and it gave him a peculiar feeling in the region of his heart that was almost pain. 'I only ever think of you as a clever, incredibly beautiful woman, and you shame us both by thinking otherwise,' he said gently and, reaching out, he caught her shoulders and drew her gently towards him. 'And if I gave you the wrong impression, I'm sorry.' He moved one hand towards her cheek, and trailed gentle fingers down until he reached her chin.

A betraying pulse began to beat at the base of her throat and a nervous flutter stirred her stomach. 'That's a first.' She tried for sarcasm, but the tremble in her voice gave her away as he tilted her chin and looked deep into her wide emerald eyes.

His eyes grew dark. He brushed her mouth gently. 'And I do believe you about Ted.'

'You do?' She stared at him, and her heart skipped a beat. He believed her. Was she hearing right? A heady excitement bubbled through her.

'Yes, I do.' Tension snaked through Marcus's large powerful body. His hand slipped from her shoulder to tighten around her slender waist, and he smoothed a few tendrils of glorious red hair from her brow. He had to keep it light, he wasn't yet ready to confess he was blinded by jealousy.

'After all, any woman with me as her lover wouldn't look twice at Ted,' he said with a husky chuckle, his slumberous dark eyes holding hers.

Eloise couldn't help it; even when she was angry, he had the ability with a word, a look, a touch to make her change her mind. Her lips twitched. 'You arrogant devil!' She shook her head but he looked deep into her green eyes and saw the humour she couldn't quite hide.

'But you like me,' he murmured teasingly, and suddenly Marcus, who had never considered if a woman liked him or not, found he was waiting, his heart pounding for her answer.

'Yes, you could say that,' she responded with a husky

chuckle of her own, and then very gently, almost reverently, he bent his head and kissed her, and she kissed him back in helpless surrender.

He gently pulled her dress off her shoulders, his dark gaze flicking over her pouting breasts, raising her in his arms, slowly with the tip of his tongue he circled the areolae of one hard nipple.

'Oh, yes,' she sighed, immediately thrown back into a whirlpool of sensations. 'Please.'

'Oh, yes,' Marcus parroted, his mouth enclosing the rigid tip and slowly licking her aching flesh, teasing with tongue and teeth until her back arched, and she was burning with the heady heat of passion and desperate need for continuance.

He slipped his arms beneath her, lifting her high so he could capture her mouth with his in a long drugging kiss as he carried her into the bedroom. He slid her down the long length of his body, letting her feel the pulsing ache of his arousal as he eased her out of her dress in one smooth movement.

He was wearing too many clothes. A low groan of frustration escaped her and she pushed her hands beneath his jacket up and around his back, dragging his head down to her, finding his mouth with her own.

Airborne again, Marcus laid her down on the bed, and in seconds joined her naked. A deep erotic sigh of pleasure escaped her, as the black hair of his chest rubbed against her turgid nipples.

Long fingers traced the length of her body, the indentation of her waist, the silky softness of her flat belly, and she trembled. She gripped his shoulders quivering with need. But he played with her mouth, licking and nibbling, then thrusting with his tongue, and all the time his long fingers slowly stroked the curve of her hip, the smooth skin of her inner thigh, but frustratingly refraining from touching her where she longed to be touched.

'Marcus,' she panted, her small hands sliding down to cover his, lost to everything but her own need.

'Tell me what you want,' Marcus rasped in a dark undertone, his breath fanning her cheek, his night-black eyes searching emerald. 'Perhaps this?'

Her whole body jerked as his seeking fingers parted the velvet folds of flesh to touch the hot, moist, pulsing point of pleasure, sending convulsive shivers lancing through her.

Her hands roamed feverishly over his shoulders and skated down his back, around his broad chest to trace the silky black line down over his taut stomach, driven by a purely female primeval need to possess and be possessed, to claim him as her own. Her slender fingers found him, curving around the satin-coated steel length of him with shivering excitement, stroking him, made bold by her need.

She felt his great body shudder, and briefly she felt an incredible sense of power. But a heartbeat later she could not think at all as his mouth caught hers in a savagely hungry kiss. Involuntarily her fingers tightened around him.

With a guttural groan, Marcus raised his head. 'You do it,' he spelt out roughly, his night-black eyes clashing with her dazed green. Shuddering on the edge in a passion-induced dream, she did…

Eloise awoke early the next morning and yawned widely. She stretched languorously and was instantly aware of the warm male body beside her. Slowly turning her head, her green eyes widened on the sleeping figure of Marcus.

He lay on his back, one arm trailing across the top of

her pillow, the other flung across the other side of the bed. The sheet was draped low across his hips, his broad hair-roughened chest rising slowly and evenly in sleep.

She glanced up at his face. With his eyes closed, and a day's growth of beard darkening his firm jaw, he looked less than his perfect self, younger and somehow vulnerable.

Heat coloured her cheeks as she recalled last night, and her own part in it. She had actually touched him intimately with hands and mouth, something she had never imagined doing, and yet with Marcus she wanted to. It was unbelievable...

He was amazing. They had made love with a passion a hunger that lasted for hours until, sated and exhausted, she had fallen into a dreamless sleep. Her love-swollen lips curved in a smile of pure female satisfaction. Hardly surprising he was still asleep, she thought, her fascinated gaze sliding over his naked torso.

Even with her body aching in muscles she never knew she had, she couldn't keep her eyes off his gorgeous bronzed body, and recalling how it felt to be thoroughly possessed by him made her shudder with remembered pleasure. Unable to resist, she reached out her hand and gently smoothed the soft black hair from the centre of his chest down to the narrow strip that disappeared beneath the sheet.

'Hmm. That's nice,' Marcus murmured, moving and pressing a kiss on the top of her head.

'I thought you were asleep.' Eloise blushed scarlet and lay back, feeling almost happy. Marcus had said last night he believed her about Ted. A giant step forward—surely it couldn't be long before he believed she was innocent of all he had accused her of?

'I was, until you assaulted me.' Marcus grinned and sat

up, pulling her up with him. The dark eyes that met hers danced with wicked humour, and she smiled back.

'Me?' she questioned in mock indignation.

'Yes,' Marcus answered, and after kissing her thoroughly he rolled off the bed. 'I'll make breakfast, you start packing. We're going to Greece.'

'You're kidding, of course,' she exclaimed, her eyes skimming over his lithe body and wondering how a naked man could still manage to portray such stunning arrogance.

'I couldn't possibly leave London at the moment,' she said easily, thinking of all the new designs she was involved with for their expanding business, and Katy's light workload because of her preoccupation with Benjamin. Which was only as it should be, Eloise thought, her mind wandering into the realms of fantasy, imagining what a baby with Marcus as a father would look like.

The thought brought her up cold, all the colour leaching from her face… She looked at him as he turned back to face her, and watched the humour vanish, and his face grow cool and distant.

His dark knowing eyes rested on her pale face. 'You can and you will, Eloise. You have far too many distractions in London.' He knew he sounded harsh, but he couldn't help it; she had looked at him, white-faced and horrified, and it gave him a peculiar feeling in the area of his heart again.

How could he have gone from wanting, needing and believing her to this hard-faced tyrant, Eloise wondered, within minutes of waking up? A night of passion meant nothing to Marcus, and his complete lack of emotion simply confirmed what she already knew.

But she lived here, Eloise reminded herself firmly. She worked here. He had to be crazy. She couldn't drop everything and swan off to Greece at his say-so…

'Don't be ridiculous.'

'I would be ridiculous if I left you here alone again. On Rykos, when I am not around, my family and friends will take care of you.' Marcus knew from experience how difficult it was to have a sex life on the tiny island without everyone knowing about it, and he was a man... For Eloise, branded as his woman, it would be impossible. No man would go near her, and that suited him just fine.

'I do not need taking care of,' she fumed. Where did he get off ordering her around? Well, she wasn't putting up with it any more and she was damn well going to tell him so, but before she could open her mouth again he'd left.

She listened to him running the shower in the bathroom, and expelled a shuddering sigh. What was the point of arguing with him? she decided with bitter resentment. After the night they'd spent together, she'd had high hopes Marcus might begin to trust her, might care about her. But he'd made it brutally clear he didn't. Her mind in turmoil—Greece apart—it had hit her when thinking about babies. Marcus was always meticulous about using protection, but last night he had forgotten...

Half an hour later, she joined him in the kitchen. As she walked towards him, clad in well-washed denim jeans and a baggy grey tee-shirt, she was aware she looked a mess, and didn't give a damn. She wasn't going anywhere and that was final.

'You're wearing that to travel?' he asked flatly. 'Hardly flattering, and jeans are far too hot for August in Greece.'

'I'm not going to Greece. I have neither the time nor the inclination,' she told him coldly, pulling out a chair and sitting opposite him at the tiny kitchen table, surprised he had actually prepared coffee, toast and a selection of conserves. He wasn't totally hopeless in the kitchen, she thought dryly, suddenly feeling hungry. She filled a cup with coffee, took a sip, and reached for a slice of toast, before bravely raising cool green eyes to his. 'Some other time, perhaps.'

Marcus's gaze narrowed and swept over her tensely held body perched on the chair. She was nowhere near as confident as she tried to appear. 'Nice try, Eloise,' he drawled mockingly. 'But it isn't a request, it's an order.'

'Tough. I have to work, and I have a commitment to Katy.'

'Need I remind you, we have a deal? Your first commitment is to me and, as for your work, you can design as easily in Greece as in London.'

His deliberate mention of their deal hit her like a cruel blow, and she despised herself for harbouring a lingering shred of hope that he would grow to love her. When was she going to learn? Pride alone made her squeeze back the tears that threatened and, lifting her head, she said, 'But I don't want to,' bravely defying him.

Hooded dark eyes surveyed her. 'You don't have a choice.'

'So this is the end of the truce,' she snapped back.

Marcus cast her a cynical smile. 'Yes, if that's how you want to see it. But why pretend, Eloise? We both know I only have to touch you to make you change your mind.'

Stunned at his arrogance, her appetite deserted her, and the toast dropped from her fingers. Her gaze skated helplessly over him. He was wearing the same clothes he had arrived in last night. He should have looked a mess. But the grey designer suit fitted him like a glove, the jacket straining over broad muscular shoulders; even the blue shirt still looked perfect. How did he do it? Or was it her?

God help her! But she was made humiliatingly aware that he only spoke the truth, and it shamed her to the depths of her soul. She felt so vulnerable. What was he doing to her? A vivid mental image of last night heated her flesh, the images so real, she could almost feel the touch of his hot, hard body against her skin.

The doorbell rang and she leapt to her feet, almost stumbling on her headlong flight through the small hall to open the door. He was insidiously taking over her life; she did not seem to have the strength to deny him, and it terrified her.

Katy walked in. 'Your paper.' She dropped the paper in the direction of the hall table, lifting her head and sniffing the air. 'Is that coffee I smell?' and she headed for the kitchen.

Eloise closed the door and bent down to pick the paper off the floor. It had fallen open, and her eyes caught a name in the centre page. Rick Pritchard. The blood drained from her face, her hand shook and, closing her eyes, she paused for a moment. Then with slow deliberation she rose and folded the paper and placed it on the table.

The name was a timely reminder. It was way past time she got herself back under control. She had allowed Marcus to break through the shield she kept over her emotions, the only person to do so in four years. She must rebuild her defence against him. But how easy that was going to be with Marcus calling all the shots? A deep, shuddering sigh escaped her and, straightening her shoulders, she took a few long steadying breaths, practising the exercises she had been taught. She could hear Katy's voice and the deep rich tones of Marcus's and then laughter.

If there were any repercussions from the unprotected sex of last night, Eloise knew she would have to leave Marcus. Which meant she would have to sell the house and break up the partnership. The sound of Katy's laughter would be a thing of the past, as would their friendship, and all because of Marcus Kouvaris. But at this particular point in time she did not care. She had more important things to worry about, like staying alive... Suddenly Greece seemed a very desirable location.

By the time Eloise entered the kitchen, Marcus had talked Katy into believing it was a marvellous idea for Eloise to go to Greece. Eloise put up a token argument, not wanting Marcus to realise she had changed her mind—not because of him or Katy, but because Eloise wanted to be anywhere but England...

A dark skinned maid escorted her up a palatial marble staircase and along a wide corridor, and into a bedroom. 'The master's,' she said with a giggle.

Eloise looked at the girl blankly. 'Thank you, that will be all,' she murmured, surprisingly not in the least embarrassed, and watched as the young maid backed out of the door and shut it behind her.

Her beautiful face impassive she glanced around. Large, it was sumptuously elegant with a huge bed on a raised dais as the main feature. She strolled across the mosaic floor and pushed open a door to a sybaritic bathroom, in black and gold, with a large circular spa bath, double shower, and marble and mirrored walls. It fitted the man, she thought idly, and re-entered the bedroom and crossed to the window that took the place of one wall. She slid it open and stepped out onto a long balcony. The air was hot and heavily scented after the coolness of the bedroom, and the view so spectacular she caught her breath.

A paved patio with a dolphin-shaped swimming pool as its centre led to a garden that was a riot of colour in the early evening sun, and gently sloped down to a low wall, and a sandy beach and the clear blue sea beyond. She glanced to one side and saw an orchard, a mass of orange and lemon trees, and in the distance she could see the small cluster of luxury villas. None so luxurious as this, she was sure, and *one* the scene of the drama five years ago that had led to the tragedy her life had become now, she thought bitterly. She looked in the opposite direction and her heart missed a beat. She recognised the cliff and the precarious path down to the hidden bay.

Abruptly, she turned back to the bedroom. Marcus had brought her to his home on Rykos... A house, he had told her on the flight across, he had designed and had built in the last couple of years. What he had not told her was it was in close proximity to the cliff and beach where he and Eloise had once shared a picnic.

Eloise had kept the memory of that one perfect day in her heart and head as a kind of talisman. In times of great pain and stress, she used to conjure up the bay in her mind, to blank the horror out. It was ironic that, after reading that hated name, Rick Pritchard, in the paper this morning and, rigid with shock, she needed her talisman view, and there it was before her very eyes—and it did not work any more.

The innocent nineteen-year-old had finally gone forever. Marcus had made sure of that; and, the truly sad part was, he had not even noticed...

CHAPTER TEN

METHODICALLY Eloise unpacked her clothes, placing them in the wardrobe and drawers provided in the dressing room, deliberately avoiding looking at the masses of male garments.

'What on earth are you doing?'

On her knees, placing the last of her underclothes in a scented drawer, Eloise glanced up. Marcus was towering in the doorway, barefoot, and obviously paused in the process of undressing. The trousers of his suit were unfastened and hanging perilously on his lean hips. His shirt was open to the waist, revealing a hard, muscular chest shaded with black hair. He was a powerful, virile male, she thought almost objectively. Then she saw the expression on his darkly handsome face, one of arrogant astonishment.

He expected to be waited on hand and foot. He had probably dropped his shoes, jacket and tie in a trail across the bedroom floor, she guessed. 'What's it look like? I'm unpacking,' she said facetiously. 'It's what we lesser mortals do.'

Hooded black eyes narrowed on hers. 'I employ staff for such things.'

'Yes, O lord and master,' she muttered under her breath.

'I heard that,' Marcus drawled silkily. 'And as long as you remember it, we'll get along fine.'

He scanned her wide green eyes, anticipating her angry rebuttal, but surprisingly she simply said, 'Okay,' and stood up.

'Wait.' He caught her arm as she would have walked

152

past him, inexplicably angered by her apparent indifference. 'The staff are employed to take care of my guests; they are happy to have a job, and will be insulted if you do not use them.' He sounded like a pompous prig, he knew, and the knowledge made him frown in self-disgust.

Eloise glanced at the hand on her bare arm, and up into his thunderously frowning face. 'Yes... okay.'

Damn it. She was doing it again, with the *okay*, and he didn't like it one bit. Thinking about it now, he realised she had been doing it ever since Katy had lent her voice to his, in persuading Eloise to agree to come to Greece with him. She had been the same on the plane.

His dark eyes narrowed intently on her lovely face for a long moment. But her usual brilliant green eyes returned his scrutiny expressionlessly; something was missing. He felt like shaking her. Instead, his hard features perceptibly darkened.

'O...kay,' he drawled cynically. 'Now share a shower with me,' he demanded with deliberate provocation, his fingers tightening on her arm.

Eloise was aware that Marcus was trying to rile her on purpose. Why, she had no idea. The only connection between them was sex, and from now on it was going to stay that way until their relationship had run to its natural conclusion, and without trust on either side that should not take too long. But for the moment she had to stay away from England; that was the most important thought in her head.

If she discovered she was unlucky enough to be pregnant, then all deals were off, KHE would have to get by without her, and she would be on her own. In the meantime, she would enjoy what Marcus offered. She could be as hard as a man, if she tried.

'Yes, okay.' She lifted her hand and placed it on his broad chest. 'Whatever you say.'

Marcus made love to her hard and fast with the water cascading over their naked bodies, he felt her climax, her fingernails tearing into his back as they both reached shattering fulfilment at the same time.

His breathing rough and audible, he shot her a blistering glance, and slowly unwound her long legs from around his waist and lowered her limp body to the floor. With one arm supporting her, he reached over and turned off the shower tap, then dropped a soft kiss on her forehead.

'We'd better get out of here and get dressed,' he said ruefully. 'I meant to tell you before I was distracted—Aunt Christine and Stella are coming for cocktails and dinner.'

Reeling under the force of her own response, to be hit with his relatives' arrival in pretty much the next breath simply confirmed for Eloise she had been right to decide emotional detachment was the only way to deal with Marcus.

Straightening, she shrugged off his arm. 'Right, okay,' she said calmly and, unconscious of her nudity, she stepped out of the shower. She picked a towel from the pile provided, wrapped it around her naked body and left the bathroom, without looking back at Marcus.

Okay—she had done it again… An incredulous frown pleating his broad brow, Marcus grabbed a towel and flung it around his hips. For the first time in his adult life he felt guilty about having sex, and he didn't like the feeling one bit.

Eloise quickly dried her body and slipped on her clothes without glancing in a mirror. She felt as if she was moving, talking, acting through a swirling fog. She had felt like this before and knew it was the shock of hearing the news about Rick Pritchard, and she had to battle to break free.

Only in Marcus's arms had she become truly aware again, a wry smile twisted her lips. Unfortunately, she couldn't spend the rest of the day in his arms. She knew from past experience it usually took about twenty-four hours for the paralysing fear to fade.

Dinner was not the ordeal Eloise had expected. Christine was a woman in her forties. She must have been Marcus's mum's younger sister, Eloise surmised. She was small and plump with gentle brown eyes, and Stella at seventeen was a younger version. It became increasingly apparent to Eloise as the meal progressed that Christine obviously had no knowledge of the state her husband had left his affairs in. She was a lovely lady and, from her comments to Marcus and to Eloise, it was obvious she had total and utter faith in Marcus to look after the financial side of her life.

After admiring the amber pendant Eloise was wearing and hearing Eloise worked as a jewellery designer, Christine remarked, 'You are the first girl my nephew has seen fit to introduce to our small family, and you are lucky. He is brilliant at business; he will help you.' She turned her warm brown eyes to Marcus. 'I am right. No?'

Eloise swallowed a lump in her throat at the expression of tender love they exchanged. And when the evening was over and Eloise stood at the door of the villa and was subjected to a hug and a kiss from Christine and Stella, plus a demand she must visit them for a meal, her throat closed up with emotion.

This would not do, she told herself, walking back inside. In any other circumstances she could have really loved Marcus's relatives... But the knowledge that her mother Chloe had had an affair with Christine's late husband and conned him out of a great deal of money made the bile rise in her throat and left her with an acrid taste on her tongue.

Meeting Christine had brought it home to her as nothing else could why Marcus held her in such low regard.

'Would you like a nightcap?' the object of her thoughts enquired as they entered the hall.

She arched her shapely brows. 'Not wise after all the wine I have consumed,' she responded flippantly. Actually, she hadn't drunk much, but she wanted to get away from Marcus for a while.

'Don't worry. I won't let you get drunk,' he advised her smoothly, his narrowed dark eyes skimming over her figure. Every shapely curve revealed by the green silk dress which was held up by tiny sequinned shoulder straps. It was so slim-fitting that there was a split up one side to enable her to walk, and he remembered the fun he had had buying it for her in Paris with a smile.

Eloise lifted a graceful shoulder. 'Yes, all right.'

His smile extinguished, Marcus's sensuous mouth tightened into a hard line. She looked at him and smiled, but it was as if she wasn't there. 'Sit on the terrace. I'll bring the drinks out,' he snapped. Without a word Eloise sat down and, instead of being pleased she had done as he said, Marcus felt irrationally angry.

Reclining on a lounger on the terrace with a glass of juice in her hand, Eloise glanced across at Marcus. He was leaning against the ornate balustrade, staring down at her. In a white dinner jacket and black trousers, he was devastatingly handsome, but the hint of anger glinting in the darkness of his eyes was unsettling. What had she done wrong now? she wondered bitterly. Not servile enough for him? Well, tough…

'You liked Christine and Stella?' Marcus prompted.

'Yes, they're both charming. In other circumstances I'm sure we could have been friends.'

'What do you mean—in other circumstances?' he demanded hardily. 'There is nothing wrong with now.'

Gracefully, Eloise rose to her feet and, after draining her glass, placed it on a nearby table.

'Okay, if you say so.'

'No, it is not damn well okay.' Marcus moved to block her path his hands closing like talons on her shoulders. 'What is with this "okay" to everything I say?' he growled with savage frustration. 'You've barely said a sentence since we left London.'

He hauled her against him and she looked up into his hard features, and was suddenly aware of the brush of his long body against her. 'Sorry, I didn't realise I was supposed to make brilliant conversation as part of our deal,' she said bluntly.

'Damn the deal, and talk to me,' Marcus groaned, his fingers gentling on her shoulders. 'This is my home, and I want you to be happy here.' His dark eyes caught and held her own. 'I want us to be happy here. Not just *okay*.' And as he said it he knew he meant it. He wanted much more from Eloise than sex. He wanted her warmth, her friendship, her *love*…

He wanted to forget their deal! Eloise was so surprised, the shock that had almost swamped her mind all day, but had begun to lift over dinner finally vanished, and she responded tentatively. 'I'm a bit tired from the flight and everything. Disorientated.'

Deep in her innermost being, she wanted to believe he was serious. She'd only ever belonged to Marcus in the physical sense, and with the warmth of his body enfolding her she was loath to give up the little he was prepared to give her. Was she going to let the ghost of the past that had haunted her all day win, or was she going to take one last chance?

'Let's go down to the beach,' Marcus suggested. 'The sea air will clear your head.'

'Ok—' She nearly said it again, and a brief smile tilted the corners of her mouth. 'A very good idea, I agree.'

Marcus slanted her a wry grin, and dropped an arm around her bare shoulders. 'Come on.'

They walked along the deserted beach in a relatively peaceful silence.

For Eloise the underlying tension was never far from the surface but, looking around her, scenting the clear night air, the only sound being the gentle movement of the sea, she realised she felt safe. She cast a sidelong glance at her companion through the thick fringe of her lashes, and knew she had Marcus to thank for her feeling of well-being, and she made a conscious decision to try and relax, live for the moment.

It was a wonderful night, a clear star-studded sky with the full moon gleaming on the dark water. Eloise kicked off her shoes and walked into the gentle waves whispering over the sand. The water was warm, and she turned playfully back to Marcus. 'Come and have a paddle.'

'I can do better than that,' Marcus said thickly, and slowly he stripped off his jacket and spread it on the sand. His shirt, trousers, everything followed.

Astonished, wide-eyed, she watched her own personal striptease show, a slow burning need igniting in her belly. He stood tall and straight not a yard away. A work of art that rivalled Michaelangelo's David, perfect in line and form, and totally unashamed of his magnificent aroused body.

His dark eyes captured hers, and she was powerless to break the contact. 'Now it's your turn, Eloise.'

Hypnotised by the burning intensity of his gaze 'Yes,' she conceded softly. Safe and sure in his protection, she caught the hem of her dress; she slipped it over her head, and threw it onto the sand, freeing her high firm breasts to the warm night air and Marcus's rapacious, hungry and very masculine appraisal.

She tucked her fingers in the top of lacy white briefs, and slowly stepped out of them one leg at a time; then, straightening up, she squared her shoulders and looked at Marcus.

In silence they simply stared at each other, totally naked, at one with the earth, sea and sky.

Marcus reached out his hand, and Eloise placed her own small hand in his palm. His night-black eyes caught and held hers, the simmering passion in his gaze igniting her own. Adrenaline raced through her veins; anticipation heated her blood. For the first time in her life she rejoiced in her own sexuality, neither afraid nor ashamed.

In that moment she saw them as two supreme beings, naked as nature intended, free from all the shackles of convention, all worldly cares, and she stepped forward.

'You are perfection,' Marcus groaned as their mouths met in a desperate hungry passion.

He shaped her swollen breasts with shaking hands, his thumbs grazing over the hard tight peaks, before lifting her in his arms, and lying her on his outspread jacket. His large powerful body stretched out beside her his shoulders shook as he lifted his head. 'Every time I see you, I want you more.'

Reaching up Eloise framed his head in her hands and urged him down to her. 'Don't talk,' she murmured. She wanted nothing to spoil the erotic dream consuming her and pressed her mouth to his, her tongue daringly searching the moist depths of his mouth.

Time suspended in another dimension, they touched, tasted, and explored and, mindless in the grip of a primeval passion, the sea water gently lapping at their limbs, they finally came together in a glorious, slow-burning, ecstatic climax that left them both shuddering in the aftermath of exquisite pleasure.

Marcus recovered first and, smiling down at her, a smile of smug male satisfaction, he kissed the tip of her nose. 'Skinny-dipping next.'

It was another first for Eloise. She had never swum naked before and later, when they made their way back to the house, dishevelled and looking as if they had done exactly what they had done…she wondered if she ever would again.

The sun was shining through the window when Eloise's eyes fluttered open.

Marcus, a fully dressed Marcus, if one could call denim shorts and a sleeveless black tee-shirt fully dressed, was standing by the bed. 'What time is it, what are you doing?' she mumbled, closing her eyes again. So much virile male pulchritude was a jolt to her system so early in the morning.

'Almost noon.'

'What?' Her eyes flew open.

'I thought you needed the rest, and your friend Katy called. Apparently she has talked Harry into letting her come out for a few days. She will be arriving this afternoon.'

Her eyes properly open now, Eloise looked at Marcus. The lover of last night had gone; his dark eyes were narrowed speculatively on her small face, his body tense.

'That will be nice,' she said politely, his obvious reserve a timely reminder to her to keep her emotional distance from the man, and she dragged the cotton sheet up to her armpits.

'Maybe, but it seems rather a sudden decision on Katy's part,' Marcus opined darkly. 'So much so, I could be forgiven for thinking you had arranged it between you. Are you really that bored at the prospect of staying alone with me?'

His black eyes roamed broodingly over her beautiful face, the fabulous red hair spread over the pillow, to where she had tucked the sheet firmly across her breasts. His throat constricted as he recalled the lushness of her body beneath the sheet. Hell! What on earth was the matter with him? Challenging her like some jealous teenager, just because she had a friend coming to stay, when he wanted her all to himself, he finally acknowledged with a frown.

Watching him frown, Eloise shivered in spite of the heat. Marcus was back to his usual cool, remote self. Yet she could have sworn in the middle of the night she had felt his arms close around her, holding her close, protecting her. Sadly she realised it had been wishful thinking on her part. Inexplicably, she felt like crying but, gritting her teeth and fighting back the tears, she sat up in bed, pulling the sheet up under her chin.

Taking a deep breath, she tilted back her head. 'You have to be joking.' She forced a light laugh. 'I wouldn't dream of inviting a friend of mine anywhere near you, unless I had to. And may I point out this is your home; Katy asked you. You could have said no.' She knew she had gone too far; he took a step forward, his black eyes blazing, and then he stilled.

Marcus stared at her as if she had sprouted horns and a tail. Her words had cut deep. She had no family, but she didn't even want him near her friends, while he had wanted to bring her to his home, delighted in introducing her to his family, and was looking forward to her meeting his friends on the island.

In that moment, Marcus, a man who had never believed in love, suddenly realised he was madly, passionately in love with Eloise. He bent forward again. 'Eloise.' He had to tell her and, reaching out, he gently stroked her red hair from her face.

Eloise flinched back.

'No,' he said sharply. 'I…' and he could not say it. The deal, everything came flooding back, and he almost groaned out loud. How could he have been such a blind fool? He didn't give a damn about revenge. It was Eloise he wanted, had always wanted, and he'd been too arrogant, too jealous, to admit as much.

'I'll go and collect Katy,' he said, pulling back. 'You rest, eat, pamper yourself—do what women do.' He must sound like an incoherent idiot, he knew, but he had so much ground to make up with Eloise, he didn't know where to start.

A grim smile twisted his lips. He needed a strategy to woo her, win her love. On the plus side, he knew he wouldn't need to coerce her into bed. The chemistry between them was explosive. Maybe a private talk with Katy might give him a few pointers.

'Pamper?' Eloise exclaimed and, watching the fleeting expressions chase across his handsome face, she was totally confused.

Glancing back at Eloise, seeing the confusion in her emerald eyes, the master strategist lost it. 'I want us to stay together, get married, everything,' Marcus said with grim determination, sitting down on the bed and pulling her into his arms.

She shook her head, unable to believe her ears. He

looked more like he had swallowed a dose of horrible medicine than a suitor. Then he kissed her.

'Damn Katy,' Marcus muttered, lifting his head, as the whirling blades of a helicopter landing broke the silence.

Eloise looked up and collided with lustrous dark eyes. Was she dreaming or had Marcus really asked her to marry him? He looked frustrated and, unbelievably for him, vulnerable, unsure. 'Katy,' she mumbled irrationally, too stunned to comprehend what he meant.

'I have to go and collect her, but think about what I've said,' he prompted, and leaping to his feet, he left.

Not for a moment admitting he had to get away, he was as stunned as Eloise looked. He had proposed marriage without a second thought. Hell, who was he kidding? Without even a first thought! His brilliant mind had been turned to mush by a pair of green eyes. Eloise drove him crazy. He must be crazy to want to give up his freedom. A few minutes after climbing into the waiting helicopter, a broad smile broke on his face. He felt nothing but joy.

CHAPTER ELEVEN

'NO BENJAMIN with you?' Marcus asked, after the usual friendly greetings to Katy. 'I'm amazed you could bring yourself to leave him at home.' He smiled as he escorted the rather frazzled-looking Katy across the tarmac to the heliport. 'It must have been a sudden decision on your part to visit Eloise,' he prompted. He still had a lingering suspicion Eloise had somehow arranged this visit to avoid being alone with him, though he did not see how. He had never let Eloise out of his sight, since yesterday morning.

'It was, and I'm only staying the one night.' Katy shot him a worried frown. 'But after I read the newspaper, I really didn't think it was something I could tell Eloise over the phone.'

'Sounds dire. Don't tell me the firm has collapsed overnight without her,' Marcus quipped.

'No, but it does concern Eloise.' Katy glanced at Marcus, and was reassured by his cheerful grin.

'You know, before meeting you I would have bet Eloise would remain a virgin till her dying day,' she confided in him chattily. 'But she's blossomed incredibly into a confident woman with you to look after her. Harry and I were amazed when she agreed to go to that film premiere with you. I would have sworn Eloise would never appear in the public eye ever again after the trauma she went though with the court case. The victim's name is supposed to remain secret, but that slime-ball's letter from prison to the gutter press threatening revenge, nearly finished poor Eloise off. But your trip to the premiere convinced us both she's finally got over her fear of men and recognition.' Katy gave Marcus a grateful smile. 'But old habits die hard; we've protected her for so long. I want to be there for her when she finds out.'

Victim? Court case? His Eloise a virgin? Marcus's mind reeled under the implication, a deep, dark, bottomless pit opening up before him. Katy obviously thought he knew what she was talking about. Glancing up, he realised they were at the helicopter.

'Finds out what?' he asked lightly, helping Katy into the helicopter and handing her a set of headphones, desperate to continue the conversation in flight.

'This is great. I've never been in a helicopter before.'

Marcus forced a smile at Katy, but he had to know why she was here. Something was terribly wrong. 'Yes, but you were going to tell me...'

'Oh, yes.' Katy sobered. 'Eloise will have told you all about the assault and stabbing.' Marcus felt the blood drain from his face, and he listened in growing horror as Katy rambled on.

'It was a terrible time, and she was so brave all through the trial. But what you can't know—I only found out late last night, when I got around to reading the paper—Rick Pritchard, the man who attacked her, who got a seven-year sentence, is to be released on Monday after serving only four years.'

'I see.' Marcus froze, the blood turning to ice in his veins.

'Yes, well, after he was sentenced, he vowed from the dock he would get Eloise, and I saw the look in the fiend's eyes. I wouldn't put anything past him. The letter he sent to a newspaper a couple of weeks later simply reaffirmed the fact. But she has you to protect her and the fact she's in Greece instead of London is actually quite fortuitous.

The swine is unlikely to find her on Rykos,' Katy opined, ending on a cheerful note. 'Oh, look, I can see the sea and dozens of little islands. It's beautiful.'

'Yes.' Marcus carefully pointed out various landmarks. He did not dare reopen the discussion on the attack. He had never felt such rage and fury in his life, or such disgust, most of it directed at himself. God, what had he done? Suddenly a lot of little things made sense. Katy's and Harry's protectiveness towards Eloise; Eloise's dislike of publicity—and he silently groaned.

The sound of the helicopter made Eloise's heart skip a beat. They were back. With one last glance in the mirror, she ran from the bedroom, and down the stairs, happy anticipation giving a bloom to her cheeks, and brilliance to her emerald eyes.

She wasn't dreaming; Marcus had asked her to marry him. The why and wherefore she would have to discuss with him but, for the first time since meeting Marcus again, her heart was bursting with hope for the future. She'd told herself not to get too excited but she couldn't help it. She'd dressed in a simple mint sheath dress, and on her feet she wore soft leather mules in the same colour. She had brushed her hair back and left it loose. She didn't want to overdo it and look as if she had dressed up especially for Marcus.

Stopping her dash for the door, she made herself walk slowly out on the terrace and around to the rear of the house, in sight of the landing pad. She watched as the tall figure of Marcus stepped down from the helicopter and swung the smaller figure of Katy to the ground.

'Fantastic,' Katy murmured, walking around the terrace with Marcus at her side, and the houseman bringing up the rear, carrying Katy's holdall. 'This is some house, Eloise!'

'Glad you like it.' Eloise grinned at Katy. 'Wait until you see the pool,' and she glanced up at Marcus. 'Perhaps we can all try it later when Katy's settled.' She smiled a little nervously, still a bit unsure about his proposal, but there was no reciprocal smile; his dark features looked coldly remote.

'Not for me. I have some work to do in my study. Nikos here will show you Katy's room, and as she is only staying one night I'm sure you two want to gossip. I'll see you both at dinner.' He strode into the shadowed interior of the house without a backward glance.

One phone call and Marcus turned pale as death. The hand holding the receiver shook with the force of his emotions. 'Fax me the lot—trial transcript, newspaper articles, everything.' Dropping the phone, he paced the length of his study like a caged tiger.

He couldn't believe it, didn't want to, but he knew it was true. When the fax machine started printing he sat down at his desk and started to read. The detective he had hired had said before Eloise was as *pure as the driven snow* and he, with his cynical mind, had thought he was being facetious. To see it in black and white in the trial transcript made him sick to his stomach. She had been a virgin when she was attacked, and technically still had been afterwards. The fiend had not succeeded.

Eloise, his Eloise, had been returning across a park alone after a game of tennis, and been brutally attacked by a depraved man, Rick Pritchard. Luckily a couple out walking their dog had disturbed him. Eloise had been rushed to hospital and the police called, and then the stab-wound to her inner thigh had been treated and she'd regained consciousness.

He buried his head in his hands, the full horror of what had happened to Eloise piercing him like a knife in the heart. The scar on her leg… She had said it was an accident. She had nearly bled to death…

Leaping to his feet, he wanted to smash something, or someone; impotent fury blazed in his black eyes. He had never felt such rage, such hatred, in his life; he wanted to kill Rick Pritchard with his bare hands. That being impossible, he once more picked up the phone. There was not a flicker of emotion in his dark sardonic features, but the implacable intent in his jet-black eyes would have scared the devil himself, as in a cold, hard voice he issued his instructions.

'A lovely pad,' Katy declared half an hour later seated opposite Eloise at the small table on the balcony of her bedroom. Nikos had thoughtfully provided a jug of iced tea and two glasses, plus a plate of various Greek delicacies to nibble on.

'I can see why Marcus wanted to bring you here, you lucky girl.' She sighed in delight at the panoramic view of sea and sky.

Eloise looked across at her friend. 'Okay, Katy, why the rush out here?' It was totally out of character for Katy to fly anywhere unless she had to.

Bright brown eyes turned compassionately to Eloise. 'There's no easy way of saying this. Rick Pritchard is due to be released from jail on Monday.'

Eloise quelled an internal shiver at the mention of the name. She should have guessed. She'd read the article in the paper herself yesterday morning. Of course Katy must have seen it and, being Katy, worried over her.

'Is that all?' Eloise tried a smile, deeply touched by Katy's concern. But if the last few months had taught her anything, it was she could no longer hide from the harsh reality of life or depend on other people to protect her.

Katy had her own family and life to lead. 'I know, Katy. I saw the article when you gave me the paper yesterday. It is not important,' she lied.

'You're sure? You're not frightened he'll come after you?' Katy asked seriously.

'Really, Katy… Do I look frightened?' Eloise prompted and, casually picking up a small stuffed vine leaf, she waved her hand around. 'Look where we are and with whom. Marcus is more than a match for any man, or woman!' She allowed a brief, knowing smile to curve her lips, before she popped the morsel of food in her mouth.

'Yes, you're right.' Katy smiled back, completely taken in by Eloise's consummate acting. 'Harry said I was worrying unnecessarily, and Marcus seemed quite cool when I told him about it. But, hey, now I am here, can we at least try out the pool.'

The food stuck in Eloise's throat and she had to swallow hard to dislodge it horrified by Katy's comment. 'You told Marcus?'

'Yes, on the way over. Why, does it matter?'

Recovering swiftly. 'No. No, of course not, but do me a favour—don't mention it to him again.' The thought of Marcus knowing her dark secret mortified her. 'He's Greek, a typical macho male, and as you can imagine any mention of an attack on his lady puts him in a bad mood.' She made it up as she went along. 'And I really don't want to talk about the case.'

But she knew she was only putting off the moment of reckoning. Once Marcus got her on her own he would want the full story. Now she understood why he had appeared cold on his return with Katy.

'Sure, if you say so. The subject's closed,' Katy said understandingly, then grinned. 'Now lead me to the water.'

They spent the rest of the afternoon at the pool, but there

was no sign of Marcus. The whole situation put Eloise under a severe strain. So far, by some miracle she had managed to fool Katy into thinking Marcus was the love of her life and everything was fine. If Katy realised everything was not as it seemed, she would question Eloise until she got the truth.

But what was the truth? Eloise thought as she stood in the bedroom, fastening polished jade earrings to her ears, a perfect match for the patterned green silk sarong-style dress she had opted to wear for dinner. So much had happened, so fast. She was plunged into turmoil by her conflicting emotions.

Yesterday morning she had told herself she hated Marcus, because he'd ordered her to come to Greece, but after reading the newspaper she'd jumped at the chance to get away. She'd spent all day in a state of shock. Then last night and the episode on the beach when she had succumbed to his blatant sexuality yet again, she'd felt no shame, but freedom. This morning Marcus had asked her to marry him, and for a while she'd believed happiness was a possibility. But when he returned with Katy, it was as if the last twenty-four hours had never happened.

Dear heaven, it was no wonder she was an emotional basket case, she told herself bitterly. She was a complete novice when it came to male-female relationships, and Marcus was a vastly experienced, complicated man. He was also a very traditional male, with a high profile position to uphold in the business world. Not the sort of man who would take for his wife a woman who had been violated and the centre of a sordid court case, she concluded sadly.

Straightening her shoulders, she left the room to collect Katy and go down to dinner, her stomach churning with nervous dread, waiting for the axe to fall. Trying to understand what drove Marcus was like riding a roller-coaster, a spectacular high then a deep, depressing trough. Never mind the fact some madman might be chasing her…

They ate dinner out on the terrace with the sea and night sky as a backdrop. Marcus looked his usual magnificent self in a lightweight linen suit, and by the coffee stage he had shed his jacket. He ruled the conversation with all the charm and wit of a true Renaissance man. Katy was completely fooled, but Eloise could sense the underlying tension in the taut set of his wide shoulders.

She hadn't had a private word with him since his bombshell proposal this morning. He'd waited until she and Katy had appeared for dinner before exiting his study with a murmured apology about changing for dinner. He was avoiding her, obviously disgusted.

Now, the few times their eyes met, his narrowed into hard darkness masking all expression. Obviously he was regretting his reckless proposal, Eloise thought sadly, but then she had not really believed him anyway. Miracles didn't happen. At least not to her.

Inwardly she heaved a sigh of relief when, after demolishing almost a whole bottle of wine single-handedly, Katy said she was tired and wanted to go to bed.

'Yes. I'm rather tired myself,' Eloise agreed, rising from her seat. She glanced across at Marcus. 'I think I'll call it a night,' she said smoothly, playing her part for the benefit of Katy. 'If you don't mind.' Her green eyes widened as she saw the flash of something almost feral in the black eyes that met her own.

'You do that, sweetheart,' he said. With perfect manners, he rose as they did, and turning to Katy wished her good night, and then, glancing at Eloise, he added, 'I am going to have a brandy. I will see *you* later.'

Following Katy into the house, Eloise heard the sarcasm

in his tone, and slanted him a sharp backward glance—
but, to her astonishment, she caught an expression of such
bitter devastation on his darkly handsome face, her step
paused. She wanted to go to him and ask him what was
wrong. Then common sense prevailed; she was imagining
things. Marcus had never needed anyone in his life, and
she caught up with Katy, and showed her to her room.

Shedding her clothes, Eloise showered, and slipped a
brief white cotton nightgown over her head. Returning to
the bedroom, brush in hand, she sat down on the bed, and
began brushing her hair. Marcus confused and tormented
her, until she could no longer think straight. She'd tried.
She'd tried to retain some control, to defend her poor heart
against the overwhelming attraction of the man, but she
was beginning to believe it was a hopeless task. She was
hopeless. Her lower lip trembled; a solitary tear rolled
down her cheek, and she brushed it away with her free
hand, then brushed her hair with more ferocity than was
strictly necessary. She refused to wallow in self-pity; she
was a survivor—she had proved that once before, and she
could do so again.

Lost in her own thoughts, Eloise did not know how long
she had been sitting on the bed, when she glanced up and
saw Marcus standing a few feet away.

He was as cold and still as a marble statue. She could
see it in his eyes, feel it in the silence. Eloise swallowed
hard vaguely threatened by his silent scrutiny. 'The bathroom's free,' she said inanely.

'So is your attacker,' Marcus hissed between clenched
teeth. 'Why didn't you tell me you'd been attacked?' he
demanded softly.

'I didn't think you'd be interested. Anyway, Katy has
told you now,' Eloise answered bluntly, staring at him as

he wrenched off his tie as if it were choking him and undid the first few buttons of his shirt.

'Katy thought I knew,' he raked at her, tight-lipped with temper. 'After a few calls, I finally received the transcript of the trial and the press reports. I have just finished reading them.'

All the colour drained from Eloise's face, and the brush fell unnoticed from her hand to the bed. 'It was a long time ago,' she tried to say nonchalantly, but the tremble in her voice was plain to hear. She hated the thought of Marcus reading every horrible torturous intimate detail of the worst episode in her life.

'Why didn't you tell me?' Marcus demanded savagely. 'Why did you lie? I asked you about your scar and you said it had been caused by an accident.'

Eloise slowly stood up, and told him the truth. 'I was shy; it was the first… I didn't want you to know, not then, but later maybe.'

'Why, why in God's name would you hide such a thing from me?' Marcus's fury was so real she took a nervous step back. He saw it, and went white, strain etched in every line of his face. He had thought she was a virgin, but had ignored it, and it only served to make him more furious. 'You were afraid of me.' He hissed in outraged disbelief.

Eloise shivered. 'No, I just wanted to forget.'

'Forget?' he bit out incredulously, 'And how the hell am I supposed to forget?' Marcus seethed, his glittering black eyes clashing with hers, and she caught her breath. She did not have to listen to this. It was as she had thought—he was disgusted by the court case, disgusted with her.

'The exquisite face, the luscious body.' His gaze slid down over her scantily-clad form and he reached out and caught her wrist as she would have whirled away.

'God, but you've got your revenge, Eloise.' He surveyed her with burning intensity. 'Have you the slightest idea how I feel? How can I forget that I all but forced you into my bed?' he demanded, his black eyes raking over her with contempt.

Eloise flinched as though she had been struck, but pride alone made her face him. She stiffened, and stared at him with ice-green eyes. Another room, another man accusing her. As if it was her fault she was a beautiful sexy girl, a tease—of course she led the defendant on. It was the past come back to haunt her yet again.

'Don't touch me. Let go of my arm,' Eloise snapped, cold anger covering the pain he was inflicting by his callous words. 'If, as you say, you read the transcript, you know that technically it was attempted rape and assault with a deadly weapon. You do not come into that category.' Eloise threw him a look of pure scorn, denying the feelings he could arouse in her even when he was behaving like the worst kind of chauvinist. 'Yet,' she concluded viciously.

Marcus released her so abruptly she fell back against the bed. He lifted his hand and drove shaking fingers through his thick hair. Hell, what was he doing, raging at Eloise? None of this was her fault. She was the victim, and he was filled with self-contempt.

'I shouldn't have said that,' he conceded tautly. 'I allowed my anger to get the better of me. Sorry.'

She raised her eyes. Marcus saying sorry was a new experience—but one look at his face and she realised he looked less in command of himself than usual. In fact he looked absolutely dreadful. 'Forget it,' Eloise muttered with a negative shake of her head, and sat down on the bed, her trembling legs no longer capable of supporting her. 'I have.' After the court case, she'd vowed never to be forced by any man into defending her actions, and she was not about to do so now with Marcus.

There was a long silence, then Marcus took a deep breath and straightened to his full height. 'I can't forget what that man did to you Eloise. I wasn't angry with you, I was furious with him, and myself.' His black eyes captured hers, and there was no doubt of the sincerity in their depths. 'I feel like the lowest of the low. I refused to believe a word you said, because all the evidence made you seem a liar. So I didn't care how I got you in my bed, as long as I did. I would be lying if I said I regretted making love to you—I don't, though I recognise I'm not much better than the man who attacked you. But you have nothing to fear from me, Eloise; I will never touch you again.'

Eloise turned paper-white, and there was an even longer silence while she digested what he'd said, and stared back at him, her green eyes curiously blank. She had been a challenge to him, but he didn't want her any more.

'It's okay,' she said finally. She had always suspected once he discovered her past he would lose interest in her. 'I'll go back with Katy tomorrow.' She wasn't going to cry, she wasn't going to beg. 'As for the money I owe...'

'You don't owe me a thing, Eloise. I've known that since Harry told me how you'd invested your inheritance to start the business and you're all equal partners that you don't care about money.'

Eloise knew somewhere in the back of her mind he was telling her something vital, but she couldn't think straight. She felt sick inside and, taking a few deep breaths, it was only by a mighty effort of will she managed to shore up the defensive wall in her mind that stopped her bawling her eyes out. 'Okay.'

She was doing it again. Marcus's dark eyes narrowed, harsh and brooding, on her pale face and finally his brilliant brain discerned instantly what she was doing. He was appalled he hadn't recognised the tactic sooner, appalled at his own insensitivity.

'No, damn it, it is not *okay*,' he swore. 'Don't do that again. I realise now why you were like that yesterday. You were in shock; it's self-protection. You knew, didn't you? You knew the rat was being set free.'

'I read the paper before we left London. Yes,' she admitted, her head bent, no longer caring what Marcus thought or felt. Just wishing he would leave, before she broke down completely.

A deep agonised groan had her lifting her head. Marcus stood, shoulders stooped, his hands covering his face, and as she watched his hands slid down to his sides. He stared down at her, his black eyes glazed with moisture, his handsome features twisted in horror.

'What is it, Marcus?' she asked hoarsely, deeply disturbed by his ashen pallor.

'God help me!' His tormented black eyes caught and held hers. 'Yesterday you were in shock and I ordered you into the shower.'

Eloise had never seen such pain and anguish in her life, and slowly it dawned on her—Marcus, her arrogant, infuriating, powerful lover, the keeper of her heart if he did but know it, was racked with guilt.

She reached up and placed her hand on his curled fist. 'I enjoyed our sojourn in the shower,' she said softly.

He continued to stare at her for a disturbing length of time, as if he had not heard; then his fist unfurled and he clasped her hand in a deathlike grip. 'Oh, God, Eloise,' he groaned from deep in his throat, and pulled her up into his arms, crushing her to him. 'I wish that were true.'

'It is,' she murmured tilting back her head to look up into his agonised face.

He stared at her for a moment in solemn silence, his eyes probing hers with a burning intensity; then, as if he could not help himself, he groaned again, his dark head descending. 'I love you so much, Eloise.' He buried his face against her throat. 'I can't bear the thought of anyone hurting you, and I know I must have hurt you. God! I took your innocence, I made you stay with me. I am no better than the scum who stabbed you.'

She felt as if all the air had left her lungs, by the fierce pressure of his arms, and she couldn't believe what she was hearing. Her mouth fell open in shock. Marcus loved her. She lifted a tentative hand to his head. She hated to see her proud, arrogant lover so distraught, and she knew what she had to do.

'Marcus, you never hurt me, and certainly not physically. I always wanted you, even when we fought. I want you to believe me.'

'You are too soft-hearted for your own good,' he groaned against her throat and, lifting his head, his black eyes lingered on her slightly parted lips. 'You need someone to take care of you,' and he brushed his mouth over hers in the lightest of kisses. 'Let it be me, and I swear no one will ever hurt you again.'

'You...you love me?' She had to ask, to be sure.

'Eloise,' he murmured thickly, his fingers brushing her hair lightly from her flushed cheeks, while his eyes devoured her. 'I love you, and I have never felt more unworthy than I do at this moment. I can only pray that you will forgive me and let me try to make you happy.'

Her green eyes widened to their fullest extent as he spoke; it was almost too incredible to believe, but it was there in the gleaming depths of his dark eyes. It was there in the arms that tightened around her almost in desperation, and she finally knew it was there in his heart. 'There is nothing to forgive,' she whispered unsteadily. 'Just kiss me and tell me again you love me.'

He kissed her with a tender passion that stirred her more deeply than anything had ever done before. Her arms linked around his neck and she lost herself in the miracle of the moment.

'I love you, Eloise,' Marcus groaned and, sweeping her off her feet, laid her down on the bed, removing her night-gown in between kisses. He stared down at her and, with a hand that visibly shook, he traced the length of her leg and the hard ridge of tissue. For a second his dark eyes flashed violently. 'God, I could kill him,' he snarled.

'Marcus.' She held out her arms to him. 'Forget him and come to me.'

He made love to her with a care a depth of passion that touched her soul. His mouth found the scar and laved the length, and more. Eloise held nothing back and gave as much pleasure as she received, until they lay sated in each other's arms, two hearts beating as one perfect whole.

'Please marry me,' Marcus rasped throatily, and Eloise moved sinuously against him.

'Another deal?' she teased, glancing up at the darkly handsome face above her, and was stunned by the vulner-ability in his night black eyes.

'No.' His sensuous mouth tightened. 'You never were, or were never meant to be.' Marcus said with scrupulous honesty. 'We need to talk.' Rolling onto his side, he propped his head on one hand and looked down at her.

'When Theo died, and I discovered what Chloe had done, I hired a detective to find her. When I was informed Chloe was dead and she had no sister, I was intrigued. The money meant little to me; I was more interested in finding you, to be brutally honest,' he said ruefully. 'You had haunted my dreams for years, seriously curbed my womanising ways, and I was curious to discover what had become of you.'

'I don't think I like the womaniser bit.' Eloise grinned up at him, but the rest was like manna to her love-starved heart.

'Yes, well, when the detective found you and informed me of your real name, and you owned a jewellery firm, I was bitterly disappointed; along with the signature on the contract it seemed to confirm that you were in league with Chloe. Then, when the detective told me you were as pure as the driven snow, I didn't want to hear any more. In my cynical mind, I thought he was being sarcastic. I decided to look you up, and come to some arrangement over what I considered should be Theo's share.'

'But I told you the truth, Marcus. My mother used my college project and she also forged my signature. It had absolutely nothing to do with me,' Eloise protested.

'I know that now.' Marcus calmed her with a finger across her lips. 'Let me finish. When I saw you by chance at the supper club, I was struck dumb; you were more beautiful than I remembered, and you were with a much older man.'

'I wasn't *with* Ted, well…'

'Shh. For the first time in my life I was hit by jealousy. And I thought of what you and your mother had done to my uncle and his family—and I was furious.'

'I told you….'

His dark head swooped and he stopped her with a kiss. 'Please, Eloise, I want to get everything out in the open between us. No more secrets.

'When I took you out to dinner, I was going to expose you as a liar and a cheat and demand Theo's money back—but, over the meal, you were so sweet, so much fun, I thought, why bother? I didn't need the money, and then, when we made love…'

Eloise smiled dreamily up at him. 'That night was so perfect. It was a miracle for me. I never expected to be able to let a man touch me, but with you it was different. I think it was because I had known you before the attack, and so you weren't a stranger. It was as though the trauma of the past didn't exist and I was nineteen again.'

His dark eyes locked with hers. 'God, Eloise! What I have put you though?' he said slowly, and she felt his muscles lock with tension. 'I know it was your first time. You were so nervous, so obviously inexperienced. I fully intended to keep on seeing you, and to forget about the fraud against my uncle.

'Then, after the phone call, when we were leaving, and you quite happily said you had obtained finance from Ted Charlton the night before. Everything you said suggested you'd slept with him. You got back to your apartment at three. You were so excited it was five before you finally slept—I wanted to strangle you. Then you signed the deal in the morning and celebrated over lunch.' His dark eyes clouded with remembered pain. 'I was gutted, thinking I must have been mistaken about your innocence, as you had spent the night and half the day with Ted to get him to invest in KHE, just like your mother, and then came to me.'

'You…' Amazement made her eyes widen. 'You actually… I wondered why you were so dismissive when you took me home.' Eloise stared at him. 'But it was nothing like that! Ted left me at the door. When I said *we* discussed Paris, I meant Katy, Harry and I. They waited up for me, as they tend to worry over me since the attack. Ted called the next day for a meeting with Harry, and then took us all out to lunch.' Recalling the conversation at the time,

Eloise realised how it might have sounded. 'But if you thought... No wonder...' she trailed off.

A wry smile twisted his sensuous lips. 'That's exactly what I thought. My ego took an absolute hammering; I didn't know if I was on my head or my heels. I needed to get away from you, to think.'

'I don't like the sound of that,' Eloise murmured, wriggling a little closer to the warmth of his naked body.

He chuckled and continued. 'I delayed going to America, and deliberately took Nadine to the charity ball, hoping you would see the photograph.'

'I did,' Eloise admitted. 'I was terribly hurt but, funnily enough, in one way I was grateful, because even if I never saw you again, you had cured me of my emotional hang-up where men were concerned. At least, that was what I told myself.'

One dark brow arched sardonically. 'I'll take that as a compliment—but I'm not sure I want to be seen as a sex counsellor.'

Eloise gave him a playful punch in the chest and let her hand linger there lovingly. 'You'd better not, Buster. I'm the only female you're ever going to counsel.'

'You're the only female I want to.' He ran a tender hand down her throat and over the soft swell of her breast.

She shivered and covered his hand with her own. 'And Nadine, what happened to her?' she asked hesitantly.

'I'm a lot older than you are, and there have been women in my life—but only on a casual basis. Nadine was one of them. I hadn't seen her for some months and I looked her up when I arrived in London, but that was as far as it went. Our first date and I saw you and no other woman would do. You're the only woman I have slept with since the moment I saw you again. Believe me.'

She wanted to believe him, and she knew some things

she would have to take on trust. 'I do.' But she still didn't understand why he hadn't come back for three months, and she asked him.

A dull tide of red ran up over his high cheekbones, and he looked less than his usual arrogant self. 'I didn't dare. But, God, I wanted to… Haven't you realised yet? You're my obsession, you drive me crazy. I love you quite desperately. After making love to you, there could never be anyone else for me. When I went to America—' he hesitated '—I was so angry, I was determined I was going to make you pay. I consulted my lawyer, supposedly on behalf of Aunt Christine, and he was of the opinion the legal case would cost more than the actual money Theo had lost, and that an out-of-court settlement was the way to go. But I told myself I didn't want to see you ever again, and I tried, I really tried. I concentrated on work to the exclusion of all else, determined to forget you ever existed. Then Ted Charlton got in touch with me and almost begged me to take over his commitment to KHE. After two months of aching for you, I thought, why not? It was a legitimate reason for seeing you. Then he told me he had slept with you, and confirmed what I suspected. All my anger surged back, a hundred times worse. I convinced myself if you slept with him for money, you could damn well sleep with me.'

It was Eloise's turn to put her finger over his lips. 'I really never slept with him.'

His mouth quirked in self-derision. 'I know that. I think I've always known, but jealousy is a powerful emotion. And, if I'm honest, deep down you terrified me; it suited me to think of you as some kind of thief, because then I could deny the very real feelings I had for you. I could pretend you were just like all the other women I have known, self-seeking and greedy. If I once admitted you were different, I knew my bachelor days would be numbered. I told myself I was buying into KHE to help Ted and to get Theo's money back, but I came to the opening of the Paris boutique, secretly hoping you would...' He lifted an elegant bronzed shoulder. 'I don't know...fall at my feet in love and gratitude,' he said wryly.

Eloise half smiled. His description was not far wrong; she very nearly had.

'It wasn't funny,' Marcus murmured intently, brushing a caressing hand gently over her firm breast, as if compelled. 'I ached to be like this with you again, but instead you looked at me like something you would scrape off the bottom of your shoe.'

Eloise sighed, stirring against him, and grinned. 'That bad, hmm?'

This confession was certainly good for *her* soul, but she wasn't so sure it was doing much for Marcus's ego. 'But you blackmailed me into your bed anyway,' she prompted him.

'By then I was determined to have you, and Ted had given me the lever, and to my shame I used it. Revenge is a very powerful emotion and I figured you owed my family.'

'So when did you finally realise you loved me?' She tried to sit up, and Marcus held her back down by simply rolling over her, his elbows either side of her shoulders and his hands cupping her head. The fully naked body contact and the warmth of his breath on her face made her lose her train of thought for a second.

A long kiss later, he stared into her emerald eyes. 'I always have; I was going to marry you when you were nineteen, but you vanished. So I denied I loved you to myself. I thought it was a sign of weakness, and I kept on denying it.' A dull tide of colour washed over his olive skin. 'Until this morning, I looked at you and I knew I was fooling no one but myself. My control snapped and I probably made the least romantic marriage proposal known to man, and I dared not wait to hear your answer in case it was no.'

'I liked it.'

'Forgive me, Eloise, and marry me.' She was stunned to see a trace of doubt in his night-black eyes. 'I will look after you, protect you, and I know I can make you love me eventually or die trying.'

'You won't have to try. I do love you, Marcus, and the answer is yes.'

EPILOGUE

KATY collapsed on to the bamboo cane sofa next to Harry. 'Let the holiday begin; give me a drink quick.'

Eloise smiled and Marcus stood up and crossed to the drinks trolley. 'What will it be, Katy—wine or something stronger?'

'G and T. I need it.'

With a sigh of contentment, Eloise watched her husband of a month mix the drink. They had married in a simple ceremony in the island church, with close friends and family, plus every inhabitant of the island. Eloise had never been happier.

Her sparkling emerald eyes followed Marcus; he never failed to stir her. This evening he was wearing tailored shorts and a soft cotton shirt, and he was without doubt the most handsome sexiest man alive, and he loved her.

As if sensing her scrutiny, he handed Katy the glass and crossed to sit down next to her, slipping an arm around her shoulder, and squeezing gently. 'All right, my love?' he enquired huskily and, running the tip of his tongue along her pouting lips, he claimed them with a kiss.

'Never better,' she whispered back, her pulse speeding up, and for a moment wished she had not invited Katy and Harry to stay for a week.

'You two are hopeless,' Harry teased. 'We came here on holiday, not to watch an X-rated show.'

Leaning back, Marcus chuckled. 'Well, we are all adults here.' Glancing with mocking intent around the terrace he added, 'The little devil Benjamin has finally gone to bed, it seems.'

'Yes, thank God.' Katy sighed, taking a long swallow of her G and T.

'I don't suppose you've heard yet,' Harry said, changing the subject. 'It was in the paper last week; Rick Pritchard apparently got into a fight outside a pub in Dover. He was found in a back alley, badly beaten, and is now in intensive care. They reckon it was foreigners, probably illegal immigrants that did it, because they've all vanished. So you won't have to worry about him any more.'

'I never did worry about him,' Marcus said smoothly. 'His sort usually get what they deserve.'

Watching Marcus, Eloise had the strangest feeling he was not the least surprised by the news.

Later when they were alone in their bedroom, she leant against him, her hand toying with the waistband of his briefs. 'Did you know about Pritchard?' she asked huskily, her own breathing unsteady, as his hands slid up under the fine silk of her nightgown to curve around her bottom, urging her closer.

'I would die if I lost you.' Marcus groaned as her fingers traced the hard masculine length of him.

'That's no answer,' she murmured unsteadily, glancing up and catching a flash of something that looked suspiciously like triumph in her indomitable husband's eyes.

'It's the only one you need,' Marcus growled and, sweeping off her nightgown, he carried her to the bed.

And he was right. Eloise sighed happily some time later, safe in his arms.

THE MILLIONAIRE'S
REVENGE

by

Cathy Williams

Cathy Williams is originally from Trinidad but has lived in England for a number of years. She currently has a house in Warwickshire which she shares with her husband Richard, her three daughters Charlotte, Olivia and Emma and their pet cat, Salem. She adores writing romantic fiction and would love one of her girls to become a writer, although at the moment she is happy enough if they do their homework and agree not to bicker with one another.

Don't miss Cathy Williams' exciting new novel *At the Greek Tycoon's Pleasure* out in December 2006 from Mills & Boon Modern Romance™

CHAPTER ONE

GABRIEL GREPPI stood outside the compact, ivy-clad Victorian house for a few minutes, his hands thrust into the pockets of his beaten suede jacket. He glanced up towards the left of the house, and saw that her room was in darkness. It would be. She would be at the stables now, even though it was after nine and the countryside was sunk in the frozen grip of winter.

The thought of her brought a smile to his lips. For her, he would go through this, but it wouldn't always be this way. He knew it. Could feel it in his bones. Knocking on the door of this house and being made to feel like a beggar, a distasteful presence to be endured by her parents with that particularly freezing politeness so typical of the British upper crust. No, things would change. He was only twenty-two and it might be a long haul, but things would change.

He hardened his jaw and pressed his finger to the doorbell, listening to it resound through the house, then he lounged against the doorframe and waited until the door was cautiously pulled open. Gabriel was tempted to ask whether they were expecting bandits to ring the bell before entering the house, but he refrained. A keen sense of humour had never been one of Peter Jackson's striking qualities, although that might just have been towards him.

'Greppi. What brings you here, boy?'

Gabriel gritted his teeth together and summoned up all his self-control not to respond with something he would live to regret.

'Could I have a word with you, Mr Jackson?' He insinuated his foot through the small opening, just in case Peter Jackson gave in to the temptation to slam the door in his face.

'What, now? Can't it wait?'

Peter Jackson gave an impatient click of his tongue and regarded Gabriel's dark, handsome face with irritation, then he reluctantly pulled open the door and stepped back. 'If you've come to see my daughter, then you can start heading back to that house of yours, boy. Laura's in bed and I have no intention of getting her out of it at this ungodly hour.'

'It's nine o'clock.'

'Precisely.'

'And I haven't come to see Laura, I have come to see you. You and your wife.' Gabriel fought to maintain his composure but, under his weathered jacket and faded jeans, every muscle in his hard body had tensed.

That stopped Peter Jackson in his tracks. He paused and narrowed his blue eyes. 'I hope you don't intend to ask any favours of me, boy, because I can tell you right now that the answer is a resounding negative. I am not in the habit of bailing out anyone financially.'

'I have not come here to ask for money.' He kept his tone as polite as he could, but the derision underneath was unmistakable and the older man's mouth tightened.

'Then say what you have to say and leave.'

This was turning out to be a big mistake. He had chosen to take the honourable path and now he wondered what had possessed him.

'Perhaps I could speak with your wife as well.'

'Oh, very well. But you'll have to be brief. My wife is not a well woman. She needs to get to bed at a reasonable hour.' He turned and began walking towards the snug and

Gabriel followed behind him, slightly taller and with the easy, graceful stride of someone attuned with his body.

'Lizzie, darling, we have an unexpected visitor. No, no need to get up. It's just Greppi.'

Elizabeth Jackson sat in one of the big, padded armchairs, a fragile figure but with the stunning prettiness of a woman who even now, in her mid-fifties, could still make heads turn. The classic English rose who exuded good breeding from every one of her fingertips. Neither invited him to sit, nor was he offered a drink, although both were, he could tell, curious to find out what the hell he was doing in their house at the unseemly hour of nine in the evening.

Peter Jackson stood behind his wife's chair, as ruggedly impressive as she was delicately pretty. 'If you're thinking of buying one of the horses, Greppi, then you're out of luck. Laura tells me that you have a knack with Barnabus, but he's not for sale. If you could afford him, which I frankly doubt. Might be a bit tempestuous, that stallion, but he'll make a damned fine racehorse with the proper training, so don't think you can cut yourself a deal cheaply simply because you know how to handle him. Or, for that matter, because my daughter chooses to associate with you. I am doing enough of a good deed by employing you to do odd jobs around the stables on the weekends.'

'I have come to ask for your daughter's hand in marriage.'

I have come to tell you that I am from another planet. I have come to tell you that I am the son of Satan. Gabriel watched their astounded expressions and figured that he might as well have confronted them with either of those two possibilities.

'I know that Laura thinks the world of you both and I would very much like to receive your blessing.' Gabriel's nerves remained steady as he stared at them both. Young he might be in years, but his life had not been an easy ride and he had learned to deal with pretty much anything that could be thrown at him. Including Laura's snobbish, insular parents who had made it clear from the very first moment they had set eyes on him that he was one of life's more lowly inhabitants.

'I love your daughter, and whilst I realise that at the moment I may not have much to offer her, I assure—'

That broke the gaping silence surrounding them. The mention of his penury. Peter Jackson flung back his head and roared with laughter, then he sobered up sufficiently to wipe a few residual tears of mirth from his eyes.

'What, are you completely mad, Greppi? Now you listen to me and you listen carefully, boy.' The older man leaned over his wife and enunciated his words very slowly, as if addressing someone whose grasp of English was faulty. 'Neither Lizzie nor myself approved of your *involvement* with Laura, but she's a big girl and there has not been much we could do about it. However, the only way you will marry our daughter is over my dead body! Do you read me loud and clear, boy? She is our jewel and there is no way on the face of this green earth that we will give our blessing to any marriage between the two of you.'

'She's only a child, Gabriel.' Elizabeth Jackson's voice was quiet but firm. 'Nineteen years old. And you're only a child as well.'

'Why don't we cut through the *child* argument and get to the heart of the matter?' Gabriel said with rigid self-control. 'You see me as an inferior citizen because I am not British.'

'That's not true, young man!' But Elizabeth Jackson's protest was as empty as a shell. The truth was stamped on her husband's face and Gabriel turned his head to one side in anger.

'You're not what we have in mind for a son-in-law, Greppi. I have no doubt that you'll make something of yourself, and good luck to you, but Laura deserves…'

'Better?' Gabriel's voice was spiked with acidity.

'Call it what you will. And I warn you, Greppi, you leave our daughter alone. We haven't wanted to interfere, but you are no longer welcome at these stables. You can find somewhere else to do your riding and earn your extra money.'

And that was the end of the discussion. Gabriel could see it in the way the old man turned towards the window, offering him the dismissive view of his back.

'Very well.' Jet-black eyes smouldered as he looked at the two of them who would both breathe a sigh of heartfelt relief when he disappeared out of their line of vision.

But this was not over. He had appealed to them for their blessing and they had turned him down. Laura would not. He would have preferred to have married the woman he loved with her parents fully on his side, but if that was not to be the case, then so be it.

He turned on his heel and walked out of the room, letting himself out of the front door. The meeting, which he had imagined would have lasted at least an hour, an hour of persuading them that, whatever their prejudices, he would devote his entire life to making their beloved daughter happy, had lasted a scant ten minutes.

The stables were set away from the house. Gabriel made sure to exit along the drive, knowing that her father would probably have leapt to the window just to make sure that he was leaving the premises, and, after a few minutes of walking through the cutting night air, he abruptly turned to his right and ploughed his way back towards the extensive stables.

He had arranged to meet her there and she would be waiting for him. The thought of that quelled some of the fire burning in his soul and he relaxed his pace, filling his head with images of her.

The stables stretched around a huge courtyard, which was occasionally used for lessons for beginners. A long, sheltered corridor bordered the sprawling sweep of the individual horses' quarters and Gabriel swiftly and assuredly made his way towards Barnabus's stall.

The light was on and she was grooming him, her long fingers stroking the mane, running along the proud length of his head.

Gabriel felt the familiar hot stirring in his loins and drew his breath in sharply, and both Laura and horse turned to look at him.

'I didn't expect you so early,' she murmured, leaving the horse and wiping her hands along her jeans. She smiled and lifted her face to his, giving a soft purr of contentment as his mouth brushed hers.

'Disappointed?'

'Hardly!'

'Do you want me to give you a hand here?'

'Oh, no. There's nothing to be done. I was just chatting to Barnabus.'

'About me, I hope,' Gabriel murmured softly, pulling her towards him and keeping her there, with his hands on her rear, so that she could feel exactly what she did to him.

She was the perfect combination of her parents. She had the height of her father and the blonde beauty of her mother. When she tilted her head back, as she was doing now, her waist-length hair rippled over his hands like strands of silk. White silk.

'But of course,' she agreed with a small laugh of delight. 'Who else? What have you been doing since I last saw you? Have you missed me?'

I've been slaving at an incompetently run engineering company. I've been poring over books so that I don't completely lose track of my Economics degree. I've been putting aside every sweat-earned penny so that I can afford to eat when I return to university. Oh, yes, and I've asked your father for your hand in marriage and it was bitten off.

That little titbit, he decided, he would keep to himself. Now, he would lose himself in her and then he would propose. Her parents would simply have to accept him because they would have no choice.

'If you're finished with Barnabus…' he murmured, tucking her hair behind her ear and nibbling it with his teeth until she squirmed.

'The office…?'

'Out here, if you'd prefer, although I cannot truthfully say that I would welcome dealing with the frostbite afterwards…'

The office comprised three rooms attached to the far end of the stables. One small sitting area for clients, a room in which the books were kept and a bathroom, all furnished with exquisite taste. Soon, Gabriel thought, they would no longer need to scurry and hide and make love like thieves in the night. He imagined her face as she heard him ask her to marry him and he felt a fierce quiver of possessiveness.

'What's the matter?'

He turned to see that she was staring up at him, all wide-eyed and concerned, and he smiled.

'Do you ever dream of us making love in a proper bed?' he asked softly, unlocking the door to the office with the key that, unimaginatively, was hidden under one of the plant pots outside. He pushed open the door and then closed it behind them, capturing her against the back of the door and kissing the nape of her neck. 'A proper, king-sized bed complete with satin sheets and a feather duvet?'

'A cramped single bed would do,' Laura murmured, sighing as his tongue trailed along her neck. 'Anywhere but here. I have nightmares about Dad bursting in when we're in the middle of…of…'

'Making love…?' he finished smoothly for her and she coiled against him with a smile. His voice always did this to her, turned her legs to water. His dark, deep voice with the lingering traces of his Argentinian background, and his smoky, sexy eyes that could stroke her body even when he wasn't touching her.

He had turned up out of the blue one wintry morning a year ago. One minute she had been bending over, grooming one of the horses, her long hair roughly braided back away from her face, and she had stood up to find him staring at her from the stable door, his hands in his pockets, his body leaning against the rough doorframe. He had heard about their stables and he had come to see whether he could earn some money helping out because he loved horses and was a natural at handling them. He had only just come up there to live. His father had been made re-dundant from his post as a teacher and, whilst he could cope until he located another job, there simply was no longer enough to cover his son's university fees. Gabriel needed to work for a year and had taken a job nearby at a small company, interrupting his university career until he could accumulate sufficient money to put himself through the remainder of his course. He had explained all of this without taking his eyes off her and without moving from his indolent stance by the door. Laura had listened and had hardly heard a word he had been saying. She had been too overwhelmed by his sheer animal beauty.

'Are you suggesting that you want to make love to me?' Gabriel whispered in her ear now, and Laura made a low, gurgling sound as he cupped her face in his hands and began kissing her jawbone with infinite, lingering tenderness. Underneath her three layers of clothing, she could already feel her breasts aching to be touched.

It was dark in the office. Dark but warm, with the small fan heater gently purring like a soothing background noise.

'What would you do if I said that I just wasn't in the mood?' Laura teased, curling her fingers into his dark hair and nudging his face up so that she could cover his mouth with hers. The kiss was fiercely passionate, tongue pressing against tongue with an urgency that spoke volumes about the four days during which they had not seen one another. An eternity, it seemed to her.

'I would call you a liar,' he teased back. He slipped his hands beneath her thick, woollen jumper and hooked his fingers under the waistband of her jeans, then he gently circled his fingers round so that he could undo the button and slide down the zip, whilst Laura made a tiny moaning sound in anticipation of what was to come. Heaven on earth. It was the only way she could describe it. Sometimes when, for whatever reason, they had not managed to touch one another for a while, they would scrabble to make love, ripping each other's clothes off in their eagerness to unite their bodies.

Tonight, Gabriel thought, was a special night. Tonight, they would take their time.

He led her towards the back of the office, where a long sofa was ranged against the wall. In the beginning, it had felt odd to make love in the place where Peter Jackson's accountant did the books. Necessity, however, was the mother of invention, and over time the oddness had faded away.

The sofa could have been specially designed for coupling. Laura had once laughingly told him that, in her opinion, Phillip Carr had stationed it there so that when he came twice a week to do the accounts he had somewhere to nod off when the boredom of the numbers began to get to him.

'Let me look at you,' Laura said huskily, stretching her long body on the sofa and staring up at him as he towered over her. 'You know I love looking at you get undressed.' She loosely clasped her arms above her head so that a slither of flat, pale stomach was visible.

'I have no idea why.' He gave a low, teasing laugh.

'And who's the liar now? You know exactly why I love looking at you. You have the most beautiful body I have ever set eyes on in my life. You're as powerful and muscular as any one of our prized racehorses.'

'Thank you very much,' he said drily, although he knew that, coming from her, this was the biggest compliment she could give him.

He shrugged off his bomber jacket, then tugged his thick jumper over his head, followed by his tee shirt, once black, now faded to a dark, uneven grey.

Laura gave an involuntary groan of physical response at his bare-backed torso, just a shadowy outline in the darkness. She had seen him bare-backed before, though. In the summer, when he had stripped off his shirt and ridden Barnabus, without her father's knowledge. Her memory could easily fill in the details of how he'd looked, his body bronzed, his muscles defined and rippling with every little movement. She watched, heavy-eyed, as he removed his trousers and the boxer shorts that were low slung on his waist, and her smile met his.

'Enjoying the view?'

Laura sighed with delicious assent and stood up, ready to wriggle out of her jeans. Her body was on fire. Just looking at him was enough to make her breathing shallow and unsteady.

'Allow me, *querida*,' he murmured. It was one of the rare times when he uttered an endearment. He was a man of passion but essentially a controlled man. Outbursts of verbal emotion were not in his nature. No phoney declarations of love for him. Laura appreciated him for that. His tenderness went beyond mundane utterances. Which was why his endearment now made her heart flutter with pleasure. She allowed him to strip off her jumper, her long-sleeved rugby shirt, which had been a legacy from her father's barnstorming days when he'd played rugby for the county, her tee shirt, leaving only her lacy bra, which barely covered the full swell of her generous breasts.

'Beautiful. You are exquisite.' He dipped his finger into the hollow between her breasts and languidly stroked her, mesmerising her with his eyes until her breath caught in her throat. 'I will never tire of looking at you, touching you.'

Laura laughed softly and caught his finger in her hand, raising it to her mouth so that she could draw it in between her lips, whilst she continued to look at him with her amazing chocolate-brown eyes. With her other hand, she lightly traced the hard muscles of his flattened stomach, down to where his manhood was sheathed with dark, vibrant hair.

'What, *never*? Even when you go to university in September to finish your course? And all those young, beautiful girls are there making eyes and flinging themselves at you?'

'Would you be jealous?' He slipped his hands down her waist and began easing her jeans off, tucking the tips of his fingers into her briefs as she wriggled out of the jeans and gently kicked them to one side.

'Oh, absolutely, Gabriel. Which is why I don't think about it.' She licked his mouth with her tongue and pushed her body against his. She was only a few inches shorter than he was and their bodies made a perfect match, fitting against each other as though specifically designed for the purpose. 'I prefer to concentrate on the here and now.' To prove her point, she drew his hands down to the front of her briefs, wantonly offering him the temptation to explore the honeyed, womanly centre wetly waiting for his expert touch.

'You're a witch, Laura.' Gabriel tugged down her underwear and then unclasped her bra, allowing her full breasts with their rosy peaked nipples to spill forth in all their bountiful glory.

'Only since I met you.' And they both knew that that was true. She had come to him as a virgin, driven into his arms by a force of attraction she had never in her life experienced before. The many boys she had laughingly dated in the past had faded into insignificance alongside the potent, raven-haired stranger who had walked into her life and taken it over.

'Right answer.' He cupped her breasts with his hands. God, he had meant for this to go oh, so slowly, but with her naked body pressing against his he had to fight to maintain control. When she rubbed against him as she was doing now, he just wanted to take her, to feel her body joined to his in heated, pulsating fulfilment.

He guided her back to the sofa, but when she made to lie down he urged her back up, sitting, so that he could part her legs and kneel between them. The perfect position in which to devote his attention to her perfect breasts. He nuzzled them as Laura flung back her head and made no effort to silence her groans of exquisite pleasure. His tongue played with the tips of her nipples and then his mouth circled first one, then the other, pulling and sucking until she began to buck gently against him with her hands firmly clasped in his hair.

No other man would ever touch her like this. She was his, he thought with a surge of possessive elation.

He placed the flat of his hands against the soft inner flesh of her thighs and, whilst she was still reeling from the effects of his mouth on her sensitised breasts, he began a more intimate exploration that had her writhing and gasping as his tongue found the protruding nub of her femininity.

In between her panting, he could hear the abandoned rawness of her voice as she verbalised her passion and that was a powerful aphrodisiac. With a final flick of his tongue deep into the moist sweetness, he rose up and thrust into her, moving strong and deep until their bodies reached the peak of mutual fulfilment.

Only when they were physically spent did he shift her lengthways onto the sofa so that he could lie beside her. A tight fit but it felt so right with his leg draped over her body.

'Wouldn't it be wonderful if we could actually fall asleep together, Gabriel? Like this? Spend the night together?' Laura cradled his head against her breasts and smiled down at him. She swept some of her tangled hair away from her face and continued to watch him as he idly coiled one long, stray tendril around his finger. He held the hair between his fingers and languorously dangled it over her nipple until she giggled.

'I could come and visit you when you're at university,' she carried on dreamily. 'Your own room. Bliss. Or else you could come and visit me at university. Taking this year off's been good, but I can't wait to stretch my wings and leave home.'

'Edinburgh is a long way to commute from London.' He touched her nipple with the pad of his thumb and felt her body still under his touch.

'What are you saying to me, Gabriel?' Laura jerked his head up so that their eyes met in the semi-darkness. 'Too far to commute? I know it won't be like it is now, with you working locally, but we'll still see each other, won't we? Fate brought us together. I know that. Why else would you have happened to see that advert for a job all the way up here, with lodgings provided? And why else would you have found your way here, at these stables, to earn some extra money, meeting me in the process? Fate.'

'Ah, but are you sure you will have time for me?' he teased. 'Studying to become a vet is not going to leave you much time for entertaining old…acquaintances…'

Laura caught the wicked gleam in his eyes and breathed a silent sigh of relief.

'So it's just as well that you're not an old acquaintance, isn't it?' She allowed herself a little laugh and relaxed back against the sofa.

'There *is* another solution, of course, to the problem of meeting up regularly…'

'Oh, yes. What's that?' She ran one foot along the length of his thigh. 'Have you suddenly discovered a vast sum of money somewhere and bought a helicopter so you can fly up to see me every evening?'

'Laura, will you marry me?'

It took a few seconds for Laura's drowsy brain to absorb what he had just said. 'You're joking, aren't you?'

'I have never been more serious about anything in my life, *querida*.'

Laura shifted herself into a sitting position and drew her

legs up. She desperately wanted to switch the light on so that she could see the expression on his face, but switching on lights was totally out of the question. The office block was not at all visible from the house, but it was still a chance they never took. Instead, she peered at him.

'Marry you, Gabriel?' He was deadly serious. His body language conveyed as much.

'Of course, it would be a bit difficult to start with, but we could find somewhere cheap to rent in London and as soon as we are settled you could re-apply to a London university to do your course. Having to come up here to work and save money has slowed me down a bit, but I have only one year left to complete and then I will be earning money. We won't go hungry, *mi amor*, of that you can be certain.'

'Gabriel…' Her voice was a low stammer as the implications of marrying him slammed into her like a fist. Her parents would die. Her mother certainly would. She knew that they had viewed her relationship with Gabriel with growing unease, and they probably weren't even aware that they were lovers. Her mother had shown slightly more fortitude than her father and had contented herself with the occasional observations that she should be careful not to become too emotionally entangled. Her father had been more outspoken. He had told her only two weeks ago in no uncertain terms that he disapproved strongly of what was going on and that he wanted her to end any relationship before it got out of control.

She could feel him pulling away from her and she reached out and gripped his hand tightly. 'God, Gabriel, I love you so much. I've never felt anything like this before. You know that. I've told you that a thousand times. More. But…'

'But…?' No, this was not going how he'd imagined, not

at all. He had expected her immediate, glowing acceptance. Yes, there would be one or two problems, but nothing that could not be handled. Nothing that they could not discuss and solve. His pride began shifting into place. He could feel it closing around him like a vice and he took a few deep breaths to steady himself.

'I'm only nineteen,' she said, half pleading. 'Can't we just…carry on like this…?'

'You mean sneaking around your parents' backs because you're ashamed to be seen openly with me?' he accused harshly, and Laura flinched back from the tone of his voice.

'That's unfair!'

'Is it?' He stood up and began putting on his boxer shorts, his jeans whilst she continued to watch him with a growing sense of panic. 'It seems to me, Laura, that you don't object to my presence in your bed, or should I say on this cursed sofa, but you object to it everywhere else in your life!' Rage had now settled firmly into place. He remembered her father's burst of laughter at the unimaginable idea that a poor Argentinian might want to marry his daughter and wondered whether it was so far removed from her own refusal. Because refuse she had. No point trying to cover it up in pretty packaging. She had turned him down.

'Stop it, Gabriel!' She sprang to her feet, shaking with dismay, and tried to get his hands between hers, but he brushed them aside and carried on getting dressed whilst she stood before him in all her naked splendour. Her vulnerability only occurred to her when he had slung his tee shirt over him, and then she hurriedly began to follow suit, flinging on her clothes with shaking hands.

'God, you even still wear your father's clothes!'

'He doesn't *wear* this! And I only put it on because it's

warm and it was the first thing that came to hand when I left the house tonight! Left the house *to meet you!*'

'Yes, under cover of darkness! Would you have been so desperate to come rushing out if I had invited you to dine with me? If you had been forced to tell *Mummy and Daddy* that you were going on a date with me?'

'Yes, I would have been just as desperate!' Her eyes glittered with unshed tears, which she swallowed back. 'But when have you ever asked me out on a date?' she flung at him. 'You come and work and sometimes we ride off together away from the house and we sleep together, but when have you *ever* asked me to go out to dinner with you?'

'You know the situation!' His voice cut through her like a knife and sent a shiver of despair fluttering down her spine. 'I have always made it clear that every meagre penny I get from the company is ploughed back into my bank account so that I can support myself financially for my last year at university!'

'*I've* offered to pay!'

'Accept money from a woman? Never.'

'Because you're so damned proud! And you're letting your pride destroy what we have now!'

'What we have? We have nothing.'

The silence stretching around them was shattering. Gabriel could hardly look at her. His optimism as he had set off earlier for her house now seemed pathetic and absurd. Even after he had been kicked in the face by her parents, he had still stupidly convinced himself that she would still be his. His wife. He had made the classic mistake of avoiding reality, which was that she was rich and he was poor and never the twain could meet. Whatever flimsy objections she was now trying to come up with.

'Don't say that,' Laura whispered. 'I love you.'

'Just not enough to prove it. Just not enough to marry me. Words without action are meaningless.'

'You make it sound so simple, Gabriel. You love me, therefore do as I say and follow me to the ends of the earth, never mind about hurting anyone along the way.'

He flushed darkly and his mouth tightened into a hard line. 'It is as simple as you choose to make it.'

'No, it's not! It's anything *but* simple! What about my university degree?'

'I told you…'

'Yes, that I could come to London and somehow it would all be sorted out! And my parents? Do I just walk away from them as well? Why can't you just…wait? Wait for a few years? My parents would adjust over time…I know they would. I would be able to finish my degree. Perhaps I could start in Edinburgh and arrange a transfer…' Her voice faltered into silence as she absorbed the hard expression on his face.

'I made a mistake.' His mouth curled into a twisted smile that was the death knell on any lingering illusions she might have been nurturing that she could somehow prevent him from walking out of that door and never turning back. 'I thought I knew you. I realise now that I never did.'

'You knew me, Gabriel. Better than anyone has ever known me,' Laura intoned dully. One errant tear slipped out of the corner of her eye and she let it trickle down the side of her face.

'Oh, I don't think so, *querida*.' The endearment that had filled her with joy only an hour before was now uttered with sneering cynicism. 'It's time for you to get back to the playground you know best. You will go to university and be the golden girl your mummy and daddy have

trained you to be and then, in time, you will marry someone they approve of and live happily ever after.'

He turned away and began walking towards the door
and that snapped her out of her daze and she rushed behind
him, past him so that she could position herself in front,
blocking his way out.

'Don't do this!'

'Get out of my way.' There was a grim determination
in his voice but Laura stood her ground, refusing to watch
him leave even though her head was screaming at her that
it was all over and that there was nothing she could do to
make him stay.

It flew through her head that she could agree to marry
him. Marry him and crash headlong into her parents' disappointment and anger. Toss aside her aspirations and follow him, as he wanted, to the ends of the earth. But the
moment was lost when she realised, knowing it to be a
fact, that he would never accept her now. All those little
indications of his pride that she had glimpsed over the
months had solidified into something she could not breach.

She felt an anger rise inside her suddenly. 'If you loved
me, you would wait for me.'

He reached out and pulled the door open from behind
her and, tall though she was, she was not half as powerful
as he was. He opened it easily, sending her skittering out
of his path.

'It can't end like this,' Laura cried desperately. Her flash
of self-righteous anger had lasted but a second before disappearing in a puff of smoke. 'Tell me that we'll meet
again.'

He paused and looked at her then. 'You should hope,
querida, that we never do…'

CHAPTER TWO

THIS was Gabriel Greppi's favourite time of the day. Six-thirty in the morning, sitting in the back seat of his Jaguar whilst his driver covered the forty-minute drive into London, allowing him the relative peace and sanity to peruse the newspapers at his leisure. From behind the tinted windows of the car, he could casually look out at the world without the world casually looking back at him.

Sometimes, in the quiet tranquillity of the car, he would occasionally reflect that the price he had paid for his swift and monumental rise to prominence had been a steep one. But such moments of reflection never lasted long. His days of idle, pointless introspection were long over and they belonged to a place he would never again revisit.

He picked up the *Financial Times* and began scouring it, his dark eyes frowning in concentration as he rapidly scanned the daily updates on companies and their fortunes. This was his life blood. Companies that had suffered under mismanagement, inefficiency or just plain bad luck were his playground and his talents for spotting the golden nugget amidst the dross were legendary.

He almost missed the tiny report slipped towards the back section. Four meagre square inches of newsprint that had him narrowing his eyes as he re-read every word written about the collapsing fortune of a certain riding stables nestling in the Warwickshire equestrian territory.

No, not a man for idle introspection, but this slither of introspection galloping towards him made his hard mouth curve into a smile. He reached forward and tapped on the glass pane separating him from Simon, his driver.

'You can take the scenic route today, Simon,' he said.

'Of course, sir.' Obligingly, Simon took the next turning from the motorway and began manoeuvring the byroads that led away from the country mansion in Sunningdale towards the city centre.

Whilst Gabriel relaxed back into the seat, crossed his long legs encased in their perfectly tailored and outrageously expensive handmade trousers, and clasped his hands behind his head.

So the riding stables were on the verge of bankruptcy, pleading for a buyer to rescue them from total and ignominious ruin. He could not have felt more satisfied if a genie had jumped in front of him and informed him that his every wish would come true.

For the first time in seven years he allowed his tightly reined mind to release the memories lurking like demons behind a door.

Laura. He stared through the window at the lush countryside gliding past them and lost himself in contemplation of the only woman to have brought him to his knees. The smell of the stables and the horses. Glorious beasts rising up in the misty twilight as they were led back into the stables. And her. Long white-blonde hair, her strong, supple body, the way she laughed, tossing her head back like one of her adored animals. The way she moved under his touch, moaning and melting, driving him crazy. The way she had finally rejected him.

His jaw clenched as he feverishly travelled down memory lane and he felt the familiar, sickening rush of rage that had always accompanied these particular memories.

'On second thoughts, Simon. Take the motorway. There's a call I want to make…'

Or rather, a call he would instruct his head accountant to make. But Andy, his head accountant, didn't get to the office until eight-thirty, and waiting until then nearly drove Gabriel to the edge of his patience.

It was not yet nine when Laura raced into the kitchen and grabbed the telephone, breathing quickly because she had just finished doing the horses and had opened the front door to the frantic trilling of the phone. Of course, the minute she picked up the receiver, she could have kicked herself. Why bother? She knew what was going to greet her from the other end. Someone else asking about unpaid bills. Lord, they were crawling out of the woodwork now! Her father had managed to keep the hounds at bay whilst he had been alive, spinning them stories, no doubt, and using his upper-crust charm to squeeze more time in which to forestall the inevitable, but the minute he had died and she had realised the horrifying extent of the debt, every man Jack had been down her throat, demanding their money. The house had been mortgaged to the hilt, the banks were clamouring for blood and that was only the tip of the iceberg.

How she had managed to swan along in total ignorance of their plight was now beyond her comprehension. How could she not have managed to realise? The house slowly going to rack and ruin? The racehorses being sold one by one? The horses in their care gradually being removed by concerned owners? She had merrily gone her way, doing her little job in the town, coming back to the security of her home and her horses, protected as she had always been from the glaring truth of the situation. God!

Her voice, when she spoke, was wary. 'Hello? Yes?'

'This is Andrew Grant here. Am I speaking to Miss Jackson? The owner of the Jackson Equestrian Centre?'

Laura ran her slender fingers through her shoulder-length blonde hair and stifled a little groan of despair.

'Yes, you are, and if you're calling about an unpaid bill, then I'm afraid you'll have to put it in writing. My accountant will be dealing with…with all unpaid bills in due course.' Like hell he would be. There was simply no money to deal with anything.

'I have in front of me an article in the *Financial Times* about your company, Miss Jackson. It doesn't make pretty reading.'

'I…I admit that there are a few financial concerns at the moment, Mr Grant, but I assure you that—'

'I gather you're broke.'

The bluntness of the statement took the wind out of her and Laura shakily sat on the old wooden chair by the telephone table. With the phone in one hand, she stared down at her scuffed brown boots and the frayed hem of her jeans. In the past four months she felt as if she had gone from being a carefree twenty-six-year-old girl to an old woman of eighty.

'Money is a problem at the moment, yes, Mr Grant, but I assure you—'

'That you will miraculously be able to lay your hands on enough of it to clear your debts, Miss Jackson? When, Miss Jackson? Tomorrow? The day after? Next month? Next year?'

'My accountant is—'

'I have already had a word with your accountant. He's managing your company's death rites, from what I gather.'

Laura gave a sharp intake of breath and felt her body tremble. 'Look, who *are* you? You have no right to make phone calls to my accountant behind my back! How did you get hold of his number? I could take you to court for that!'

'I think not. And I have every right to contact your accountant. The demise of your company is now public knowledge.'

'What do you want?'

'I am proposing a rescue package, Miss Jackson…'

'What do you mean by a "rescue package"? Look, I really don't know a great deal about finances. Perhaps it would be better if you contact Phillip again and then he can explain to me…'

'On behalf of a very wealthy client, who wants to meet with you personally to discuss what he has in mind.'

'M-meet with *me*?' Laura stammered in confusion. 'Phillip has all the books. It would be extremely unorthodox to—'

'The sooner you are able to arrange a meeting with my…ah…client, the quicker your problems will be resolved, Miss Jackson, so could I propose…' he paused and down the end of the line she could hear the soft rustle of paper '…tomorrow? Lunchtime?'

'Tomorrow? Lunchtime? Look, is this some kind of joke? Who exactly *is* this so-called client of yours?'

'You will have to travel to London for the preliminary meeting, I'm afraid. My client is an exceptionally busy man. If the deal shows promise, then, naturally, he will want to see the stables for himself. Now, there's a small French restaurant called the Cache d'Or just off the Gloucester Road in Kensington. Could you be there by one?'

'I…'

'And if you have any doubt as to my client's financial worthiness or, for that matter, the reliability of this proposed deal, then I suggest you call Phillip Carr, your accountant, and he should be able to set your mind at rest.'

At rest was the last place her mind was one hour later,

after she had called Phillip and plied him with questions about the identity of the apparent knight in shining armour who wanted to buy one desperately ailing riding stables in the middle of nowhere.

'He can't be serious, Phillip. You've seen the place! Once glorious, now a destitute shambles. Not even a good reputation left to trade on! Just an empty, sad shell.' Laura felt the prickle of tears welling up when she said this. She could hardly bear to remember the place when it had been in its heyday, when her mother had still been alive and everything had been all right with the world. When everything had been all right in *her* world, a lifetime ago it seemed.

'He's certainly serious at this point in time, Laura, and, face it, what harm is there in checking it out?'

'Did you manage to find out who exactly this man is?'

'I have simply been told that his estimated wealth runs into several million, if not more, and I've been given a succinct list of his various companies.' Phillip sounded unnaturally sheepish and Laura clicked her tongue in frustration. She and Phillip went back a long way. He was now about the only person she could trust and the last thing she felt she needed was his reticence.

'Why the secrecy?'

'Because he is considerably powerful and he says that it's essential that no one knows of this possible deal.'

'I don't understand.'

Phillip sighed, and she could imagine him rubbing his eyes behind his wire-rimmed spectacles. 'Look, meet the man, Laura. He might just save the day and you have nothing to lose. The fact is, without some kind of outside help you'll lose everything. The lot. House, contents, your precious horses, any land you have left. It's far worse than I originally thought. You're standing on quicksand, Laura.'

Laura felt a shiver of fear trickle down her spine. Thank heavens her father had not lived to see this day. However much he had squandered everything, she refused to hate him for it. He had been caught up in one long vortex of grief after her mother had died, and what had followed, the gambling that had been exposed, the addiction to alcohol that he had always been able to hide beneath his impossibly cheerful veneer, all of it had been his own sad response to emotional turmoil.

She became aware that Phillip was talking to her and she just managed to catch the tail-end of his sentence.

'…and the worse is yet to come.'

'What do you mean? How could things get any worse?'

'You could be held liable for some of his debts. The banks could descend on you, Laura, claim your earnings. If this man seems genuine, then be more than open-minded about his offer. Entice him into it. It could be your last chance. I frankly don't see anyone else taking it on.'

Twenty-four hours later, with those words ringing in her ears, Laura dressed carefully and apprehensively for what could turn out to be the biggest meeting of her life. Her wardrobe sparsely consisted of a mixture of working clothes, which she wore to the office where she held down an undemanding but reassuring job three days a week as secretary for an estate agency, and casual clothes, which took the brunt of her work with the horses and showed it. Sensible dark skirts, a few nondescript blouses and then jeans and baggy jumpers. She chose a slim-fitting dark grey skirt, a ribbed grey elbow-length cardigan with tiny pearl buttons down the front and her high black shoes, which escalated her already generously tall height to almost six feet.

Hopefully, this powerful businessman would not be too

short. Towering over a diminutive man would do her, she conceded wryly, no favours at all.

Her nerves were in shreds by the time she arrived at the restaurant, after two hours of monotonous travel during which she'd contemplated the gloomy future lurking ahead of her.

As she anxiously scanned the diners, looking for an appropriately overweight, middle-aged man reeking of wealth, Gabriel, removed to the furthest corner of the room and partially out of her sight behind an arrangement of lush potted plants resting on a marble ledge, watched her.

He had not known what to expect. He had awakened this morning positively bristling with anticipation. Not a sensation he had experienced in quite a while and he had relished it. Money and power, he had long acknowledged, didn't so much corrupt as they hardened. Having the world at your beck and call produced its own brand of jaded cynicism.

He sat back in his chair, watching her through the thick, rubbery leaves of the plants alongside him, and a slow smile curved his handsome mouth. Seven years and this moment was well worth waiting for. Yes, she had changed. No longer did she have that waist-length hair, which, released, had always been able to turn her from innocent young thing into something altogether more sexy. No, but the blunt, straight, shoulder-length hair suited her. His eyes darkened as they studied the rest of her. The lithe body, the full breasts pushing out the little, prim grey cardigan, the long legs. He felt a surge of violent emotion and deliberately turned away, waiting for her now, with his whisky in one hand.

He sat back in the chair and swallowed a mouthful of his drink, mentally following her progress as she was ushered towards his table.

Their eyes met. Brown eyes widening in disbelief clashing with coal-black, thickly fringed ones. Gabriel smiled coldly as she stood in front of him, casting one desperate glance back over her shoulder and then back to him.

'Gabriel? My God, how are you?' The residue of shock was still rippling through her body as Laura looked at the spectacularly handsome man lounging in the chair in front of her. She clutched the back of the chair and managed a small, tentative smile.

'So, Laura, we meet again.' His hard black eyes raked over her body with casual insolence before returning to her face, and continued to watch her over the rim of his glass as he took another sip of his drink. 'You seem a little…disconcerted.'

In fact, she looked as if she might faint at any moment.

'I wasn't expecting…I thought…' Laura stared back at him, transfixed by his face and those mesmerising black eyes that had always made her feel hot and unsteady. Had it been *seven years* ago? It seemed like just yesterday. She cleared her throat. 'When this meeting was arranged, I had no idea…'

'That you would be coming face to face with me? No, you wouldn't have.' Gabriel gave an indolent shrug of his broad shoulders. 'But I am being very rude. Sit down.' He watched as she hesitated fractionally, knowing what was going through her head. She didn't want to be here. If she could have, she would have fled the restaurant as fast as she could. But she couldn't. She was trapped by her own financial circumstances in a cruel twist of fate that not even he, in his most vengeful moments, could have conceived.

'Sit,' he ordered silkily, when she continued to hover by her chair like a frightened rabbit caught in the headlights of a fast-moving car. 'After all, as old *friends* we have much to talk about.' She still had that peculiarly en-

ticing air of innocence and sensuality. Her extreme blonde-
ness in combination with those large, almond-shaped chocolate-brown eyes had always been eye-catching because
they contrasted so sharply with the contained intelligence
on her face. For the first time, Gabriel lowered his eyes as
his body treacherously began to respond to her.

'What do you want, Gabriel?' A pink tongue flicked out
to moisten her dry lips, but she obeyed his order and cautiously slid into the chair.

'Why, I thought my accountant made it perfectly clear
what I wanted...' Gabriel beckoned a waiter across and
ordered a glass of white wine for her, Sancerre, then he
smiled lazily. 'After seven years I am finally able to offer
you a drink. A drink in a smart, fashionable and excruci-
atingly expensive restaurant. As many drinks as you would
like, as a matter of fact. Is that not extraordinary...?'

'I would have preferred mineral water.'

Gabriel ignored her small protest.

Did he know what he was doing to her? Yes, of course
he did, Laura thought shakily. It was pay-back time. She
felt a shiver of apprehension feather down her spine as she
was swamped by memories. God, he had been beautiful.
She slid her eyes surreptitiously to him. He still was.
Suffocatingly and excitingly masculine. All male. Every
pore of him breathed virile sexuality and he hadn't
changed. No, he *had* changed. Power and wealth had hardened the ferociously handsome features of his face and the
eyes staring at her were cold and assessing. A wave of
nausea rushed over her.

'You look a little pale. Take a sip of your wine.' His
voice snapped her out of her memories and brought her
crashing back to reality. 'Please accept my sympathies on
the death of your father,' he said, observing her coolly,
whilst his fingers stroked the side of his glass.

'Thank you.' Laura paused to take a sip of wine. 'I see you…you've done very well. I had no idea…'

'That a poor boy like me working to make ends meet so that he could afford to complete his university course would turn out good in the end?'

'That's not what I was going to say. How is your father?'

'Back in Argentina and doing very well.'

'And you? How are you? Are you married? Children?' In her head, he had never married. Laura realised, with shock, that he had been in her head ever since he had stormed out of her life. She had allowed herself to be persuaded by her parents that his disappearance had been for the best, that she had her future, that they had never been suited, that she would forget him in time, but she hadn't forgotten him. And her memories of him were still of the raw youth who had swept her off her feet. Not of this man sitting in front of her with the world at his fingertips.

Gabriel's jaw hardened. Married? Children? Those were dreams he had nurtured a long time ago, dreams he had uselessly expended on the woman floundering in the chair opposite him. He had been naïve enough at the time to imagine that she had shared those dreams. Until reality had kicked him in the face and he had been forced to swallow the bitter truth that he had been nothing but an amusing plaything for a rich young girl. Her dreams of happy families had not included wedding a poor Argentinian. Not enough class. His hand tightened around his glass and he quickly swallowed the remainder of his drink.

'No,' he said abruptly. He signalled to the waiter for menus and, after they had placed their orders, he sat back in his chair and loosely linked his fingers on his lap. 'So…our fortunes have changed, have they not? Seven years ago, eating out at a restaurant like this would have been out of my reach.' His dark eyes gave a quick glance around their expensive surroundings before returning to her face. 'Who would have ever imagined that here I would one day sit, with you opposite me, in the role of...what shall we call it, Laura? Penitent?'

'Why are you so bitter?' Laura's eyes met his and skittered away in a rush of helpless confusion. 'It's been years...' She sighed. 'Look, I don't want to rake over old ground. Phillip tells me that you're interested in buying the riding stables. I might as well warn you that they're not what they used to be.' She wished desperately that he would stop staring at her.

'Why am I so bitter...?' he mused. His voice was lazy and thoughtful, but his dark eyes were coldly hostile and a shiver of dread slithered down Laura's spine. 'Why do you *think* I'm bitter?'

'Because your pride was dented when...' Her voice faltered and she nervously tucked a loose strand of hair behind her ear.

'Say it, Laura,' he commanded silkily. 'After all, it has been a long time since we last set eyes on one another. What could be more natural than to go over old ground?'

'What's the point of all of this?' She whipped her napkin from her lap and flattened it with the palm of her hand on the table. 'Do you have any intention of buying the stables, Gabriel, or did you decide to get me here so that you could watch me squirm? Humiliate me because I once turned down your proposal of marriage?' There. It was out and they stared at one another in lengthening silence.

She would not allow him the satisfaction of playing cat and mouse with her. He had no intention of buying any stables. He had simply used that as a pretext to get her here so that he could spend a few hours watching her squirm because she had wounded his volatile, Argentinian pride.

'I'm going.' She stood up and scooped up her handbag from the table. 'I don't have to stay and suffer this.'

'You're not going anywhere!' His voice cracked against her like a whip and she glared down at the impossibly handsome, ruthless face staring back at her with narrowed eyes.

'You can't tell me what I can and cannot do, Gabriel!' She leaned over, squaring her hands on the table, her body thrust towards him. It was a mistake. It brought her too close to him, too close to that sexy mouth of his and, as if sensing it, he smiled slowly.

'Times really have changed, in that case,' he murmured, his black eyes flicking to her parted lips, then dipping to view the heavy breasts gently bouncing beneath the cardigan. 'I remember when I could tell you *exactly* what to do, and you enjoyed every little instruction, if I recall…'

Bright pink feathered into Laura's cheeks as their eyes tangled and she drew her breath in sharply.

'But…' he was still smiling, although his expression was cool and closed '…that's not what this is all about, is it? This is about the riding stables, which is why you are going to sit back down, like a good little girl. This is about your future, and believe me when I tell you that you have no choice but to endure my company.'

Laura felt all the energy drain out of her. He had the upper hand. Whatever card she pulled out of the pack, he carried the trump. The fact that he loathed the sight of her was something she would have to grit her teeth and put up with because he was right, she had no choice.

'That's better,' he drawled, when she had returned to her seat. 'Now, I propose that we discuss this over lunch in the manner of two civilised adults.'

'I am more than happy to do so, Gabriel. *You're* the one who's intent on dragging the past up at every opportunity.' She was still trembling as she sat back and allowed the large oval plate of filleted sole to be placed in front of her. It smelled delicious, but her appetite seemed to have utterly deserted her. 'Perhaps we could agree to call a truce on discussing the past,' Laura intoned tightly.

'You are not in a position to offer agreements on anything.' He had ordered the halibut and he dug his fork into the white flesh, savouring the delicate flavour. He should have been delighted to have won this round, to have pulled the plug on her outburst and forced her to obey him, but, aggravatingly, there was no such sense of satisfaction. He stabbed another mouthful of food into his mouth. 'But let us get to the matter in hand. What is the position with the riding stables?'

'You know what the position is. It's a mess. Phillip must have explained all of that to your accountant or whoever the man was who made the phone call.'

'How much of a mess?'

'A lot of a mess,' Laura confessed grudgingly and half-heartedly continued eating. Her stomach felt inclined to rebel at the food being shovelled into it, but she would not let him get to her again. 'The racehorses have all gone. Sold. Four years ago. Most of the other horses were removed over time. I still have a few, but I doubt I shall be able to hang onto them for much longer. And the house…well…it's still standing, but just.'

'What happened?'

'Are you really interested?' Her eyes flashed at him. She couldn't help it. 'Or do you want all the grisly details for your scrapbook on how much the Jackson family fell? So that you can chuckle over it in the years to come?'

'Now who is guilty of dragging the past up?' Gabriel

taunted silkily. 'I am not asking questions any interested buyer would not ask.'

'And are you *really* interested in buying, Gabriel?'

Good question. He had toyed with the idea. Andy had been appalled at the thought of investing money in a decrepit stables that would probably never show any return for the money ploughed in, arguing that such enterprises failed or succeeded by word of mouth and that, because Gabriel was not a part of the racing scene, it was doomed to failure. And Gabriel had been able to see his logic. He had also been unable to resist the opportunity to avenge himself for a rejection which he had carried inside him like a sickness for too long. But had he really been serious about buying the place?

Now, he realised that he was deadly serious. A couple of hours in this woman's company was not enough to sate his appetite. He looked at her, at the strong, vulnerable lines of her face and the supple strength of her body, and suddenly wondered what other men had touched her. He would touch that body again, he would feel it move under his hands, but this time unaccompanied by the emotions of a boy. He would touch her as the man he now was. He would take her and she would come to him on his terms and when he was finished with her, then *he* would be the one to reject her. If it took the purchase of the riding stables, then so be it. It was hardly as though he could not easily afford it.

'I am interested in buying,' he agreed smoothly. 'So explain what happened.'

'Mum died. That's what happened.' Laura closed her knife and fork and wiped her mouth. 'Her heart. We both knew that it was…that she was weak, but I think Dad just never accepted the reality of it. He always thought that something would come along, some magical potion and everything would be all right. But nothing came along, and when she died he just couldn't cope. He lost interest in the place. He said it all reminded him of Mum and he began going out of the house a lot. I thought it was to see horses, visit old friends. Since he died, I discovered it was to bet.' She sighed and pressed her fingers against her eyes, then propped her face in her hands and stared past Gabriel with a resigned, thoughtful expression. 'He gambled away everything. Amazing to think how quickly a thriving concern can go down the pan, but, of course, the world of horses doesn't operate along the same lines as a normal company. The racehorses were sold.'

'He gambled away *all* of the profits from those thoroughbreds?'

'Not all.' Laura's eyes slid towards him and she shivered. Despite the stamp of ruthlessness on his face, he still possessed bucket-loads of that sexual magnetism that had held her in his power. He was her enemy now and making no bones about it and she would rather have died than have let him see that he could still have an effect on her. 'He made two investments that were disastrous and plunged him even further into debt. I guess, that was when the spiral of gambling to win really began.'

'And you were not aware that all of this was going on?'

'I never imagined there was any reason to be suspicious!' Laura returned defiantly. 'I wasn't at home doing the books. How was I supposed to know that the money was disappearing?'

'Because you have eyes and a brain?'

That stung because it was the refrain that played over and over in her own head. But did he have to say it? But then, why shouldn't he? His past and present had now merged to give him the freedom to say whatever damn thing he wanted to and she could do nothing but accept it because she needed him. Her hand curled into a ball on her lap.

'Obviously not enough of either,' Laura said icily.

'What happened to your plans for becoming a vet?' Gabriel asked, abruptly changing the subject.

'I had to…to cut short university because of Mum and then…well…' She shrugged and lowered her eyes, not wanting to think about what might have been. 'Dad needed me.'

'You have been at home all these years? Helping out?' He sounded amazed and Laura flushed, remembering all her grand plans.

'Of course I haven't just been at home!' she snapped. 'I…I have a job in town.'

'Doing what?'

'Is this part of the normal line of questioning by any prospective buyer?'

'Call it curiosity.'

'I'm not here to satisfy your curiosity, Gabriel. I'm here to talk about the riding stables. There's still a bit of land and of course the house, but that's about it. It's all heavily mortgaged. Now, do you still want to proceed or not?'

'You're here to satisfy whatever I want you to satisfy and make no mistake about that. I know everything there is to know about the financial state of your riding stables and, without my money, life will be very bleak indeed for you. So if I ask you a question, you answer it. Now what job do you do?'

'I work in an estate agency, if you must know. I'm a secretary there. Since Dad died I've had to cut short my working hours so that I could spend more time at the stables, but I still work three days a week.'

And what a sight for sore eyes she must make in the place, Gabriel mused suddenly. Stalking around like one of those thoroughbreds she had spent her life looking after. Driving those poor, hapless men crazy.

'A secretary,' he said sardonically. 'What a disappointing end to all your ambitions.' His voice was laced with irony and Laura bit down the response to fly at his throat.

'I happen to like it there,' she said tautly.

'Satisfying, is it? As satisfying as it would have been to work with animals? Shifting bits of paper around a desk and fetching cups of coffee?'

'Some things are not destined. That's just the way life goes and I've accepted it.' Laura met his gaze stubbornly. She would never have guessed that her stormy, passionate lover could have transformed into this cold stranger in front of her. 'I may not have risen to dizzy heights and made lots of money like you, but money isn't everything,' she threw at him, and in response he gave a short bark of dismissive laughter before sobering up.

'At least not now,' he amended coldly. 'Not now that you have no choice but to fall back on that little homily, but somehow it doesn't quite sit right on your shoulders, Laura. Perhaps my memory is a little too long.' He leaned forward, planting his elbows on the table and closing the space between them until he was disconcertingly close to her. 'I remember another woman, to whom money was very important and maybe I have more in common with that woman now, because money *is* important, isn't it, *querida*? Money drove us apart and now it brings us together once again. The mysteries of life. But this time, I hold you in the palm of my hand.' He opened one hand before squeezing it tightly shut whilst Laura looked on in mesmerised fascination. 'Tell me, how does it feel for the shoe to be on the other foot?'

CHAPTER THREE

PHILLIP should have been handling this. Phillip should have been the one showing Gabriel around the stables and the house, gabbling optimistically about how much of a turnaround could be achieved with the right injection of cash. Wasn't that supposed to be a part of his job?

But Phillip was not going to be around. Away on business, he had apologised profusely. He had no idea why she was so intimidated at the thought of showing her prospective buyer the premises. It wasn't as if he were a complete stranger. And, after all, she *did* work in an estate agency, even if showing people around properties did not actually constitute one of her duties. She would be absolutely fine, he had murmured soothingly.

But Laura didn't feel fine. She had had precisely three days after that nerve-shredding meeting with Gabriel to realise that the last thing she felt about selling to him was fine.

The fact was she had not been able to get him out of her mind. In under half an hour, he would be driving up that long avenue towards the house, and she still didn't feel prepared. Either physically or mentally.

She had carefully collated all the paperwork given to her by Phillip in connection with the accounts for the riding stables and laid them out neatly on the kitchen table. She had tidied the house in an attempt to make it appear less shabby, although the sharp spring sunlight filtering through the long windows threw the faded furnishings into unflattering focus. She had taken her time dressing, for-

saking the security of working clothes for the comfort of
trousers and a loose checked shirt. She had still found herself with one and a half hours to spare.

Now, she waited with a cup of coffee, her stomach
churning with tension and then twisting into knots when
she finally spotted a sleek black Jaguar cruising slowly
towards the house.

Laura took a deep breath and reluctantly responded to
the ring of the doorbell, pulling open the door once her
face had been arranged into an expression of suitably de-
tached politeness. She had spent so many hours reminding
herself that, as far as Gabriel Greppi was concerned, she
was an object of dislike that she had automatically assumed that her body would obediently follow the dictates
of her head and not react when she saw him. She was
wrong. Her eyes flickered over him as he stood in front of
her, casually dressed in a pair of khaki trousers and a short-
sleeved shirt that revealed the dark, muscular definition of
his arms. A faint perspiration broke out over her body and
she stood back, allowing him to brush past her and then
stand in the hall so that he could slowly inspect it.

'Did you...find the house okay?' Laura asked nervously,
closing the front door.

'Why shouldn't I have?' The black eyes finished their
leisurely tour of the hall and he looked at her with a cool
expression.

'No reason. I collected most of the paperwork from
Phillip. It's all in the kitchen, if you want to go and have
a read.'

'In due course,' Gabriel drawled lazily. 'Right now, I'd
appreciate something to drink and then you can show me
around.'

'Of course.' She walked ahead of him and he followed
her into the kitchen, appreciating the view of her long legs

and well-toned body. He had had three days to savour his plans for seduction. Three days during which even the demands of his beloved work had paled into the background. The more he had contemplated it, the more beautifully just it had all seemed. One rejection deserved another and he had been given the opportunity to achieve it. The wheel had turned full circle and he would reap the benefits of sweet vengeance. Despite the massive control he applied in his working life, he was innately a man of passion, and his response to the situation did not disconcert him in the slightest. Laura was unfinished business and he would finish it at last, once and for all.

'What would you like to drink?' she was asking him, watching as he skirted around the large central island in the middle of the kitchen and towards the French doors that led out onto the open fields at the back.

'I assume there is some kind of structural report on the house amidst that stack of papers on the table,' he said, turning around to look at her.

'What kind of structural report?' Laura stammered, frowning.

'The kind that will tell me whether this house is in need of serious renovation, or whether its state of decay is confined to the superficial. You can appreciate that such information will necessarily reflect any price I might be willing to pay.'

'The house isn't falling down, Gabriel.'

'How do you know? These old properties need a lot of attention and, from the looks of it, it has had less than zero.'

'You're determined to rub it in my face, aren't you?' she asked tightly, moving over to the table so that she could begin sifting through the inches of paperwork to see whether she could locate anything about the material state of the house. She raised her eyes to his resentfully. 'You just can't resist reminding me that you could make or break me, can you?'

'Is that what I'm doing? I thought I was merely asking for information about the property.' He looked at the bruised, hurt eyes and felt a sharp twinge of something he did not want to feel. 'Leave it,' he said abruptly, 'it can wait. For now, I would very much like something to drink. Tea would be nice.'

'You never used to like tea.' The words were out of her mouth before she could think and colour slowly crawled into her face as she spun around and began fiddling with the kettle. God. Please. Don't let the past sneak up and grab me by the throat. 'How do you take it?'

'Very strong with one sugar.' Gabriel sat down at the table. That little stack of paperwork would just have to wait. He wouldn't be able to concentrate on any of it anyway. Not with her moving around in front of his roving eyes like that, reaching up to fetch mugs from the cupboard so that he could see a little pale slither of skin, as firm and as toned as if she were still the young girl of nineteen he had once completely possessed.

When she sat at the kitchen table, she made sure to take the chair furthest away from his, and gazed down at her fingers cradling the mug. The silence was excruciating. She could feel his eyes on her and she wondered what he was seeing. Certainly not the uninhibited young girl she had once been. Could he sense her fear? And if he did, would he know where it stemmed from? Would he guess that he terrified her because she was realising how much she still responded to him? Physically? As though the intervening years had never existed?

'When did your father…leave to return to Argentina?' she asked in a stilted voice, simply to break the silence.

'A year after I completed my university course.' Gabriel stood up and Laura jumpily followed his movements with her eyes as he prowled through the kitchen, like a restless tiger moving as a way of expending its immense energy. 'He did not manage to find a satisfactory post to fill the one he had lost and he returned to be with the rest of his family. I went on to work at a trading house and discovered that I possessed a talent for working the stock market. A quite considerable talent. I was rewarded with the financial backup to start my own business.' He sipped some of his tea and directed a cutting smile at her. 'While your fortunes were falling, mine were on the rise. Is life not full of little ironies? But, I forgot, you would rather I did not mention my successes, which you can only view as a measure of your own failures. Or rather, those of your family.'

'That's not true. I'm very pleased for you.'

'Pleased because I am now in the position to rescue you from your financial mess?'

'Stop it, Gabriel!' She stood up and moved towards him, bristling with anger. 'You talk about discussing things like two civilised adults but that's the last thing you're interested in doing, isn't it? You haven't even glanced at all those papers on the table!'

'I told you. I'll look at them in due course. Not that it makes an appreciable difference. I know the state of your finances, Laura. You owe everyone money. I am stunned that the place continued to exist for as long as it has. But then, your father must have benefited from the fact that he was on personal terms with his bank manager, not to mention all his suppliers.' He sipped his tea and looked at her flushed face over the rim of his mug. 'What would you do if I decided not to buy?' he asked.

'I expect Phillip would find another buyer.'

'Really? Has he had much interest so far?'

'I don't know.' Laura stared down at him with her arms protectively folded across her chest.

He could see that she was braced for another attack and he resisted the urge to oblige. He would have her, but to have her he would have to gain her trust. She was right. He was not behaving like a civilised adult. Having prided himself over the years on his ability to remain aloof, to detach himself to a position from which he could dispassionately control his surroundings, he was now acting like an adolescent suffering from a severe bout of pique.

He drained the remainder of his tea and stood up. 'Shall we look around the rest of the house now?'

It was impossible not to be aware of him as they walked up the winding staircase that led to the first floor. Instead of following her, which would have been bad enough, he walked alongside her and the flanks of his muscular thighs were only inches away from brushing against hers.

Had he simply been a good-looking man, Laura was sure that she would have been immune to his predatorial charm. But she had once known and touched every inch of that powerful body, and the memory of it waged a silent and savage war inside her against the reality of the situation. He had come back into her life a hostile and aggressive stranger and she could not afford to allow nostalgia for the past destroy her sense of perspective.

Although the land around the house was extensive, Oakridge House itself was relatively small. Five bedrooms, all with individual fireplaces, two bathrooms and a nest of smaller rooms on the ground floor, the largest of which was the formal drawing room, which had not now been used for years.

Laura started with the guest rooms and she maintained a nervous silence as he slowly inspected each one in turn.

Then the bedroom that had once been shared by her parents.

'This house must have seemed very big when your mother died,' Gabriel commented, gazing around him at the floral curtains and matching bedspread, and the dressing table, which, though cleared of everything, still looked as though it were waiting for someone to sit at the stool and peer into the angled mirror. 'Did it not occur to your father that he should sell the place and retire on the generous profit he would have made? Instead of remaining here and squandering the lot?'

'I suggested it to him.' Laura remained by the door, rigid with tension. 'But he said that he couldn't bear to leave the memories behind.'

'Ah. So he did the next best thing by running the place into the ground.' He walked towards her, noticing the way she shrank away from him and it took a superhuman effort not to allow his surge of rage at that to cross his face. 'And how do you feel about living here now?' he quizzed as he walked towards her bedroom.

'I have no choice, as it happens.' Laura watched as he pushed open the door to her bedroom and stepped inside. This felt like the deepest invasion of her privacy, but even so she felt a betraying wave of emotion rush through her at the sight of him looking around him, looking at the bed she still slept on. 'I...no one is really interested in buying the house with all the stabling...' she found herself chattering on witlessly, just to stop her eyes from flicking towards the bed and imagining him lying there, naked, with her next to him. 'It...Phillip says that it's too isolated to appeal to families, who like...like being surrounded by other houses...the whole package seems to put them off...' Her voice trailed off as he walked towards her, impossibly sexy, his eyes fixed on her softly parted mouth.

Her eyes slid sideways, avoiding him, and she licked her lips nervously.

'So why not just cut up whatever land you have left and sell it to a building company? I am sure someone, somewhere, would love to erect thousands of little starter houses here.' He was now within touching distance of her and he could sense the tension oozing out of her. Was it sexual tension? he wondered. He leaned against the doorframe, so that he was now impossibly close to her.

'It's…it's green-belt land…and besides, Dad expressed the wish in his will that the place be sold lock, stock and barrel as riding stables.'

'How considerate of him, lumbering his only offspring with the burden of trying to find the buyer in a million. You seem a little edgy. Am I making you nervous?'

It would have given him a kick of satisfaction to know that he was the reason for her shallow breathing and fluttering eyelids, but, frustratingly, he realised that he was no longer the young man he once was, sure of her responses to him. For all he knew, she could be itching to escape his presence for completely different reasons. Trapped by the man she had once rejected and loathing the sight of him because he held her future in his hands. His lips thinned into a forbidding line.

'Of course not,' Laura breathed, inching away out into the corridor. 'But…but it's getting a bit late. Perhaps we ought to have a quick look around the stables…before the light fades…'

Gabriel pushed himself away from the door. Whatever she felt for him now, he would make sure that time worked its magic on her, time and his persuasive powers to seduce her back into his arms, back into his bed and towards the inevitable rejection. He would allow her to wriggle but then he would reel her in. He wondered how her body would feel after all these years, and felt himself harden at the thought.

'No need to show me the land,' he commented. 'Just the stables and, of course…the other outbuildings.' He saw her pause fractionally when he said this and he knew, with a fierce stab of undiluted satisfaction, that she was thinking the same thing that he was. The offices. Home of their stealthy love-making seven years ago. She might have eradicated him from her life when he had made a nuisance of himself by daring to propose marriage to her, but she still couldn't quite forget the passion they had shared, could she?

It was still light when they got outside, but he had not arrived till a little after four and the light was already beginning to fade.

'I only have the three horses left,' Laura was telling him, with her back to him as she walked past the empty stalls. 'Two are so old that they probably won't make it through this winter, and I really shouldn't be spending money on feeding them, but…'

'But you cannot bear the alternative.'

Laura turned to look at him, her eyes flashing with anger. 'That's right, Gabriel! I can't bear the thought of having them put to sleep! I know that it doesn't make financial sense and I suppose, to a man like you, anything that doesn't make financial sense isn't worth considering, but I'm afraid I've still got some compassion left!'

'Unlike me?' He looked at her and fought the urge to kiss her very firmly on that quivering pink mouth. God, even after all the muddy water under their bridge, he was still attracted to her! It confused him and confusion was not an emotion with which he had much familiarity.

'Unlike you!' she agreed with vehemence. 'You never used to be like this, Gabriel. What happened?' She had intended to throw that at him with scathing disdain, but instead she winced as she heard the genuine curiosity in her voice.

'Life happened,' he said abruptly.

'I'm surprised you never married.' A slight, cool breeze lifted her hair from her shoulders and Laura wrapped her slender arms around her body.

'Because I am such a catch?'

'You're good-looking and eligible. I would have thought that you would have had hundreds of women beating a path to your door in search of a band of gold.'

'Oh, but I have,' Gabriel drawled smoothly. 'I prefer my life to be uncluttered, however, so I usually try and end things before the beating-down of the door occurs.'

Of course he would have had numerous lovers, but she still felt a jolt of searing jealousy at the thought of them all, lying in bed with him, making love.

'Now, shall we continue with our tour of the empty stables? Or are there any more pressing questions you feel you need to ask?'

'I was simply being polite,' Laura muttered. 'If we're going to be doing business together, then we might as well be civil to one another, wouldn't you agree?'

'Doing business with one another?' He began strolling down the corridor that ran along the stabling blocks, peering into the forlorn, vacant stalls, seemingly checking each one for signs of imminent collapse.

'Hold on. We *are* doing business with one another, aren't we?' Laura hadn't budged and he eventually turned around to look at her. 'That's what all this is about, isn't it?' she persisted, her heart thudding as he slowly approached her. 'You *did* say that you were serious about buying the place, didn't you?'

'I also said that it would depend on its condition. I'm a

businessman first and foremost, as you were at such pains to point out. It's hardly likely that I'm going to throw my money into a pit from which I shall never be able to recover any of it, wouldn't you agree?' His mouth curved into a smile and Laura gave a little shrug of her shoulders, uneasily aware that he was toying with her even though what he had said was absolutely true and would have been said by any prospective buyer. Anyone would demand to see the goods and approve them if they were to invest money.

'My horses are just along here,' she said, leading the way. 'I know the stables look a bit desolate, but with sufficient money they can easily be brought up to standard.'

'Is that the selling blurb your accountant asked you to give me?'

'It's the truth.'

'They're a far cry from how they used to be seven years ago,' Gabriel remarked, pausing when she did to look at one of the older horses. He watched and saw the suspicious glitter in her eyes give way to tenderness as she pushed open the stable door and began stroking the horse. He could hear her murmuring under her breath.

'Did you keep Barnabus?' he asked softly, stepping into the darkened stable beside her and running his hands along the flanks of the horse whilst his eyes remained fixed on her down-turned head. He was assailed by a sudden rush of memories and breathed in sharply, tearing his eyes away from her just as she raised hers to his face.

'He's two stalls along.' She stood up and her expression resumed its wariness as she led him out, shutting the door behind her.

'It must be a bitter pill to swallow…all this…' The words were jerked out of him and her wary expression deepened.

'What do you think, Gabriel?' This time she didn't enter either of the stalls, standing well back when Gabriel walked in to run his long fingers over Barnabus's black head. It was too painful to watch.

'What do I think…?' he mused, leaving the stall with reluctance. Riding was in his blood. He would have liked to have mounted the stallion and ridden him across the fields, but there were more pressing things to do. 'I think…' he continued speculatively as he walked slowly towards the offices, making sure that he kept as close to her as he reasonably could—he wanted to make sure that she felt his presence '…that you find yourself in an impossible situation. This is your home, you have grown up here, the riding stables formed part of your childhood. I think you would do pretty much anything to hang onto them. Am I right?' They had reached the offices but, before entering, he turned to look at her.

'Naturally, I would like to see them brought back up to the standard they once were…' Laura responded hesitantly, not really knowing where this was going.

'Of course you would.' He smiled coolly at her. 'Because the alternative would be disastrous for you personally, wouldn't you agree? No roof over your head, for a start.' He pushed open the office door and stepped inside.

Just as he remembered. A little shabbier, but by far the least run-down of all the buildings. He paused in the middle of the room and looked at her over his shoulder. 'Come inside, Laura, and shut the door behind you. It's getting a little cold out there.' He turned his back to her and heard the soft click of the door being shut.

From the outer reception room, he strolled into the office, still there with its desk and files and the sofa, spread against one wall. He could sense her standing by the door, hovering, waiting for him to complete his perusal of the room, and he wondered savagely whether she had ever really missed him. She would have come into this office after he had left, and thought...what? Anything? Would she have felt some twinge of regret and wistfulness? Or would any such emotions have been quickly and easily replaced by relief that he had walked out of her life before he had become too much of a liability?

The thought of that made him clench his fists in his trouser pockets. He turned very slowly around until he was looking at her with a veiled expression.

'So tell me, Laura, what *would* you do to hang onto this place? And keep your lifestyle intact? I mean, three days a week working as a secretary surely cannot pay you very much. What would you be able to afford to buy in town? Or even to rent, for that matter? A one-room studio flat somewhere? Maybe you might be forced to share a house with someone...'

Laura eyed him uneasily as he casually strolled closer towards her. Every muscle in her body had tensed and she could hear herself breathing quickly, drawing in shallow bursts of air, which seemed barely sufficient to keep her standing on her wobbly feet.

Gabriel extended his arms, propping himself against the wall and trapping her so that she was forced to look at him, could barely move without colliding with some part of his aggressively masculine body.

'I...I haven't really...given it much thought...' she stammered as his black eyes bored into her.

'Well, think about it now.' He allowed her a few seconds of silence whilst he continued to stare at her. 'Having the bank repossess the place. You would get a pittance, you know. Probably enough to cover some of the debts but certainly nothing left over on which you could reasonably live. You might even be forced to pay off some of the creditors out of your own meagre personal funds. So…what would you do to hang on here?' His eyes dropped to her trembling mouth, then down to her breasts, which were heaving as she inhaled deeply to gather her self-composure, which had been blown to the four winds.

'Wh-what do you mean?' Her voice was little more than a choked whisper. Her glazed eyes couldn't leave his face.

'I mean that I still want you…' He removed one hand and shockingly placed it lightly at her waist, slipping it under her shirt so that he could run his finger along her waistline.

'I don't come with the property, Gabriel.' She could have accompanied that assertion with a forceful push, but for some reason Laura found that her hands were powerless to move.

'Ah, but would you *like* to?' His hand slipped further up the shirt until he could feel the weight of her breasts pressing heavily against his fingers. Her eyes were fighting him, but her body was singing a different tune, he realised. Her body still remembered what it felt like to be joined with his.

And his, he thought with a blow of startling clarity, had never forgotten. The women he had slept with during those intervening years had never fulfilled him the way this woman quivering under his touch had. The thought angered him and made his resolve harden. He cupped one breast in his hand and gently massaged it. Her breasts, like ripe, succulent fruit, had always turned him on and they were turning him on now. God, he could feel his erection stiffening in response.

'You can't buy me, Gabriel.' Laura's voice did not convey a convincing message of denial. Her nipples hardened into taut peaks of arousal, betraying her every instinct to run away as fast as she could from this man.

'Are you telling me that I don't turn you on, Laura? If that is what you're saying, then I don't believe you.' To prove his point, he rubbed the pad of his thumb over her throbbing nipple and smiled like a cat suddenly in possession of a large saucer of cream. Yes, she felt the same. His hands, which had caressed other bodies, now felt as though they had been designed to mould just this one. He dipped into the lacy covering and scooped out one large breast and felt a fierce kick of pleasure as a small moan escaped her lips. Lips that were begging to be kissed. Just as her nipples were begging to feel the pressure of his fingers playing with them, rubbing them until they ached with sensitivity.

He lowered his head and his mouth met hers with a hunger that he hadn't realised he had. His body pushed hers back against the wall and with a groan of sheer yearning Laura twined her arms around his neck, her tongue feverishly and urgently clashing with his.

Oh, yes, it felt good to taste him again. She was still reaching for him when he pulled away and she slowly opened her dazed eyes.

'Still the same fiery woman,' he murmured, drawing away and leaving her to hurriedly try and resurrect some of her scattered wits. Laura looked at him with her arms folded protectively across her breasts. Her heart was still thudding wildly behind her ribcage, but reality was beginning to sweep away the cloud that had made her fling caution to the winds.

He had kissed her to prove a point and prove it he had in no uncertain terms.

Gabriel could see the conflicting emotions race across her face like shadows but he felt no real sense of satisfaction. So she still wanted him, had not been able to resist him the minute he had laid his hand on her, but he wanted more. More than just the knee-jerk reaction afforded by two people obviously still attracted to one another. He wanted her body and soul.

'If you think I'm going to come to bed with you so that you buy this place, then you're mistaken, Gabriel.' Her words snapped him out of his reverie during which he had been thinking of her standing before him, naked, willing and ready to do whatever he wanted. Until the time came when he turned her away.

'I would not dream of asking any such thing of you,' Gabriel replied, lowering his eyes. 'You will come to bed with me because you still want me.'

'I hate you, Gabriel,' Laura whispered and in that moment she did. Hated him for being able to control her after all this time. He had once spoken about marriage and setting up house together, but on his terms. Even then, she doubted that he had known the meaning of love, love as something beautiful to be shared and for which sacrifices had to be made. He had wanted her enough to make her his possession, but had not loved her sufficiently to wait, to allow her to ride the storm of her parents' disapproval in her own time, to gain the qualifications that would have meant everything to her.

It had all become apparent over time that wanting someone was not enough. And now here he was, wanting her again but allied to that urge to possess, to take what he wanted, was a cruel streak that desired retribution for the damage she had done to his pride.

Yes, she hated him, she told herself fiercely, or, at least, she desperately needed to hate him.

Her utterance was like a knife twisting in his stomach. 'I do not know why,' he said acidly, 'when I am prepared to rescue you from your situation.'

'If you buy this place, then you're doing it for yourself,

Gabriel. What will you do with it? Convert it into a leisure centre? Turn it into a country house so that you have somewhere to spend weekends away from London? Or do you really care what happens to it? Will it just be enough to know that for a moment in time you could indulge your desire to have control over me?' She pulled open the office door, desperate to get out of the place and away from his suffocating masculine presence.

'I already own a country house,' Gabriel drawled, watching her retreat and allowing her the temporary victory of imagining that her retreat might be permanent.

'You don't live in London?'

'Naturally, I have a penthouse there for when I have to stay in the city, but my primary residence is in the country.'

Laura edged out of the room and into the cooling air outside. He followed her and she angled around him to lock the office door, pulling back so that she could create some vital distance between them as they walked back to the house.

'And you…you commute to London every day?' Keep the conversation on an impersonal level, she told herself feverishly. 'It…it must be exhausting.'

'I live in Berkshire. It's not a million miles away from London and, at any rate, I have a driver who takes me in to the city. Except, of course, when I decide to stay in my apartment in Chelsea.'

'If you're working late?' The house was thankfully within sight and Laura had never been more grateful to see it.

'Working late or…playing late,' he murmured, sliding his eyes across to her and watching as two bright patches of colour appeared on her cheeks.

Playing late. There was no need for him to expand on

that. Laura could well visualise the type of games he played and the sort of women he played them with. Sophisticated, beautiful women, the female counterparts of himself.

'So what would you do with the place?' she reverted to her original question.

'Allow me.' His hand brushed hers as he pushed open the front door and Laura felt an alarming quiver of sexual awareness race through her veins, making her jerk back. He stood aside and she scuttled past him into the hall.

'I would keep it as a riding stables, of course,' he harked back to her original question. 'It would require a considerable amount of money to bring the place back up to a respectable standard, but it is feasible.'

'And when do you think you'll be able to give me an answer on, uh, whether you're interested in buying or not?'

'After I've looked at all the paperwork,' Gabriel said lazily. 'Which reminds me, I need to get it all from the kitchen.'

'Uh, yes, of course. I'll just go and fetch it.' Anything to get away from him so that she could clear her head! She hastily gathered all the paperwork together and was rushing, head down, back into the hall, intent on shoving the lot into his hands and escorting him to the front door post-haste, when she more or less catapulted into him coming towards her.

The shock made her stumble and he caught her, wrapping his solid arms around her body to steady her.

'What are you doing?' she shrieked, pulling back and instantly regretting her desperate outburst as his coal-black eyes raked over her flushed face. She could have sworn that the devil could read every panic-driven thought in her head!

'You came hurtling out of that kitchen like a bullet,' he

said drily, propelling her gently back but keeping his hands firmly on her arms. Her face was flushed with defensive anger, which was slowly replaced by the dawning realisation that she had overreacted to his simple attempt to prevent them both from crashing to the ground. Like it or not, he thought with grim satisfaction, he was turning her world on its head. She might feel nothing for him emotionally, but he had awakened a dormant passion and if she thought that he was going to allow it to go away without first getting exactly what he wanted, then she was in for a shock.

'The papers?' She was looking at him in a dazed fashion. Now she blinked as he reminded her of the reason she had been rushing out of the kitchen and she quickly thrust the lot into his hands. 'I'll be in touch…soon.'

CHAPTER FOUR

LAURA sat at her desk, staring ahead at her computer screen and trying to focus on what was in front of her. Some agreement about a house that had just been sold. She had just typed it, but she really didn't have much of a clue as to what she had actually typed.

Three days and still no phone call. Phillip had told her that he would make the call to Gabriel on her behalf, to find out what his intentions were for buying the stables, and she had hotly denied him permission to do any such thing. She would not beg. She would not encourage Gabriel's notion that she was so desperate for him to purchase that she would do anything. Her behaviour three days previously, when she had fallen into his arms like a sex-starved nymphomaniac, still terrified her because she could see it happening again. And she would have to fight against any such thing with every bone in her body.

Lord, she had spent so long trying to expunge him from her mind. When he had walked out of her life, she had been desperate with grief, but she had hidden her desperation well. Her mother's health had been failing, and her father had already told her in no uncertain terms that any shock might prove the final straw and running after Gabriel Greppi would surely constitute shock. She had listened to them, aching and silent, and their soothing words that it was all for the best, that she was young, that she had her whole life ahead of her, that their two worlds could never meet and he was from a different world from the one she knew, had gradually numbed her into staying put.

And at the back of her mind grew the nagging suspicion that if he had truly loved her, he would have understood why she had refused his proposal. She had pleaded with him to stay and he had abandoned her. Then her mother had died and everything had slowly gone into free fall.

Seeing him again had been more than a shock, and realising the depth of his hatred for her even greater. But far more shocking was the fact that when he had touched her, every fibre in her body had burned and come alive and she had responded. God!

She printed off the letter in front of her, determined not to let him invade her mind, and was scanning Hugo's spidery handwriting to begin another letter when the door clanged open and she looked up to see the object of her fevered thoughts standing in the doorway. It was so unexpected a vision that she had to blink several times, convinced that the darkly sexy shape framing the doorway was an illusion.

No chance. Not unless everyone else in the office was simultaneously having the same illusion because a quick glance around showed six faces all turned in his direction and Hugo was briskly exiting his office, hands outstretched, obviously sensing someone with a lot of purchasing power.

Gabriel's black eyes found hers but he remained where he was, his sheer presence rendering total silence amongst her normally garrulous colleagues.

'Do come in! I'm Hugo, Hugo Ross. Come in, come in!' Hugo's booming voice broke the silence and they all returned to what they were doing. All except Laura, who could feel a sizzle of treacherous excitement exploding in her veins as Gabriel continued to watch her bewildered face.

'Hugo.' His voice was drily polite, but he did manage

to tear his eyes away from her sufficiently to concentrate on the blandly handsome man bearing down towards him. 'I hate to disappoint you, but I'm not in the market for a house…'

To be fair, Hugo took the disappointment well. He fell back and shrugged with a rueful smile. Gabriel was well aware that she was stunned to see him here where she worked. He was no longer looking at her but he could sense her eyes on him, wondering, no doubt, what decision he had come to in connection with the stables.

'Are you quite sure? We have some glorious properties around just at the moment.' Laura had seen that Hugo had already sized up the cut of Gabriel's cloth and she had no doubt that those glorious properties would begin at the million pound mark.

'I'm sure you do,' Gabriel returned smoothly, 'but I'm here on personal business.'

All eyes swivelled interestedly onto her as she stood up and plastered a bland smile on her lips.

'Hugo,' she said, moving into action and searingly aware of Gabriel's dark eyes riveted on her. 'This is Gabriel Greppi. Remember I told you that he might be interested in buying the stables?'

'Ah, yes, so you did.' This time Hugo's blue eyes were speculative as they focused on Gabriel. He was well aware of the extent of the financial difficulties hanging over the stables and Laura could see him making a careful judgement of the man in front of him. Judgement of the man as her prospective rescuer and of the man as simply a man and she felt a twinge of sympathy for him.

He had employed her initially as a favour to her father and they had become friends and he had made it clear that they could be more than just friends if she'd wanted. She had not and he had taken her refusal in good spirit, proving in the end to be one of the steadiest friends she had had over the years.

'I thought you might have telephoned,' she addressed Gabriel, 'or perhaps called Phillip to let him know...'

'Oh, I prefer to deal face to face with you in this matter.' He turned to Hugo with an icily polite smile. 'If you don't mind, Laura and I will discuss this matter in private. Get your bag,' he told her and, when she glanced uncertainly towards Hugo, he repeated the command, leaving her no choice but to obey.

'What time will you be back, Laura?' Hugo pointedly turned his back to Gabriel, a gesture that did not appear to disconcert Gabriel in the slightest. Hugo placed his hand on her arm with a look of concern on his face and over his shoulder Laura met Gabriel's stony expression with bland disregard.

If he thought that he could purchase her with the property, then he was wrong, and he was doubly wrong if he thought that he could control who touched her and who didn't. He might be pulling her out of a quagmire not of her making, but that didn't make him her saviour. Just the opposite, she thought, and a cold shudder of apprehension trickled down her spine.

'She'll be back when she's back and only to collect her things,' Gabriel announced shortly, moving around so that he was standing beside them both.

'I beg your pardon?'

'You heard me, Laura. I am taking you out to lunch to discuss my decision and you will not be returning to this job here.'

'Don't be ridiculous!' The door clanged open and a couple walked inside, holding hands and looking bright-eyed and optimistic. First-time buyers. Hugo, torn between sorting out the dramatic situation unfolding before him and seeing to the young couple, who were shortly followed by an elderly man and his wife, reluctantly left them alone.

'I am not being ridiculous,' Gabriel informed her with no effort to lower his voice.

'Shh! Gabriel,' she hissed, 'I can't just walk out of here and never return.'

'You *will* return. I told you—to collect your things.'

'Will you keep the volume down?'

Gabriel felt his lips twitch as he took in her flustered face. 'You never did like scenes,' he mocked. 'And, no, I will not keep my voice down, so, in order to avoid one, I suggest you do as I say.'

And with Hugo now glaring at her whilst trying to placate his prospective buyers that the dark, handsome man with the arrogant tilt of his head did not actually work for him, Laura resigned herself to grabbing her bag from the chair and stalking out of the office, ahead of him.

'How dare you?' She turned on him the minute they were outside, hands on her hips and her body thrust forward in a stance of pure aggression.

'How dare I come up here with the glad tidings that I am going to buy your riding stables? I thought you would have been overjoyed to see me.' He had thought nothing of the sort. He had known precisely what her reaction would have been to look up and see him standing there in her cosy little workplace. But he had discovered that he'd wanted to see where she worked. Another piece of the jigsaw that was slowly coming together to form the complete picture.

'You know what I mean, Gabriel!'

'Where do you want to go for lunch? I will rely on you to suggest somewhere quiet where we can have a talk…about business.'

'I'm not hungry!'

'Well, I am. So humour me.' With that he began striding along the high street, attracting stares from most of the women who walked past him, bar those too old or too young to notice.

Laura half ran until she caught up with him. Tall she might be, but her strides were no match for his, especially in her slightly heeled court shoes, which she was not accustomed to wearing.

'What about this place?' He stopped in front of a spacious wine bar that advertised its specials of the day with a blackboard on the pavement.

'You can't make me give up my job, Gabriel!'

He ignored her and she wanted to literally scream with frustration. If this was his primitive, caveman way of getting his own back on her after seven years, by controlling every aspect of her life, then he was doing a very good job of it, she thought furiously.

'We'll talk inside,' he informed her, glancing back at her flushed face over his shoulder as he stood aside to allow her to walk past him into the wine bar.

Laura maintained a simmering silence as they were shown to a table towards the back of the wine bar and handed two oversized menus, which she barely glanced at.

'Is it all right for me to talk now?' she asked sarcastically, leaning forward so that her breasts rested against the surface of the table and her straight, impossibly fair hair swung around her face.

'Just so long as you don't raise your voice. We wouldn't want to create a scene.' He glanced across at a waitress, who almost tripped over her feet in her haste to get to their table and take their drink order. Champagne. To celebrate. To which Laura automatically replied that she never drank alcohol at lunchtime since it made her feel sleepy.

'Does that matter? You are more than welcome to fall

asleep in my car on the way to the house. Once you have collected your possessions from your office and said a rueful goodbye to your fellow employees.' Not to mention your employer, Gabriel thought to himself, recollecting the hand on her arm and the expression of fondness in Hugo's eyes when he had looked at her. The thought that there might be something going on there made his lips tighten and he forced himself to relax. He would get to that later.

'I am not going to be leaving my job, Gabriel. That was not part of the deal.'

'It is now.' He sat back to allow their waitress to place two champagne flutes on the table and waited until she popped open the bottle and poured them both some of the bubbly golden liquid. 'After I had a look around the stables, well, I was frankly alarmed at their state of disrepair. You may not have noticed, but there are cracks on the ceilings, what looks suspiciously like rising damp in some of the rooms, not to mention parts of the roof that look as though they have exceeded their sell-by date by several years.' He played with the stem of his champagne flute, allowing his words to hit home and settle in, then he took a leisurely sip of his drink and proceeded to run his finger lightly and absent-mindedly around the rim of the glass.

'Naturally, I will have to have the place professionally surveyed, but I estimate the house alone will cost thousands in terms of refurbishment, and that is not taking into account possible structural faults.' He leaned back into his chair and linked his fingers loosely on his lap. 'A massive job.' He shook his head. 'I very nearly decided against buying, but…' Actually, he had thought no such thing. The sweet challenge of winning her back only to discard her was too irresistible.

Laura gulped down a generous mouthful of champagne and almost choked in the process.

'I still don't see what all of this has to do with my job,' she persisted in a panicky voice. 'I am very grateful that you've decided to buy the stables and you can sort out all the ins and outs with Phillip, but...' She trailed off into helpless silence as he sat there, politely listening to her and shaking his head in the thoughtful manner of someone dealing with a person who was missing something glaringly obvious.

'You're part of the bargain, Laura.'

'What do you mean? I'm not part of any bargain. I have my own life...'

'Oh, but you don't.' There was a cutting smoothness to his tone that she didn't like. *What did he mean that she was part of the bargain? Did he think that he was going to sleep with her, have her as his concubine or else no deal?*

'I don't understand.'

'Well, then, I had better explain, hadn't I?' But he would take his time, watch her stewing over his words, watch her wondering whether he intended to make her into a sex slave as a fair exchange for digging her out of the hole in which she had become submerged. *Sex slave.* The thought filled him with sudden warmth and he leaned forward, instantly invading her space. 'The sort of business that your family was involved in does not operate along the same lines as a normal company, as you yourself pointed out. For a start, it can only work if the person in charge knows about horses and, more importantly, knows people within the world of horses and horse-racing. Are you beginning to get my drift here?'

Only too clearly. 'There are plenty of people around who would jump at the chance of working for you. I could easily put you in touch with them.'

'But my solution rests a lot closer to home than that...'

He smiled with dangerous intent. 'Who better to help re-construct the tatters of the riding stables than yourself, Laura?' He beckoned the waitress across and, having treated her to a full-wattage smile of pure charm, gave his lunch order and waited in polite silence whilst Laura stammered out hers, frankly the first thing she could spot on the menu.

'Another glass of champagne?' He tipped some more bubbly into her empty glass and said soothingly, 'There's no need to look so worried. I have absolute confidence in you.'

'That's not what's worrying me, Gabriel…'

'Is it not? What, then?' He inclined his head to one side and frowned in supposed puzzlement. Laura could easily have tipped her glass of champagne over his arrogantly beautiful head. He knew precisely what she was worried about. She was worried about the trap that she felt slowly closing in around her, but she knew that to mention any such thing would have him throwing back his head and roaring with laughter. He would deny any such thing, would accuse her of being melodramatic, and to all intents and purposes he would have good reason because what he was offering her was a generous deal with the opportunity to remain living under her own roof and helping to res-urrect the riding stables she had grown up loving.

On paper, it all sounded wonderful. In practice, a little voice was issuing warnings at a rate of knots.

'Perhaps I could help out in my spare time,' she con-ceded lightly. 'I'm sure Hugo would be flexible with my hours, if I needed to have time off now and again.'

'Not good enough, Laura. Getting the stables back up to running standard is going to be a full-time job and you know it. People are going to have to be employed, contacts are going to have to be revived…' And the thought of her popping out to do her job with Hugo there to mop up any flagging spirits would not do at all. In fact, the mere thought of it made his stomach clench in violent knots.

'I will ensure that you are paid handsomely for your work, of course...'

'So in other words, I shall become your employee.'

'If you want to put it like that.'

'Is there another way of putting it?'

'You could see it simply as being offered the chance of a lifetime to get the stables back on the map where they belong...'

'In other words, I have no choice.'

'Naturally you have a choice. We all have choices. You can choose to reject my offer, in which event I shall be forced to return to London empty-handed.'

So in other words, no choice. Laura sighed and gulped down a bit more of the champagne. She could already feel it going to her head but she didn't care.

'So what happens next?'

'You mean after you go and collect your things from work?'

'After I go and tell Hugo what's happening. I don't *have* anything at work, as such.'

'He already knows what is happening.' Gabriel narrowed his eyes on her flushed face. God, but how he would have liked to have plunged straight into her beautiful head and found out what exactly was going on in there. He couldn't imagine her being attracted to a man like Hugo, making wild love with him, but then maybe she now liked them safe and bland and unexciting.

'I don't intend to disappear without any sort of explanation to him. I've worked there for years now and he's been...good to me...'

'And in what ways has he been "good to you"?' Gabriel's mouth twisted and Laura glared back at him.

'You have a one-track mind.'

'I recall a time when you liked that...' he murmured, and she couldn't help it. A faint pinkness invaded her cheeks. Oh, yes, she remembered that time well. Too well.

'That was then and this is now,' Laura informed him crisply. 'After I quit my job, what then?'

'What then? Why, we sign papers. Mine are all prepared, including the stipulation that you work for me running the place. I can have them faxed to your accountant by lunchtime tomorrow. More immediately, we return to the house. My surveyor is booked to inspect it this afternoon. As soon as the deal is signed, I can begin throwing some food to the baying wolves and you can begin sleeping easier at night knowing that the bailiff will not be knocking at your front door.'

Their food arrived but all Laura could do was toy with the Caesar salad on her plate. Her mind was buzzing with thoughts, most of them vaguely alarming.

'You should eat more than that,' she heard him saying and Laura blinked in surprise at the sudden change in conversation. One minute informing her that he was now in charge of her life, or at least a hefty part of it, and the next minute chiding her for not eating enough for all the world as if they were two normal people, having a normal conversation in a normal situation.

'Is salad all you have been living on since your father died?'

'Why do you ask?' Laura retorted suspiciously, only to sigh at her overreaction to a perfectly polite question. 'It's easier.' In fact, she had lost weight since her father had died. Everything had fallen on her shoulders and somehow rounding up the day with a hearty meal for one had not been top of her agenda.

'You've lost weight.'

'Since when?'

'Since I last made love to you seven years ago.'

Laura nearly gagged on the bluntness of his statement. Had he done that on purpose? Because he knew that it would send her entire nervous system into a rapid nose-dive? But when she looked at him, it was to find him returning her gaze with complete innocence.

'I happen to like the way I look,' she retorted. 'You're entitled to your own taste in women if you like them plump.'

'Voluptuous,' Gabriel corrected mildly.

'I was never voluptuous, so your tastes must have changed over the years!'

'Oh, you were. Curves in all the right places…breasts a man could fill his hands with.' His voice was low and lazy and at the mention of her breasts he openly looked down at hers before flicking his dark eyes back to her flushed face. 'Your breasts at any rate are still as wonderfully bountiful as they used to be…'

'This is a ridiculous conversation,' Laura choked hotly. 'We were supposed to be discussing business.'

'We were. Now I thought we might move on to more general conversation.'

'If your idea of general conversation is discussing my figure, then…then…'

'Then…?'

'Then you're wasting your time because I'm not going to join in!'

'Perhaps it *was* a little rude of me, but really, you need to take care of yourself. I don't want you collapsing on me when you need to have all the strength at your disposal to deal with the work ahead.'

'Have you got some sort of...plan...or timetable?' Laura grasped the opportunity to steer the conversation away from the dangerously personal observations he had just thrown at her. She was mortified to discover that, unwittingly, he had stirred something inside her that had had her melting, thinking thoughts best kept hidden.

'You're the one in the know when it comes to horses. What do you suggest?' She was making a big effort to calm down. The blushing hue of her cheeks was subsiding and her normal colour was returning, but she still couldn't quite meet his eyes. Gabriel watched it all and he realised that at least part of his pleasure, if not all of it, was derived from the knowledge that he was getting under her skin. He also realised that he *wanted* badly to get under her skin, that his purely male response to her went beyond any desire for revenge. He wanted to taste the sweetness of that full mouth once again. That brief moment of passion three days earlier had only served to tease his appetite and to remind him of how intensely satisfying the act of making love had been with her.

He dragged his mind back to what she was saying and realised that he had been staring at her with an utterly blank expression when she tilted her head to one side and frowned.

'Are you listening to me?'

'Oh. Yes. Of course. You were saying...?'

Was he so bored that he couldn't even keep his mind focused on what she had just spent five minutes rattling on about? Laura wondered.

'I was saying that I can get in touch with all our old suppliers and hopefully convince them that they can resume doing business with us again. But before then, I would have to begin the process of wooing old clients back. Some of them will have gone for good, but I personally know a few who were truly sad about…about the way things turned out and privately told me that if ever the business picked back up, they would return their horses. God, Gabriel…it's such a huge job. I just don't know…'

Her eyes clouded over and he found that he didn't like that. He almost preferred the resentment to the sadness. Not, he reminded himself grimly, that the disintegration of the stables had anything to do with *him*, but he felt a sudden rage for the old fool who had done this to his daughter.

'You can do it,' he said gently. 'If anyone can do it, you can. I have utmost faith in you, Laura.'

'But I have no real idea where to start. There's so much…' She chewed her lip, fighting back the overwhelming urge to burst into tears. His anger she could handle. She didn't like it but, in a funny way, she understood it. His gentleness she found much more disconcerting, as she found her own sudden temptation to lean on him, get strength from him, let him hold her and soothe her problems away.

I must be mad, she thought shakily. He declared himself the enemy and made no bones about it. How on earth can I be thinking of leaning on him? She shook her head to clear it and raised her eyes to his.

'I can't do a thing, anyway, without…without finance.'

'It will be taken care of,' Gabriel informed her, calling for the bill and removing one of several platinum credit cards from his wallet to pay. He glanced at his watch. 'We just about have time for you to pay a visit to your office and then we will head to the house.' Back to the business in hand. For a second there he had felt a compelling need to gather the wretch up in his arms and kiss her troubled expression away. Lessons, he reminded himself harshly, are never learnt by forgetting the past.

'And don't forget,' Gabriel informed her as he pulled up just a few metres down from the estate agency, 'there is no time for any lingering farewells. I will give you five minutes.'

'Or else what?' Laura retorted, swinging open her car door and putting one long leg out of the car.

'Or else I shall come in and get you.'

And he would, too, she thought sourly as she dashed into the office. In fact, the beast would probably enjoy it. Drawing himself up to his full height, flinging his arrogant dark head back and crooking one imperious finger in her direction. In other words, bringing the entire place to a complete standstill.

She had just enough time to assure Hugo that she would call him later in the evening to explain all and to promise her work colleagues that she would keep in touch. Judging from the avidly curious expressions on their faces, she wryly thought that she would have no choice. If she didn't call them, they would make sure to call her!

She arrived back to find Gabriel standing outside, indolently leaning against the polished black driver's door of the car, and she immediately slowed her pace.

'Seven minutes,' she informed him, 'and forty-six seconds.'

'Good of me to allow you the extra two minutes and forty-six seconds, wouldn't you agree?' But he grinned wickedly when he said this and Laura felt her body surge into sudden, maddening response.

'You deserve a medal,' she muttered, hiding her confusion by sliding quickly into the car. 'What time is the surveyor coming?' she asked, once he was inside the car and gunning the engine.

'Probably there already,' Gabriel said nonchalantly.

'If not on his way back to London having got there and found no one at home.'

'Oh, Anna will wait.'

'Anna? Your chartered surveyor *is a woman*?'

'No need to sound so surprised.' Gabriel briefly slid his eyes across to her. 'This is the twenty-first century. Women have invaded the working place and many now hold down substantial jobs.'

'I know that!' Laura snapped.

'And I happen to be an extremely non-sexist employer. Everything rests on credentials, as far as I am concerned.'

Laura bit back the temptation to inform him that he could have fooled her, considering he had all the macho arrogance of someone living in another century!

'She will probably find it useful to have a look around the outside of the house and establish visually what might need doing,' he was saying now. 'She is very thorough and I trust her utterly to provide me with an unadorned statement of what will need looking at and how much I should expect to pay.'

The image of a middle-aged professional woman briskly walking around with a notepad in one hand and a pen tucked into the top pocket of her severe suit was dispersed the minute they pulled into the courtyard to find a gleaming silver Porsche parked at an angle. Before Laura could readjust her mental impression of what to expect, the woman in question rounded the corner and she wasn't wearing anything remotely resembling a severe suit. An appreciative smile curved Gabriel's lips and then he was walking towards her, arms outstretched, speaking in quick, unintelligible Spanish. And whatever he was saying, it didn't have much to do with bricks, mortar and rising damp, Laura considered sourly, lagging in the background.

At least not judging from the warm tinkle of laughter that punctuated the woman's rapid phrases.

'Laura, come and meet Anna.' He still had his arm around the other woman's waist and his mouth was still relaxed with a smile.

'This,' he said with a gesture meant to embrace the house, 'is Laura's legacy and my next purchase. What do you think?'

Close up Anna was a little older than Laura had originally surmised, but just as pretty. Small, olive-skinned, with dark eyes and dark hair that was loosely tied at the nape of her neck but with loose tendrils escaping that promised long, rebellious curls when released. And she was voluptuous. Full breasts under the tight-fitting cream jersey and tan jacket. Laura suddenly felt sick and had to force herself to smile and shake the dainty hand extended towards her.

'It needs a bit of work,' Anna was saying, all business now and commanding no less of Gabriel's attention for it. She turned to point at various bits of the house, efficiently indicating damage that Laura had not even been aware of. 'May I have a look inside?' she finished and Laura nodded curtly, leading the way whilst the other two fell back and began chatting in low tones. Low, *intimate* tones, it seemed to Laura.

She practically flung open the front door and, once in, was chagrined to be told that she could perhaps go and prepare a pot of coffee whilst the two of them made a more detailed examination of the house.

'Perhaps I ought to come along,' she suggested with saccharine sweetness. 'After all, I *have* lived in this house all my life and I would be very interested to know what repair work might have to be done.'

'No need,' Gabriel drawled. He had managed to disengage himself from the raven-haired bombshell and Laura was besieged by a further attack of acidity at the thought that he would probably resume intimate contact the minute they were out of sight. 'It may have been your house, but as of tomorrow it will be in my possession. It is far more pertinent that I find out firsthand the extent of damage.'

'I will have my report ready within a week,' Anna addressed her with a smile. 'It will be quite detailed.'

'And I'll be allowed a copy, will I?' Her voice dripped sarcasm although Gabriel appeared blithely unaware of that. In fact, he seemed in remarkably high spirits, Laura thought as she politely stared him down with her hands planted firmly on her slim hips.

'Naturally.' For sheer devilry, he once again slipped his arm around Anna's waist before guiding her towards the spiral staircase winding up to the first floor. God, he wanted to look back over his shoulder just to see if she was still standing there, all bewitching defiance, simmering. But he didn't.

In fact, he kept his arm wrapped around the brunette's waist and only removed it when they had cleared out of sight. And only then did he begin quizzing Anna about her husband, Rodolfo, and their eighteen-month-old son. If his cousin was slightly bemused by her exuberant welcome, she concealed it well, chattering happily about family business, whilst casting her well-trained eyes into corners and nooks and crannies and up the fireplaces for any hazards waiting to be uncovered.

'What games are you playing, Gabriel?' she finally asked him curiously as they inspected the last of the rooms one and a half hours later, having agreed to call it a day.

'Games, my dearest cousin?'

'Games,' she declared firmly.

'Cat and mouse,' he said succinctly, aware that that only covered the tip of the iceberg.

'And which one is the mouse?' she teased.

'Do I resemble a mouse to you?'

'No, but then I have never seen you play this type of game with a woman before. Do not enter into something only to discover that you do not know the rules.'

'Trust me, Anna.' His eyes gleamed in anticipation of the woman waiting in the kitchen. He could feel her presence calling him. 'I am in total control…am I not always?'

CHAPTER FIVE

AN HOUR and a half spent condemned to the kitchen, side-lined into the role of onlooker in her own home, had done nothing for Laura's temper. She had usefully prepared something for herself to eat later, then had sat at the kitchen table contemplating every little thing she now thoroughly disliked about the man who had once been the centre of her life.

The fact that he was canoodling in one of the rooms with a curvaceous brunette, flaunting his sex life in front of her as a stark reminder that she was nothing to him now except a bitter taste in his mouth he was determined to eradicate, only made her more sour.

Laura remembered something her father had told her months after Gabriel had walked out of her life. She had been staring out of the kitchen window, lost in the familiar cloud of depression, when Peter Jackson had surprised her from behind. Her infernal moping around had to end, he had informed her angrily, it was not doing anyone any good at all, least of all her mother. Had she ever stopped to think, he had snapped, that she was busily mourning the loss of a man who had had his eye on the main chance? That this so-called love of her life had wanted the status and position she offered and that if she had been anyone else he would not have looked at her twice?

No, it certainly had not occurred to her then, but it was occurring to her now.

There was no shred of nostalgia in him for the past they had once shared, no hint that he remembered her wide-eyed adoration with any affection, because, she had thought in the solitude of the kitchen, he had never really cared about her.

By the time Gabriel and Anna finished their extended tour of the house, Laura was stiff-lipped with the battery of thoughts that had been whirling around in her head.

She stood up when she heard their footsteps, arms folded. And he *still* had his infernal arm around the woman's waist!

'Something smells good in here,' Gabriel said, disengaging himself. 'Anna, you'll stay for some coffee, won't you?' Her body language was speaking volumes, he thought with satisfaction. Arms folded, face rigid with disapproval. Yes, he was utterly and pleasurably in control. The thought did wonders for his sense of well-being.

'I can't, Gabriel.' The brunette smiled apologetically. 'It's late and I face a long drive back to London.' She gave him a look of intimate and indulgent affection that had Laura's teeth snapping together.

'What is the state of the house?' she asked with freezing politeness. 'Mr Greppi seems to think that it's on the verge of collapsing.' *Gabriel?* Did he really expect her to believe that all his employees addressed him by his first name in tones of warm intimacy? He might see himself as Mr Ultra Modern Man with his staff, but did that stance include running his hands all over their bodies in full view of whoever might be watching? If so, then she was surprised he didn't spend half his time in a court somewhere fighting off harassment suits. Not that this particular woman looked in the least upset by his intentions!

'Far from it,' Anna said warmly, collecting her bag and briefcase from the counter. 'There's nothing fundamentally wrong with your house.'

'*My* house,' Gabriel corrected, shooting Laura a rueful

smile that the correction had to be made, one that she countered with icy blankness.

Anna shook her head and said something in Spanish, then she turned to Laura. 'My report should be ready within a week, but there really will be no need for any extensive repair work. The window sills need looking after. Some of them have rotted through, and I noticed that some small parts of the roof will need replacing, but aside from that any damage is superficial. Years of neglect take their toll.'

'Yes, I realise that.'

'Now, now, there is no need to sound so offended,' Gabriel mocked. 'Anna is just doing her job. Now, perhaps you could get that coffee ready whilst I see Anna out?'

'If I'm going to be working for you, then we need to get a few things straight,' was the first thing Laura told him when he reappeared in the kitchen a few minutes later.

She had taken up residence by the kitchen table, but even with the distance between them she was still agonisingly aware of his suffocating masculinity. Especially now that there was no third party around to dilute it.

'Ah, coffee. Just what I need.' He picked up the mug, took a sip and then moved in her direction, making sure that he passed fractionally too close to her before pulling out one of the chairs and sitting down.

He wasn't wearing a tie, but he undid the top two buttons of his shirt, tugging open the neck and running his long brown fingers along the underside of the fabric whilst Laura watched in helpless fascination, before dragging her mind back to the grievances she had rehearsed.

'Point one,' she informed him, 'is that I'm not your servant. Don't think that when you happen to be around you can snap your fingers and I'll run and make you, and whoever else happens to be with you, a cup of coffee.'

Gabriel looked at her lazily whilst he continued to slowly sip his coffee. He wondered whether he should just inform her that really she did not have much option when it came to her list of duties, and then decided that constant confrontation was not going to achieve what was becoming increasingly important. Namely, her. In bed with him. Wet, willing and naked.

He was the cat, yes, and admittedly she was the mouse, but she would be oh, such a very eager mouse when she came to him.

He smiled at the thought of that, which was disconcerting enough to make Laura stop in her tracks. She had expected him to jump in with another little reminder of her indebtedness to him, which included making however many cups of coffee he wanted. In fact, she had prepared quite a good argument to counteract any objections. What she hadn't expected was for him to smile, a slow, gleaming smile that sent a shiver of treacherous awareness rippling through her.

'You are absolutely right,' he said, maintaining his killer smile.

'I am?'

He nodded.

'Yes, of course I'm right. I don't intend to be used, Gabriel, or to do any running and fetching for you.' She could hear herself blustering but then, dammit, did he have to sit there and look so damned agreeable?

'I would not expect you to. Indeed, if I gave you the impression that I was…throwing my weight around, then I apologise. Profusely.' He could fully understand why she was staring at him with such suspicious incomprehension. He had done nothing *but* throw his weight around since he had set eyes on her again, and it wasn't going to do. He didn't want her cowed and spitting hate at him. He wanted her sweet and compliant and deliciously abandoned.

Besides, what was the good of rejecting someone who viewed him with intense dislike? It would amount to no rejection. For the second time, she would simply be relieved to see the back of him. She might be aware of him, in fact *was* aware of him…he could feel it in those hot little surreptitious glances she occasionally slid across to him when she wasn't aware that he was looking…but as long as he continued to wield the rod of power, she would resolutely fight the attraction with every ounce of strength.

Sure, he wanted to remind her at every turn that she was now dependent on him, but every little reminder only drove her that bit further away. Only a fool sabotaged his own game plan with pointless hollow victories.

'Oh,' Laura said, taken aback.

'What were those other points of yours you wanted to mention?'

'Nothing,' she mumbled, gulping down the remainder of her coffee. 'Well…' She looked outside at the darkness that had fallen and wrapped itself around the house. 'It's getting late. Perhaps you should be setting off…'

Gabriel could see her tense in anticipation of another confrontation and so he obligingly got to his feet.

'You're right.'

Laura felt that she should be breathing a heartfelt sigh of relief. Why then did she feel just a little bit disappointed at the speed with which he had taken her up on her suggestion? Surely she didn't *want* him to hang around any longer? That would be downright masochistic!

'It will take me at least an hour and a half to get back,' he chatted casually as he headed out of the kitchen and towards the front door. He would have liked to have given her something to think about after he had gone, a light kiss somewhere innocent yet deeply arousing, perhaps on the side of her neck. Nothing that would indicate the desire for anything else. But there was no point in barging through the sudden window he had created for himself.

Having been so thoroughly wrong-footed, Laura was now overcome by an attack of guilt. It was already after eight and she had offered him nothing to eat. She should at least have suggested that he share the economical dinner she had made for herself. In fact, she had opened her mouth to offer the invitation when caution made her stifle back the words.

'So tomorrow,' he said, turning around to face her, 'perhaps you could meet me at your accountant's office?' Her slightly flushed face and half-parted lips were appealing enough to almost make him forget his resolve not to frighten her away. That mouth was begging to be plundered. His hands ached from wanting to plunge into that prim top of hers and expose the soft, heavy breasts with their tempting, pert nipples. He stuck his hands severely into his pockets.

'What time?'

'Nine-thirty. He will be expecting us. My fax confirming the purchase as well as all the contracts with stipulations should have reached him some time this afternoon. In case I failed to mention it, you and I will have to agree on a price for the furniture contained in the house. At least, those items of furniture you wish to sell, of course. Naturally, you can keep the rest here until such time as you wish to remove them.'

'You mean when you're ready for me to move out?' She saw that he had flushed darkly at her words and wondered whether he was perhaps not immune to the slightest twinge of guilt that he was going to be throwing her out of the only house she had ever lived in.

Did she realise, Gabriel wondered, what a vision of temptation she presented when she dropped her guard? He couldn't help it but he could see the swell of her breasts and his torrid imagination made him flush. 'There is no rush for you to contemplate any such move,' he said briefly, turning to open the door just in case he did something he regretted. 'This is not an ordinary house purchase. You will be in charge of running this show and the best place for you to be will be right here, for obvious reasons. But we can discuss all of this tomorrow.'

'Right. Yes. Of course.' Perfectly businesslike. Obviously he no longer felt the need to remind her at every turn that he was the one in the position of doing her a favour. In fact, he obviously no longer felt the need to dwell at all on the fact that they weren't strangers. He was a businessman first and foremost and this had all now become business.

Laura waited by the open doorway, watching as he strode towards his car, got in and began driving carefully out of the courtyard and down towards the road at the bottom of the long drive.

Now that he had gone, the house seemed suddenly very empty. She ate her meal to the deafening sound of silence and went to bed thinking unwelcome thoughts of Gabriel and the Porsche-driving chartered surveyor with the easy smile and the darkly sexy body. They made a stunning match. Both olive-skinned, both raven-haired, both obviously at ease in each other's company.

Not that Gabriel and his love life were any concern of hers, she told herself firmly the following morning as she made her way to Phillip Carr's office in the centre of town.

She had half expected him to arrive late, but in fact he was already there by the time she was shown into Phillip's office, sitting with his back to her, relaxed and confident.

'I've been looking through the papers,' Phillip greeted her warmly, delighted with the solution to a problem over which he had been regularly losing sleep. 'Everything seems to be in order. In fact, Mr Greppi has been most meticulous in his attention to detail.'

Gabriel was smiling at the older man, receiving the compliment with nonchalant modesty, but out of the corner of his eye he was vibrantly aware of Laura slipping into the chair alongside his. Her pale hair gleamed like silk and he approved of what she was wearing. A short-sleeved rose-coloured dress that was simple but fitted, emphasising the narrowness of her waist and the length of her legs, which seemed to go on for ever. Despite what he had said about her losing weight, there was no chance she would ever be mistaken for one of those stick-thin models, two of whom he had dated in the past and neither of whom had done much for him. Her body was a bit more streamlined than it had been seven years ago but she was too full-breasted to ever look skinny. And she still had the athletic firmness of someone accustomed to an outdoor life. He slid his eyes away and began to pay more attention to Phillip, who was now going over some of the details of the contract with his client.

When he got to the part about her salary, Laura gave a little squeak of astonishment, rapidly followed by an objection.

'No way,' she said firmly, turning to face Gabriel for the first time since she had entered the room. He was dressed for work and looked no less impressive for it. Dark charcoal-grey suit, crisp white shirt, dark blue tie with a small, clever pattern running through it. He swung his chair to look directly at her, one eyebrow raised in apparent enquiry.

'No way…what?' he asked, sitting back and lightly linking his fingers on his lap.

'Phillip, would you mind giving Gabriel and myself a few minutes of privacy?'

'Is that really necessary, Laura?' Phillip asked. 'I honestly cannot see what the problem is here and the sooner we go through this contract, the sooner we can have the deal signed, sealed and delivered, so to speak.' Before, he added to himself, our knight in shining armour decides to have a change of heart. Everything, so far, looked too good to be true and in Phillip's experience canny businessmen rarely indulged in deals that were too good to be true. Not unless they were the eventual winners, which certainly was not the case here. He tried to signal as much to Laura with his eyes but she was steadfastly ignoring him and, with a click of his tongue, he reluctantly stood up.

'So,' Gabriel said, pushing his chair back so that he could cross his long legs, ankle resting on knee, fingers still linked on his lap as he lightly rubbed the pads of his thumbs together, 'what is the problem here? I confess I'm baffled.' He tilted his head to one side and devoted every nerve in his body to looking at her.

'Baffled!' Laura gave a snort of disbelief. 'Oh, please. I know exactly what you're doing here, Gabriel. Overpaying me so that I'm even more indebted to you than I already am! You're offering to give me *five times* more than I was getting working for Hugo, and that's when I was working *full-time* there!'

He shook his head. 'This is a record. The first time anyone has attacked me for *overpaying* them!'

'You mean you've been attacked for *underpaying*?' Laura smirked, distracted.

'No…actually, I usually manage to get it just right.'

'Mr Perfect Employer. I wonder why I'm not surprised

to hear you singing your own praises. Could it be that I'm getting accustomed to your ego, which is as big as a house?'

'I am Argentinian! You insult my pride...' But he grinned when he said this and Laura found herself grinning back, caught up in a moment of perfect wry and mutual understanding. Until she remembered the matter at hand.

'Anyway, you're distracting me...'

'Oh, good,' Gabriel murmured wickedly, 'success at last.'

Which brought a bright flare of colour to her cheeks as the velvety ambiguity of his words struck home. 'I *mean* you're distracting me from what I was saying. Which is that there's no need to be so ridiculously generous. It's enough,' she continued, taking a deep breath, 'that you're buying the riding stables, that you're going to try and turn it around, that you've offered me this lifeline.' Laura lowered her eyes. 'And in case I haven't said this before...thank you.'

'What was that?' He leaned forward, cupping one ear with his hand.

'You heard me.' A small smile tugged the corners of her mouth.

'Accept my generosity,' Gabriel said, holding onto her softening and feeling something tug deep inside him. 'There is nothing self-serving about it. The job will be a big one. I am merely compensating you in a manner I judge fit.' He gave her a crooked smile. 'Please.'

'You should at least give me a probationary period,' Laura offered. 'You may not approve of the way I handle things...'

'Why not?' He raised his eyebrows in lazy amusement. 'Are you planning on going down a few illegal routes? A spot of bribery or blackmail? Sleeping with a few contacts to generate business?'

'Of course not!' Laura flushed. 'I would never dream of doing anything of the sort!'

'You mean the bribery and blackmail or the sleeping with contacts…?'

'Both! All! You know what I mean.'

'Then I see no reason why you should be on any probationary period, but…' he shrugged '…if it makes you happy then we can agree on a three-month probation.'

'During which you would expect me to achieve…what? Precisely?'

'Why don't we discuss that later? In the meanwhile, we might just as well get Phillip back in so that we can finish here. I take it your little argument over pay is sorted…'

'I suppose so,' Laura said limply.

The remainder of the meeting, which lasted a full two and a half hours with only the odd snatched break for some coffee and biscuits, moved at a dizzying speed. Sums of money were thrown around that made her gasp. Guided by Phillip, she signed on the various dotted lines he indicated, barely aware of the various contracts she was reading. By the time she and Gabriel were shown out of the office, Laura felt as though she were unsteadily coming off a roller-coaster ride.

The fish, Gabriel thought as he followed her out onto the pavement, was on the hook. All he had to do now was enjoy the unparalleled experience of reeling it in. And reel it in he would. With every signature, he had been grimly aware of the fortuitous sequence of events that had brought him to this point. He now owned the house that had once been barred from the likes of him, and in a manner of speaking, whether it was politically correct or not to even think it, he owned the woman who had once casually and cruelly turned him away. Or perhaps he didn't own her, he thought with brutal honesty. But he would.

'Are you heading back down to London now?' Laura asked, breaking into his thoughts. 'I suppose it's been difficult for you to find the time to keep coming up here.'

He noticed that she was heading towards her car, the old relic of a Land Rover her father used to drive, and which she had presumably been obliged to continue using because of her straitened financial circumstances.

'That car will have to go,' he said abruptly.

Laura stopped in her tracks and looked at him with her mouth open. 'I beg your pardon?'

'The car. It will have to go.'

'What do you mean *the car will have to go*? That car works perfectly well. Well-ish, anyway. And in case you hadn't noticed, I don't have a replacement waiting in the wings. Besides, it's very sturdy, which is what I need living where I do.' Laura began walking towards it, trying hard not to notice the rust spreading along the bottom of the driver's door.

'It won't do.' Gabriel swept his eyes over the denim-blue vehicle with an expression of disdain.

'Is this part of your continuing plan to strip me of everything?' Laura flared up at him angrily.

The accusation was so close to the truth that Gabriel had the decency to blush, but he stood his ground, his mouth thinning in determination. 'It is no such thing. I simply feel that your driving around in that heap of crumbling metal is not exactly going to give any prospective clients the right impression of a business on the road to recovery.'

They stared at one another until Laura helplessly lowered her eyes. 'I can't just go out and buy another car,' she protested stubbornly.

'Why not?'

'Because...'

'Our business here has not been completed. We are about to pay a little visit to the local bank where I will set up a substantial account for you from which you will withdraw whatever money is necessary to cover costs. Your salary will be transferred directly into the bank account you now possess.' He looked at the mutinous set of her mouth and shook his head. 'There is no point in trying to fight me every inch of the way,' he informed her softly. 'You will never win.'

'No,' Laura jeered, 'because you're bigger and stronger and infinitely richer. Am I on the right track here?'

'Pretty much.' He shrugged.

'You can set up bank accounts, snap your fingers and make me do your bidding, force me to part with just about the only thing I possess to my name now that the house has gone.'

'The house but not the contents,' he reminded her. 'And you still have the clothes you wear.'

'Which you will doubtless decide to make me get rid of somewhere along the way?' His failure to answer, in fact to look as though her jabbing attack had even remotely dented his formidable self-composure, was added fuel to the fire. 'I may obey you,' Laura said through gritted teeth, 'and I may be grateful for everything you've done, but I'll never like you.'

His only reaction was the tiny pulsing muscle in his jaw, an indication that her words were getting to him.

He would not rise to her bait. She could glower until the cows came home, Gabriel thought, but to no purpose because he was not going to indulge in a heated argument with her.

Besides, in a strange way, he knew how she was feeling.

He knew that her anger stemmed from her helplessness, from her sudden vulnerability. When she'd still had the house and the land and the decrepit sign announcing the riding stables that were no more, she'd still felt, psychologically, that she'd still had *something*. That ownership had passed to him, of all people, was therefore more than galling.

The sudden, startling insight into the woman fulminating not five inches away from him aroused a compassion he had no time for.

'Let us go to the bank,' he said in a tight voice.

'I want to go home.'

'I know you do,' Gabriel said gently. But then his face hardened. 'And you will. Just as soon as we have sorted out our finances.'

An implacable wall, Laura thought. She could rail and storm and beat her fists against it, but it would never budge. Her shoulders drooped and she nodded in resignation.

'And then,' he announced with supreme arrogance as they walked the short distance to the bank, 'we will go and buy you a car.'

The bank manager, who miraculously seemed to have a huge window in his day in order to jump to Gabriel's commands, was as fawning and beaming as Phillip had been.

'You,' Laura said sarcastically, during the five-minute pause in the conversation during which the impressionable and youthful bank manager had seen fit to rush off and order his secretary to halt all his calls until otherwise told, 'are obviously the most exciting thing that has happened to Tony Jenkins this year. If he bends over backwards any more, I think the back of his head will touch the ground.'

Gabriel looked at her appreciatively and grinned. He had

forgotten how damned funny she could be when she tried. 'Perhaps he is impressed by my good looks and winning personality,' he commented drily.

'Perhaps he's even more impressed by all those numbers you're giving him.'

'Shallow man,' Gabriel murmured in a low voice, his dark eyes making her go hot all over. 'Someone should tell him that money is not everything.'

'I hate it when people quote me.' But she looked away quickly and was inordinately relieved when the subject of their discussion reappeared.

'And now,' Gabriel said as soon as they had stepped outside, Laura now in possession of so much money with which to commence this venture that her head was spinning, 'for the car.'

'There's no need for that just yet, is there?' she said, trailing powerlessly along behind him, reluctantly impressed by the awesome business acumen he had displayed over the past few hours. 'I mean,' she continued breathlessly as she walked quickly to keep up with his easy, purposeful stride, 'I can sort of look around in the next few weeks...'

'I have always found that it is best to strike whilst the iron is hot.'

'And what if *I* don't want to strike!'

Gabriel paused to look at her. God, but he was enjoying himself. In fact, he didn't think that he had enjoyed a morning's work quite as much as he had today. He had almost forgotten his long-term plan, the stakes he had begun planting that would reap their own reward, namely her acquiescence. When she stopped fighting him, he could almost begin to recapture that heady, pleasurable and utterly treacherous attraction he had felt for her. An attraction that went far beyond the physical.

It was a mistake he was not about to make.

'Then, naturally, I will respect your wishes,' he said smoothly.

'As you would any of your employees'?'

'I always listen to what others say,' Gabriel confirmed ambiguously. 'If you want to have a breather before you begin looking for a car, then by all means.' He glanced down at his watch. 'In fact, it is almost time for lunch. Why don't we go somewhere and have a bite to eat? Mmm?'

Laura suddenly and inexplicably felt the sharp edge of panic rip through her. The sun was bright and hard and emphasised every angle of his face. And what she saw disturbed her. More than that, frightened her.

'Don't you have to get back to London?' she asked nervously. He had an empire to run, for heaven's sake! Surely he couldn't spend all his time swanning around up here in the manner of a country squire with nothing better to do?

As if he had read her mind, he said wryly, 'I am the boss. I can come and go as I please and there is still too much to do here for me to leave at the moment.' But she was right. Sophisticated though communications were, he still needed to be physically present in his office some time soon and once there he would find himself bombarded with all the minutiae that he had hitherto enjoyed but which would take his mind off the business in hand.

He would have to speed things along.

He gave her a shuttered look. 'What about that little Italian just at the corner over there?' Very deliberately he placed his hand on the small of her back, and even though he felt her tense under the slight pressure of his touch, he didn't remove it. In fact, his contact widened until he was guiding her across the road with his hand circling her waist.

A purely routine gesture, Laura thought frantically. They had just completed a huge deal by any standards and he was probably just trying to show some sign of friendliness. It was her fault if her body was reacting like dry tinder being set ablaze. He had a girlfriend already anyway. The thought of that steadied her and as soon as they had crossed the road she politely pulled out of his grasp.

They could carry on like this for ever, Gabriel thought suddenly. One small move on his part followed by five large steps back on hers. She had been warned off him from the start and any ceasefire between them was doomed to falter.

He snapped his teeth together in angry impatience. Biding time was all well and good but it wasn't his style. By tonight, he promised himself. He would taste those lips by the end of the evening and then he would begin his assault on her senses.

'Tell me,' he said as soon as they were shown to a table, 'what is the state of your love life?'

'What?' Flabbergasted, Laura looked at him in pure amazement.

'Your love life,' Gabriel repeated. 'What is the state of it? By which I mean, do you have a lover?'

'I know what you mean! I was just stupefied that you have the nerve to ask!'

'Well, I do,' he said calmly.

'It's none of your business.'

'I wish I could be as phlegmatic about it as you are…' He paused and Laura felt an unnerving tug of anticipation as she wondered feverishly where he was going with this one. Would he be jealous if she *did* have a lover? He had always had a jealous streak a mile wide and she couldn't stop the sizzle of intense excitement at the thought of

arousing his jealousy now, ridiculous though any such notion might be.

'But it makes sense for me to know, as your employer.
If you were…involved with a man, I would obviously try
and curtail too many trips that necessitate overnight
stays… Oh, come on, Laura, it is a purely practical question.' Dark eyes lazily inspected her face.

'I…well, at the moment, I'm not actually involved with
anyone, so I would be free to overnight anywhere should
the situation require it. Not that that was really any business of yours. I mean, I don't ask *you* about Anna, do I?'

'Anna?' For a few seconds he had no idea what she was
talking about.

'Oh, don't pretend to be all innocence, Gabriel.' Let him
say it, she thought viciously. Then this unwanted pull of
attraction will go away under the burden of reality. 'You
know who I mean. The dusky bombshell you were cuddling up to at the house. I believe she goes under the title
of your chartered surveyor!'

'Oh, *that* Anna.' He smiled slowly and positively purred
with the satisfaction of having drawn her out into the open.
'My cousin.'

The game was on. He was back in full control and ready
to pounce.

CHAPTER SIX

'YOUR cousin.' Laura tried to give a snort of disbelieving laughter, but she was rapidly reaching the conclusion, the mortifying conclusion, that he was telling the truth. 'Ha,' she finished weakly.

'You didn't think...no, surely not!' Gabriel leaned closer to her. 'I am shocked!'

He didn't look shocked. In fact, he looked remarkably pleased with himself. Without too much effort, Laura could quite easily have hit him over the head with something very hard. Instead, she composed herself and stared at him haughtily. The man was playing games with her, which was bad enough. Worse, though, was the fact that, instead of her feeling insulted and outraged, the wicked glitter in those black eyes was shooting to the very heart of her, making her skin burn.

'Men *do* have affairs with women who work with them. Or *for* them. It's not unheard of.'

'Ah, you do not give me sufficient credit.' He sat back and continued staring at her as a waitress approached their table and took their orders of lasagne, which was the first thing that came to Laura's head and Gabriel, without glancing at the menu, fell in line. All the better, she thought sourly, to get rid of the waitress so that he could continue his little pretence of nursing wounded feelings.

'I have always made it a policy of mine never to get sexually involved with a member of staff,' he said piously. 'It can lead to all sorts of complications.' He hoped she wouldn't remember that when she was lying, spent and fulfilled, in his arms.

'There's no need to explain yourself to me,' Laura mumbled ungraciously.

'Anna and I have always been close. When she came to England to study and qualified as a chartered surveyor, I was delighted to be able to offer her a job with the company. In fact,' he said confidentially, 'I am godfather to her little boy.'

'Lovely,' Laura said.

There was a fractional silence, during which she was intensely aware of him looking at her whilst she gazed down in apparent fascination at the tips of her fingers resting on the table.

'You weren't...' he allowed the pause to drag on until she reluctantly raised her eyes to his '...*jealous*, were you?'

'Of course I wasn't jealous!' Laura scoffed. 'Why on earth should I be?'

Gabriel spread his hands in a flamboyantly Latin American gesture of bafflement.

'I don't have any claims over you, Gabriel, any more than you have over me. Yes, we were involved a long time ago. And yes, we're involved now, but in a completely different way. This time, it's all about business. You're now my paymaster.'

He didn't like that. Not one little bit. She could see it in the immediate narrowing of his eyes.

'I do not care for that term *paymaster*.'

Laura shrugged. 'It's the truth. You now are the lord and master of what used to be my home and you are perfectly entitled to bring anyone there you want to. You could bring an entire harem of women!'

She could feel him positively fulminating as they ate their lunch in virtual silence.

This was not how Gabriel had envisaged their conversation going. With every short, blunt, factual observation she had managed to distance herself from him in a way nothing he could say would have succeeded in doing. Now, as he broodingly cast his eyes on her face, downturned as she half-heartedly toyed with some food at the end of her fork, as if debating whether or not she should eat any more, he could sense her getting more and more remote.

She was drawing lines between them and he knew that, once those lines were drawn, she would set them in cement. And, God, he didn't want her behind any lines. He couldn't understand it, but the threat of her remoteness was wreaking havoc with his composure.

He pushed aside his half-finished oval plate of food and sat back in the chair, watching her as she made sure not to look at him.

'Is it not ironic that we are doing now what we should have done all those years ago?' he asked softly, and she raised startled eyes to his.

'What's that?'

'Sharing a meal.'

'I told you, circumstances have changed.' She went back to her labours with the food whilst inside her giddy little leaps were taking place.

'You asked me before how it was that I had never married. Let me ask you now, how is it that *you* never married?'

Laura shrugged.

'What does that...' he imitated her shrug '...mean?'

'It means that the opportunity never arose.' She couldn't stomach another mouthful. 'What would you like me to begin with first, Gabriel? I mean, should I concentrate on fixing up meetings with people to try and regain business, or should I start working on the land to bring it up to scratch? You need to give me my list of duties so that I can—'

'Dammit, woman!' Gabriel exploded. 'Would you stop behaving as though you're...you're...?' For the first time since he could remember, his cool power of articulate speech deserted him completely.

'Your employee?' Laura said helpfully. 'But that's exactly what I am.'

'There is no need for you to put on this ridiculous act of bowing and scraping!' he growled, realising that she had somehow managed to get him into a corner. How, he had no idea.

'I'm not bowing and scraping. I'm asking you to define my duties in order of importance. Besides, I would have thought that it might have made your day to have me bowing and scraping.'

It damned well should have done, Gabriel thought ruefully. When he had picked up that newspaper and read about the riding stables, it had certainly been top of his aims to see the wretch in a position where the tables had been reversed.

Somewhere along the way, things had changed. He most certainly did not want to see her bowing and scraping.

'Well, you are wrong,' he told her brusquely. 'If you want me to tell you what I expect from you, then I will, but I would prefer that we discuss it together.'

'You mean pretend that this is a normal situation and that you haven't just bought me out lock, stock and barrel for the sole purpose of getting your own back?'

'Dammit, Laura...'

'I'm sorry. I'm just a little edgy because this deal has

now been done and I've become a lodger in my own house, on my own land.'

'You would have been in that situation anyway,' Gabriel pointed out darkly. 'The place had to be sold and chances are you would have got a lot less on the open market. And you would not have been living there. You would now be out searching for somewhere you could afford.' He couldn't bear the trace of sadness in her eyes even though he was honest enough to realise that he had been instrumental in putting it there. She didn't see him as her rescuer, she saw him as her gaoler and it was like a knife twisting slowly in his gut.

'I know.'

'Then stop punishing me for offering you a good deal. And you are not a lodger in your own home, dammit, Laura. You belong there and you are to look on it as yours.'

'But it's not, is it?'

Gabriel counted very slowly in Spanish to ten. 'Okay. I think we ought to concentrate on getting the house into a good condition first of all. It's going to be the least time-consuming of the tasks and the most immediately rewarding. So what about we leave this place, head back to the house and then we can have a look around and decide what is to be done? And if you tell me that it's up to me because I am now the owner, then I will personally throttle you.'

'Oh, I'm quivering with fear, Gabriel.' But the fight had gone out of her voice. She could feel him tiptoeing his way towards her, trying to make her see his point of view, and his sudden vulnerability was more moving than any of his aggressive thrusts at her had been. She raised her eyebrows in amusement and he offered her a crooked smile in return.

'Good. That's more like it.'

'Oh, you approve of women quivering in fear, do you?'

He looked at her for so long and in such concentrated silence that she became aware of the subtle change in the atmosphere. From combatants to ex-lovers. The intangible electricity made her flesh crawl and Laura lowered her eyes quickly.

'Let's get out of here.' He beckoned for the bill, paid it and then stood up.

All through the drive back to the house he made polite, surface conversation, asking her what improvements she would like for the house, but the undercurrent between them still rose and fell, until by the time he screeched to a halt outside the house he thought he would pass out from wanting to touch her.

So much for the master seducer, he thought ruefully. He couldn't wait to leap out of the car so that he could try and clear his head. Whilst she…she seemed utterly in control, barely speaking, occasionally glancing out of the window with a thoughtful expression on her face, which made him want to stop the car immediately and demand to know what she was thinking.

'Shall we have a look straight away?' Laura asked as soon as they were in the hall. 'If I know what you want, then I can get going first thing in the morning.'

Gabriel gritted his teeth together in frustration and watched as she kicked off her formal shoes so that she was now barefoot.

'Let's start with downstairs.'

'I'll just go and fetch some paper.'

'Oh, for God's sake, is that really necessary, Laura?'

'It'll help me remember if I just jot down what you say.' Their eyes clashed for a few seconds, and then she fled to the kitchen where she dug around until she managed to excavate a sheet of A4 paper and a pen.

This was proving to be even harder than she could ever have dreamt in a million years. If she could have held onto her hostility. If he could just have done her the favour of remaining a one-dimensional cardboard cut-out—ex-lover with an axe to grind. But no, he had to turn things on their head, he had to be gentle and amusing one minute only to switch back into arrogant aggression.

She returned to find him in the sitting room, staring around him. 'I came here that last day to see your parents. Did you know that?' Gabriel had not meant to utter a word about that fateful, humiliating episode, but now that he had he could see that he had shocked her.

'You came *here*?' She shook her head in bewilderment. 'Whatever for?'

'To ask for your hand in marriage.' His mouth twisted cynically and he continued to watch her face as it was suffused with colour. 'Naturally I was thrown out on my ears.'

'I didn't know.'

'No. I did not expect your papa to confide that little titbit to you.'

'He didn't dislike you, Gabriel, he just thought…'

'That his baby could do better?'

'Isn't that what all fathers think?' Her eyes flashed suddenly. 'If *you* had a young daughter and the situation was the same, wouldn't *you* have reacted in exactly the same way?'

'Naturally not,' Gabriel said shortly, but her retort had him turning away. 'Anyway, it is all water under the bridge. For the moment, we have other things to talk about.'

'You're the one who raised the subject.'

'It's history. Tell me what you suggest for this room. I find it too dark and depressing.'

'It's your house,' Laura said stubbornly, and he shot her a glowering look from under his lashes.

'And I am ordering you to tell me what you think.'

'I like greens,' she said finally, when the option was either to say what she thought or remain locked in silence, which she knew he had no intention of breaking. 'And creams. Autumnal colours. Mum liked all this floral stuff and when she became, well, really ill, she said it cheered her up to look at the flowers on the walls.' Laura's mouth trembled and she frowned down at the piece of paper in her hand.

'I'm sorry.'

She had barely noticed how close he had come to her. He filled her nostrils with his masculine scent.

'You can cry, *querida*. Tears are nothing to be ashamed of.'

'Of course I'm not going to cry.' She shook her head briskly and looked up at him. It was the gentle compassion in his eyes that did it. She blinked and felt the hot sting of tears begin to seep from under her eyelids, and suddenly his arms were around her, pulling her towards him.

Laura allowed herself to be folded against his broad chest. She hooked her arms around his waist and he seemed to just wrap himself around her, one hand on her back, the other pressed against the side of her head, whilst his fingers weaved through her hair. She could hear him making soothing noises under his breath, which only made matters worse because the oozing of her tears became more of a torrent until her body was shaking from crying.

Eventually, she edged herself away, only conscious now of how closely their bodies had been entwined, and raised her eyes to his.

'I'm very sorry. Not very professional.' She tried to give

a self-deprecating laugh, which emerged as a croak of sorts.

'Here.' He reached into his pocket and handed her a handkerchief, which Laura gratefully accepted, but he continued holding her tightly against him. It felt good. Better than good, he thought.

'I'm fine now,' she said in a more normal voice.

'Sure?' Gabriel tilted her face with one finger under her chin and then softly brushed away the remainder of dampness on her cheeks with the pad of his thumb.

'Sure. Thanks for the hankie. I'll wash it and return it to you.' She had to remove herself from this clinch. Her breasts were pushed against his chest and, now that she was no longer sobbing like a maiden in distress, she was all too aware of them reacting with perky vigour to his body. As was the rest of her. Where his fingers had traced her cheekbones, her skin burned. She wanted to just tiptoe and capture that beautiful, arrogant mouth with hers. She wanted to close her eyes and lose herself in him.

She made a concerted effort to draw back and succeeded.

'I'm not sure what came over me,' she apologised with a watery smile.

'Memories,' Gabriel said gruffly, sticking his hands into his pockets. A perfect opportunity missed, he thought regretfully. He was definitely losing his touch. He had had her there, in his arms, as vulnerable as a newborn babe and, instead of seizing the opportunity, he had played the understanding gentleman, had *wanted* to play the understanding gentleman. He wondered whether years of being the object of pursuit had dulled his talent for the chase.

'The room could certainly do with an overhaul, though,' Laura said, moving away. 'What would *you* like to see

here? I…' She sighed and frowned. 'The furniture will
look odd if the room is done up around it. Old-fashioned.'

'Then sell it, Laura. Put the proceeds into your bank
account.'

For when I'm thrown off the premises, she thought. Because she had no doubt that off the premises was exactly
where she was heading, despite all his talk about treating
his house as hers. Nor would she allow three seconds of
sympathy to get to her and make her forget that their relationship now was just precisely what she had told him,
namely a business arrangement.

Her eyes skittered across to him and she licked her lips.

'Why don't I just leave you in charge of the decorating?'
he suggested.

'Because I don't know the first thing about interior design. And I wouldn't feel comfortable…taking charge of
somewhere that's not my own.'

'Oh, God. Here we go again.'

'No, really, Gabriel. I'm not about to start…'

'Reminding me that I'm the big, bad wolf who has de-
prived you of your family home?'

Instead of rushing headlong into defending her position,
Laura smiled sheepishly. 'Right. What I'm saying is that
I'm not exactly…you know, the height of fashion…' She
could feel every word turning into a tongue-twister as he
stood stock-still and regarded her with that dark, disturbingly penetrating look of his that made her toes curl.

'The height of fashion…? What has fashion got to do
with anything?'

'A lot. It has a lot to do with…I mean, Gabriel, look at
you and look at me.' He duly cast his eyes down his body
then ran his eyes over hers, paying a lot more attention to
every inch of her. When he finally met her eyes, she was
blushing furiously.

'Yes, there are some obvious differences but I would put those down to gender.' He raised one eyebrow in amusement and Laura remained staunchly unmoved by the provocatively inviting glitter in his eyes.

'You want the best. It's obvious from the way you dress, Gabriel. I…I've led an outdoor life and never had much time for how I looked.'

'Where are we going with this one?'

'I don't know anything about furnishing a house to the sort of standard a man like you would expect!'

'A man like me…' Gabriel mused coolly. 'You forget that I did not always possess this wealth.'

'And now you do,' Laura persisted stubbornly, 'and I'm sure you would want furnishings that reflect your…your status.'

'Oh, naturally,' he mocked, 'I could not possibly want somewhere comfortable and soothing when I could have something very expensive and probably very ostentatious. I do not intend to make this a permanent base, but when I do come here, I assure you I will not be looking to surround myself with heavy velvet drapes and silk on the walls. Nor will I want the taps to be gold-plated.'

'Why do you always have to jump to the other extreme?'

'Why do you always have to pigeon-hole? If you do not feel confident about decorating this place, then feel free to hire an interior designer.' He shrugged, as if suddenly bored by the conversation. He didn't want to be here discussing wall colours and furniture requirements, he thought suddenly. As long as they continued trawling from room to room with Laura clutching that stupid sheet of paper, they would remain on opposite sides of an insurmountable wall. He, the boss in charge, she the employee who had been bailed out. And it didn't matter one jot if her eyes kept sliding over to him of their own accord. She would keep her instincts at bay and listen to her head.

'Is that what you did with your own house? Hired an interior designer?'

'I have no time to sit in shops poring over wallpaper books and shopping for little artefacts. I gave my designer free rein and she did the rest.'

'And you like it?'

'Of course I like it! If you want, I could give you her number and she could do the same here.'

The thought of someone striding through the rooms, casting a baleful eye over the furnishings and then replacing the lot with expensive equivalents made her blood run cold. Or maybe she just had an economical streak.

'I'll do what I can,' she conceded, 'but don't blame me if you disagree with my tastes.' He inclined his head in a nod. 'And when it comes to choosing bigger things, then you'll have to find the time to pick them yourself.' Another nod. 'Good.'

'So that's settled?'

'For the moment.'

'Then why don't we leave here and do something altogether more productive...and enjoyable?'

His restlessness had evaporated. He felt invigorated. The house had been closing him in, closing them both in with its reminder of their reversed fortunes. What better solution than to go outside and leave its depressing presence behind? And what better way to voice the suggestion than in words of such blatant ambiguity that she could do nothing but flush at the latent connotations?

'What did you have in mind?' Laura asked warily.

'Well...the sun is shining. And I hanker to ride Barnabus again...I haven't ridden in months, not since I was in Argentina. Is he still as fiery as he once was?'

'You want to go *riding*?' Laura squeaked.

'Outrageous, I agree, but, yes, I do. For one thing, it's a waste to be inside when we can be outside and for another, I could use the opportunity to see the land and try and work out what needs doing.'

'Oh. Yes. Of course.' She glanced down at her clothes. 'I'll just go and get changed, shall I?'

A perfectly sensible suggestion, she told herself as she hurriedly shoved on a pair of jeans and an old sweatshirt. It was bright but breezy and very concealing. So why then did she feel just a little bit apprehensive? She couldn't keep the past totally locked away, could she?

He was waiting at the foot of the stairs for her, and he made damned sure that he gave her only a cursory glance.

'You're not really in the right gear,' Laura informed him, *en route* to the stables.

'I didn't think that I would end up on a horse or else I would have dressed differently.'

'You mean you have scruffy clothes?'

'Tut-tut. There you go. Pigeon-holing again.' But his voice was lazily amused. 'And for your information, I happen to have quite a lot of scruffy clothes hanging in my wardrobe.'

'Oh, really.' The sun, the ease of his conversation, the faint buzzing of the bees in the background, made her feel relaxed. 'Shabby jeans and faded tee shirts?'

'Absolutely. The shabbier and more faded, the better.'

She couldn't help it. She laughed, pushing open the stable door and expertly getting Barnabus ready before leading him out into the courtyard.

'Do you want me to come riding with you?' she asked, suddenly realising that she had expected to but that he might want to ride on his own. A lot of people preferred the peace of solitude rather than riding with someone else and having to make conversation.

'I would not go otherwise. Saddle up one of the others.'

'Old Lily won't be able to keep up with Barnabus,' Laura warned him, watching greedily as he stroked the horse, speaking to it in those low, soothing tones that sounded like waves lapping against the shore, getting it to trust him before he mounted.

She hurried off and was returning with her own horse just in time to see Gabriel mount Barnabus, his every move solid and confident and exquisitely graceful. Whatever gripes her father had had over Gabriel, he had never been able to deny that Gabriel was good with horses. Better than good. He seemed to belong on them.

Laura stood, riveted, as he settled onto Barnabus's back, the reins lightly held in one hand whilst he stroked the horse's mane with the other.

'Are you going to mount or are you going to stare at me for the rest of the day?'

His laconic question, when she hadn't been aware that he had been so much as looking in her direction, jerked her back to reality and she mounted her own horse with alacrity, pressing her knees firmly on either side to urge it forward.

'Ready?' He grinned with infuriating amusement. Her gut feeling was to launch into a lecture on the size of his ego, which had encouraged him to hallucinate that she had been watching him when in fact her thoughts had been a million miles away, but since it would have been patently untrue she contented herself with tugging the rein in her hand and nodding.

'Shall we skirt the boundary fence to the left and follow it round to that oak tree? The oak tree *is* still there, I take it?' He wondered if he could concentrate on anything as banal as fencing when this woman was riding alongside him. Lord, but she looked beautiful. The sun captured the fairness of her hair until it seemed to dazzle the eyes and her body looked alive on the back of her horse, every muscle firm and toned. Quintessentially the very opposite to every woman he had dated since he had loved and lost her.

Ah, but he hadn't lost her, had he? he reminded himself silkily. Because here she was, the wind blowing back her hair, her body slightly arched as she galloped at a steady speed alongside him. Sexy in the way only a totally natural woman could be sexy and soon to be his until such time as he no longer considered her a lost love, simply someone else he would have slept with along the way.

'The fencing is in a bit of a state,' Laura told him, pointing out the obvious as they both slowed to a trot to inspect it. She had worked up a sweat riding and now shoved up the sleeves of the jumper. 'Dad looked after it when we still had horses but over the years he only managed to keep up rudimentary repairs.' She turned to face him. 'I must have been a complete idiot not to have noticed what was going on.'

'We all make mistakes.'

Was it her imagination or did she detect something else behind that throwaway remark? Was he referring to her? A past mistake he had once made?

'Shall we continue?' she asked tightly, and he nodded as he shrewdly assessed the extensive repair work that would have to be undertaken.

They circled the huge area. There were entire tracts of fencing that had rotted over time. The money that should have been used to fix them redirected into betting and alcohol. When Gabriel thought about it, he could feel a murderous urge towards Peter Jackson, but aligned to that was a certain sympathy that he neither invited nor welcomed. The man must have been distraught to have let the whole lot go. The riding stables had been his life.

By the time they finally reached the oak tree he had seen enough to have a pretty good idea of the state of the rest.

He dismounted, tethered his horse, thereby ensuring that she did the same, and then sat down at the base of the tree, his legs drawn up, his arms resting loosely on his knees.

'Your trousers will be filthy when you get up,' Laura remarked, smugly aware that she was far more appropriately dressed.

'Sit down by me,' Gabriel commanded lazily. 'We need to talk about how we're going to approach the job of upgrading the land.' Which, he reckoned, should take about ten minutes. And after that...? He intended to stick to his plans for seduction and not be distracted by the buzzing inner voices that kept holding him back. He looked at her from under his lashes as she slowly walked towards him. He noted the unconscious elegance of her gait, the way she held her body like a dancer, utterly indifferent to how other people regarded her.

'It's been impossible trying to do anything about it,' Laura said apologetically. 'Since Dad died, I seem to have spent all my time in a nightmare of trying to work out finances.' She sighed and Gabriel made an angry noise under his breath.

'God, didn't the man have any idea what this would do to you? Leaving you in a situation like that?'

'He never thought he would just...I guess he thought that he would have time to get things back on track and so I would be spared the worry.' She looked down at the fields sprawled in front of them. From a distance, it all looked perfect. It was only when you got closer that you could see the signs of decay. It was the same for the house and the stables. 'You don't have to tell me that it's a far cry from how things used to be around here seven years ago.'

'I was not about to tell you any such thing.' He got up, brushing himself down, only to reposition himself on the grass, lying on it with his hands folded behind his head and his long legs crossed at the ankles.

'Shouldn't we be heading back now?'

'Oh, I think I'll enjoy this sun for a bit longer. Of course, you are free to head back whenever you want.' It was a gamble, but he didn't want her in any way to feel that she had been manipulated. Nevertheless, his body seemed to twist into several thousand knots in the few seconds of silence during which she decided what to do. If she got up and rode back to the house, then he would be forced to stay, at least for a short while and, whilst the scenery was enchanting, its appeal would vanish like a puff of smoke if she weren't here to enhance it.

'Oh, I might as well wait for you,' Laura said eventually, and he wondered whether she could hear his profound sigh of relief. He turned on his side, propping himself up on one elbow so that he could look at her.

'Why don't you come out of the shade of that tree and enjoy the sunshine? It is not that often we get weather like this in spring.'

'I know,' Laura agreed, pushing herself up and strolling over in his direction. 'Last year it rained solidly for spring. If you think the fields are bad now, you should have seen them then. They looked like a jungle.' She sat down, still keeping her distance, he noticed idly. 'Old Tom McBride came and trimmed them back for next to no pay.'

Gabriel allowed his eyes to stray to the bottom half of

her body, encased in faded, tight jeans and topped with laced-up old leather walking shoes. She was still sitting up with her arms stretched out behind her to support her body. His eyes lingered for a few seconds on the definition of her stomach under the sweatshirt, then moved lazily upwards to the swell of her breasts. Bra or no bra? he wondered. Difficult to tell under that thick cloth. Her head was flung back, her eyes closed as she enjoyed the sun.

'What is your relationship with the estate agent?' Gabriel asked.

Laura's eyes flicked open and she turned to look at him. 'Any estate agent in particular?'

'The blond one who looked as though he perhaps had not started shaving yet.'

'I don't know any estate agents who fit that description.'

'Little liar,' Gabriel drawled. 'Was he your lover? Was that how you got the job working there?'

'I should come across there and smack you on the face for implying that,' Laura said.

'Well, why don't you?' he invited with a soft laugh that sent goose-pimples racing across her skin. 'You can hit me as hard as you like for being such an insufferable, insulting boor…and then I can take my revenge for being hit…'

'Oh, yes,' Laura said on a breathless little laugh. Her heart was racing and every shred of common sense was telling her that she was playing with fire. But the way he was looking at her, his black eyes roving lazily and caressingly over her face, sent shivers of excitement through her that were shattering common sense.

'What would you do?' she taunted. 'I know you, Gabriel, however much you've changed over the years. You wouldn't dream of laying a finger on me…'

'Oh, I wouldn't dream of it, would I?' He pushed himself up and moved closer to her, close enough to touch her if he wanted to but not so close that she would feel his presence as a threat. Every muscle in his body felt alive. He would take this woman and under all the reasons he had logically worked out for himself, under all his arguments about levelling scores and evening scales, he was burning with the sheer, overpowering craving to take her simply because he found her irresistible…

CHAPTER SEVEN

'GABRIEL, n-no…'

'But I haven't done anything.' His slow smile was so devastating that it made the breath catch in Laura's throat. He'd mesmerised her. He mesmerised her then and he mesmerised her now, even though she knew that the divide between them stretched like a yawning gulf. The impassioned young boy had developed into a cynical predator and his motives were at best based on animal lust and at worst…she shivered to think.

But, God, the way his eyes were lingering on her face made her feel as though she were standing close to an open fire and on the edge of a precipice.

'I—I'm not a complete idiot,' Laura stuttered weakly, hugging herself.

'I never implied that you were. What are you wearing under that baggy sweatshirt of yours?'

'Wh-what?'

He gave a low, sexy laugh and continued to look at her. One long, hot look of burning intensity that seemed to send the heat spreading from the tips of her toes to the top of her scalp.

'Are you wearing a bra? You never used to when you went riding. I remember you once told me that you dreamed of riding on a beach, naked, and that the closest you could ever get to that was to ride without a bra under your jumper. But then, in those days, there were always a lot more people around. Now…here we are, alone on this little hill…'

'This is not an appropriate conversation.' She made a desperate effort to get back to normality but she couldn't tear her eyes away from him and her heart was pounding so hard that her ribcage felt as though it might crack at any moment. 'We're not the same two people now that we were then. I work for you. Have you forgotten? And you told me that you would never have a relationship with an employee.'

'Oh, but I am not talking about having a relationship. I am talking about making love. And rules, at the end of the day, are made to be broken.' He wasn't about to let her imagine for a minute that any kind of relationship was in the offing. He had offered her one of those once and had been rejected. This time, he would be brutally honest and he would let her come to him in the full knowledge that what he wanted and *all* he wanted was her delectable body.

He trailed his finger along her spine and smiled. 'No bra. I thought so. Some things never change.'

'Stop it!' Laura spun around so that she was facing him. That light touch had felt like an invasion, and, horrifyingly, an invasion she craved. 'Is that how you live your life, Gabriel? A series of episodes with women in bed? How sad.'

'Why is it sad?' Her mouth was spitting insults, he thought with gratification, but her chocolate eyes were telling another story, and he continued to devastate her with his look. 'Because you think that sex has to be accompanied by emotions? And since you never married, are you telling me that you have not slept with another man since me?'

'Of course I have,' Laura retorted scornfully, and his body stilled. He really hadn't expected her to say otherwise, but for reasons he could scarcely identify the thought of her lying in the arms of another man brought a surge of jealous bile rising to his throat.

'The effeminate little man at the estate agency?'

Trust Gabriel Greppi to be contemptuous of someone like Hugo, she thought with sudden anger. Just because Hugo was not built along the macho lines that he was and did not have the overpowering self-assurance that made him see the world and its female inhabitants as his own personal playground.

Oh, how he would love to think that she had spent seven years in a deep freeze, pining.

The fact that it was mostly true, something she was only now beginning to realise, made her even angrier.

'No, not Hugo!' she snapped, thrusting her face towards him.

'Who, then? And if he was so meaningful, where is he now?' It took all his strength not to give in to basic instinct and shake the answer out of her.

'His name was James Silcox, if you must know!' And what a mistake he had been. After four years of celibacy, she could see, in retrospect, that she had drifted into the relationship partly in a desperate attempt to alter the rut into which her love life had sunk and partly because her father had approved of him. It had been a disaster. His talent for being amusing had not concealed a clever mind, as she had optimistically imagined. He had been good-looking, witty and as empty as a shell. The relationship had lasted all of six months and then dwindled into a sporadic friendship, which was all it should ever have been in the first place. It had not escaped her notice that since her financial problems had come to light, even that had disappeared. She was no longer a desirable connection.

'And I don't know where he is now,' she finished truthfully.

'What happened? Were you too forceful for the poor boy?'

'Me? Forceful?'

'You don't play feminine games,' Gabriel told her, reaching out to brush some hair away from her face. 'And men tend to like their women to play feminine games.'

'You mean, batting eyelashes and pretending to be helpless even when they have nerves of steel?'

'Something like that.' He hadn't anticipated quite so much conversation. Women, he had always found, or at least those he had dated in the past, had always followed his lead, and lengthy conversation had never been high on his agenda. But then hadn't he always known that this particular woman was unique? In fact, he had forgotten how much he enjoyed just talking to her. 'Also...' he let his eyes drift casually over her baggy sweatshirt and faded jeans '...they tend to be impressed by a more...feminine look.' He knew that one would get to her and he grinned broadly when her expression reflected the expected reaction of sulky affront.

'Oh, well, thank you very much for that, Gabriel. You've just put your finger on why I haven't managed to find Mr Right. My taste in clothes hasn't been up to par. And I suppose all these little episodes in your sad, sad love life have had exquisite dress sense?' Was he aware of the flirtatious thread running through this conversation? she wondered frantically. Instead of fuming over his undisguised insults, she was blossoming! The teasing, lazy look in his black eyes gave his words a sexy, bantering intonation that had every nerve in her body singing.

'They have,' he agreed gravely.

'And what would that exquisite dress sense be comprised of?' she asked, stung by the comparisons she knew he must be making in his head between herself and his past conquests.

'Oh, the usual. Tight little dresses with plunging necklines and high, high heels.' And not one of them could light a candle next to this woman sitting right here, he thought suddenly, with her concealing clothes and lack of make-up. The thought of those heavy breasts, unfettered beneath the loose-fitting sweatshirt, turned him on in a way that no tight dresses and revealing necklines ever could. He savoured the moment when he could push up the thick cotton and feast his eyes on her bountiful body.

Laura wanted to ask him if he was so enamoured of voluptuous women in figure-hugging clothes, why then did he want to sleep with *her*? But she was too afraid of his answer to ask the question. God, was she so pathetic that she preferred to ignore the truth staring her in the face? Which was that he simply wanted to revisit old pastures and prove to them both that he could still have her if he wanted, no strings attached?

'Well, in that case, why don't you mount Barnabus and ride back to the house so that you can get away quickly and find yourself a suitably well-dressed woman?'

'Actually,' Gabriel drawled, his skin positively crawling with pleasure at this show of pique, 'there's something that is even sexier than tight-fitting clothes on a woman...'

'And what's that? Not that I'm interested.'

'*No* clothes on a woman.' The words dropped into the charged pool of electricity between them and he watched as the ripples began to fan out. 'No clothes on a woman, out in the open, surrounded by fields and trees.' The games were done and, whether she knew it or not, she wasn't going to slip away from him. 'The smell of warm sun on a naked body and the feel of grass under bare skin.'

A fine film of perspiration broke out over her body as

her imagination took wild flight. Her head was screaming at her to run away as fast as she could, but she couldn't move. She could just watch him close the small distance between them, and her eyes drooped as his mouth covered hers.

His hunger drove her backwards until she was lying on the grass, his body half over her as he pushed his tongue against hers and explored the warmth of her mouth with an urgency that was matched by her own. Her hands pressed against the side of his face and she arched back in sheer pleasure as he began kissing her neck and behind her ear.

'Do you want this, *querida*?' he murmured hoarsely. 'Because if you don't, then you had better tell me now. Before we both reach the point of no return.'

'Yes,' Laura whispered raggedly. 'No. Oh, I don't know, Gabriel.'

He stopped and looked down at her until her eyes flickered open. 'Tell me,' he commanded roughly, running one thumb along her eyebrow, and she turned her face into his hand and kissed his palm.

'Yes,' she admitted unsteadily. 'I want you, I want *this*.' And she knew exactly what *this* was, the act of making love, nothing more, nothing less.

'And I want to hear you say it,' Gabriel told her huskily. 'I want to hear you moan with delight. God, I want to feel you tremble under my arms, Laura.' Balancing on his elbow, he began to unbutton his shirt with his other hand, his fingers trembling until the shirt was finally hanging open and Laura curved her arms beneath it, delighting in the feel of his naked torso. She had watched him and imagined, but actually feeling him was beyond imagination, as was the dizzying sensation of coming back to a place where she belonged.

She eased his shirt off his shoulders, savouring each glimpse of hard, bronzed skin, and watched as he shrugged if off.

'Not exactly fair,' he murmured with a wicked gleam in his eye that had her blushing like a virgin bride instead of a woman who had lain countless times in this man's arms before.

'What's not fair?' she responded with a wicked, teasing smile of her own. She reached up to lick his mouth with the tip of her tongue and smiled as a low moan escaped him.

'My performing a striptease while you remain covered up like a Victorian damsel.'

He moved into a kneeling position, his legs straddling either side of her and watched, fascinated, as she drew the sweatshirt slowly upwards, exposing the firm paleness of her flat stomach, then those breasts, which he had been lusting after ever since he had first laid eyes on her again. A hot burst of desire exploded inside him, shocking him with its intensity. His hands itched to touch, but he restrained himself, savouring the prospect of possession. Instead, he continued looking at her, breathing unsteadily whilst she lay passively and bewitchingly beneath him.

'Having fun?' he smiled crookedly and she stretched languidly in response, raising her hands over her head. She wanted to faint from the intense pleasure of just having those eyes roam over her semi-nude body.

'Are you?' she replied. Stupid question. Whatever he felt for her, whatever dubious reasons he had for making love with her, there was no doubt in her head that he still wanted her and, Lord, how she still wanted him. Sheer physical need was now in the driver's seat.

'Never had so much fun in my life before.' Their eyes

met and she gave him a smile that was enchantingly, teasingly feminine.

She reached down to cup her breasts with her hands, inviting him to do more than just watch, and Gabriel sank towards her offering with a groan of submission, burying his face against her soft mounds and nuzzling them with his mouth and tongue until Laura was whimpering with pleasure.

The ragged sound that was wrenched from her lips as his mouth closed over one tautened nipple was the sound of absolute abandonment.

Gabriel dimly heard it and felt like a young adolescent on the brink of orgasm just from the touch of his fantasy woman. In the distant past, when they had stolen their love-making sessions in the office, their passion had been muted by the unspoken thought that they might, just might, be interrupted. Now, with miles of deserted fields around them, they could be as vocal as they wanted and her cries of pleasure were like music to his ears.

But he wasn't going to rush a minute of this.

He took his time, devoting his undivided attention to her beautiful breasts and loving the feel of her writhing beneath him and begging him not to stop. As if he were even capable of stopping!

He licked her breasts and then trailed his tongue along her stomach, which tasted warm. And her smell was the smell of pure woman, without any of those lingering traces of perfume that did nothing for him.

He undid the top button of her jeans, then the zip, and gently eased them down her long legs until he could easily pull them off and toss them to one side.

'That's not fair,' Laura said huskily, repeating his teasing observation of earlier on, and he grinned at her.

'So it isn't,' he drawled, catching her eyes and holding

them, although not for long. The need to look at that beautiful, bronzed body was far too tempting just to make do with his eyes.

She watched with greedy yearning as he shrugged off his already unbuttoned shirt, then deliberately took his time with his trousers. With unconscious provocation, Laura's fingers strayed to the top of her underwear and she casually slipped them under to caress the fair, soft curls as she continued to drink him in with her eyes.

God, the woman couldn't possibly know what she was doing to him, Gabriel thought with another savage thrust of undiluted desire. He watched the idle movement of her hand under the flimsy cotton of her underwear and any thoughts of taking his time disappeared under the need to touch her again.

His trousers were kicked aside, quickly followed by his silk boxer shorts until he was standing in front of her feverish gaze in all his proud, masculine and very impressive nudity.

A slow, satisfied and eminently cat-like smile curved her wide mouth.

Wasn't it supposed to be the other way around? Gabriel thought wryly. Wasn't *he* supposed to be the cat in command of its very luscious prey?

'Touching yourself, *cara*?' he enquired lazily as he sank down to join her on the warm grass and he covered her hand with his own.

'Of course I'm not!' Laura protested. She stroked the side of his face and felt a lump gather at the back of her throat. All this would become was another memory to add to the collection, she thought sadly. She meant nothing to him and he had made that perfectly clear.

He took her hand and kissed the tip of each of her fingers with such infinite tenderness that she could almost kid herself that there was some emotion there.

There was nothing to be gained from dwelling on it, she thought, pulling him fiercely towards her and kissing him, liking it better when he yanked off her last remaining item of clothing.

'Want to play rough, do you, little tiger?' He laughed softly into her mouth.

'It's been a long time.'

'Feel free to make as much noise as you want,' he returned, moving directly over her so that his hardness brushed against her belly and set up a series of sweet sensations inside her. He hooked his arms under her back so that she curved up towards him and began to ravage her breasts.

Then, without any thought of teasing her further, he moved down to part her thighs with his hand and began plundering between her legs. He felt it when she curled her fingers into his hair and then she began obeying his strict instructions that she should make as much noise as she wanted.

At some point, lost in the daze of tasting her, he felt her tug his head up to tell him that he had to stop, that he was driving her crazy, and then it was *his* turn to be ravaged by *her*.

It was something he had not experienced for a very long time. The women he had dated in the past had preferred him to make all the moves and that had always suited him perfectly, unconsciously maintaining the control that had become part and parcel of his dominant personality.

Now *she* was taking control and he found himself enjoying every minute of it as she straddled him and, after taking her fill of every inch of his body, sank onto his engorged manhood and began moving in a way that was unbelievably erotic.

Her breasts dangled tantalisingly by his face, brushing his mouth until he caught one in his hands and began suckling on the tight bud, whilst her body continued to move over him, grinding harder until they reached that point of no return and crossed it.

Laura finally lay down on him, spent and satiated, and he stroked her hair.

'So,' she said seriously, rolling off him to lie on the grass at his side, 'I guess it goes without saying that what we did was…a big mistake…' She sat up and reached for her clothes, only to find herself pulled back down as one big hand descended on her shoulder.

'What do you think you are doing?' They looked at one another, both on their sides, facing each other.

'We have to get back to the house, Gabriel. I was getting dressed. We…we shouldn't have done what…what we just did. You know that.'

'Why not?'

'Because sex is just going to complicate everything.'

'Oh, is it, now?' He idly began to stroke her breasts, enjoying the way her body was reacting to his feather touch. Forget what she was saying about sex complicating everything. She still wanted him. It was obvious in the way her nipples were hardening under his lingering finger and in the way her breathing was beginning to sound raspy.

For a while just then he had been so lost in the rapture of touching this woman, feeling her naked body, that he had almost forgotten the whole point of the exercise. This, he reminded himself, was the woman who had turned him away and it was only now, being with her again, wanting her the way he did, that Gabriel could see how affected his life had been by the rejection.

'Yes, it is,' Laura said, shifting to move, and he caught her wrist with his hand and, after kissing her palm, turned his eyes to hers.

'Why? Did you not enjoy what we just did?'

'You know I did.'

'Mmm. I know.' He smiled lazily and began stroking her thigh until she gave an involuntary gasp of pleasure as her body responded. He leant forward and kissed her delicately on her mouth until she lay back down so that he could lean over her and continue his exquisite exploration of her lips with his tongue.

And this time their love-making was slow and languorous. He touched every inch of her with such infinite gentleness that her body wanted to explode from sheer *want*. When she would have tugged him up from those most intimate caresses a woman could have, he captured her restless hand with his steady one and continued caressing her, devoting himself entirely to bringing her so close to the peak of orgasm that she was panting, only to replace his inquisitive tongue with little kisses.

By the time she lay spent by his side, the fragile spring warmth was beginning to recede and, by mutual consent, they both got dressed and began the ride back to the house.

'I'll help you muck them out,' he told her, the first words they had exchanged since their shatteringly prolonged love-making.

'Honestly, you don't have to. I…I'm perfectly capable of handling it on my own.'

'I realise I don't have to, but I want to.'

It was a relief that the physical demands of tending to the horses allowed Laura time to try and get her frantic thoughts into some kind of order. Not that she wasn't helplessly aware of Gabriel working right there alongside her. Somewhere along the line, he had removed his shirt and it seemed that wherever she looked her eyes crashed into his bare-backed torso with its hard, muscular strength and tightly packed muscle.

'Right,' she said weakly, after forty-five minutes of solid work conducted in silence, 'I think we can call it a day here.'

Gabriel stood back and looked at her. Her hair was damp with perspiration and she had shoved up the sleeves of her sweatshirt. With deliberate slowness, he put back on his shirt, leaving it unbuttoned.

'Feels like old times,' he drawled. 'I haven't mucked out for years.'

'I'm surprised you never bought any horses,' Laura said, grasping at this little straw of conversational normality. She dragged her eyes away from him and moved towards the stable door.

'I thought about it,' Gabriel replied, watching her as she carefully avoided his gaze. 'But horses need constant attention and upkeep and...' he shrugged '...my working hours are too unpredictable.' He walked behind her and closed the door behind him. He could read DISCOMFORT written all over her in huge capital letters, and perversely wanted to snatch her back to him.

He rested his hand loosely on her neck and felt her flinch. Dammit, she hadn't been uncomfortable back there out in the open! Oh, no, she had been abandoned and uninhibited and utterly in his possession!

'Relax,' he told her softly.

'Relax? How can you possibly expect me to relax?' Laura swung round to look at him, her eyes wide with confusion.

'Easily,' Gabriel said smoothly. 'We have just had mind-blowing sex. You should be feeling very relaxed.'

'I should be heading for the nearest river to jump in,' Laura said bitterly. 'We should never have made love. It was a mistake and it won't happen again!'

'We will discuss this inside. When we have both had a shower and something to eat.'

'There's nothing to discuss,' Laura muttered, turning away, hugging herself tightly.

For the moment, Gabriel thought, he would leave her nursing her thoughts of regret and actually thinking that their love-making might really be a one-off episode.

'And shouldn't you be heading back to London?' she flung at him.

'In due course. But definitely not in this state.' He looked down at himself, covered in bits of straw, and Laura reluctantly admitted that he had a point. Not to mention the small fact that the house belonged to him anyway, so he could have however many damned showers he wanted!

'I'll get you a towel,' she said as soon as they were in the front door.

'And get one for yourself whilst you are about it.' He looked at her without smiling, but the intent was stamped all over his face.

'What are you talking about?' A frisson of excitement and alarm ripped through her.

'As we are both in dire need of a shower, then I suggest we do it together.' And when she opened her mouth to protest, he covered it swiftly with his own and felt her body melt. Oh, yes. Did she really think that she could run away from him now? Did she really imagine that he would allow her to do that?

'Didn't you hear a word…th-that I just said, Gabriel?'

'Heard and absorbed every word, *amante*. Which is not to say that I agree with a single one of them.' To emphasise his point, he slipped his hands under her jumper and placed his hands under the crease of her breasts. 'What we did was not a mistake. We wanted one another and we still want one another, and there is no point in your pretending otherwise.' He could feel the rapid beating of her heart under her ribcage.

'We can't bring the past back.' Laura heard the unsteady tremor of her voice with dismay. She should be thrusting him away, flying up those stairs as fast as her legs could carry her, but she couldn't move a muscle.

'Nor can we forget it,' he replied fiercely. 'Why don't you tell me that it was all a mistake…now…?' His hands covered her breasts and he began rousing her with masterful precision, touching her nipples and setting them aflame with longing. They half walked, half stumbled, still united, until he was pressing her back against the wall, and with her in that position he moved one hand to her thigh and began rubbing her there, there where she could do nothing but respond, his fingers firm as they pushed against the crease of the denim until she was half crying out.

She surrendered. He felt it the instant her arms wrapped around him and she blindly searched for his mouth.

'Now, what about that shower?' he broke away to murmur and she looked at him with a dazed expression, then smiled.

His tactics, he admitted minutes later as the warm water shot jets down at them both in the shower cubicle, left a lot to be desired, but all was fair in love and war.

Strangely, though, he didn't just want her to yield to him because she couldn't resist the tug of what they did to one another in the sack.

'Your hair needs washing,' he said, swivelling her away

from him and reaching for the bottle of shampoo so that he could trickle some into her wet hair and begin massaging. 'And this is not the way to do it,' he murmured huskily, when she gave a sensuous little whimper of pleasure and curved her back against him so that he had no choice, as a red-blooded male, but to wrap his arms around her and bury his mouth against her neck.

'You're right.' She squirmed until she was facing him, slippery with soap and water, and their quick shower, as it turned out, took them a lot longer than they had anticipated.

This was what he wanted. Or so he told himself in the warmth of the kitchen, holding a glass of chilled wine in his hand and looking at her as she busied herself in the kitchen, having insisted that he sit down and let her cook.

At his beck and call. One touch, and she was on fire. Click his fingers and she would melt in his arms.

So why was there still a thread of dissatisfaction gnawing away at the pit of his stomach? Had he not achieved exactly what he had wanted? If he turned his back now and walked away, he knew that she would be the one to hurt, so why the ache? He owned the house, the land, her body. He had got his revenge and now he felt sullied, somehow, by it.

'There was no need to put yourself to all this trouble,' he said abruptly, and she turned to face him with a frown.

'What's the matter? What's wrong?'

'Nothing is wrong. Why should anything be wrong?' he asked irritably.

'No reason whatsoever,' Laura replied, covering the frying-pan with a lid and drying her hands on a towel. She reached for her wineglass on the counter and took a sip of wine, then she perched against the ledge of the counter and folded her arms. 'You're free to go any time you want,

Gabriel,' she said coolly. 'Don't imagine that because we've slept together that there's any need for you to try and play the gentleman now. In case you'd conveniently forgotten, *you* were the one who suggested staying on for something to eat.'

'And in case *you'd* conveniently forgotten, *you* were only too delighted at the suggestion.' Flushed, as she had been, after their third bout of love-making! For some reason, the thought of her murmuring things she thought he wanted to hear when in the throes of passion made his teeth snap together in fury.

It was something of which Laura did not want to be reminded. Let that be a lesson to her, she thought angrily. Nothing between them was normal and it was pointless pretending that it could ever be! They were not some domesticated little couple playing at happy families. They had made love but love was the last thing that came into the act. The thought of him sitting there, squirming because he would rather be off now that he had slept with her, filled her with mortification.

'It seemed sensible!' she shot back. 'Not that I have much choice, anyway! After all, this *is* your house. I am only acting the part of dutiful employee.'

'And was that what you were doing earlier on?' he rasped. 'Acting the part of the dutiful employee?'

Laura was the first to look away. She didn't want to see the jeering cynicism stamped in those beautiful black eyes. More importantly, she didn't want him to see the furious, blinding panic in her *own* eyes.

God, she thought with dawning, incredulous horror, I've fallen in love with him. All over again. Maybe, she thought with clammy dismay, she had never fallen *out* of love with him. She had just managed to submerge it all until he came back into her life and then, well, it had just been a question of time before she'd catapulted back into his arms. She could have coped better if she had thought that she had been acting the part of the dutiful employee!

'No,' she whispered numbly.

She had turned away and Gabriel, his body tense, wanted desperately for her to turn back to him so that he could read what was going on in that seductive head of hers. He took a few deep breaths to calm himself and to regain some of his self-control.

'Look,' he said to her back, 'there is no point in us arguing with one another.' Why the hell wouldn't she look at him? The thought that he might have blown it filled him with sudden, suffocating dread. 'I just did not want you to feel that you had to slave over a kitchen stove to cook food for me when I would more than happily have taken you somewhere to eat.'

'I had to cook for myself anyway,' Laura muttered, which shoved his simmering anger a few notches higher. She had succumbed to lust and so, heck, why not invite him to eat with her? Not as if she were putting herself out!

'Women, home-cooked meals and me do not mix.' Pride slammed into place with ferocious ease. 'It's been my experience,' he said dismissively, 'that a woman who cooks food wants more than I am ever prepared to give.'

'In which case,' Laura replied with equal dismissiveness, 'you have nothing to fear from me in that area.'

'Because all you want is sex?'

Because it's all I can get and that's better than nothing. 'Why not?' She shrugged and began putting plates and cutlery on the table. Brave words but she couldn't meet his eyes. She couldn't bear to see the relief in his eyes that she wasn't going to clutter his high-powered life with unwanted complications. 'We're both adults,' she said with a tight smile. 'Isn't it good that we understand each other?'

CHAPTER EIGHT

GABRIEL frowned at the computer screen in front of him. He could vaguely register the detailed report staring back at him and the numbers indicating that a takeover made six months previously was beginning to show the profit he had predicted, but his eyes were glazed.

When the phone rang, he leapt at the receiver and grabbed the opportunity to shove his chair back at an angle that offered him a view through the opened door into the sitting room where Laura was busily discussing colours and paints with three men.

He had decided, he had told her, that he needed to be on hand to supervise the beginnings of work being done on the house. This wasn't a company takeover, he had told her grandly, he was personally involved with this particular purchase, he had to be there for her to consult freely whenever she felt she needed to. When she had drily reminded him of the need to trust his workforce, namely her, he had swept aside the objection with a careless wave of his hand and words to the effect that it would be easier for him to work from the house as opposed to having her travel down every single time she needed to make a decision about something. That was the whole point of communications these days, he had explained, stilling the protest she had been about to utter. E-mail facilities, fax machines, computers allowed total mobility.

Within twenty-four hours he had moved in lock, stock and barrel, propelled by an urgent need that he himself did not fully comprehend. He just knew that he had to be around her.

Now, he stretched out his long legs on the dining table, which was big enough to implement as his desk, and looked, with satisfaction, at the tall, lithe blonde who was obviously having absolutely no trouble whatsoever in dealing with three of the men she had employed. She needed his presence here like a fish needed a tree, he thought to himself as he went through the motions of dealing with his secretary on the other end of the phone. But she needed his body. Of that there was no question. When the day was done, she would slide into bed with him, warm and willing and insatiable in her demands. It should have been enough. In fact, he knew that he should be tiring of her, getting ready to deliver his final trump card, namely his withdrawal, and thereby complete the business he had set into motion.

When he replaced the receiver, he remained sitting as he was, his fingers linked loosely on his lap, and pondered the niggling question of why her physical acquiescence was proving to be more of a frustration than if she had denied him her body totally.

Because, he reflected, he wanted her mind as well. Did she give tuppence for him at all? Was there anything there for her apart from the great sex? When she chatted to him and laughed at some of the things he said, was it done out of some obscure sense of obligation or duty or, worse, guilt because sex should be accompanied by at least some measure of amicability? Lord, the questions nagged away at him until he finally stood up in utter frustration and strode into the sitting room.

'What's going on in here?' he asked with a strained smile. 'Anything that I should be aware about?' Just being within a few feet of her made his fingers itch and he shoved his hands firmly into his pockets whilst he continued to survey the room, now stripped of its wallpaper, in the manner of someone who knew what they were looking at.

'I'm sorry.' Laura smiled. 'Did we disturb you? It must be a little disruptive trying to work in the room opposite. Why don't you close the door to the dining room?'

'I did not come here to isolate myself away from what is happening,' he muttered irritably, his dark eyes sliding across to dwell on the bewitching picture she presented, all ruffled hair and overalls that should have diminished her appeal but instead heightened it. 'After all, it *is* my house.' Had he just said that? A sullen, infantile observation that had her narrowing her eyes fractionally? 'What are these colours on the walls?' he asked, pointing at the streaks, and he allowed himself to be carried along with the flow as she began discussing what should be used where, whilst the plasterer made him run his hands along the walls, which would need resurfacing, and the electrician pointed to various sockets and made intelligent sounding remarks about the wiring in the house.

Out of the corner of his eye, Gabriel watched her face become animated as she discussed what could be done and tried to prise time scales out of the three men.

He could hear the sound of yet more men working on the floor above, pulling up the worn carpets and stripping the walls of yet more wallpaper.

On the spur of the moment he made a decision.

'I think we can leave the workforce here to get on with the basics,' he announced, pulling her to one side.

'Leave them and do what? My job is to be here, supervising.'

'I am temporarily altering your duties,' Gabriel informed her. He captured her arm with his hand and ex-

plained to the three men that they would be on their own
for a few hours and could they manage. 'You know where
everything is,' he continued, still grasping her hand just in
case she attempted to wriggle free to play the damned dil-
igent employee. 'Tea, coffee, milk. Help yourself in our
absence and we will see you later.'

This, Laura fulminated as she hurriedly changed in the
bathroom into some clean, fairly respectable clothes, was
the problem. All was fine when they were making love.
Everything could be forgotten then in the midst of explosive passion, but the minute they were in a normal situation
he just couldn't help reminding her who was boss. She
worked for him and he never spared a thought for how she
felt. Why should he? she asked herself repressively. She
was his employee by day and his sex slave by night until
he tired of one or both duties and dismissed her. Emotion
did not enter into it and feelings were never, ever discussed.

The minute she stormed down the stairs, Gabriel could
see that her simmering anger at his high-handed attitude
was heading for boiling point, and he countered it with a
conciliatory smile.

'My apologies for behaving with such despicable arrogance,' he told her before she could let rip. 'Forgive me?'
His dark eyes appreciatively took in the vanilla cord trousers and the blue and cream checked shirt that she had
slung casually over a figure-hugging cropped blue vest.

'I told you it was a bad idea moving in here. You don't
need to keep a constant watch on me. I'm not going to do
anything outrageous with your precious décor!'

'You look enchanting.'

'I beg your pardon?'

'Enchanting and utterly, utterly irresistible.' He smiled
very slowly and watched as the storm in her eyes gave

way to pink-cheeked silence. 'Would you be horribly offended if I told you that I had to come in there and take you somewhere private so that I could thoroughly seduce you?'

'I would tell you that completing this job would take for ever if you didn't learn to control your...'

'My...?' Gabriel prompted silkily.

'Your carnal urges.' Just saying it, though, made her feel like jelly inside. And the beast knew it! 'Where are we going anyway? I really feel as though I ought to be supervising these men just to make sure that nothing goes horribly wrong.'

'They are stripping walls, pulling up carpets and doing the odd bit of plastering,' Gabriel said wryly, slipping his arm around her waist and leading her outside to the car. 'There is a limit as to how confused they can get by those very simple tasks.' Before he unlocked the car, he swung her around to face him. He couldn't help himself. It felt like years since he had touched her, even though it was only a matter of a few hours.

'Have you ever been ravished in a car?' he murmured, threading his fingers through her hair and tilting her face up to his.

'You still haven't told me where we're going,' Laura said unsteadily. A few well-chosen words and she was putty in his hands! It was pathetic. Or maybe it was just love and love had no qualms about turning a sane human being into an unthinking idiot.

'So I haven't.' He released her, unlocked the car and then opened the door for her, leaning down once she had tucked her long legs inside. 'But you'll be pleased to hear that I have not stolen you away simply to satisfy my needs.' Yes, he thought sourly, he could turn her on all right, just as he always had been able to years ago.

Her velvety brown eyes looked at him in bewilderment. 'You mean we're actually going somewhere?'

'Call it a drive to have a look at some interior design. And there will be no need for us to rush, because whilst you were changing I told Pete Clarke to make sure that the house is locked and everyone out when he leaves this evening. I thought it better, really, because it is a bit of a drive and who knows, *cara*, we might want to stop *en route*?'

'Certainly nowhere that involves pulling up down a narrow side lane,' Laura admonished as soon as he was in the car and pulling out of the drive, but just thinking about it was enough to bring a smile to her lips. 'I'm way too old for that kind of thing and, besides, we're both far too tall for making love in the cramped back seat of your car. Even if it *is* a very big car.'

'You might be tall but you're as supple as a piece of elastic,' Gabriel replied, his eyes fixed on the road. He gave a wicked grin that set her pulses racing. 'But maybe you're right,' he conceded ruefully.

'So tell me where we're going, Gabriel.'

'We are going to my place in Berkshire. I want you to have a look at my house and tell me what you think, about the style of the décor.'

'You mean get an idea of what you like?'

He shrugged. 'Actually, I hired a team of people to do the house for me. Lack of time.' Or inclination, for that matter.

'And do you like what they've done?' Laura felt a burning curiosity to see this man whom she adored in his surroundings.

'It is very grand.'

'You don't sound awfully certain, Gabriel.'

'I thought I liked it, but now I'm not too sure.' Quite

an admission and one that took him by surprise. He had never had any complaints about his mansion before but now, having seen her at work with her colour charts and wallpaper books, he had been overtaken by the feeling that his mansion, kitted out in the most lavishly expensive style by the most sought-after professional interior designers, was not suited to his tastes after all.

'If you don't like the way it's been decorated, then what's the point of taking me there?' Laura asked, and he began irritably drumming the steering wheel with his thumb.

'I thought you might enjoy getting away from the riding stables for a day,' Gabriel said and he immediately wondered whether she was as conscious of the petulance in his voice as he was. 'I mean, when was the last time you got away, Laura?'

'Got away from the house?'

'House, county, country, whatever!'

'There's no need to start shouting.'

'*I am not shouting!*' A simple plan, he thought, to close the books and put the past behind him, and look at where he was now! The woman had managed to get under his skin in ways he could never have imagined! From being a man permanently in control, he had become someone who swung from mood to mood with alarming irregularity, not that she even noticed, never mind cared!

'Oh, good.' She glanced wryly at him and their eyes met in a split second of perfect accord which, ludicrously, made him want to stop the car and give her a hug. A hug, he thought with exasperation! Since when did *hugs* feature in his grand plans of seduction and revenge.

'Well…' Laura chewed her lip and thought. 'I *have* been to London within the last year…'

'Have you? Who with?' He was in there before his brain

could tell his mouth to keep silent, but when he glanced sideways at her she hardly seemed to have registered his querulous demand.

'As for leaving the country…no, I can't remember the last time I actually left the country to go on holiday anywhere.' Laura sighed. When she had been growing up and living in the lap of luxury, trips abroad had been regular annual events. Both her parents had been disinclined to leave the riding stables for too long in the care of someone else, but even so they had always had two weeks in the sun somewhere over winter and a week during the Easter holidays. 'Why? Are you offering?' she teased, and when he remained silent she realised that she had crossed an invisible boundary. And one she should have seen from a mile off, she thought miserably. Holidays would have constituted something more than just sex and there was no way that he would have considered that option.

'What if I did?' Gabriel asked with mild curiosity. The thought of going on a holiday with the woman sitting next to him was like a promise of paradise and he had to grimly remind himself that he had felt just like this seven years ago when the prospect of marriage had beckoned.

Laura, looking at the stern profile, could almost read what was going on in his head. The thought of going anywhere with her that might indicate a normal relationship was abhorrent to him. It was written in block letters on his unsmiling face. Did he imagine that she would jump at the chance for an all-expenses-paid vacation now that she was indebted to him?

'I would refuse, of course,' she said lightly, turning away and staring with unseeing eyes at the fast-moving countryside around them. 'A dutiful employee never abandons her job when it's only just started.'

Her glibly spoken answer hit him like a hammer in his gut but he forced himself to nod curtly in agreement.

'How much further do we have to go?' Laura asked as his taut silence thickened around them. In the blink of an eye the light-hearted banter between them had evaporated and she knew, once again, how fragile it really was, how easily it was obliterated by one wrong word or one dangerous sentence. 'Tell me about your house. How long have you been living there?'

Gabriel expelled his breath and shook his head slightly. 'What can I say about my house? I bought it five years ago when the property market had slumped. I thought it would prove to be a worthwhile financial investment, and I was right. It has…eight bedrooms and I lose count of the reception rooms. A lot.'

'And you entertain quite a bit? I can't imagine you entertaining. You would frighten all your guests.' She saw his shoulders relax and a small smile replace the hard expression on his face. Ridiculously, she felt a spurt of pleasure that she could manage to shift his mood. He surely couldn't be that emotionally cold towards her if he could respond to her in that way, could he? Could he?

'Should I take that as a compliment?' he asked, flicking her a glance.

'Depends. Do you want to be thought of as scary?'

'Sometimes it helps in business,' Gabriel told her truthfully. 'Especially when you are an outsider. No matter that I have lived here for years. I am an Argentinian and you, of all people, should know how strong the old-school tie can be.' But there was no bitterness or resentment in his voice when he said this.

'I can't imagine that anyone would let old-school ties stop them from dealing with you, Gabriel, and you know it. You're way too charismatic to be ignored.'

'Now *that* I do take as a compliment. Although…' he lingered musingly before continuing '…you seem to be doing a rather good job of ignoring me at the moment.'

'Really. And what should I be doing?'

'My thigh feels a little stiff at the moment.' This was better. He was discovering that when it came to the physical, he was supremely in control, but whenever the emotional started creeping in, which it seemed to do a little too often for his liking, then his control disappeared like a puff of smoke. 'Must be all the driving,' he said helpfully. 'Perhaps you could massage it just a little…?'

'Isn't that a little dangerous when you're at the steering wheel?' Laura asked innocently and Gabriel grinned, back in the driver's seat in more ways than one.

'Perhaps you're right.' Just as well that there was a convenient turning less than five minutes later, and, because they had avoided the motorway, it was simplicity itself to go down sufficient winding turns to leave all signs of traffic behind.

'I know what you said about being too old and too tall,' Gabriel drawled, killing the engine and relaxing back against his car door so that he could look at her with lazy thoroughness, 'but I couldn't resist the temptation to discover whether you were right…'

A little over an hour later, Laura found out that she was neither…and nor was he.

When, she thought to herself as they approached the roundabouts and traffic lights that were the hallmark of suburbia, would she be able to look at this man and resist him? When would she be able to hear his voice, redolent with its soft, sexy come-on, and not feel every bone in her body melt?

More disturbingly, what was going to happen to her when he got sick of revisiting old territory and vanished,

leaving her behind to pick up the pieces and start again?
It seemed that they were living in a vacuum, where sex
was the integral force, but whilst she was spinning away
into the fantasy realms of love, he was merely enjoying
her for a short while, enjoying the thought of controlling
the woman who had turned him down. He wasn't spinning
away anywhere.

She was barely aware of the change in the scenery. From
passing estates to more open land where houses lay un-
glimpsed down avenues leading away from the main road.

His car turned down one of these imposing avenues and
Laura blinked with a start to the view of a sprawling, ranch-
style mansion, which loomed imposingly ahead of them.

'Your house?' She gaped incredulously and Gabriel half
smiled.

'My house,' he agreed, slowing the car to park to one
side of the drive. 'Like it?'

'It's very…impressive,' Laura said with resounding understatement. 'Very…big. Well, huge, really.'

She had to stand and stare once she was out of the car,
whilst he patiently waited, watching her through narrowed
eyes.

'It seems a bit magnificent for one person,' Laura finally
volunteered, following him towards the imposing front
door.

'Like I said, I originally bought it as a financial investment and as such it has been worth every penny.'

'There's more to life than money.'

'Really? I have yet to encounter it.' He opened the front
door and stood aside to let her through.

Breathtaking enough on the outside, it was a designer's
paradise on the inside. Wooden floors gleamed and seemed
to stretch endlessly and matched perfectly with the heavy
cream of the wallpaper, and through open doors she could

glimpse a harmony of rich colours and thick curtains that hung to the ground in swirls.

The house had been cunningly designed on various levels, so from where she stood, with her back to the front door, Laura could see the staircase curve towards the left, where a luxurious sitting area overlooked the main entrance and presumably led to one wing of the house, before winding up towards the right wing of the house.

'If this is the sort of thing you like,' she joked nervously, 'then you're going to hate Oakridge House when it's finished. Lord, Gabriel, I almost feel as if I should remove my shoes just in case the shiny polished wood gets scuffed.' It was meant as a light-hearted observation but she could see from the thinning of his mouth that he hadn't cared for it.

'Don't be ridiculous, Laura. Come on, I will show you to the kitchen and we can have something to drink before we have a look around.' This was a mistake, he thought grimly. She hated this place and he was disgusted to find that he was now seeing it through her eyes as well and not much liking what he saw.

They bypassed rooms, into which Laura sneaked quick, fascinated peeks until they came to the kitchen, which, much as she might have expected, was everything anyone could want from a kitchen. Wood, chrome and cream gleamed with showroom brightness.

'Lovely,' she said faintly, and he glowered at her.

'You hate it. Why not be honest and admit it? I won't get annoyed.' He was so annoyed, in fact, that it felt good to add, with deliberate casualness, 'What you think does not affect me at all.'

'I don't hate it,' Laura said stubbornly, folding her arms. Did he have to spell out his position with such relentless indifference? 'And I would love a cup of coffee,' she continued, 'if you can locate it. These counters seem very clear of anything useful. I mean—' she could feel her hurt gathering some much-needed momentum '—what the heck is that?' She pointed at a silver gadget on the counter by the stove, which was so dazzlingly bright that you very nearly needed sunglasses to look at it.

'It's a…ah…juice extractor.'

'And that?'

'Cappuccino maker.'

'Which you're going to use to make my cup of coffee?'

'I prefer the ordinary kettle.' He had ruffled her beautiful feathers with his dismissive put-down, and Gabriel felt a twinge of disproportionate delight.

'Then why on earth did you waste your good money on a cappuccino maker? Huh? If you preferred *the ordinary kettle*? More money than sense.'

'I did not *buy* it, as a matter of fact.'

'Oh, I see. It just landed on your counter one morning from outer space.'

Gabriel threw back his head and laughed. 'It *does* look a little terrifyingly alien,' he agreed.

'And do you know how to use it?'

'I…'

'You don't know!' Laura crowed, grinning. 'What did I just say about more money than sense? I bet you're scared to go anywhere near it in case it explodes if you press the wrong button!'

'You are utterly incorrigible, woman.'

'And utterly right as well. So what other gadgets do you have concealed in this high-tech kitchen which you're too scared to use?'

Gabriel couldn't help it. He grinned sheepishly back at her and shrugged. 'The microwave can be a little uncooperative sometimes,' he admitted ruefully, wondering how on earth he had ever managed to feel remotely comfortable in a kitchen where most of the appliances seemed designed to repel casual use.

'So how on earth do you manage to fend for yourself?' Laura asked, folding her arms and subjecting him to a penetrating, quizzical stare.

The urge to tell her that what he needed was a good woman to fend for him was so strong that it left him shaken.

'I have staff,' he muttered, and she nodded with superior condescension.

'Handy.'

'It is one of the privileges money buys.' Gabriel wondered how she would look in an apron, cooking for him, tending to his every need. Try as he did to turn the image into a purely sexual one, all he could picture was the leggy blonde in front of him sitting at a kitchen table, a beaten old pine kitchen table, listening to him talk about his day, soothing away his stress.

Good God!

'Maybe we should leave the coffee for later,' he muttered, turning away so that she couldn't see any tell-tale darkening of his cheeks. 'I might as well show you around the rest of the house and, please...' he slid his eyes over to where she was standing, looking at him with her head inclined '...feel free to speak your mind.'

'Okay,' Laura replied airily. 'I will.'

Twenty minutes later and Gabriel was beginning to regret his open invitation. She had voiced her opinions on everything, from the colour of the walls to the choice of paintings hanging on them, from the design of the furniture to its level of comfort. In the sitting area she had bounced experimentally on the long pale blue sofa and pronounced it too firm.

'It may look attractive,' she had told him, sweeping imperious eyes over the sofa and chairs, which, from his vague recollections, had cost a small fortune, 'but sofas should be squashy. If you would prefer something along these lines, then you'd better tell me now, so that I know what to order or, rather, which stores to send you to for you to decide.'

'I cannot possibly make a decision like that on my own. I wouldn't know where to begin.'

'Now I'm supposed to see you as the Helpless Male?' Laura had shot him a disbelieving, sceptical look. 'You still haven't answered my question. Firm or squashy?'

'Squashy.'

'Patterned or plain?'

'What…' he had almost fallen into the trap of telling her to choose anything *she* liked, but had caught himself in the nick of time '…would you suggest? You are the designer.'

'Something warm and patterned,' Laura had said. 'Something with ethnic overtones, maybe in terracottas and greens.'

'Fine.'

And every room had been subjected to the same critical eye. By the time they were heading up the stairs to the bedroom wing of the house, Gabriel was fast developing a keen sense of loathing for most of his furnishings.

After guest room number two, Laura stood in front of him, frowning, her hands on her hips.

'I'm getting very mixed messages here, Gabriel,' she informed him.

His reply was wary. He was being bombarded by mixed messages himself, none of which he welcomed. 'What about?' he asked, his eyes narrowing.

He breathed an inner sigh of relief when she said, looking around the pristine room, 'I don't dislike anything I've seen, but I would never have chosen this kind of décor myself. It's very…impressive and tasteful, but I find it all very cold and lacking in the comforts I associate with a home. But you've lived here for years and so you must like it. In which case, perhaps I'm not the best person to use for doing the inside of Oakridge House. Maybe you need someone professional.'

'I have every confidence in you, *querida*.' The endearment, combined with those dark, sexy eyes, did what they always did. Made her forget what she had been saying.

'To choose stuff *I* would like, Gabriel, which, judging from what I've seen of your house here, *you* would absolutely hate. And let's face it, Oakridge House *is your* house, not mine. I don't want to finish my job only to discover that I haven't done it to your liking.'

'Why don't you leave me to worry about that?' He was beginning to hate those lines of demarcation that he had been so keen to establish only a few weeks ago. 'And do not start rambling on about your duties as my employee,' he continued repressively.

'I can't just overlook that little technicality,' Laura said tightly. 'You're paying me a fabulous salary, rescuing me from penury and I want to repay you by doing a good job.' God, it was so easy to get carried away on the wings of day-dreaming, and of reading signals that just weren't there. Discussing domestic issues was a sure-fire way to forget exactly what their situation was, and Laura felt compelled to pull herself back from the brink of massive, dangerous self-deception.

'Then as your employer,' he mimicked with thinly veiled anger, 'who is paying you a fabulous salary and rescuing you from penury, I order you to furnish the house precisely how you want to. Use your flair and imagination and I am happy to leave the outcome up to you.' He turned away and began striding along the corridor, with its plush white carpeting and pale ochre walls.

'There's no need for you to storm off in one of your Latin American moods,' Laura called to him, which instantly made him stop in his tracks and dragged a reluctant smile to his lips. He turned slowly to face her and realised that she had not moved an inch from where she had been standing at the door to the guest room.

'Just as there is no need for you to constantly harp on about your status as my employee.'

They stared at one another from one end of the corridor to the other.

She could have told him that seeing her reduced to that status had been the object of his exercise, and that the only reason he was now choosing to overlook the little detail was because they were lovers and even he must feel some guilt at making love to the woman he had sought out for purposes of revenge.

But she held her tongue.

To have said any of those things would have made their already precarious bubble burst into a million smithereens and she wanted to hold onto the bubble for as long as she could.

Eventually, she shrugged lightly and stepped towards him.

'If you don't mind my taste, then I'll furnish your house just as I would furnish my own,' she said, walking towards him, and she was rewarded with one of those blisteringly sexy smiles that almost made her falter in her tracks.

'I think it is time you saw the master bedroom,' Gabriel murmured, not taking his eyes off her approaching figure for a second. 'It is the one room in the house I actually chose for myself.'

He reached out sideways to push open a door to his right, watching her intently as she came towards him and only turning away when she too turned to gape at the room in front of her.

Gone was the impersonal beauty of the previous rooms she had explored. Here was a room that breathed masculinity. The bed was very low to the ground and the dark, swirling colours of the quilt demanded touching. A rich, dark wooden chest of drawers banked one wall and the pale carpet was almost unseen beneath a massive Persian rug that dominated the floor space. Heavy, deep blue velvet drapes completed the feeling of eroticism.

'You like it?' he whispered into her ear and all Laura could do was nod in wonder at the vibrant mix of colours, none of which seemed out of place although most of them clashed.

'The quilt cover is silk,' he said softly. 'It feels magnificent against bare skin. Would you like to try?'

The mere thought of them writhing naked on top of the silk made her skin begin to tingle, and with supreme confidence he took her hand and led her over to the bed, leaving her to stand by it only for as long as it took him to draw the curtains, plunging the room into instant darkness.

'A sensual boudoir,' Laura said as he lit four bulky candles of varying heights on the chest of drawers. 'Was this your intention when you…created it?'

Gabriel nodded and omitted to mention that it had been a chaste boudoir. He had never brought any of his women back to this house, preferring to see them in his penthouse in London. She was the first, but damned if she would know that.

He moved to where she was still standing and pulled off the shirt, groaning involuntarily as his hands slipped under the vest to find the heavy warmth of her bare breasts.

He rolled his thumbs over the tightened peaks of her nipples and half closed his eyes as she slipped the vest over her head and tossed it to the ground. Then the trousers. Down they came, followed by the lacy underwear. She had been right. Making love in a car did not lend itself to the delight of seeing her exquisite, naked body.

'And what would you like me to do on this silk duvet of yours?' Laura murmured seductively.

'For starters, just lie on it and let me see you.'

It felt as beautiful as it had promised. Laura stretched on the bed, watching him through half-closed eyes, and began moving sensuously for his languid viewing. When her hand trailed along her stomach to ruffle the fine fair hair that guarded her sex, Gabriel sank onto the covers with a grunt of savage passion and captured her wandering hand with his own.

'You little hussy,' he growled. 'Do not even think about touching yourself. That is for my enjoyment only.'

And he was about to prove that very point when the doorbell shrieked into the thick silence and Anna's voice crackled on the intercom in the bedroom, laughing and asking Gabriel, 'Where are you?'

CHAPTER NINE

LAURA walked tentatively towards the kitchen. The sound of Anna's voice had galvanised them both into action. In Gabriel's case, it had been a simple matter of running his fingers through his hair whilst swearing darkly under his breath about interruptions, and then going downstairs to open the front door.

In Laura's case, she had slipped back on her clothes with the nervous tension of a teenager being caught on the couch with her boyfriend when her parents should have been safely out. It was ridiculous, she told herself severely. They were both consenting adults. Which just went to bring home to her in all its ugly clarity the clandestine nature of their relationship. They were fine romping around in the sack just so long as reality didn't manage to break through.

She peeped into the kitchen to find that Gabriel was nowhere to be seen, although Anna was sitting comfortably at the kitchen table, quietly composed with her fingers linked on the glass surface.

'This is a ridiculous table to have in a kitchen, wouldn't you agree?' The dark-haired woman smiled and Laura relaxed and walked in. 'I told Gabriel to get rid of it years ago, and, in all fairness, he agreed every time I mentioned it, but, like all men, did nothing about the advice.'

'Hi.' Laura smiled back cautiously. 'I'm sorry. We weren't…expecting you…but it's lovely to see you again.' She hovered, not too sure what to say. Anna was right. Kitchens should be comfortable and chrome and glass did

154

not constitute comfort, but it would have been ludicrous to embark on a conversation about a kitchen table. 'Where…where is Gabriel?'

'I sent him out.'

'You sent him out?'

'To get some oil for my car,' Anna explained. 'The little red light started appearing on my way here and, being a woman, I have no idea how to put oil in.' She shrugged and gave Laura a conspiratorial smile that suggested she was more than adept at putting oil in her car. 'Besides, I wanted to talk to you without my cousin glowering in the background. Shall we have some coffee?' She stood up and headed towards the cappuccino maker and began operating it in a professional manner, fetching coffee from one of the cupboards and mugs from a drawer.

'You drove here to talk to me?' Laura asked in bewilderment. 'What about?'

'How do you take your coffee?'

'White, no sugar. Thank you.' Laura sat down and tilted her chair so that she could look at what Anna was doing.

'I needed to see Gabriel, actually. In fact, I telephoned the house, but you must have just left. The foreman there told me that you were heading down here. Apparently Gabriel had said that he was to lock up behind him because they were going to Berkshire and might not be back in time before they were due to leave. Naturally, I assumed that you would be coming here and I thought I would kill two birds with one stone. Discuss some business with Gabriel and also grab some time with you. Here you go, coffee almost as you would get it in a restaurant. Without the grated chocolate on top.' Without giving Laura time to ponder the little issue of why Gabriel's cousin wanted to talk to *her*, she rested the mug on the table and sat down.

She looked as stunning as she had done the first time

Laura had set eyes on her. Her brown hair was neatly tied back, though this time in a more casual French braid, to suit her more casual outfit of pale brown cord trousers, flat brogues and a cream, thin jersey top with a fine ribbed pattern running vertically down.

'So. How is the house coming along?'

'That's what you wanted to discuss?' Laura breathed a sigh of relief. 'Well, Gabriel suggested that we do the easy bits first, so at the moment I'm working on updating the house.' She grimaced and then smiled. 'Nothing has been done on it for as long as I can remember. All the wallpaper is being stripped and a lot of the furniture will be replaced. I shall keep a few of the old pieces that belonged to Mum and Dad and then sell the rest, although a lot of it will fetch token amounts. There's very little market for second-hand furniture these days.'

'And how do you feel about it? You know, working and renovating a house that used to belong to you?' Anna sipped some of her coffee whilst looking at Laura levelly over the rim of the mug.

'I look on the bright side. That things could have been a lot worse for me. At least I have a roof over my head and, when my job at the stables is over, I should have saved sufficient money to get a small place of my own.' Why did she get the feeling that they were skirting around an issue? Nibbling the appetiser in preparation for the main meal? And why did she get the feeling that the main meal was not going to be to her liking?

'And Gabriel has moved in, I gather?'

Laura flushed and drank some of her coffee. 'He said he wanted to be on hand so that he could have input into what was going on. He said that it would have been difficult to travel up when he was needed from London and that it was easier to communicate with his office via computer.' She half expected Anna to give a snort of laughter at that, but was disconcerted to find that she just continued looking thoughtfully at her, as if weighing up something in her mind.

'And you two...have become close, have you?'

Laura felt a brief flare of anger at the intrusiveness of the question, but it was immediately quenched by the gentle look in the other woman's eyes.

'I don't mean to be nosy,' Anna apologised. 'But Gabriel did explain a bit of the relationship between the two of you...that you used to know each other a long time ago...'

'I was still a teenager at the time. Gabriel came to the stables occasionally.'

'My cousin is a very passionate man, Laura...' Anna looked a little embarrassed at this observation but she drew in a deep breath and continued anyway. 'Under any other circumstances, I would leave him to get on with his life, but I like you and I disapprove of his tactics.'

'His tactics?' So here it was. The starter course was finished and they were on to the main meal and Laura knew exactly where it was heading.

'He rescued you from your situation so that he could avenge himself of what he saw as an insult delivered many years ago...' She paused and looked at Laura with blazing honesty. 'He can be a very persuasive man, full of charm. Too much charm, really, and I am only cautioning you against falling in love with him because he will hurt you.'

Too late for that little warning, Laura thought restlessly to herself, not that it would have helped anyway. She had never fallen out of love with him.

'I know you think that I am being intrusive, poking my nose in matters that do not concern me, but...' she sought around for a tactful way to say what she wanted to say

'…you strike me as a gentle, maybe emotionally vulnerable girl, even after all you have been through…'

Laura counteracted this accurate observation by gulping down some coffee and then staring fixedly at the pattern on her mug before reluctantly raising her eyes to meet Anna's.

'I can take care of myself.'

'Even when it comes to Gabriel?' She sighed. 'I gather that he is getting you out of his system and, in so doing, it would be easy for you to absorb him into yours and he will…he will never marry you.'

There. The finality of her words hung in the air between them and Laura drew her shoulders up.

'I'm not a fool. I know that. So it's just as well that I haven't made the mistake of falling in love with him, isn't it?'

'Isn't it just.' Gabriel's voice from the kitchen doorway exploded like a bomb in the kitchen and he walked towards them, his angled face devoid of expression. His hands were thrust into his trouser pockets and he didn't even dare look at Laura because to look at her would have been to be consumed with rage.

Had he expected anything else from her? He had wooed and seduced a woman who felt nothing for him but lust and all his plans for revenge lay in ruins around his feet because, fool that he was, he had actually committed the same cardinal sin he had committed years before. He had misread her signals and allowed himself to be lulled into loving her all over again.

He didn't know who filled him with more rage. Her or himself.

'Because Anna is absolutely right.' He stopped directly in front of Laura and steeled himself to meet her brown, dismayed eyes. 'I will never marry you.' Then he turned to his cousin with a hard expression. 'And you were totally out of order in coming here so that you could interfere in matters that do not concern you. Running around behind my back and stirring up trouble is not part of your job specification.'

'I could not live with my conscience if I had said nothing, Gabriel.'

'Which is hardly my problem. Now I think it is time you left.'

'I need to talk to you about a couple of our clients.'

'Not now.'

Anna stood up and glared accusingly at her cousin. In all fairness, Laura thought, she did not appear in the least intimidated.

'I'll leave,' Laura suggested, clearing her throat and standing up. She had slept with this man, loving him and knowing that he did not return her love, knowing that he was playing with her, but she had managed to justify her responses to herself because neither of them had crossed the dangerous barrier of discussing their emotions and what they felt or didn't feel. Now, though, with everything spilled out into the open, turning a blind eye to reality was no longer an option.

'Leave and go where?' Gabriel asked coldly and she flinched at the expression in his eyes.

'Back to Oakridge.'

'And how do you imagine you will get there?' he asked icily. 'Sprout wings and fly?' He knew that she was desperate to retreat and that whatever they'd had between them was well and truly over. He could read it in her brown eyes, which could barely meet his without sliding away. *So it's over*, he thought. Well, it was inevitable. But he felt as if a light was being turned off inside him. Light or not, though, he would not ask her back into his bed.

'I could wait and perhaps, Anna, you could give me a lift to the nearest station when you're leaving?'

'She will do no such thing. She is leaving right now and you will stay as planned.'

'Gabriel, let her go.'

'Goodbye, Anna. You know where the front door is. Feel free to use it. You can telephone me in the morning to discuss whatever business you wanted to discuss.' He didn't even bother glancing at his cousin when he said this. He just continued pinning Laura with his eyes into frozen immobility.

She felt rather than saw the other woman reluctantly leave the kitchen, but, instead of feeling relieved that at least one member in the cast of this awful, unfolding drama was out of the way, she was overcome with sudden, wild tension that made her legs shake, and she collapsed back onto the kitchen chair.

'You look nervous,' Gabriel said into the tautly stretching silence and he forced himself to offer her a mimicry of a smile. 'I have no idea why. You surely must have known all along that what we had was not going to go anywhere.'

'Of course I knew that, Gabriel.'

'So why do you look so shell-shocked? Nothing my cousin said should have disturbed you.' He hated himself for his reluctance to let her go. With controlled calmness, he walked across to a cupboard, extracted a bottle and proceeded to help himself to a generous serving of whisky, to which he added a couple of blocks of ice, but nothing else. He needed it. In fact, he had never needed a drink as much as he now needed this one. The stark realisation of how he felt about the woman sitting in muted silence only feet away from him had struck him where he hurt most.

At the very core of his masculine pride and at the heart of his formidable self-control.

'And don't think that you can start bleating on about being used.' He swigged back a mouthful of the drink. 'You threw yourself willingly at me.'

'I wasn't about to start bleating on about anything.'

'Then why the strained expression? I told you myself once that you meant nothing to me.' Just saying it made him feel a bastard but, in some crazy way, punishing her was to punish himself and it was something he was compelled to do.

'I know, but...'

He felt a flare of treacherous hope and squashed it ruthlessly. 'But you thought that you could change my mind? Is that it?' he taunted. 'Did you imagine that I would get so enraptured with your warm, available body that I would begin to hear the distant sound of wedding bells?'

'You sound as if you hate me, Gabriel,' Laura whispered. 'How could you have made love to me if you had hated me?'

'You flatter yourself. Hate is a big emotion.' He gave an expressive shrug of his big shoulders. 'We had an arrangement by mutual consent in which emotion did not play a part.'

'I think it's time I left.' She hoped that she would find the control of her legs that she needed and was relieved when they did not sink from under her as she rose to her feet and walked woodenly towards the kitchen door, skirting around so that she did not come within touching distance of him. 'I'll walk to the station if you're not prepared to drop me. Or I can get a taxi. Would you mind if I use your phone?'

'I take it that you do not wish to continue our love-making, which was so rudely interrupted an hour ago?'

Gabriel felt that his heart were being physically wrenched out of his chest.

'I think it's best if we stick to what we should have stuck to from the start,' Laura said, pausing to look at him, loving every ounce of the proud, cruel man standing across the kitchen from her. 'Business. If, that is, you still want me to work for you at the stables.'

'Why should that have changed?' He deposited his glass on the counter and then leaned against it, propping himself up by his hands. 'Of course, it might be a little awkward, in view of our new-found business-only relationship, if I were to carry on working at the house, so I will have my things collected some time tomorrow.'

He was letting her go without a backward glance, Laura thought in anguish, and, amidst all her emotions, at least surprise wasn't one of them. He had never lied to her. She was the one who had been guilty of lying to herself.

'And I shall drop you to the station myself. Never let it be said that I am not the perfect...' his mouth twisted cynically '...gentleman.'

The short ten-minute drive to the station was completed in total silence and he stopped the car only to allow her time to get out, not even killing the engine to imply that he might stick around if even to see that she got safely on a train back to the house.

The only words he spoke were to inform her that he expected to be kept advised of what was going on with the decorating of the house and that all major decisions were naturally to be referred to him, as her boss.

'Naturally,' Laura responded with equal cool and she held her head high as she walked away from him, only allowing her emotions to spill over when she was on the train heading back.

At least he would no longer be working under the same

roof and she would be spared having to live alongside him, without the joy of knowing his body at night. How easy it had been for her to ignore the truth and kid herself that it didn't really exist.

Anna had simply forced a situation and she should have been grateful for that because love just grew with time and her love would have known no boundaries.

It was late by the time she reached the house. The workmen had all left, thankfully, although the house hardly felt like a home with the wallpaper stripped from a lot of the walls and the downstairs carpet in the process of being removed.

Laura was barely aware of the chaos, however. She bypassed the kitchen, ignoring the rumbling in her stomach, and headed straight for the bedroom. Luxuriating in a bath seemed like a needless waste of time, so she had a quick shower instead, and then got into her pyjamas, which were items of clothing that she had not recently been wearing.

Gabriel had told her that he had liked to feel her nakedness next to him even when he was asleep, and she had been all too happy to oblige. Now they were a mocking reminder that all of that was over. She was back to pyjamas and loneliness with the added bonus of a future filled with anguished memories and regret.

Gabriel, she was sure, was not lying in his king-sized bed with its silk duvet, nursing thoughts of misery and loss. Hopefully, he was not flicking through his little black book and seeking out her immediate replacement. No, she more imagined him sitting in front of a computer somewhere in the house, in another of those designer-clad, soulless rooms, working.

He would have been. He should have been. If only he could manage to stand up without falling over. Alcohol never had been his way of dealing with anything but, from the relative comfort of a chair in one of the sitting areas, it seemed like a damned good idea. It blurred his feverish, maddening thoughts into a manageable numbness. Unfortunate that it also had such a numbing effect on his limbs, aside, that was, from his arm, which seemed to function perfectly when it came to topping up the whisky glass.

All he needed now was to fall asleep and be spared the occasional pain when a coherent thought managed to find its way to his brain, to remind him of what he had lost and to jeer at him for having got himself in such a position that he had been vulnerable enough to feel the pain of losing.

She didn't love him. Never had, never would. She had just enjoyed the sex he had provided. He had heard it with his own two ears, and, drunk or not, he was not so far gone that he couldn't remember that much. He had preached to her a load of bull that it shouldn't have made a scrap of difference, but he could have been preaching to himself because it did. He could never touch her again now that he knew, for sure, how emotionally indifferent she was to him, but he couldn't imagine a world in which she was not there to touch and talk to and laugh with. He shook his head in a dazed fashion and wondered whether another small drink might not send him into the arms of sweet, forgetful sleep. Unfortunately, the bottle, he realised, was empty, and he was too damned heavy-limbed to do anything about replacing it.

At a little past midnight, he finally drifted to sleep with the grim realisation that morning was not going to bring a whole lot more peace of mind.

But he would never go back to her. Even if being apart from her killed him in the process. He would have his things removed and keep in casual touch via telephone, or better still e-mail, even if that meant buying her a computer and getting someone to have it up and running. If he had to come face to face with her, he would bring someone in tow, preferably a very sexy woman, just to prove once and for all how little she had meant to him and to safeguard himself from doing something he might later regret. Such as fall back under her spell.

In a confused way, it all seemed to make sense when the alcohol was still swimming through his bloodstream, and in the morning, when he finally surfaced, he had enough wit to get on the phone and order his secretary to arrange for his things to be returned to London.

Which was why, soon after three in the afternoon, Laura was at hand to witness the quick and efficient departure of all evidence that Gabriel had ever set up office in the house.

She watched as every electronic item was carefully dismantled and boxed, and then signed the relevant sheet with an unsteady hand.

Then she sat at the now-empty dining table with her chin propped up in the palm of her hand and allowed her mind to drift away on its own unhappy course.

Only the sound of the telephone ringing brought her back to life, and when she heard Anna's voice down the line she almost wept at the vague contact with the man she loved.

'I'm phoning to say how sorry I am for…not minding my own business,' Anna said anxiously. 'I had no idea how deep in you both were. And I certainly never expected that Gabriel would sneak up on us the way he did.'

'I'm not in deep,' Laura denied weakly. 'So we slept together, but we're adults. It's not unheard of, you know, sex between two consenting adults who are attracted to one another, even though there's no emotional commitment. It doesn't mean…it doesn't mean that…' She couldn't complete the rest of her empty protest.

'Oh, but it does. I could see for myself, Laura.'

'I… Oh, why am I lying? What's the use? I was always in love with him, but everything comes to an end and there's no need to apologise, Anna. You did what you thought was the right thing to do and…*both*? We weren't *both* deep in anything. *I* was deep in, but you heard Gabriel yourself and I can't even say that he strung me along because he didn't. I think a part of me was just always waiting for him to come back, so that I could pick up where we left off, unconditionally.'

'So now you are back at the riding stables and he has remained at that gruesome mausoleum of his in Berkshire, am I correct?'

'You're correct.'

'And presumably the fool has had all his things removed from the house?'

'They've just taken away his fax machine, his computer, all the office equipment…'

'And you let them?'

'Of course I let them!' Laura said robustly. 'What else was I supposed to do? Fling my arms across the door and refuse them entry to a house that doesn't even belong to me? Two strapping men?'

'And you have not considered fighting for Gabriel?'

'Fighting how?' Laura wailed. 'He doesn't want me!'

'If Gabriel did not want you, he would never have returned in the first place. He would have read about the stables, had a chuckle and moved on to the next page. If he did not want you, his eyes would not have burned with anger when he realised that you wanted to leave his house with me. Gabriel is a blind idiot and one day, when all this is over, I am going to get him to grovel at my feet in gratitude for being the interfering old bag that I am!' And she sounded so spirited and so convincing that foolish thoughts began to multiply in Laura's head and she seized the thread of hope they promised with both hands, rushing to get her diary when Anna suggested that they meet up and chat.

She flicked through the pages, then flicked back through them and a little cold film of perspiration broke out all over her at what she was seeing for the first time.

Her period. Where was it? For years she had adhered to her mother's guidelines about always writing the commencement of her period in her diary because *a woman could not afford not to be tuned into her reproductive system.* But they had been very careful. From the very first, he had taken the necessary precautions. Well...not from the *very first*, Laura thought slowly. No, that first time had been when they had gone riding and she had surrendered. Which had been...a few weeks ago.

But she had had no symptoms. No sickness, no tiredness, no increased appetite. Nothing.

'Hello? Are you still there?'

'Yes,' Laura said faintly. 'Look, someone has just banged at the front door. Can I get back to you with a date? I'd love to meet up.'

Her heart was pounding when she replaced the receiver, although when she told the foreman that she was just stepping out for half an hour or so her voice sounded perfectly normal.

Stepping out to go to the nearest pharmacy, even though she knew in her gut that the trip was unnecessary. Unless her reproductive system had decided to go on a short holiday to cope with all the recent emotional turmoil, she was pregnant.

Nevertheless when, a little over an hour later, she saw

two clear blue lines appear in the two windows of the device that boasted a ninety-nine per-cent accuracy rate, Laura gave a little moan of shock.

So what happened next?

What happens, a little voice in her head said, is you pick up that telephone and you arrange to meet Gabriel. No point waiting for him to call at some point in time, because that point in time was never going to arrive. Gabriel's pride was as big as a mountain. He would never come back to her, and, despite what Anna had said, she really didn't know *what* his feelings towards her were. Yes, he wanted her, or at least he had done. And he was not as indifferent emotionally to her as he pretended to be. That, at any rate, was what she was going to have to believe when she picked that phone up in five minutes' time.

He wasn't in. Big anticlimax. But his secretary must have detected the urgency in her voice because she gave Laura his mobile phone number.

This time he did answer and in a voice that left Laura in no doubt that, whatever he was doing, he was not going to have the time to listen to what she had to say.

'You need to cultivate a better telephone manner,' were her first nervous words and she punctuated the observation with shaky laughter.

Hearing her voice was so unexpected that it took Gabriel a few seconds before he realised that he was talking to the woman who had plagued his thoughts the night before. He had missed a breakfast meeting because he had just not been able to get out of bed in time to make it to the Savoy and he had only just managed to get to his second scheduled meeting for the day, at an impressive smoked-glass building in Canary Wharf.

He abruptly halted his long stride through the offices of DuBarry, obliging the personal assistant who was leading him through to the boardroom to stop as well, and cupped the cell phone in the palm of his hand.

How dared she? How dared she telephone him, *using his mobile phone number no less*, when he was about to go into a very important meeting, after he had made it absolutely clear that he wanted nothing more to do with her? That she could take a running jump off the side of a very steep cliff! Had she no respect for a single word he had spoken?

'What do you want?' God, it was bloody good to hear her voice.

'I hope I'm not interrupting anything.'

'You are, as a matter of fact. Now get to the point, Laura.' He made sure to invest his voice with supreme indifference, overlaid with just the right amount of irritation that would indicate a busy man who had no time for some insignificant ex-lover. He placed his hand over the receiver and whispered to the personal assistant, a ferociously competent-looking woman in her mid-fifties with disciplined hair and a face that would terrify the most hardened of men, that she would have to go ahead of him and explain that he was dealing with a very important call, and would be in as soon as possible.

'I want to talk to you.'

'You have my e-mail address. You will have to learn to make decisions without running to me every two seconds. I thought I had made it perfectly clear to you that you and I are finished and the less contact I have with you, the happier I will be. Now, if that is all...'

Laura gritted her teeth together and clenched her fist. 'I want to see you and it's not about the house.'

'Oh, no? Then what do you want to talk to me about?' He glanced at his watch and realised that he would have to get a move on if he was to complete this meeting in time for his next one. Still. Disgusted though he felt with himself, there was no way he could dismiss her. Just the sound of her voice was sending his system into overdrive.

'I want to talk to you about us,' Laura said bluntly.

'I really have no time for this,' Gabriel said dismissively. 'I am very busy.' The personal assistant reappeared and he glowered at her.

'I don't care how busy you are, Gabriel. I'm not prepared for things between us to end this way.'

'*You* are not prepared?'

'That's right. *I* am not prepared and I shall just keep pestering you until you…meet me.'

'Oh, very well. I will drive up to the house this afternoon. I should be there early evening, but I can warn you now that there will be no point to the meeting.'

Laura was shaking by the time she dropped the receiver back onto its handset. She didn't dare start having doubts about what she had done now that she had done it, but she couldn't help herself. They crept in like pernicious tentacles of ivy and sought to wrap themselves around the fragile little fragments of courage she had tried to instil within herself.

By the time the workmen were leaving the house, she had analysed and re-analysed every nuance of every expression she had ever seen cross his face, searching desperately for signs of hope that he might care about her. She could deal with his pride and his indifference, provided at least some of it was just a veneer, but what if his indifference really did run bone-deep? What if Anna had been utterly wrong?

Eventually, as Laura quickly changed into a pair of jeans and a fresh top she abandoned her pointless train of thoughts and told herself that, at the end of the day, she had no choice but to see him anyway. She was carrying his baby and there was no way she would want to keep him in ignorance of that fact, even if there was a chance that she could have. A father deserved every chance to know of the existence of his child, just as the child would deserve every chance to know of his or her father. Any other route was unthinkable.

She was peering through the side window when Gabriel's car drew up and her heart clenched as he stepped out of the driver's seat and glanced once around him. He had come straight from work. He was still in his suit, although the tie had been removed and the top two buttons of his white shirt were undone. She imagined him restlessly tugging it off as he drove up to the house.

Her courage of earlier on was disappearing at a rate of knots, and by the time she went to the door, where the doorbell was imperiously issuing its summons, it had completely vanished. She literally had no idea what to say as she pulled open the door and was confronted by the harsh, cold expression of two dangerously dark eyes staring at her.

'Gabriel. Hi.'

'You said that you wanted to talk, so here I am. It has been a long trip up through traffic and it will take at least an hour and a half to get back home, so shall we get this talk over and done with as soon as possible?'

Making it clear what his intentions were, Laura thought with plummeting self-confidence. He had come but he was not going to stay the night, whatever she had to say…

CHAPTER TEN

THE kitchen was one of the few rooms as yet untouched by the workforce and Gabriel followed Laura into it, keeping a telling distance and focusing on the bitter pill that he had been forced to swallow and that still stuck in his throat like a bone. What did she want to talk to him about? If she thought that she could wriggle back into his bed and his life, then she was way off target. God, how had he managed to get himself into this hole? The answer, he thought savagely, was quite simple: he had found a spade, dug it and jumped in whilst telling himself that he was totally in control.

His faraway plan to avenge himself for the insult delivered to him seven years previously could not have gone more disastrously wrong. Instead of using her ruthlessly so that he could eventually discard her in his own sweet time, he had caved in once again and the only means he had of extricating himself from the mess was to walk away from it as quickly as his long legs could carry him.

Even looking at her now, the way her body moved like a gazelle in front of him, mesmerised him.

His overriding urge was to close the distance between them, swing her around and make her his.

'Have you eaten?'

She was looking at him, all wide brown eyes and appealing hesitation.

'I am fine. Why don't we just have a cup of coffee and you can tell me what was so important that you felt you had to drag me out here?'

God, but he wasn't making this easy. Laura gritted her teeth together and thought of the little life growing steadily inside her. The thought of tossing that little fact his way made her want to faint.

'Sure, but, if you don't mind, I'll just fix myself something to eat as well.' She knew that he wasn't even looking at her as she busied herself by the counter, making them both a cup of coffee and rustling together the vegetables she had previously chopped and prepared.

The opening remarks she made, about nothing in particular, were met with monosyllabic answers and a tone of disinterest.

This was the behaviour of a man who cared?

Eventually, she turned around, her plate in her hand, and sat facing him at the table.

'So,' Gabriel remarked, finally affording her his attention, 'why don't you just say what you have to say and get it over with, Laura? Instead of the both of us playing this game of polite strangers.'

'Because we're not, are we, Gabriel?'

The directness of her reply took him aback and he narrowed his eyes at her upturned face as she continued to look at him levelly across the table.

'We're lovers.'

'*Were* lovers. You need to get the tense right.'

'What changed, Gabriel? One minute we were on the brink of making love and the next minute you had turned into a raging bull and what we had was gone in a puff of smoke. Was it so meaningless to you?'

A dark flush spread over his high cheekbones. 'If this is going to be a post mortem on a failed relationship, then you are wasting your time.'

'Why? Because you think that I should meekly walk away and accept that I meant nothing to you?'

'I dislike women who cannot face the end of a relationship.' Gabriel shrugged with exaggerated indifference. 'All good things come to an end.' He had won, he thought. He had her in the palm of his hand. That had been his intention. So why was he feeling so damned hollow? Because he had fallen in love with her. Again. Her body was never going to be good enough and he knew that if he allowed her back in, she would wreak further devastation on his heart. But, God, he didn't want to leave this house, this kitchen, *her*.

'Why?'

'Why what?'

'Why do all good things have to come to an end? Are you implying that the only relationship you will ever consider with a woman is one that *isn't* good?'

'Relationships are possible without all the trappings that society forces us to accept.'

'By trappings you mean…what? Love? Marriage?' The last thing she wanted was for this conversation to be reduced to the level of a hypothetical debate, but he just wasn't going to give an inch. If she mentioned the word marriage, he would oblige her by talking about it as an institution, if she mentioned love, he would analyse the meaning of the word and then dismiss it. She shook her head in frustration and rested her forehead lightly on the palm of her hand.

'Have you brought me here so that you can hear me tell you again that I have no intention of ever asking you to marry me?' Gabriel's mouth twisted cynically and she flinched, but held her ground.

'I would never expect you to ask me to marry you, Gabriel,' Laura returned softly.

'Then what?' he grated irritably. He was beginning to

feel uncomfortably hot, and he ran one long brown finger inside the collar of his shirt.

Laura chose to ignore that pointed question. His voice might be callously dismissive and his eyes were as hard as ice, but he was uncomfortable. She could sense it and that gave her failing courage a bit of a boost. She loved this man and she was going to fight for him, and if it didn't work out the way she hoped, then so be it. Better to fight and lose than to walk away and then spend the rest of her life regretting her passivity.

'So if relationships and commitment and marriage isn't about love, Gabriel, what is it all about?'

He shrugged and stood up. He had to. He had to move. The contained energy inside him was killing him.

He restlessly began to prowl through the kitchen, hands shoved aggressively into his pockets, whilst his dark eyes swept over the blonde figure sitting quietly on the chair.

What was she trying to say to him? That she couldn't do without his body? That she was prepared to beg and plead just so that she could get her daily fix of sex? But if sex was what she was after, then why hadn't she greeted him at the door in the clothes of seduction? Small, revealing and provocative?

'Who knows?' he answered ambiguously. 'Maybe the best relationship is one based on business.'

'I thought that that was precisely what we had,' Laura replied drily.

'Not quite the sort of business I had in mind,' Gabriel said smoothly. 'I meant business that involves a two-way profit.' He picked up a small flowerpot resting on the counter, in which a clump of basil was struggling to grow, and inspected it in some detail before putting it down.

'Gabriel, sit down. I can't concentrate when you're

stalking through this kitchen like a cat burglar on the look-out for the family heirlooms.'

'What is there to concentrate on?' He felt a fierce tug of excitement and fought it tooth and nail.

'I don't want what we have to end,' Laura began, drawing in a deep breath and watching as Gabriel pushed back his chair and proceeded to inspect her through half-closed eyes. 'And before you open your mouth to speak, let me just finish.'

He could have told her that the last thing he was going to do was open his mouth. Behind the scowling façade, he was hanging onto her every word.

'Seven years ago, you walked away and I let you. I let you because I was young and marriage was something that I had never, ever even contemplated. Maybe my parents had something to do with it, I don't know. But I was a fool.'

'Especially when you look at me now,' Gabriel intoned grimly.

'That has nothing to do with it,' Laura told him impatiently. 'I don't care whether you made a million or not. What I care about is that you…came back. And I know why you came back…' All of this was hard and it took every ounce of courage she possessed to lay every card on the table, but this part was the hardest. Acknowledging the cold, ugly truth that had brought him to her aid. She could feel a lump of self-pity gather at the back of her throat and she choked it down.

'You came back,' she continued in a whispered monotone, 'because you wanted revenge and what better revenge than to have me in a position of indebtedness to you. The shoe was on the other foot, as far as you were concerned, and you could have the last laugh. But what matters to me is that you came back. I realised that I loved you then and I never stopped loving you.' She glared at him, daring him to sneer at the admission that had drained her, but he didn't. He looked lost for words.

'You expect me to believe that? I heard you tell Anna just the opposite, *querida*.' He didn't dare give way, but his heart was soaring like a bird. He wanted to jump up, sing, wrap his arms around her, all at the same time.

'When?'

'When? What do you mean *when*? Yesterday, of course. When the two of you were having your cosy chat in my kitchen.'

'I spoke to Anna this morning and told her everything. Well, almost everything.' Laura sighed and ran her fingers through her hair. She was perspiring, as if she had run a marathon, and her hands were shaking. 'I told her how I felt about you. I can't change how you feel, whether you believe me or not, but...' she met his eyes steadily, without blinking '...I love you, Gabriel Greppi, and I wouldn't be able to live with myself if this all fizzled out and you never knew how I really felt. When I told Anna that I wasn't involved with you, I was lying. It's as simple as that. I had a moment of pride. I might have thought that you...would have recognised the passing weakness.' She paused long enough for the silence to settle, and then said shakily, 'Aren't you going to say anything? Even if all you have to say is that you don't believe a word I'm saying?'

'I cannot ask you to marry me...I asked you once...' *A moment of pride!* He had a lifetime of pride. He couldn't ask her to marry him, not again, even though he believed every word she had just spoken. The truth of it was shining in her eyes. But his pride.

'Is that all you have to say, Gabriel?' Laura stood up. 'Nothing else? You damned, stubborn...okay, you win. I've told you how I feel and if you have nothing to say, then you were right, it's over.' She had gambled everything. What price one more gamble?

His head shot up and he stood up as well, moving swiftly over to her.

'I…'

'Marry me.' Laura looked at him with blazing challenge. 'What we have is good, very good, and it'll get better. Take a chance.'

'You're asking me to marry you?' His face darkened and he dropped his head.

'That's right. Marry me.'

'Or else what?'

'Or else you'll regret giving up the greatest love you will ever know.' She tentatively placed her hand on the side of his face and caressed his skin.

'No,' he murmured hoarsely.

So this was it. She had taken the gamble and lost.

'Right,' Laura said hollowly.

'I mean, no, I would not just regret giving up the greatest love I will ever know…I would regret a great deal more than that…' He tilted her chin so that she was looking at him and what she read on his face, the tenderness and love, made the breath catch in her throat. 'I lost the only thing worth having the day I walked out of your life, my darling.' He buried his head into her neck and then, when he had gathered his self-control, that priceless commodity that had been in very short supply ever since he had gone barging back into her life, he raised his head once again to catch her eyes with his.

'I came back, yes, for the lowest of reasons. I thought I was over you and that I was simply closing a chapter. God help me, I saw myself as the all-powerful one who had returned to settle old scores. But the fact is, there were no scores to settle. I should never have let my pride kill our relationship then. I should have listened to what you were saying because every word you said was right. We were both young. We could have waited a little longer, grown to know each other better, but I was having none of it. When I think that this cursed pride of mine would have caused my own destruction a second time, my blood runs cold.'

'You love me,' Laura said with a wondering smile.

'I adore you. When you called me on my mobile this morning and told me that you wanted to see me, to talk, I couldn't wait for my meetings to be over. I couldn't wait to be in your presence again because it's only when you are around that I feel alive.'

'And you'll marry me?'

'You don't intend to let me wriggle away again, do you, *querida*?' This time he gave a low, velvety chuckle that made her go to liquid inside.

'That's certainly one of the reasons.'

'One of the reasons?'

'Would you mind if we sat down? I feel as if my legs are going to buckle from under me.'

Thank goodness the kitchen stools were generously built. Big enough for Gabriel to comfortably sit with Laura on his lap. She rested her head on his shoulder and realised, suddenly, that the full extent of his love was about to take a serious knock. Marriage, passion and a three-year honeymoon spelled a different story from marriage, a swelling stomach and midnight feeds.

'Better?' he murmured into her ear. 'Perhaps we should go upstairs, lie down on the bed. Altogether more satisfactory for what I have in mind, now that I have been browbeaten into marrying you, you beautiful witch.'

'Okay, but first there's something else I have to tell you.' She sat up and looked him straight in the eye. What she saw was a tiny, black-eyed infant with a mop of curly dark hair and a gummy smile. 'If we get married, it might be an idea for it to be sooner rather than later.'

Comprehension took a matter of seconds. She could see it dawning in his eyes and then he grinned with radiant, unchecked joy. 'You are pregnant?'

'I did the test this morning. I…it happened the first time we made love, when we didn't use any protection. If you don't want to marry me now that you know, then I'll understand. It's a big responsibility and it's just been dropped on your lap like a bombshell.'

'Not want to marry you?' He placed his hand on her stomach, still flat and toned. 'There is no way I would *not* marry you, and the fact that you are pregnant with my child, *our* child, is the icing on the cake.' He stroked her stomach in slow circles and Laura's breathing quickened, a little fact that did not escape his notice.

'Perhaps we *should* go upstairs,' she murmured, catching the satisfied expression on his face and blushing.

'Oh, yes? And what did you have in mind when we get there?'

'You know exactly what I have in mind!' She led him up the stairs, holding his hand, and only paused to look at him when they were on the threshold of the bedroom. 'I shall lose my figure,' she warned him and he nodded.

'So perhaps I ought to explore you thoroughly now, mmm? Before our baby starts pushing out your stomach and making those breasts of yours heavy and big with milk? I find the thought of you pregnant very erotic, as a matter of fact…'

And he then proceeded to show her how erotic he found her. But nothing could be as erotic as the thought that at long last the dream of happiness had become reality and that from here onwards their steps forward would be taken together…for ever.

EPILOGUE

'GABRIEL, darling…' It was three-seventeen in the morning. Laura could glimpse the illuminated hands of the clock on the table next to her beloved husband, whose naked body was warm next to hers. She brushed her lips against his cheek and then grimaced as another contraction hardened her stomach.

Nearly two weeks overdue and a girl, Gabriel was forever telling her with a grin, because only a female would keep everyone waiting for as long as she had done.

'Gabriel, don't panic, but…'

It must have been the word *panic* that did it because his eyes flicked open and the first words he uttered were a heartfelt, *'Dios!'*

'I'm only just beginning,' Laura said soothingly, gritting her teeth together as another contraction ripped through her, and watching with amusement as Gabriel leapt out of the bed and began flinging on his clothes, only switching the light on as an afterthought.

'Laura, my sweetest, God, you are in pain.'

'It happens around this time of the pregnancy.' She began edging herself off the bed and he raced to her side, half tripping over his trousers, which were not fully on.

'You're wincing. You're trying to be brave but you're wincing. I am not blind! I can see!'

'Calm down.'

'How can I calm down? Your bag. I'll get your bag. Where *is* your bag? Of course I know where your bag is! Stay calm, Laura, don't panic!'

He had solicitously helped her pack her bag over a month ago, insisting on adding so many unlisted items to the contents that in the end she had warned him that he might have to buy a trunk to hold it all.

'I'm not…'

'And do not get dressed!' he ordered from their *en suite* dressing room, from which he was fetching the bag as well as jumpers and coats for them both. 'I will help you!'

'I think I can manage.' Sometimes she wondered why she bothered to say certain things when she could always so accurately predict his responses. As she expected, he completed the job of getting her nightdress off, his voice laced with frantic panic as he demanded to know whether she was up to changing or whether they should just fling a coat over her and hurry to the hospital. Maybe, he fulminated, they should take the helicopter.

'I don't think the hospital has anywhere for helicopters to land,' Laura said lovingly.

'I'll carry you to the car.'

'I can walk, you idiot. Just support me a little.'

Seven months of wedded bliss and she was still awestruck at the love that could so easily have eluded her, a love that seemed to grow with each passing minute. Their wedding had been simple and attended only by his closest family members and their mutual friends and she had enjoyed every second of it, basking in his tenderness and adoration, which he made no attempt to hide.

She could sense his frustration as he navigated the dark lanes, and finally the wider, better-lit roads, that he couldn't take the pain away from her. By the time they reached the hospital, he was far more jittery than she was and she had to murmur softly that there was no need to worry, that everything was perfectly straightforward and, really, the staff there knew how to deal with women in labour.

'How can you be so calm?' he accused, seething with annoyance at the seemingly languid manner in which they were checked in whilst he tapped his foot and glowered.

'One of us has to be.'

'I am calm.'

'Oh, yes, as calm as someone on the verge of a nervous breakdown.' Their eyes met and Gabriel felt his heart swell with love, then finally things started happening. They were shown to the labour ward and after a brief examination, from which he was excluded by some very decisive drawing of curtains around the bed, the next few hours raced by with the terrifying speed of a runaway train.

And there was nothing he could do! Only be with the woman he loved, hold her hand, mop her brow and try to remember all those pearls of wisdom he had read in the various pregnancy books he had devoured, much to his wife's amusement, and most of which he had now comprehensively forgotten.

'She's doing fine, Mr Greppi,' one of the two midwives told him at some point in the proceedings, 'but you look as though you could use a cup of tea. She'll be here for at least another couple of hours. Why don't you go down to the canteen and have something hot to drink?'

'I'm here for the duration.'

'Well, just don't go fainting on me.'

'I never faint. Shouldn't there be a consultant in here?'

'I've delivered more babies than you've had hot dinners, young man.' But the middle-aged woman grinned and winked at him. 'She'll be fine.'

Never in his life had Gabriel felt more racked with nerves and never in his life had he ever been so reduced to speechless awe than when, an hour and a half later, he glimpsed his baby as one final push expelled his son. Eight pounds, eleven ounces and groggily unaware of his surroundings until he drew in his breath and released an outraged shriek.

'It's a baby boy,' the midwife said, bustling with him and then handing him wrapped in a blanket to Laura. 'What a lot of hair.'

Laura looked down at the small bundle lying against her, fists closed and eyelids fluttering, and smiled.

'We have a son.' Pride and joy threatened to make his eyes water. 'Didn't I tell you that it would be a boy?' He stroked Laura's blonde hair away from her face, which was still glistening with perspiration, and she glanced up at him with a tender smile.

'Did you?'

'Of course I did,' Gabriel said gruffly. 'And look at that mop of black hair. He looks just like his father.' He bent to kiss his wife and then the small, warm cheek of his baby and watched in fascination as the little bundle wriggled and stretched and then settled back into position.

'My family,' he said with a lump in his throat. 'My perfect family.'

RYAN'S REVENGE

by

Lee Wilkinson

Lee Wilkinson lives with her husband in a three-hundred-year-old stone cottage in a Derbyshire village, which most winters gets cut off by snow. They both enjoy travelling and recently, joining forces with their daughter and son-in-law, spent a year going round the world 'on a shoestring' while their son looked after Kelly, their much loved German shepherd dog. Her hobbies are reading and gardening and holding impromptu barbecues for her long-suffering family and friends.

Don't miss Lee Wilkinson's exciting new novel *The Bejewelled Bride* out in November 2006 from Mills & Boon Modern Romance™

CHAPTER ONE

WARM June sunshine poured in through the open window, a beneficence after the late and miserably cold spring. In nearby Kenelm Park a dog yapped excitedly, shrill above the continuous, muted roar of London's traffic.

Glancing from her second-floor window, Virginia saw between the trees the flash of a bright red ball being thrown, and smiled, before returning to her cataloging.

A moment later the internal phone on her desk rang. Reaching out a slender, long-fingered hand she picked up the receiver. 'Yes?'

Helen's voice said formally, 'Miss Ashley, there's a gentleman here asking if we have any paintings by either Brad or Mia Adams. I've explained that there are none listed, but he'd like to know if we're able to acquire any.'

During the past ten years the Adams' work had become widely sought after, and Virginia had grown used to the idea of her parents being well known—at least in the world of art.

'I'll come down,' she said.

Helen Hutchings, a nice-looking forty-year-old widow, handled casual sales of the good contemporary art that the Charles Raynor Gallery displayed, while Virginia dealt with specialist requests or queries.

Checking that no wisps of silky ash-brown hair had escaped from her neat chignon, and donning the heavy glasses that changed her appearance and made her look considerably older than her twenty-four years, she left her office, slender and business-like in a charcoal-grey silk suit.

The long oval gallery had a balcony running around it and was open to the skylights, where today the oatmeal-

5

coloured blinds were in place because of the bright sun-shine.

Peering over the wrought-iron balcony rail, she saw that a few people, mainly tourists she judged, were browsing. At the far end, she caught a glimpse of a tall, well-built man with dark hair who was standing by the reception desk.

His stance was easy, anything but impatient, yet he had an unmistakable air of *waiting*.

As she reached the stairs, which at the bottom were roped off with a crimson and gold tasselled cord that held a notice saying Private, he turned to glance in her direction.

Ryan.

There was no mistaking that lean, hard-boned face, the set of the shoulders, the carriage of that dark head, the strong yet graceful physique.

Though it was much too far away to see the colour of his eyes, she knew quite well that they were midway between dark blue and violet.

Her breath caught in her throat. Virginia stopped dead, gripping the banister rail convulsively.

Even after her flight from New York and her return to London she had been afraid of seeing him, on edge and wary of every tall, dark-haired man who came into sight.

Only over the last six months or so had she started to feel relatively safe, confident that she had left the past behind her.

Now it seemed that her confidence had been premature.

Her heart was beginning to pound and, a rush of adrenalin galvanising her into action, she turned and fled back to the safety of her office.

Sinking down at her desk, her stomach churning sickeningly, she prayed that he hadn't seen and recognised her.

If he *had*, Ryan wasn't the kind of man to walk quietly away. Remembering how he'd said, 'I'll never let you go,' she shuddered.

In spite of all that had been between them she had left

him. Unable to bear the pain of his perfidy, afraid to confront him for fear of what damage it might do to the family, she had run without a word.

He wouldn't easily forgive her for that.

But if he *hadn't* recognised her, the situation could be saved...

Hoping against hope that Charles was back from his early afternoon appointment, she reached for the internal phone.

There was no answer from his office, which was on the ground floor, and she tried the private showroom and then, in mounting desperation, the strongroom.

When, his voice sounding abstracted, he answered, 'Yes... What is it?' Virginia could have wept with relief.

'I'm sorry to disturb you, but could you possibly find time to see a prospective customer who's waiting at reception?'

'What does he or she want?' he queried in his rather dry, precise manner.

'He asked if we can acquire any Adams paintings.'

Sounding surprised, Charles said, 'Surely you can deal with that?'

'It's someone I...once knew, and I'd rather not have to meet again.'

Though Virginia had done her best to play it down, with the perception of a man in love, he picked up the urgency. 'Very well. Leave it to me.'

Fear darkening her grey-green eyes almost to charcoal, she wondered, why, oh, why, out of all the art galleries in London, had Ryan chanced to come into this one?

Since her return to London two-and-a-half years ago, she had used her middle name as a surname and had virtually lived in hiding. No one knew where she was. Not even her parents.

She had been staying in a cheap hotel off the Bayswater

Road and, with very little money and Christmas coming up, had been badly in need of a job.

The employment agency she'd approached had sent her to the Raynor Gallery where she had been interviewed by Charles himself.

She had told him about the course on the practical and administrative side of art she had taken at college, and had explained, without giving any details, that she had just returned from the States.

After studying her thoughtfully while she spoke, he had offered her a post as his assistant.

After she had been working for him for almost a year, the gallery had started to handle the Adams' work, and when Charles had suggested that *she* should be their contact she had been forced to tell him at least part of the truth.

'Virginia, my dear,' he protested, 'as you're their daughter, surely—'

'I don't want them to know where I am.'

They were acquainted with Ryan, and that made any communication with them potentially dangerous.

Charles frowned. 'But won't they worry about you?'

'No, I'm certain they won't. You see we've never been a family in the real sense of the word.'

Seeing he was unconvinced, she explained, 'Mother was fresh out of art school when she met my father, who was over from the States.

'They'd both been painting since they were children, and lived for art. That's probably what drew them together.

'After they married they lived in Greenwich Village for several years before coming back to settle in England. By the time I was born they were well into their thirties.

'I was a mistake. Neither of them wanted me. If mother hadn't been brought up to believe life was sacred, I think she might well have had an abortion.'

'Oh surely not!' Charles, a mild-mannered, conventional man, sounded shocked by her bluntness.

'They were both so wrapped up in their work that a baby was an unlooked-for and unwelcome complication in their lives...'

Though she spoke flatly, dispassionately, he could feel her abiding sense of rejection, and his heart bled for her.

'They were well-off financially, and their solution was a series of nannies, and a girl's boarding school as soon as I was old enough.

'I was on the point of leaving school and starting college when they went back to New York to live.'

'They left you behind?'

'I was nearly eighteen by then.'

'But surely they helped to support you? Financially, I mean?'

'No, I didn't want them to. I preferred to take evening and weekend jobs and stay independent...

'So you see, not knowing where I am now won't worry them in the slightest. In fact I doubt if they ever give me a thought.'

'Very well, if you're sure?'

'I'm quite sure.'

'Then, I'll deal with them personally.'

'You won't say anything?' she asked anxiously.

'Not a word. Your secret's safe with me.'

She felt a rush of affection for him. He was a thoroughly nice man and, knowing that he would keep his promise, she breathed easier.

Until now...

The latch clicked.

She glanced up sharply, her heart in her mouth.

It was Charles, neat and conservative in a lightweight business suit, a lock of fair hair falling over his high forehead giving him a boyish air that belied his forty-three years.

Seeing her face had lost all trace of colour, he said reassuringly, 'There's no need to look so concerned. He's gone.'

Perhaps, subconsciously, she had been half expecting Ryan to come bursting in, and relief was washing over her like a warm tide when a sudden thought made her query anxiously, 'He didn't ask about me?'

Dropping into the chair opposite, Charles raised a fair brow. 'Why should he?'

She worried her lower lip. 'I'd started to go down when I realised who it was. I thought he might have seen and recognised me.'

'He made no mention of it,' Charles assured her calmly. 'And, as he appears to be the type who wouldn't have hesitated to ask about anything he wanted to know, I think we can safely assume he didn't.'

Watching Virginia relax perceptibly, he wondered what had passed between her and the powerful-looking man he'd just been talking to.

From her reactions it was clear that her feelings had been a great deal deeper than her casual 'someone I once knew' had implied. It might even be part of the reason she had refused his offer of marriage...

Hoping for further reassurance that Ryan's visit *had* been just chance, she asked, 'What did he actually say? How did he act?'

'His manner was quite straightforward and purposeful. He told me his name was Ryan Falconer, and that he'd like to acquire, amongst other things, some of the earlier Adams paintings. I promised I'd put out some feelers and let him know the chances as soon as possible...'

'Is he staying in England?'

'For a few days, apparently. As well as his home address in Manhattan, he gave me the phone number of a Mayfair hotel.'

Mayfair. She repressed a shiver. Practically on their doorstep and much too close for comfort.

'Though he's primarily a businessman, a Wall Street investment banker, I understand, he's interested in art and owns the Falconer Gallery in New York... But possibly you knew that?'

'Yes.'

When she failed to elaborate, Charles went on, 'However, I gather the paintings he's hoping to buy are for his private collection. He mentioned one by Mia Adams that he'd particularly like to own, *Wednesday's Child...*'

She froze.

'Falconer believes it was painted seven or eight years ago, and is one of her best. Though I must say I've never heard of it... He made it clear that money's no object, so I've promised to do what I can. Of course, even if I'm able to locate it, the present owner might not be willing to sell.'

Something about Virginia's utter stillness made Charles ask, 'Do *you* remember it by any chance?'

Taking a deep breath, she admitted, 'As a matter of fact I do. I sat for it. I wasn't quite seventeen.'

His light blue eyes glowing with interest, he exclaimed, 'I didn't realise your mother had ever used you as a model!'

'It was just the once. I'd been invited to spend the summer holidays with a school friend—Jane belonged to a big happy family, and I was looking forward to it—but at the last minute the visit had to be cancelled, so I went home.

'Mother said that as I was there she might as well make use of me. I tried hard to do just as she wanted, but for some reason she disliked the finished portrait, and she never asked me to sit again.'

'What did *you* think of it?'

'I didn't see it,' Virginia said flatly. 'She told me that it needed framing, and the next time I went home, it had been sold...'

And now Ryan wanted to buy it.

That fact disturbed her almost as much as seeing him again...

But maybe it was just chance that had made him specify *Wednesday's Child*? Maybe he didn't know that she had been the sitter?

Almost before the thought was completed, a sure and certain instinct told her it was no chance. He *knew* all right.

She shivered.

Watching her face, Charles asked shrewdly, 'If I am able to locate and acquire that particular painting, how do you feel about Falconer having it?'

With careful understatement, she admitted, 'I'd rather he didn't.'

'Then, I'll tell him I had no luck.'

Recalling the problems and financial losses that Charles had suffered over the past year, she swallowed hard and made herself say, 'No, if you *are* able to acquire it and he's willing to pay well, you mustn't let my silly prejudices stand in the way of business.'

'Well, we'll see,' he said noncommittally. 'Things might well be looking up.'

Before she could question that somewhat cryptic statement, he glanced at his watch. 'It's almost four o'clock. I'd best be getting on.'

Rising to his feet, a tall, spare figure with slightly rounded shoulders, he suggested with the solicitude he always displayed for her, 'You're looking a bit peaky, why don't you go home?'

Thoroughly unsettled, her head throbbing dully, and never having felt less like work, she said gratefully, 'I've got a bit of a headache, so I think I will, if you really don't mind?'

Smiling, he shook his head. 'As it's Monday, I'm quite sure Helen and I can deal with anything that may crop up in the next hour or so.'

At the door, he paused to say, 'Oh, by the way, I won't be coming home at the usual time. I've agreed to have dinner with the client I saw earlier this afternoon...'

Her heart sank. Somehow, after what had happened, she needed his comforting, undemanding presence.

'And as it's my turn to cook—' when Virginia had first moved into his spare room, they had reached an amicable arrangement whereby they cooked on alternate evenings '—I suggest you get a takeaway, on me...'

Well aware that his sensitive antennae had picked up her unspoken need, she asked with determined lightness, 'Will you run to a Chinese?'

He grinned. 'I might, if you promise to save me some prawn crackers.'

'Done!'

'I don't expect to be late but, if by any chance I am, don't wait up for me. You look as if you could do with an early night. Oh, and if you're not feeling up to scratch, take a taxi home.'

Charles was so genuinely kind, so caring, Virginia thought as the door closed behind him. He would make a wonderful husband for the right woman.

He was an excellent companion, easy to talk to and good-tempered, with that rarest of gifts, the ability to see another person's point of view.

Added to that, he was a good-looking man with a quiet charm and undeniable sex appeal. Helen, she was almost certain, was in love with him, and had been for the past year.

It was a great pity that *she* couldn't love him in the way he wanted her to.

A few weeks before, as they'd washed the dishes together after their evening meal, he had broached the question of marriage, diffidently, feeling his way, afraid of scaring her off.

Until then she had thought of him as a confirmed bachelor, set in his ways. It had never occurred to her that he might propose, and he'd been skirting round the subject for several minutes before she'd had the faintest inkling of what had been in his mind.

'I hadn't realised how much I lacked companionship until you came along... Since you've been living here...well, it's made a great difference to my life... And you seem happy with the arrangement...?'

'Yes, I am.' She smiled at him warmly.

Bolstered by that smile, his blue eyes serious, he finally came to the point. 'Virginia...there's something I want to ask you... But if the answer's no, promise me it won't make any difference to our friendship...'

'I promise.'

'You must know I love you...'

She had suspected he was getting fond of her, but had regarded it as the kind of affection he might have felt for any close friend.

'Don't you think it might be something to do with propinquity?' she suggested gently.

Shaking his head, he said, 'I've loved you ever since I set eyes on you...' Then formally, he said, 'It would make me very happy if you would agree to marry me.'

Just for an instant she was tempted. It would be lovely to have a husband, a home that was really hers and, sooner or later, children.

Though she liked her chosen career and had worked hard to gain the knowledge and the eye that had put her on the road to success, it had always taken second place to her dream of being part of a close and happy family.

But it wouldn't be fair to Charles to marry him. He deserved a wife who would love him passionately, rather than a woman who felt merely affection for him.

In no doubt of her answer now, she took a deep, steadying breath. 'I'm sorry...more sorry than I can say...but I can't.'

'Is it the age difference?'

'No,' she answered truthfully. If she'd loved him enough age wouldn't have mattered.

He hung the tea towel up carefully, and pushed back the lock of fair hair that fell over his forehead. 'I had hoped, in view of how well we get along, that you might at least consider it. But perhaps you don't like me sufficiently?'

'I both like and respect you, in fact I'm very fond of you, but—'

'Surely that would be enough to make it work?' he broke in, his blue eyes eager.

She half shook her head. 'Fondness isn't enough.'

'I'm prepared to give it a try. A lot of marriages must be based on less.'

'No, it wouldn't be fair to you...'

Seeing the discomfort on her face, he patted her hand and said firmly, 'Don't worry. I promise I won't bring it up again.

'But don't forget I love you. I'd do anything for you... And if you should ever change your mind, the offer's still open.'

He was a wonderful man. A man in a million. She *wanted* to love him. But love was something that could neither be ordered nor controlled.

She knew that to her cost.

Seeing the dangers, she had tried not to love Ryan... Without success.

But she wouldn't think about Ryan.

As though amused by her decision, Ryan's dark face with those blue-violet eyes smiled back at her mockingly.

Her only coherent thought on first meeting him had been that never before had she seen eyes of such a fascinating colour on any other person...

Damn! there she was doing it.

Gritting her teeth, she closed and locked the window, then gathering up her shoulder bag, made her way down the uncarpeted rear stairs and out of the green-painted staff door onto the cobbled street.

Kenelm Mews, with the backs of buildings on one side and the iron railings of Kenelm Park on the other, was filled with slanting sunlight and the summer-in-the-city smell of dust and petrol fumes and melting tarmac.

Instead of turning the corner into the main road and either looking for a taxi or heading for the bus stop, as she usually did when Charles didn't drive her home, she hesitated.

With its sun-dappled flower beds and shady trees Kenelm looked green and pleasant. If she walked home across the park, it might help to clear her head and relax some of the remaining tension.

Suddenly impatient with her glasses, she stuffed them into her bag and set off through wrought-iron gates that stood open invitingly.

Passing the Victorian bandstand, and the velvety smooth bowling greens where sedate cream-clad figures were standing in little groups, Virginia took a path that skirted the small boating lake.

She walked briskly as though trying to outpace her thoughts. But try as she might, they kept returning to Ryan and his reason for coming into the gallery. Why did he want *Wednesday's Child*?

So he had an image of her? Something to metaphorically stick pins into?

The thought of so much pent-up anger and hatred directed towards herself, frightened her half to death. Her legs starting to tremble, she sank down on the nearest bench, staring blindly across the lake.

She had hoped that time would lessen the animosity she guessed he must feel towards her.

But why should it?

Time hadn't lessened the way she felt.

The bewilderment, the sense of betrayal, the resentment, the hurt...

Without warning, hands came over her eyes and a low, slightly husky voice, a voice that would have made her turn back from the gates of heaven, said close to her ear, 'Guess who?'

Her heart seemed to stop beating, robbing her brain of blood and her lungs of oxygen. Faintness washed over her, swirling her into oblivion...

As the mists began to clear, she found herself held securely against a broad chest, her head resting on a muscular shoulder, the sun warm on her face.

Gathering her senses as best she could, she tried to struggle free.

An elderly woman walking past with a liver-and-white spaniel on a lead, gave them a quick, curious glance and, deciding they were lovers, walked on.

When Virginia made a further, more determined, effort, the imprisoning arms fell away, allowing her to sit upright.

Her heart pounding like a trip hammer, her breath coming in shallow gasps, she stared into Ryan's tough, hard-boned face. A face she knew as well as she knew her own. A face she had often looked into while they'd made love.

The thick dark hair that tried to curl was cut fairly short, but by no means the shaven-headed look she so disliked; his chiselled mouth was as beautiful as she remembered, as were those long-lashed eyes, the colour of indigo.

Eyes that would have made the most ordinary man extraordinary. Except, of course, that Ryan was far from ordinary. Even without those remarkable eyes he would have stood out in a crowd...

He put out a hand, and with a proprietary gesture brushed a loose tendril of brown curly hair back from her pale cheek.

She flinched away as though he'd struck her.

His expression pained, he protested, 'My dear Virginia, there's no need to act as if you're afraid of me.'

'So you did catch sight of me in the gallery,' she said hoarsely.

'Just a glimpse before you bolted. Running away seems to be your forte.'

Biting her lip, she asked, 'Why didn't you say anything to Charles?'

His voice ironic, he told her, 'I thought I'd surprise you.'

He'd certainly succeeded in doing that. Though the air was balmy, she found herself shivering. 'How did you know I'd be in the park?'

'I waited in the mews until I saw you leave the gallery, then I followed you.'

'*Why* did you follow me?' she demanded.

White teeth gleamed in a wolfish smile. 'I thought it was high time we had a talk.'

'As far as I'm concerned, there's nothing to say.' She jumped to her feet and took an unsteady step.

'Don't rush off.' He reached out, and his fingers closed lightly but inexorably around her wrist.

'Let me go,' she said jerkily. 'I don't want to talk to you.'

He drew her back to the bench and, careful not to hurt her, applied just enough downward pressure to make it expedient to sit.

When she sank down onto the wooden slats, he smiled a little. 'Well, if you really don't want to talk, I can think of more exciting things to do.' His eyes were fixed on her mouth.

Her voice shrill with panic, she cried, 'No!'

'Shame,' he drawled. 'Though it seems an age since I last kissed you, I can still remember how passionately you used to respond. You'd make little mewing noises in your throat, your nipples would grow firm and—'

She went hot all over and, seeing nothing else for it,

threw in the towel. 'What did you want to talk to me about?'

'I want to know why you ran away. Why you left me without a word…'

Normally, he had a warm, attractive voice, a voice that had always charmed her. Now the underlying ice in it sent a chill right down her spine.

'Why you didn't at least tell me what was wrong.'

Feeling a deep and bitter anger, she wrenched her wrist free and rounded on him, eyes flashing. 'How can you pretend to be so innocent? Pretend not to know ''what was wrong''?'

He sighed. 'Perhaps you could save the histrionics and just tell me?'

Unwilling to reveal the extent of her hurt, her desolation, she choked back the angry accusations, and said wearily, 'It's over two years ago. I can't see that it matters now…'

Of course it mattered. It would always matter.

'We're different people. The girl I was then no longer exists.'

'You've certainly altered,' he admitted, studying her oval face: the pure bone structure, the long-lashed greeny-grey eyes beneath winged brows, the short straight nose, and lovely passionate mouth.

'Then, you were young and innocent, radiantly pretty, almost incandescent…'

If she had been, love had made her that way. Happiness was a great beautifier.

'Now you've—' His voice suddenly impeded, he stopped speaking abruptly.

But she knew well enough what he'd been about to say. Each morning her mirror showed her a woman who had come up against life and lost. A woman whose sparkle had gone, and who was vulnerable, with sad eyes and, despite all her efforts to smile, a mouth that drooped a little at the corners.

She swallowed hard. 'I'm surprised you recognised me from just that brief glimpse.'

'I almost didn't. That severe hairstyle and those glasses change your appearance significantly, and the "Miss Ashley" had me wondering. If I hadn't been expecting to see you—'

'So you *knew* I was there?' she broke in sharply.

'Oh, yes, I knew. I've known for some time. Did you really think I wouldn't find you?'

Rather than answer, she chose to ask a question of her own, 'What made you come into the gallery?'

'I decided to check things out on a personal level.'

'You told Charles that you wanted to buy *Wednesday's Child*.'

'So I do.'

'Why?'

'Surely you can guess. Will he be able to get it for me, do you think?'

'I've no idea.'

'But not if you can help it?'

When she made no comment, he added with a smile, 'Though I guess I won't need *Wednesday's Child* when I've got the real thing.'

Afraid to ask what he meant by that, she remained silent, looking anywhere but at him.

'From Raynor's manner,' Ryan went on, 'I rather gathered you'd kept quiet about our...shall we say...relationship?'

'It's not something I like to talk about.'

He pulled a face at her tone. 'So how much did you have to tell him in the end, to get him to see me in your place?'

'I just said you were someone I'd once known and didn't want to meet again.'

'How very understated and cold-blooded.'

'It happens to be the truth.'

She saw his face grow taut with anger, before a shutter came down leaving an expressionless mask.

'I would have said I was rather more than someone you'd once known even if you're using the word known in its biblical sense.'

She moved restlessly, desperate to get away, but knowing she stood no chance until he was willing to let her go.

'That's all in the past,' she said tightly. 'Over and done with.'

'Hardly.'

'It's over and done with as far as I'm concerned.'

He shook his head. 'That's where you're wrong. I want you back.'

'What?'

Though he had sworn, 'I'll never let you go,' the fact that she *had* gone, had run away and left him, should surely have hurt his pride to the point where he wouldn't want her back under any circumstances?

'I want you back,' he repeated flatly.

Stammering in her agitation, she cried, 'I'll never c-come back to you.'

'Never is a long time,' he said lightly.

'I mean it, Ryan. There's nothing you can do or say that will make me change my mind.'

'I don't think you should bet on it.' His little crooked smile made her blood run cold.

'Please, Ryan…' She found she was begging. 'I've made a new life for myself and I just want to be left to enjoy it.'

'You once told me you disliked being on your own.'

'I'm not on my own.' The words were defiant, meant to make an impression.

'Let's get this straight, we *are* talking about merely sharing accommodation?'

'*I* wasn't,' she said boldly. If he believed she was seriously involved with someone else he might leave her alone; she wouldn't let herself be hurt again.

He froze into stillness, before asking quietly, 'So, who are you sleeping with?'

'It's none of your business.'

'I'm making it my business.' Those indigo eyes pinning her, he repeated, 'Who?'

'Charles.'

Ryan laughed incredulously. 'That middle-aged wimp?'

'Don't you dare call Charles a wimp. He's nothing of the kind. He's sweet and sensitive, and I owe him a big debt of gratitude. He gave me a job and a home when I was desperate.'

'I'm quite aware that you share his house—my detective has followed the pair of you home often enough—but knowing you as I do, I hesitate to believe that *gratitude* is enough to get you into his bed.'

'It isn't just gratitude. I happen to love him. Passionately,' she added for good measure.

Ryan's mocking smile told her he didn't believe a word of it. 'So, when did you two become lovers?'

'Ages ago.'

'Then, how is it you have separate bedrooms?'

'What makes you think we have separate bedrooms?'

'I don't think. I *know*.'

'How could you possibly know a thing like that?' she scoffed.

'With a bit of encouragement, the domestic help can be an excellent source of information. Mrs Crabtree, in particular, enjoys a good gossip.'

Virginia's heart sank. Mrs Crabtree, a cheerful, garrulous woman, came in several times a week to clean and tidy.

Seeing nothing else for it, she admitted, 'All right, so we have separate bedrooms. Charles is conventional enough to want to keep up appearances.'

'That's not surprising. He's old enough to be your father.'

'He's nothing of the kind.'

'Rubbish! He must be forty-five if he's a day.'

'Charles is forty-three. In any case, age has nothing to do with it. He's a wonderful lover.'

Even as she spoke she felt a stab of conscience. It was hardly fair to Charles to *use* him in this way; perhaps she should just tell Ryan the truth… But she'd gone much too far to back down now.

Recklessly, she added, 'And he's not hidebound enough to believe that lovemaking should only take place in bed.'

A dangerous light in his eyes, Ryan said, 'I hope for everyone's sake that you're lying.'

'Did you seriously expect me to be living like a nun?'

'You were when I met you.'

'In those days I was abysmally naive and innocent. But you taught me a lot, and it's much more difficult to give up a *known* pleasure.'

Watching him weighing up her words, wondering…she struck at his ego, 'Or did you think you were the only man who could turn me on?'

'I certainly didn't think Raynor was your type.'

'That just shows how wrong you can be. Charles and I are very good together. He wants to marry me.'

A dark flush appeared along Ryan's high cheekbones. 'Over my dead body. I've no intention of letting anyone else have you.'

Rattled, she found herself catching at straws. 'But you said yourself how much I've changed. I'm not even pretty any longer.'

'No, you're not merely *pretty*. Now you have the kind of poignant beauty that's haunting.'

She half shook her head. 'Even it that were true, the world's full of beautiful women.'

One in particular.

'In the past I've had my share of beautiful women. But

I find that, after you, none of them will do. It's you I want in my bed and in my life.'

'I don't understand *why*,' she cried desperately.

His voice cold as steel, he said, 'For one thing, there's a score to settle. You owe me.'

CHAPTER TWO

WHITE to the lips, she whispered, 'A score to settle?'

'Why should that surprise you? You must have known that leaving me as you did would make me look a complete and utter fool?'

She couldn't even deny it. Part of her had *wanted* to pay him back. *Wanted* to wound him as much as he'd wounded her. *Wanted* to destroy his world, as he'd destroyed hers.

Afraid that he might read it in her eyes, she looked away, watching a small boy in a blue T-shirt and red shorts run towards the lake. He was clutching a shining new toy yacht, obviously a birthday present, and a stick.

As he knelt on the low parapet to launch the vessel into the water, his mother, who was wheeling a baby in a push-chair, called, 'Be careful, Thomas. Don't fall in. The water's deep.'

When—his will was proving stronger than hers—Virginia's eyes were drawn irresistibly back to Ryan's, he pursued. 'Apart from that, when you just disappeared and I had no idea where you were or what had happened to you, I nearly went out of my mind with worry. Since then I've spent two-and-a-half years and a small fortune looking for you.

'Now I've found you, I want you in my bed. I want to make love to you until you're begging for mercy and I'm sated. Then I want to start all over again. Does the thought of being made love to until you're begging for mercy turn you on?'

Heat running through her, she said thickly, 'No! I can't bear the thought of you touching me.'

25

His handsome eyes gleamed. 'Knowing that will give me great satisfaction, and add immeasurably to my pleasure—'

A simultaneous yelp of fright, a splash, and a high-pitched scream cut through his words.

Ryan was on his feet in an instant and running towards the lake as the woman with the pushchair continued to scream hysterically.

He said something short and sharp to her that stopped the screaming, and a second later he had cleared the parapet and had plunged into the water.

Rooted to the spot, Virginia watched him haul the small dripping figure from the lake and set him on his shoulders. Judging by the roars of fright the child was letting forth, he was mercifully uninjured.

The water was somewhere in the region of three-and-a-half feet deep, and came past Ryan's waist, as he waded a few steps to rescue the capsized yacht.

Letting go of the pushchair, the woman, now sobbing loudly with relief, hovered, arms outstretched ready to embrace her son.

Belatedly, Virginia's brain kicked into action, and realising that no real harm had been done, she grabbed her bag and leaving Ryan to cope, bolted.

Hurrying as fast as she could to the nearest of the park's side entrances, she made her way between the ornate metal bollards and out onto busy Kenelm Road.

A black cab was cruising past and, hailing it, she pulled open the door and jumped in, breathing hard, her heart racing.

'Where to, lady?'

'Sixteen Usher Street.'

Sinking back, drenched in perspiration, she glanced in the direction of the park. There was no sign of pursuit and, starting to tremble in every limb, she sent up a silent prayer of thanks. She'd escaped.

But for how long?

Ryan knew all about her. Where she worked, where she lived, her movements… He had said he wanted her back, and he wasn't a man to give up.

Just seeing him again had shaken her to the core, but the knowledge that he wanted her back had been even more traumatic.

It had been so entirely *unexpected*. Never once had she considered the possibility that he might want her back again.

It was unthinkable. The very idea made her blood turn to ice in her veins. All he wanted was revenge. He didn't even love her.

If he'd loved her, it might have been different…

But if he'd loved her she would never have left him in the first place…

Her hectic thoughts were interrupted by the taxi turning into Usher Street and coming to a halt in front of number sixteen.

It was a quiet street of cream-stuccoed town houses with basements guarded by black wrought-iron railings, and steps leading up to elegant front doors with fluted fanlights.

Charles had inherited the house from his parents, some five years previously. A confirmed bachelor, at least until Virginia had come along, he'd talked about moving somewhere smaller, easier to manage. But in truth he was comfortable there, and it was reasonably close to the gallery.

Recalling agitatedly what Ryan had said about his detective following her, Virginia suddenly felt uncomfortable.

She scrambled out of the taxi and, having reached through the window to pay the driver, ran up the steps to let herself in.

Feeling invisible eyes boring into her back, her palms grew clammy, and pointing the truth of the saying, more haste less speed, it took several attempts to turn the key in the lock.

Her heart throwing itself against her ribs, she dropped

the key into her purse, slammed the door behind her, and hurried through the hall and into a large attractively furnished living-room with long windows.

Dropping her bag on the couch she crossed the room and peered cautiously from behind the curtains, half expecting to see a strange man opposite, lurking behind a newspaper.

Apart from a woman walking past whom she recognised as a neighbour, the sunny, tree-lined street was deserted.

With a feeling of anticlimax, Virginia told herself satirically that she was either getting paranoid, or had been watching too many detective series on the television.

But her attempt to josh herself out of it failed dismally. The threat to her new-found security was chillingly real and couldn't be laughed away.

Becoming aware that her head was now throbbing fiercely, she went into the kitchen to make herself a cup of tea and swallow a couple of painkillers.

Then, uncomfortably hot and sticky, she decided to have a shower and wash her hair. Physically, at least, that should make her feel better.

She stripped off her clothes and, removing the pins from her hair, shook it loose before stepping beneath the jet of warm water.

As she reached for the shampoo, she found herself wondering about Ryan. He must have been saturated...

Had he walked back to his hotel? Or braved it out and hailed a taxi? Was he at this precise minute also taking a shower?

In the old days, alone in his Fifth Avenue penthouse, they had enjoyed showering together...

While the scented steam rose and billowed, her own hands stilled as she recalled how *his* hands had roamed over her slick body, caressing her slender curves, cupping her buttocks, stroking her thighs, finding the nest of wet brown curls, while his tongue licked drops of water from her nipples...

Shuddering at the erotic memory she turned off the water and, winding a towel turban-fashion around her head, began to dry herself with unnecessary vigour, rubbing the pale gold skin until it glowed pink.

Having decided not to bother and get dressed again, she found the Christmas present Charles had given her, a chenille robe-cum-housecoat in moss green and, pulling it on, belted it.

Her feet bare, her naturally curly hair still damp and loose around her shoulders, she was descending the stairs when the phone in the hall began to chirrup.

Reaching out a hand she was about to pick up the receiver when it occurred to her that it might be Ryan, and she hesitated.

Who else was likely to be calling? Who else would know she was home before her usual time?

It kept chirruping, and its sheer persistence tearing at her nerves, she snatched it up.

'Virginia?' It was Charles. His well-modulated voice sounded a shade anxious.

'Yes,' she said hurriedly. 'Yes, I'm here.'

'Is anything wrong?'

She took a deep breath. 'No, of course not.'

'You didn't seem to be answering.'

'I've just got out of the shower.' It wasn't exactly a lie.

'Oh, I see.'

'Is there a problem?' she asked.

'No. Not at all... I was just ringing to make sure you were all right.'

'Yes, I'm fine.'

'Certain?' With his usual sensitivity he had picked up her jumpiness.

Resisting the impulse to tell him about Ryan and beg him to come home, she said with what cheerfulness she could muster, 'Absolutely. Any idea what time you'll be back?'

'I should be home somewhere around eight-thirty. Don't forget to save me some prawn crackers.'

'I won't,' she promised. 'Bye for now.'

As she replaced the handset, the grandmother clock whirred and began to chime six-thirty.

Might as well ring for her takeaway now, she decided. It usually took between thirty and forty minutes for an order to be delivered, and she'd only had part of a roll for lunch, the remainder having been fed to a family of sparrows who, nesting in the eaves above her office window, had learnt to line up along the sill, bright-eyed and expectant.

Not that she was hungry.

But something to eat might help to get rid of the hollow, stomach-churning feeling that had persisted since Ryan had said, 'Guess who?' in the park.

The number of the restaurant was written in Charles's neat numerals in the book by the phone, but it was Ryan's face that swam before her eyes as she tapped in the digits.

'The Jade Garden. Good evening…' a singsong voice responded.

Her mind still obsessed by Ryan, Virginia, who was usually clear and precise, made a mess of her order and was forced to stumble through it a second time.

Returning to the living-room, she prowled about plumping cushions and tidying magazines, far too restless to sit still.

What would Ryan do next? she wondered anxiously. There was no doubt in her mind that he wouldn't let matters rest. He wanted her, and his sense of purpose was terrifying…

Though she had lied through her teeth about her relationship with Charles, it hadn't had the desired effect. Ryan either hadn't believed her, or hadn't wanted to.

Either way, her assertions had failed to provide the anchor, the safeguard, she had been so desperate to put in place.

But even if he *had* believed her, would that have stopped him? Remembering the look on his face when he'd said, 'I've no intention of letting anyone else have you', she felt her skin goose-flesh.

Just seeing him again, feeling the force of his will, had made her doubt her ability to hold out against him if he kept up the seige.

No! she mustn't think like that. If necessary she would tell Charles the whole truth, and beg for his forgiveness and support.

He was far from being the wimp that Ryan had so contemptuously called him. In fact, in a different and less obvious way he was as strong as Ryan, with a quiet determination and a tensile strength.

But how could she ask Charles for help, ask him to pretend to be her lover, when she had denied him that privilege by refusing his proposal of marriage?

All at once she was filled with a burning shame that she'd even considered involving him any further. Somehow she *must* manage without his help.

There was one thing in her favour. Usually a brilliant strategist, this time Ryan had made a bad mistake. He had admitted that he was out to make her pay for leaving him, and forewarned was forearmed.

Though his attraction was as powerful as ever, knowing his intentions would enable her to hold out against him, to freeze him off...

The peal of the doorbell interrupted her thoughts.

Her takeaway had come a lot quicker than usual. But of course it was still quite early. They wouldn't yet have had a build-up of customers...

She fumbled in her bag and purse in hand, went to open the door.

Taken completely by surprise, her reactions were a trifle slow and, before she could slam the door in his face, Ryan had slipped inside.

Over six feet tall and broad-shouldered, he seemed to fill the small hall.

Closing the door behind him he stood leaning with his back to the panels. Wearing stone-coloured trousers and a two-tone, smart-casual jacket, he looked tanned and fit and dangerous.

'Get out!' she cried in a panic. 'You have no right to force your way in here.'

'I didn't exactly *force* my way in,' he objected, adding coolly, 'Though I might well have done had it proved necessary.'

Surveying the robe, her shiny face and the wealth of ash-brown hair curling loosely around her shoulders, he remarked, 'You look about ready for bed. But of course Raynor doesn't take you to bed, does he? He has more...shall we say...inventive ideas.'

When, her soft lips tightening, she said nothing, he goaded, 'Tell me, Virginia, where does he usually make love to you? In the kitchen? Lying in front of the fire? On the stairs?'

'Stop it!' she cried.

'After what you told me earlier, you can't blame me for being curious.'

Wishing fervently that she'd kept her mouth shut, she said, 'I want you to go. Now! Before Charles gets home. He won't be long.'

Ryan shook his head. 'It's no use, Virginia, my sweet, I know perfectly well that he won't be in until much later...'

How did he know?

'And, even if that wasn't the case, do you seriously think the prospect of Raynor coming home would scare me into leaving?'

No, she didn't. Lifting her chin, she threatened, 'I could always call the police.'

'You *could*,' he agreed, 'but somehow I don't think you will. After all, the police have a lot more to concern themselves about than what they would undoubtedly class as a trivial domestic problem.'

In past skirmishes he had proved to be quicker witted than she was, and in any battle of words he almost invariably won. But she couldn't allow him to win this time.

'It isn't "a trivial domestic problem,"' she said through gritted teeth. 'It's an illegal entry into someone else's home.'

'How can it be an "illegal entry" when you opened the door to me yourself?'

'I thought it was my takeaway.'

Eyeing the purse she was still holding, he said, 'I see. Well, if you have a meal ordered, perhaps you'll invite me to stay and share it?'

Her agitation increasing, she cried, 'No, I don't want you to stay. I don't know why you came in the first place.'

'For one thing, we hadn't finished our conversation—'

'There's nothing further to say. I'll never come back to you, so you're just wasting your time.'

As though she hadn't interrupted, he went on, his voice quietly lethal, 'And for another, I'm not prepared to let you keep running out on me.'

For the first time she realised he was furiously angry, and she quailed inwardly.

He stepped towards her, dwarfing her five feet seven inches, and with a hand beneath her chin, he forced it up. His eyes were focussed on her mouth, his dark face sharp and intent.

Guessing his intention, she begged, 'No! Oh, please, Ryan, don't...'

But his hand slid round to her nape, tangling in her silky hair, and his mouth swooped down on hers, taking possession, stifling any further protests.

The purse she had been clutching like a lifeline thudded to the floor and, despite all her efforts to hold aloof, the blood began to pound in her ears and the world tilted on its axis.

Head spinning, she was engulfed, gathered up and swept away on a tide of conflicting emotions, while every nerve ending in her body zinged into life.

At first his kiss was hard, punitive, a way of venting his anger, the arm clamping her to him like an iron band.

But when, scarcely able to stand, she made no attempt to break free, his arm loosened its hold slightly and, instead of being a punishment, his kiss became passionate, his skilful tongue sending shivers of excitement and pleasure running through her.

Leaving her nape, his hand slid inside the lapels of her robe, following her collarbone, moving down to find and fondle the soft curve of her breast.

He seemed to be deliberately avoiding the tip and, desperate for his touch, her whole being was poised in an agony of waiting.

When, finally, his experienced fingers began to lightly tease the sensitive nipple, causing sensations so exquisite they were almost pain, her stomach clenched and a core of liquid heat began to form in her abdomen.

Now he was making her feel all that he wanted her to feel, and he took her little gasps and whimpers into his mouth like the conqueror he was.

Lost and mindless, she was hardly aware when his free hand undid the belt and eased the robe from her shoulders, allowing it to fall at her feet.

His mouth had moved away from hers to rove over the smooth flesh he had exposed, when, shockingly, the doorbell rang.

Ryan's recovery was light years ahead of Virginia's. Stooping, he gathered up the robe and, wrapping it around her, gently hustled her across the hall and into the kitchen.

Pulling on the robe with shaking hands, she belted it

tightly and, sinking down in the nearest chair, groaned aloud.

So much for holding out against him.

Oh, dear Lord, what had she been thinking of? If it hadn't been for the interruption, Ryan could have taken her right there on the hall carpet and she would have allowed it.

No, more than allowed it, *welcomed* it.

Oh, you fool! she berated herself. She had planned to freeze him off, to make it clear that she was no longer under his spell.

Instead her abject surrender must have boosted his confidence, made him even more certain that he could win...

Only he mustn't. Much as she wanted him—and she did still want him, maybe she always would—she mustn't let him win.

Through her tumult of mind she was aware of the front door opening and Ryan's voice saying, 'Thanks. How much do I owe you?'

By the time he came through to the kitchen carrying a brightly coloured cardboard box with a handle, she had gathered the remnants of her dignity around her like a tattered cloak.

Standing up, she faced him squarely. 'I want you to leave, now, this minute.'

Unpacking the various foil containers onto the pine table, he said mildly, 'I like Chinese food and, as you appear to have ordered enough for two, it would be a shame to waste it.'

Looking dazedly at the number of containers, she realised that her repeat of the order had caused confusion and had resulted in them delivering far too much food.

Watching her face, he asked ironically, 'Was it a Freudian slip? Did you subconsciously want or expect me to be here?'

'No, I certainly didn't. If I wanted anyone here, it would be Charles.'

She could tell by the way Ryan's mouth tightened that her answer had annoyed him, but all he said was, 'Do you have any bowls and chopsticks?'

'In the cupboard,' she answered shortly. He might insist on staying, but that didn't mean she was prepared to make him welcome.

Slipping out of his jacket, he hung it over the back of a chair before opening the cupboard door.

Along with the bowls was a small electric hotplate. Infuriatingly at home, he took it out and, having plugged it in, arranged the foil containers on it.

Loosening the lids, he suggested, 'Why don't you sit down and tell me what you'd like to start with?'

Still standing, she said curtly, 'I don't want anything to eat. I've lost my appetite.'

He raised dark level brows. 'That's a pity. Still if you're *quite* sure you don't want to eat, we could always start a precedent.'

Alarmed by the silky menace in his tone, the glint in his eye, she demanded, 'What do you mean, start a precedent?'

'Don't you think it would be a nice change to be carried upstairs and made love to *in bed*?'

All the fight going out of her, she sat down abruptly.

White teeth gleamed as he laughed. 'No? Oh, well...' Taking a seat opposite, he queried, 'So what's it to be? The sesame prawn toast looks good.' Leaning towards her, he offered her a piece.

His dark silk shirt was open at the neck, exposing the strong column of his throat. Remembering how she had sometimes buried her face against it when he'd made love to her, her mouth went dry.

Lifting her eyes, she met his ironic gaze, and felt the colour flood into her cheeks.

'You look warm,' he observed innocently. 'Do you have any nice cool wine?'

Somehow she managed to say, 'There's a bottle open in the fridge.'

He found a couple of glasses and filled them with Chablis. Then, having helped them both to chicken and cashew nuts, he picked up his bamboo chopsticks and, sorting out one of the fat, gleaming cashews, reached across the table.

Without conscious volition, her mouth opened and he popped it in.

His action was like a blow to the solar plexus, winding her and making her heart thump erratically.

Eating their first meal together in New York's Chinatown, she had mentioned that she only ordered that particular dish because she adored cashew nuts.

Loverlike, he had fed her the nuts from his own bowl. After that it had become a kind of tender ritual.

Except, of course, that it had only been play-acting. He might have wanted her, he undoubtedly had, but he had never loved her, had never felt any real tenderness for her. He had just wanted to use her.

But she had refused to be used, though it had broken her heart to leave him...

As though following her train of thought, Ryan said abruptly, 'You still haven't told me why you ran the way you did.'

'You ought to know.'

'If it was what I can only presume it was—'

'Did you think I wouldn't mind?' she burst out. 'Think I'd play along, let you use me and say nothing?'

He frowned. 'I haven't the faintest idea what you're talking about. You'd better explain.'

Infuriated by his denial, she jumped to her feet. 'I've no intention of *explaining* anything. I want you to go, and if you won't go, then I will!'

As she turned away, he said quietly, 'Sit down and finish your meal.'

Their glances met and clashed.

She wanted to disobey his order, to walk away, but she couldn't leave, and she found herself subsiding into her chair.

After a moment, he asked softly, 'Why didn't you at least let me know you were safe?'

'Why do you suppose?'

'You didn't think I might worry about you?'

'I tried not to think of you at all.'

'What about the rest of the family?'

When she said nothing, he went on, 'They were all very upset and concerned that you'd gone without a word. Beth in particular...'

'I'm sorry about that. I liked your stepmother.' It was the truth. In fact, with one exception, she'd liked the whole family.

'She had another heart attack,' he added flatly.

Virginia caught her breath.

Seeing the apprehension on her face, Ryan said quickly, 'A fairly mild one, thank the Lord.'

'Then, she's all right?'

'She made a good recovery. Which is just as well.'

'You mean if she hadn't, you would have held me responsible?'

'I *do* hold you responsible.'

Virginia flinched at the bitter irony. It had been mainly to safeguard his stepmother's fragile state of health that she had chosen to run as she did.

'Do Janice and Steven?'

'What do you think?'

Her heart sank. Still, it was better that they should blame her, a comparative stranger, rather than know something that would almost certainly tear their close-knit family apart.

One half of her still wondered incredulously how Ryan had been able to do what he did. But perhaps he'd found it impossible to help himself? Love could be a powerful, overriding force...

As could the need for revenge.

Though more sinned against than sinning, she had wrecked all his carefully laid plans and, in his own eyes at least, had made him look a fool.

Not something a man like him would easily forgive.

She shivered.

'You're surely not cold?' Ryan asked.

'No.'

'Ashamed?'

'Why should *I* be ashamed?'

'I can think of several good reasons. First and foremost that you treated a woman, who had taken you to her heart, in such a callous fashion...'

Perhaps, in retrospect, she *should* have left a note, made up some excuse for going... But, shocked and stunned, feeling mortally wounded, she hadn't known what to say.

'I'm sorry if it seemed that way. I never meant to hurt her...'

A shrill bleating cut through her words.

'Excuse me.' Reaching into his jacket pocket he produced a mobile phone. 'Falconer... It has? Good... Yes... Yes... Be with you shortly.'

Dropping the phone back in his pocket, he rose to his feet and pulled on his jacket. 'I'm sorry I have to leave quite so soon.'

'I'm afraid I can't say the same,' she informed him trenchantly.

Paying her back for her show of spirit, he came round the table and with studied insolence slipped his hand inside the lapels of her robe and cupped her breast.

Knowing that he was waiting for her to jump up and

protest, summoning every last ounce of will-power, she sat still and silent.

Smiling a little, he bent his dark head and his mouth brushed hers. 'When you're in bed on your own tonight, dream that I'm making love to you.'

'Not if I can help it,' she spat at him.

'If you're frustrated enough, you might find it impossible not to.'

'I'm *not* frustrated.'

Smiling, he rubbed his thumb over the nipple until it firmed. 'You were always very responsive.'

Unable to stand any more, she jerked away and, dragging the lapels together, jumped to her feet. 'Aren't you forgetting something? Or should I say, someone?'

His blue-violet eyes narrowed.

'Charles might not be a young man by your standards, but he's fit and in his prime. If I am frustrated I won't need to stay that way.'

She saw a white line appear round Ryan's mouth and, fiercely glad that he was furious, laughed in his face.

With a sound almost like a growl, he took her upper arms, his fingers biting into the soft flesh, and warned softly, 'Don't even *think* about it. From now on I intend to be the only man in your life, so if Raynor does get any bright ideas about making love to you, it will pay you to say no, and mean it.'

Dragging her right up against him, he kissed her once more. This time his kiss was hard and unsparing, rocking her to her very foundations. Then suddenly she was free.

'Be seeing you,' he said mockingly.

A moment later she heard the front door open and close.

Badly shaken, she went through to the hall on unsteady legs. Ryan was gone, but she noted abstractedly that her purse had been picked up and placed neatly on the telephone table.

Trembling now as reaction set in, she sank down on the

bottom step of the stairs and stared blindly into space while her thoughts whirled.

Oh, dear Lord, what was she to do? Ryan's unwelcome visit had proved at least two terrifying things: that he was in deadly earnest; and that her chances of resisting him were practically nil.

It had been that way from the start. She had looked at him and had loved him, heart and soul.

Recognising at some deep, subconscious level that he was the one she had been waiting all her life for, she had given herself to him with a joyous certainty, and the hope of a happy ever after.

But that happy ever after had been short-lived. A bare two months from its rapturous start to its bitter ending...

And now, unless she could find some way of keeping Ryan at bay, the torture would start all over again.

She would still be there, and even if his feelings for the other woman—love or obsession, call it what one will— had died, the situation would still be quite intolerable.

No matter what he said about wanting only *her*, Virginia knew that she would never again be able to believe nor trust him. And he must know that... It might even be part of his revenge to have her on the rack of jealousy and torment...

No, no, she couldn't, *wouldn't* go back to him.

But, even as she tried to make herself believe it, she knew she was like a moth that, unable to help itself, was drawn irresistibly and fatally towards a candle flame.

CHAPTER THREE

GRITTING her teeth, she tried to reject that frightening image. Somehow she must help herself. Find a way out of still loving Ryan.

If only she had loved Charles enough to marry him... But it wasn't so much a case of not loving Charles, as of still loving Ryan.

Though how could she go on loving a man who hated her? Who only wanted to hurt her? It was utter madness. That kind of self-destructive love could end up wrecking her whole life.

If she allowed it to.

But even if she was strong enough to hold out against him, all she had to look forward to was an empty future.

As far as she was concerned, love and sex went hand in hand. She wasn't one for casual sex nor for affairs, but she was a young woman still with natural needs.

True those needs had been smothered and suppressed for over two-and-a-half years, but how quickly they had flared into life as soon as Ryan had kissed her.

If she didn't want to live like a nun, marrying Charles, a man she was fond of and respected, was the obvious answer. She would be safe then, her future more hopeful, with the prospect of children and a happy, family life.

As for her reservations about it not being fair to him, well, she had told him honestly how she felt, and he'd said he was willing to try...

So why not? It might be no grande passion, at least on her side, but if she could make him happy...

The clock chiming eight roused her. With a bit of luck, Charles would be home in about half an hour.

Getting to her feet, she went back to the kitchen and, making a determined effort to think about the brighter future she had envisaged, rather than the unhappy past, began to wash up and clear away the debris of the meal.

She had only just finished and plugged in the kettle when she heard the sound of Charles's key in the lock.

Hurrying through to the hall, she smiled at him. 'You're back nice and early.'

Hearing the relief in her voice, he was glad that he'd hurried straight home rather than going on to a pub, as his companion had suggested when their business was over.

'How did your appointment go?'

'Very well.'

'That's good.'

She sounded distracted, he thought, as though her mind was on other things.

Studying her pale, drawn face, he asked gently, 'Headache still bothering you?'

'No, not really. I took some tablets when I first got home. By the way, the kettle's on if you'd like some coffee?'

'Love some.'

Wearing the robe he had bought her, and with her curly hair tumbling around her shoulders, he thought she had never looked so lovely. Nor so fraught. Something had happened to seriously upset her.

Wondering if she wanted to talk about it, or if she would prefer to be alone, he asked carefully, 'Were you thinking of having an early night?'

Shaking her head, she explained, 'I didn't bother getting dressed again after my shower.'

'Then if you're not off to bed, why don't you have some coffee with me?'

'Yes, I'd like to. There's something I want to tell you.'

He hung up the jacket of his suit, and was starting to follow her into the kitchen when she said hastily, 'I'll bring it through to the living-room.'

The kitchen was still uncomfortably full of Ryan's presence.

When she had filled the cafetière and had put the coffee things on the tray, she carried it in and set it down on the low table.

The west-facing room, always pleasant in the evening, was full of low sun, which threw a distorted pattern of oblong window panes and leafy branches onto the magnolia walls.

She poured the coffee, stirred sugar and cream into his, and handed it to him.

'Thank you. I don't know what I've done to deserve being waited on,' he remarked humorously.

Too tense to sit still, she left her own cup untouched and, wandering over to the window, stood looking out while the silence lengthened.

Now the moment had arrived, she had no idea how to broach the subject.

Watching her and guessing her difficulty, he said, 'What was it you wanted to tell me?'

Still she hesitated. Suppose he'd had second thoughts about his proposal? Decided it had been a mistake?

Well there was only one way to find out. Turning, she took the bull by the horns. 'When you asked me to marry you, you said if I ever changed my mind the offer would still be open...'

Thrown, because it was the last thing he'd expected her to say, it was a second or two before he assured her, 'It is.'

As she let out the breath she'd been unconsciously holding, his blue eyes filled with a dawning hope, he asked urgently, '*Have* you changed your mind?'

'Yes. I will marry you, if you still want me to.'

'Darling!' He was on his feet and gathering her close, eager as a boy. 'Believe me, I've never wanted anything more.'

He held her firmly, with no sign of diffidence, and his kiss was pleasant, almost exciting.

After a while he stopped kissing her to ask, 'What made you change your mind?'

'Well, I…I got to thinking… I'd like a husband and a home and a family… You do want children?' she added a shade anxiously.

'I'd never actually thought about it,' he answered honestly. 'But if that's what it takes to make you happy… How many were you thinking of?' He sounded like a man on a high, a man who could hardly believe his luck.

'At least two, possibly three or four.'

'Why stop at four?' he teased.

'Charles… You are quite certain this is what you want? A wife and family, I mean?'

'Quite certain. Forty-three isn't too old.'

'No, of course it isn't.'

'But I'm not getting any younger, so how soon will you marry me?'

'As soon as you want.'

'What kind of wedding would you like?'

'A quiet one.'

'You don't want a white dress with all the trimmings?'

Knowing she must tell him the truth, she said flatly, 'White is the sign of virginity.'

'And you're not a virgin?'

'No. I'm sorry if that bothers you.'

'My darling, I'm not Victorian enough to support the old double standard. Though I've been fairly circumspect in my dealings with women, I certainly haven't lived like a monk, and I wouldn't expect a woman of twenty-four never to have had lovers—'

'Not lovers in the plural,' she said quietly.

'One special one?'

'Yes.'

His heart sank. Several lovers that didn't really matter

was one thing… One special lover that, judging by her face, mattered a great deal was another.

Remembering Virginia's reaction to the dark, powerful-looking man who had come into the gallery that afternoon, he said, 'It was Ryan Falconer, wasn't it?'

Moistening her dry lips, she nodded.

He drew her over to the settee and when she sank down on the soft cushions, took a seat by her side. 'I think you'd better tell me about him.'

The last person she wanted to talk about just at that minute was Ryan, and half hoping for a reprieve, she stammered, 'I—I don't know where to start.'

'Start at the beginning,' Charles suggested quietly.

Seeing no help for it, she gathered herself, and began. 'It's getting on for three years since we first met. I'd left art school and was working in the Trantor Gallery, when late one morning a man came in…'

While she told him the bare bones of it, memory fleshed out the details and she relived the past as though it was the present…

The gallery was quiet, as it usually was towards noon, just an elderly couple browsing, and a small group of men in business suits discussing the relative merits of two abstract paintings.

Sitting behind the polished-wood reception desk, Virginia was checking the contents of a catalogue when the smoked glass door opened and a man came in and strolled across.

Tall and well-built, with thick dark hair that tried to curl a little, he was dressed in the latest smart-casual De Quincy jacket and handmade shoes.

As he got closer she could see he was somewhere in his early thirties, with a tough, masculine face, strong features and a beautiful mouth.

He was one of the most attractive men she had ever seen.

No, more than just attractive, he was what Marsha would have termed drop-dead gorgeous.

'Miss Adams?' The most incredible blue-violet eyes, with faint laughter lines at the corners, smiled into hers.

Virginia found it quite impossible not to stare into those eyes and, instantly captivated, her mouth went dry, and her heartbeat quickened.

Wits scattered, she stammered, 'Y-yes.'

'My name's Ryan Falconer. I'm acquainted with your parents.'

'They live in New York,' she said stupidly.

White teeth flashed in a smile. 'Yes, I know, I had lunch with them a couple of days ago, and they told me where to find you...'

He had a nice voice, warm and slightly husky, with a not-too-pronounced American accent.

'There's something I'd like to discuss with you, so perhaps you'll allow me to take you out to lunch?'

Excitement and disappointment mingling, she said, 'I usually just have a yoghurt...'

'Well, I had thought of something a little more substantial,' he mocked gently, 'but if a yoghurt is all you can eat...'

Flustered because he was laughing at her, she explained, 'It's not that. You see at the moment there's no one to take my place. Marsha's ill, so I'm only able to have about a ten-minute break.'

He glanced around the gallery. 'You surely can't be here all alone?'

'Oh, no. Both Mr and Mrs Trantor are in the office.'

'Which is?'

'The door on the left.'

'I'll have a word.'

Quickly, she said, 'I'd rather you didn't.'

He cocked a dark level brow at her. 'You really don't want to have lunch with me?'

'It's not that. But I don't think they'd agree to my going out—'

'Oh, I think they might.'

Bearing in mind the exorbitant rent she had to pay for her small and somewhat dingy two-roomed flat, she begged, 'Please, Mr Falconer, I've just taken over a furnished flat, so I can't afford to lose my job—'

'Ryan, please. And there'll be no question of you losing your job.'

Before she could protest any further, he advanced purposefully on the door, tapped and walked in, rather as if he owned the place.

Holding her breath, she stared after him helplessly.

He returned quite quickly, with Mrs Trantor leading the way. To Virginia's amazement the woman usually referred to as the Dragon was smiling, even fluttering a little.

'No, of course I don't mind, Mr Falconer. I'll be happy to take care of reception myself. Off you go, Miss Adams.'

Stumbling over her thanks, Virginia hurried to fetch her jacket and bag, pausing only to pull a comb through her silky curls. A few seconds later she was being escorted outside.

It was a cold, crisp day in early October, with sunshine lighting the autumn colours, and drifts of brown leaves lying beneath the plane trees.

'I thought we'd go to The Pentagram?' Ryan Falconer suggested casually.

The Pentagram was rated as one of London's top restaurants, but walking on air just to be with this fascinating stranger Virginia wouldn't have cared if they'd gone to the burger bar.

'If that's all right with you?' he added politely.

'It sounds wonderful, but…'

'But?'

'I'm not sure if I'm well enough dressed,' she admitted a shade awkwardly.

Glancing at her off-the-peg aubergine suit and cream blouse, he said, 'You look fine to me.'

A black executive-type limousine was drawn up a short distance away. As they approached, the liveried chauffeur jumped out and held open the door.

Feeling rather like a latter-day Cinderella, Virginia was handed in. After a brief word with the chauffeur, Ryan Falconer slid in beside her, and a moment later the sleek car drew away from the kerb and into the traffic stream.

Turning his head, he smiled at her. A smile that set her pulses hammering, and made her feel suddenly, unaccountably breathless.

He was so close, his physical presence so overwhelming, that she felt as dizzy and disorientated as if she was sitting perched on the edge of a precipice.

Yet, her perceptions heightened, she registered the length of his lashes, the way his ears were set neatly against his dark head, the shallow cleft in his strong chin, the little creases each side of his mouth that deepened when he smiled…

Becoming aware that she was staring at him as though mesmerised, she dragged her gaze away, and felt herself go hot all over.

His lips twitched and, certain that he could guess exactly how she felt, she said as coolly as possible, 'You mentioned there was something you'd like to discuss with me?'

'There is,' he agreed, 'but it'll keep until after lunch.'

With a faint recollection that The Pentagram was somewhere on the other side of town, she queried, 'How long will it take to get to the restaurant?'

'About twenty minutes,' he answered casually.

Twenty minutes! 'Mr Falconer, I'm not sure if there's time to—'

'Ryan,' he insisted. 'And don't worry, there's plenty of time. Mrs Trantor gave you the rest of the afternoon off.'

'The rest of the afternoon off?' she echoed in amazement. 'How on earth did you persuade her to do that?'

He grimaced ruefully. 'And here I was, hoping you'd put it all down to charm.'

Remembering Mrs Trantor's face, she said, 'I'm sure charm had a lot to do with it.'

'Not half as much as the thought of doing business with me. All I had to do was mention that I was looking to buy a Jonathan Cass.'

She blinked. If he was 'looking to buy' one of Jonathan Cass's paintings, apart from the fact that he couldn't be short of a million or two, that put him straight into the connoisseur class.

'Then, you're a lover of art?'

He considered that. 'More a businessman. As far as art's concerned, I buy whatever will make a profit, unless it's for my own private collection. In that case I buy only the things I like.'

'Is the Cass…?'

'For my own collection. Though I may hang it in the gallery for a while to promote interest.'

'You have a gallery?'

'On Madison Avenue. That's the reason I know your parents. They put on a joint exhibition there a few weeks ago.

'Tell me something, Virginia…may I call you Virginia?'

She nodded. 'Of course.'

'Why didn't you tell the Trantors that your parents are Brad and Mia Adams?'

'I didn't think it was relevant.' Then, quickly, she asked, 'How do you know I didn't tell them?'

'It's quite obvious. If they knew, they wouldn't be treating you like some glorified receptionist.'

'Unfortunately at the present that's what I am.'

'How long have you been at the gallery?'

'Almost four months.'

He frowned. 'Why stay? You surely didn't spend those years at college just to sit behind a desk and answer inane questions?'

'No, I didn't. But jobs in the art world aren't that easy to come by.'

'More doors would be open to you if you made it known who your parents are.'

She shook her head stubbornly. 'Particularly as I have no *creative* talent, who my parents are shouldn't make any difference. What I've learnt and am capable of, should.'

'I totally agree, but I still think you're making it hard for yourself.'

'No, I'm just refusing to make it easy.'

She saw the mingled respect and admiration in his eyes, before he remarked, 'You know, you're really quite exceptional. Most people would use every trick in the book to gain an advantage...

'But, then, I hadn't expected you to be like most people. With talented parents like yours—' Breaking off, he added firmly, 'And I don't mean that in the way you're thinking.'

A little stiffly, she asked, 'How do you mean it?'

He turned those extraordinary eyes on her, making butterflies dance in her stomach, before continuing obliquely, 'I imagine it wasn't easy being brought up by two such art-absorbed people?'

Without waiting for an answer, he went on, 'I gather you were an only child, so you must often have felt lonely and neglected?'

'Yes, I did,' she admitted. And found herself telling him something that, up until then, she had never told another living soul. 'I had everything I needed as far as material things went, but they never had any time for me, never sat me on their knees or cuddled me.'

'I guess people who live for art, or have any other overwhelming interest, for that matter, tend to disregard their children.'

'You sound as if you speak from personal experience.'

He smiled wryly. 'I guess we're two of a kind. Though I had everything that money could buy, until I was nearly ten the only thing I knew about love was how to live without it.'

Understanding exactly how he'd felt, her heart went out to the forlorn little boy he must have been.

Reading her sympathy, he took her hand and gave it a little squeeze, making her heart turn over, before going on, 'My father's two main interests in life were making money and politics. He spent most of his time either on Wall Street, or attending political rallies, so I saw hardly anything of him.

'That wouldn't have mattered quite so much if my mother had made time for me. But she too had an absorbing passion for politics.

'If she wasn't actively campaigning or fund-raising, most of her time was devoted to playing hostess at glittering social occasions, where she could hobnob with past and, hopefully, future presidents.

'Once she had reluctantly provided my father with the son and heir he needed, I was given over to the care of nannies, and later, various tutors...'

A strange sensation came over her as she watched his face and listened. She *knew* this man as if his soul was a mirror image of her own... But that was just being fanciful, she told herself firmly. Yet the feeling that he was the other half of herself persisted.

'I was almost ten when she was killed in a plane crash,' Ryan went on. 'But I'd seen so little of her, that after a few months I could hardly remember what she looked like.

'It was only when my father remarried that I discovered what real care and warmth felt like.

'Beth, an English widow with a young son and baby daughter from a previous marriage, always had time for me.

She took me to her heart and gave me all the love I'd lacked up until then... Ah, here we are...'

They had drawn up in a quiet, tree-lined street in front of a handsome porticoed building that looked more like a private house than a restaurant. Only the five-pointed star and the name in gold letters above the door identified it.

'I'm sorry,' he apologised, as he helped her out.

'For what?' she asked, puzzled.

'My intention was to talk about you. Instead I've bored you stiff talking about myself.'

Shaking her head, she said, 'I haven't been in the least bit bored.'

'You're either very nicely mannered or a diplomat. I'll be able to judge which when I get to know you better.'

The suggestion that he intended to get to know her better had her walking on cloud nine as they made their way into an elegant marble-floored foyer.

'Mr Falconer... How nice to see you again.'

They were greeted by the dapper, silver-haired manager, a cream rosebud in his buttonhole.

'Nice to see you, Michael.'

The two men shook hands.

'Are you over for long?'

'A few days.'

'Then, perhaps we'll see you again?'

'I certainly hope so.'

Alerted by a discreet beep, the manager said, 'It seems I'm wanted. Please excuse me. Alphonse will show you to your table.'

Rubbing his hands together, he gave Virginia a little bow, and departed at a trot.

The *maître d'*, appearing like a genie from a lamp, led them through to a dining-room with a rich Turkish carpet and a crimson and gold decor.

There were eight widely spaced tables, six of which were already occupied, and at the far end of the room several small velvet covered couches were grouped cosily around a blazing log fire.

Their table, covered by a spotless damask cloth and set with fine crystal and a centrepiece of cream rosebuds, was by one of the long windows.

As soon as Virginia was seated, the *maître d'* disappeared, and a younger waiter appeared with two glasses of pale amber sherry on a silver tray.

'I hope you like dry sherry?' Ryan asked in a stage whisper, as the man departed.

'Yes, I do.'

'Every single thing that's served here is of the finest, which makes it a rewarding experience, but there's no choice.'

'You mean no one knows what they're getting until it arrives?'

Making it into a game, he said, 'Not unless you ask, which counts as being chicken, or peek at another table, which is frowned on.'

Almost certain he was pulling her leg, she said serenely, 'Well, there's not much I don't like...'

'I do admire a woman with a spirit of adventure.'

'Apart from fresh oysters,' she tacked on.

His dark eyes gleamed between their long thick lashes. 'Oysters are something of a speciality here.'

She barely repressed a shudder.

'I hope I'm not making you nervous?' he enquired innocently.

'Not at all,' she lied, adding, 'if the worst comes to the worst I can always leave them.'

'Not if you want to get out of here alive.'

Certain now that he was pulling her leg, she smiled, a lovely smile that showed her white, even teeth, dimpled the corners of her mouth, and made her grey-green eyes dance.

Softly, he said, 'You're quite enchanting when you smile.' Then watching a tinge of pink appear along her cheekbones, he said, 'I thought that went out with the Victorians.'

'What went out with the Victorians?'

A little amused smile tugging at his lips, he told her, 'The ability to blush at a compliment. I find it most…refreshing.'

Ruffled by that smile, she snapped, 'Don't you mean *entertaining*?'

'That too, but in the nicest possible way,' he agreed, refusing to be put out by her tart tone.

Fighting back, she said, 'Well blushing is the only piece in my repertoire, so don't expect me to get the vapours, or scream if I see a mouse.'

'If you see a mouse here I'm the one who's likely to do the screaming,' he said humorously.

As she stared at him in disbelief, he explained, 'It wouldn't do much for the reputation of the place, and as I've a stake in it…'

'A stake in it? I thought you lived in New York.'

'So I do, but as an international investment banker I've got a finger in a lot of pies.'

As he finished speaking, a seafood torte arrived, accompanied by a chilled white wine.

'Okay?' Ryan queried.

'Fine, thank you,' Virginia answered politely. She soon discovered it was more than fine. It was absolutely delicious.

With impeccable timing, the torte was followed by a cheese soufflé, incredibly tasty and as light as air, and a fruit compote with Madeira. A small sorbet was served between each course.

It would have been sacrilege to talk, and neither spoke as they savoured the superb meal, but Virginia was heart-stoppingly conscious that Ryan's eyes were more often on her face than his plate.

Only when coffee had been served and they had moved to sit in front of the fire, did he ask laconically, 'Well?'

'That was a totally new experience,' she admitted.

'And?'

'You were right about it being a rewarding one.'

'I'm glad you think so. Incidentally, I've just had a new experience.'

When she looked at him enquiringly, he told her, 'You're the first woman I've brought here who hasn't chattered non-stop throughout the meal.'

She was wondering if he thought her dull company, when he added, 'Who was it who called his wife, My gracious silence?'

'I don't know,' she admitted, feeling a little glow of pleasure at his words. Though they had only just met, his approval meant a lot to her.

Stretching long legs towards the fire, he queried, 'Tell me, Virginia, have you ever been to New York?'

Somewhat thrown by the sudden change of subject, she answered, 'No, but I've always wanted to.'

He nodded as if satisfied, before asking, 'How would you like to work there?'

'I'd love to, but...' Then, uncertainly, she asked, 'Are you offering me a job?'

'Don't you want one?'

With a sudden suspicion, she said, 'It depends on why you're offering it.'

'You think it's because of your parents?'

'Isn't it?'

'Earlier you said, ''Who my parents are shouldn't make any difference. What I've learnt and am capable of, should.'' I go along with that.'

His dark brows drawn together in a frown, he added, 'Do you honestly believe that as far as I'm concerned, it matters one iota who your parents are?'

Feeling foolish, she said, 'But presumably they must

have mentioned me? Otherwise you would never have known I existed.'

'I'm not denying that we talked about you.'

'I can't imagine why,' she said flatly. 'It's over three months since I heard from them.'

'They seemed very proud of what you had achieved. I understand you got some special student award?'

'Yes.'

'For what, exactly?'

'The assignment was to set up from scratch an exhibition by an unknown artist.'

'What did that involve?'

'Putting into practice everything I'd learnt about selecting canvases, framing, lighting, printing techniques, cataloguing, publicity, etc. The main thing of course, was to make the show a success financially as well as critically.'

'Did you enjoy it?'

'Very much.'

'Would you like to do the same thing on a regular basis?'

Trying to hide the rush of excitement, she asked carefully, 'Is that the job you're offering me?'

'Yes.'

'Why?'

'Because my assistant curator, Miss Caulfield, who has been with me for the past four years, is leaving to get married. Her future husband is Canadian, and they're moving to Vancouver to live.'

'I mean, why me? There must be any number of more experienced people who would be only too pleased to take a post like that.'

He shrugged. 'I dare say that's true, but I've always believed in giving new blood a chance.'

Speaking her thoughts aloud, she said, 'It sounds fantastic, but I'd need somewhere to live.'

'There's an apartment that goes with the job, which incidentally carries a salary of—'

He named a figure that to Virginia seemed astronomical and, apparently reading her surprise, went on, 'It isn't cheap to live in New York, but I think you'll enjoy it.'

He spoke as if she had already accepted, she noted dazedly and, while she found it hard to believe that a man like Ryan Falconer had gone out of his way to look her up and offer her such an opportunity, she was choked by excitement.

It was a chance in a million. Not only would she be going to live in one of the most exciting cities in the world and doing the very job she wanted to do, but she would be working for him...

Though was that a good thing? the voice of caution asked. She was already dangerously smitten, and a man of that age, a man as attractive as Ryan, would almost certainly be either married, or involved in a long-term relationship.

But even if by some miracle he was neither, she was just an ordinary working girl, and therefore way out of his league. If she allowed her feelings to run away with her, she could get badly hurt. So would it be sensible to accept his very tempting offer?

Even while she asked herself the question, she knew in her heart of hearts that it would be anything but... And she was no risk-taker...

He broke the lengthening silence to ask quietly, 'But perhaps you feel you can't accept my offer because of your parents' involvement, slight though it was?'

'No, I—'

'I can assure you they didn't try to sell you...'

She could believe it. They didn't care about her enough to do that.

'In fact, though they told me where to find you, they haven't the faintest idea that I was even thinking of offering you a job...'

Then with the slightest hint of impatience, carefully controlled, he asked, 'So what do you say?'

Knowing quite well that she should refuse, she threw caution to the winds, and said eagerly, 'Yes, thank you, I'll take it.'

He smiled, and just for a moment she could have sworn he looked immensely relieved. But she must have misread his expression...

Holding out his hand he suggested lightly, 'Well, now you've made your decision, let's shake on it.'

With a strange feeling of going to meet her fate, she put her hand into his, and felt a little tingle of electricity run right up her arm.

His physical effect on her was devastating, and common sense warned her she was playing with fire. But, she realised with a sense of inevitability, she was already too deeply involved to care.

Her practical streak kicking in, and wondering how long it would take to save the air fare, she asked, 'When would you want me to start?'

'As soon as possible. Next week, preferably.'

'Oh...'

'Don't worry, I'll tell the Trantors you won't be going back, and make it right with them.'

'It's not just that,' she began awkwardly.

'There's some other complication?' His tone sharpened. 'A boyfriend perhaps?'

'No. At least no one serious.'

His manner growing relaxed once more, he said, 'You mentioned having a furnished flat... It's rented, presumably?'

'Yes.'

'So that presents no problem... I hope you're not one of the people who loathe flying?'

'No. At least I don't think so. I've never really flown anywhere.'

'But you do have a passport?'

'Yes. Just before I left college I went travelling with a group of other students in a ramshackle bus that broke down almost every day.'

'Sounds like fun.'

'It was.' She smiled at the memory.

Watching her face, and thinking how exquisite she was, he asked, 'So what exactly is the difficulty?'

'I'm afraid I haven't the money for the air fare,' she admitted reluctantly.

'My dear Virginia, I don't expect you to pay your own air fare. In fact I'd planned to take you back with me on the company jet.'

Bemused, she thought it sounded more as if he'd mounted a determined campaign to get her, rather than merely offering her a job opportunity. But perhaps that was how these high-powered American businessmen talked?

'Can you be ready to travel by Friday?'

Today was Wednesday. Apart from notifying her landlord that she was leaving, and packing her few personal belongings, there was little to do.

'Yes, I can be ready.'

'Good.'

Curiosity overcoming her innate shyness, she asked, 'What would have happened if I'd said I couldn't?'

He smiled. 'I would have put the jet on hold.'

Seeing how staggered she looked, he added in that ironic, self-mocking way she was starting to get to know, 'I'm the boss, and getting what I want is the name of the game.'

CHAPTER FOUR

THE company jet, though looking small against the commercial giants, was the height of luxury, with its own chef, a well-fitted *en-suite* bedroom, and a Monet hanging in the lounge.

Their flight across the pond, as the pilot called it, was smooth and uneventful but as far as Virginia was concerned, given the circumstances, it was the most thrilling thing she had ever done in her life.

Not that she'd done that much, she admitted, when Ryan, noting her suppressed excitement, teased her about it.

When they reached John F. Kennedy airport, a silver chauffeur-driven limousine was waiting to take them into the city.

'Though the birds-eye views are striking,' Ryan told her, 'I decided against the helicopter. Beth, who remembers driving into town for the first time, says it's an experience that shouldn't be missed.'

As far as Virginia was concerned even that was an understatement. New York, with its soaring buildings and superb skyline, was everything she had expected and more. A city by the sea, it had a luminous quality of light she hadn't even begun to envisage.

She felt she should pinch herself, but was afraid to in case she woke up. If this was a dream, she never wanted it to end.

Since taking her to The Pentagram, Ryan had scarcely left her side. No lover could have been more attentive.

When she had hesitantly asked if he hadn't something more important to do, he'd answered with a grin, 'The most important thing is making sure you don't change your mind.'

Why was it important that she shouldn't change her mind? she had wondered. Or had it been just a light, meaningless remark?

Probably.

Still he showed every sign of wanting her company, and for the past two evenings had insisted on taking her out to dinner. Each time he had delivered her safely back to her flat at a most respectable hour.

She had warned herself repeatedly that it would be madness to fall in love with him, until it was borne upon her that it was already too late.

Totally enslaved, liking him as well as loving him, all her usual rules of conduct had flown out of the window and, having discovered that he had neither a wife nor a current lady friend, if he had asked to stay, she would have found it difficult to refuse.

But he didn't. And the sensible part of her was grateful. It would have been the height of stupidity to get involved with a man like Ryan.

Yet she was already involved, emotionally if not physically, and had been since the moment he'd walked into the gallery.

Already, with no guarantee of it lasting, she would have sold her soul to be in his arms.

A truly modern woman might have made the first move, but she wasn't the type. She had neither the courage nor the confidence. Indeed, in the circumstances, a kind of perverse pride forbade it.

Apart from anything else, he might not be interested in her as a woman.

Though on more than one occasion she had glimpsed a little flame in those indigo eyes that had set her pulses racing, and had made her think the attraction might be mutual.

Still, so long as Ryan held back, she was safe.

But while he'd made no attempt to deepen the relationship, his attitude couldn't be called businesslike. He treated her with a kind of quixotic, self-mocking camaraderie, that at once pleased and puzzled her.

She couldn't bring herself to believe that he treated all his prospective employees in that way, so what made her different?

Though it seemed to make no sense, the only reason she could come up with was her parents. Not wanting to rock the boat, however, she had said nothing.

The traffic was very heavy as they drove into town, and it was late afternoon by the time they reached Fifth Avenue, with its bustling pedestrians, its spectacular buildings, and brilliantly lit shop windows.

All the colours of the rainbow seemed to be reflected in the towering glass skyscrapers, while in Central Park the trees glowed gold and bronze and scarlet in the last dying rays of the sun.

Well used to keeping her emotions hidden, for once in her life Virginia was unable to do so. Fascinated by the beauty and vibrancy of that famous avenue, its air of being *en fête*, she exclaimed, 'Isn't it wonderful?'

Ryan smiled. 'Then, you won't mind living here?'

Thinking he meant the city, she exclaimed, 'I'm sure I'll love it.'

Then, eagerly, she asked 'Where exactly will I be living?' Somehow, in the excitement and upheaval of the last forty eight hours, it was something she hadn't got round to asking.

'Here.'

'Here? You surely don't mean on Fifth Avenue?'

'I do mean on Fifth Avenue,' he contradicted. 'In fact in this very building,' he added, as they drew up outside a skyscraper with glittering window displays each side of an imposing entrance.

'It's known as Falconer's Tower. It was built just over thirty years ago when my father decided to put some of the profits from his investment in paper mills into real estate...'

While the smart young chauffeur opened the door and stood rigidly to attention, Ryan handed Virginia out and, hiding a slight smile, said gravely, 'Thank you, Carlson. Will you have the luggage sent straight up?'

'Certainly, Mr Falconer.'

Craning her neck to peer up at the glass tower, Virginia said, 'It's so tall. How on earth do you fill so much space?'

'There's a car park below the shopping mall and, above, office and business accommodation. Next comes a comprehensive leisure complex. Then the top two floors are divided into four separate apartments.

'I'm living in the penthouse at the moment...' Watching her face, he added deliberately, 'You have the small apartment next door.'

As she gaped at him, a hand beneath her elbow, he escorted her across the sidewalk and into a chandelier-hung private lobby, where a stocky, middle-aged security guard gave them a laconic salute.

'Afternoon, Mr Falconer.'

'Afternoon George. How's the new son and heir?'

Beaming proudly, George answered, 'Fine. Just fine. Starting to look like his old dad.'

'Could do worse. By the way, this is Miss Adams. She'll be living upstairs.'

'Right, Mr Falconer. I'll let the others know.'

While the elevator whisked them smoothly upwards, Virginia tried to catch her breath. She had expected a single room 'walk-up' in one of the less salubrious areas. In her wildest dreams she had never imagined living on Fifth Avenue next door to Ryan.

The whole thing was incredible. It made no sense. He wasn't treating her like an employee at all. And once again she wondered, why not?

But maybe his present assistant curator was still occupying the apartment that went with the job?

'Is this a temporary arrangement?' she queried.

He slanted her a glance. 'What makes you ask?'

Then instantly on her wavelength, he said, 'Oh, I see. No, it isn't temporary. The building where Miss Caulfield is living now has been earmarked for redevelopment, and as the unit next to mine happened to be standing empty...'

Why was an apartment in such a prestigious building standing empty? she wondered.

As though reading her thoughts, he explained, 'We had expected Janice, my stepsister, to move into it when she finished college, but she's changed her mind about staying in New York.'

A twinkle in his eye, he added, 'It may have something to do with a handsome young diplomat who, in a month or so, is returning to Washington. In the meantime she's keeping Beth company...'

As he finished speaking the elevator sighed to a halt and the doors slid open.

They emerged into a spacious, marble-floored foyer, where ornamental trees in tubs were interspersed with statues of Greek gods.

'A bit over the top, don't you think?' Ryan asked, pulling a face. 'Apparently it was my mother's idea and, as I'd just been born, my father decided to indulge her whim. However, I've always loved this.' Above a central staircase, a huge round window provided a dramatic view over the roof tops. 'I used to call it my sky window.'

On the opposite wall, there was a series of smaller matching inner windows on either side of a large handsomely carved door.

'That's the penthouse suite. It was the main family home when my father was alive. In those days he and Beth did a lot of entertaining.

'But after he died, a couple of years back, Beth, who

had suffered a mild heart attack, decided to move out. She wanted somewhere smaller and cosier…

'And this is where you'll be living.' He steered Virginia to a slightly more modest-looking door on the left and, having opened it, led the way inside. 'Let me show you around. As I said, this apartment's quite small, but it is on the corner of the building, so you get good views in both directions…'

Feeling rather like Alice in Wonderland, she left her shoulder bag in the hall and followed him, only to discover that her 'quite small' apartment was much bigger and grander than she could ever have imagined.

Though it had only one bedroom, that and the other three rooms, a living-room, a dining-room, and a well-stocked kitchen, were large and airy and luxuriously furnished.

Both outer walls of the living-room had sliding glass panels that opened onto a pleasant terrace and roof-garden with views that, rather than merely good, Virginia would have called fantastic.

The sun had gone down now leaving the sky streaked with pink and plum and palest green, while all over the city a myriad of lights were starting to spangle the encroaching dusk.

'Like it?' Ryan asked.

Speechless, she nodded.

'When you've had a chance to relax and settle in I'll take you to Clouds for dinner.'

Clouds, she knew, was equally famous as the Rainbow Room.

Her cup was running over, when he added casually, 'On the way out we'll stop so you can meet the rest of the family.'

Somehow she found her voice. 'The rest of the family?'

'Beth and Janice have an apartment on the floor below, and my stepbrother, Steven, and his wife Madeline, live next door to them.'

So she would be living surrounded by the whole of the Falconer clan, Virginia thought dazedly.

'They're expecting us to call in, so they'll all be assembled. Don't worry, it's not as bad as it sounds,' he added cheerfully. 'None of them actually bite, and I'm sure you'll like Beth...'

It was obvious from the way his face softened that he was very fond of his stepmother.

As she followed him back to the hall, he added, 'In fact I hope and believe you'll all get on well together.'

Seeing he was waiting for a response, and sensing that for some reason it was important to him, she said with more conviction than she felt, 'I'm sure we will.'

If that was what Ryan wanted, no matter what happened, she would do her best to get on well with them.

But how would they feel about it?

It was clear from what he'd said previously that they were a family who moved in wealthy upper-class New York society circles, who mingled with presidents and the like.

While she, though she had had the benefit of a good education, was a virtual nobody to them, who worked for a living. And what was worse, she was Ryan's employee...

The bell rang, breaking into her uneasy musings.

'This will be the luggage,' Ryan remarked and, opening the door, directed a blue-uniformed youth with a trolley. 'Leave those two pieces, Rawdon will deal with them. The other two need to come in here... Where would you like them?' He raised an interrogative eyebrow at Virginia. 'The bedroom?'

'Please.' She tried to sound crisp and businesslike.

When Ryan had first shown her the bedroom, the sight of the big double bed and the erotic images it had immediately conjured up, had made her blush.

Catching his eye, and guessing by the gleam in it that

he had been following her train of thought, she had blushed even harder and had hurried out.

As soon as the cases had been deposited, some dollar bills changed hands, and with a chirpy, 'Thanks, Mr Falconer,' the youth departed.

Standing by the open door, Ryan said, 'Well, I'll leave you to unpack and make yourself at home… Oh, and you'll need this.' He dropped the latch key into her hand.

'Thank you.'

Suddenly, and perhaps for the first time, the whole thing seemed real. For better or worse she was here in New York, starting a new and thrilling job, living on Fifth Avenue, next door to Ryan…

She smiled up at him, her face reflecting all the excitement and anticipation, the gladness and joy of being here with him.

Making no move to go, he stood looking down at her radiant face, his own face strangely taut.

When he bent his head slightly, she thought for one heart-stopping moment that he was about to kiss her.

Instead, he touched her cheek with a single finger, sending a frisson of pleasure running through her. 'It's been a long day and you'll probably need an early night, so I'll call for you about seven.'

While she stood like a statue, he went out, closing the door quietly behind him.

Rooted to the spot, it was a little while before she could pull herself together enough to head for the bedroom.

Only when she approached her cases to start unpacking did she realise she was still holding the key Ryan had given her, clutching it so hard that it had made a white imprint in her soft palm.

It was just before seven when the doorbell rang. Wearing the only cocktail dress he hadn't seen and, after taking a lot of time and trouble, satisfied she was looking her best, Virginia went to answer.

Dressed in a well-cut dinner jacket and stylish shirt, his thick dark hair curling a little, Ryan stood smiling down at her, making her pulses race and her knees grow weak.

As well as being breathtakingly handsome, he looked so cool and self-assured, that her small reservoir of confidence evaporated on the spot, and she found herself asking anxiously, 'Will I do?'

He looked her over from head to toe, taking in her glossy ash-brown hair, her lovely face with its greeny-grey eyes and wide, passionate mouth, her slender figure in the simple green sheath, her lack of jewellery, and thought he'd never seen anything more beautiful.

Raising her hand to his lips, he kissed the palm.

The romantic little gesture took her breath away.

'There won't be a man there who doesn't envy me,' he assured her.

Watching her long lashes sweep down and a tinge of pink come into her cheeks, he felt such a surge of desire that his voice was almost rough as he asked, 'Have you a coat?'

She produced a soft fun-fur jacket which he helped her into, before suggesting, 'As the family live only one floor below, shall we walk down?'

All her previous apprehension returning, she nodded, trying unsuccessfully to hide her nervousness.

With a reassuring smile, he tucked her hand through his arm, and together they descended the marble staircase to a foyer no less impressive than the one they had just left.

Ryan had barely touched the bell of the nearest door when it opened, giving the impression that the occupant had been waiting with some eagerness.

'You must be Miss Adams. Do come in.' A smiling, silver-haired woman drew Virginia into a charming hallway. 'I'm Elizabeth Falconer, Ryan's stepmother…'

There was no sign of the cool standoffishness that Virginia had dreaded, in fact just the opposite.

'But please call me Beth, if you'd care to. Almost everyone does...'

Elizabeth Falconer who, after more than twenty years in the States, still spoke with an English accent, was short and slender, with soft brown eyes and a pretty, gentle face.

She had an unmistakable air of warmth and generosity, which marked her as a woman who loved more than she hated, and gave more than she took.

Virginia liked her on sight.

'Come through and meet the rest of the family.'

There were three people in the large attractive living-room.

A striking blonde in her early thirties was sitting on the couch, a magazine open on her knee.

Standing by a built-in bar, a pleasant-looking man of medium height, with fairish hair and blue eyes, was serving drinks.

And perched on a pouffe in front of an open fire, a regal-looking tortoiseshell cat on her lap, was a young woman with below shoulder-length dark hair.

'Jump down, Sheba.' Pushing the affronted cat off, the girl scrambled to her feet and came to meet them.

'This is my daughter, Janice,' Beth Falconer said fondly.

With the same gentle face, the same brown eyes, and the same petite build, Janice was a carbon copy of her mother.

'Hi!' she said with a friendly smile. 'So you're Virginia.' Then cryptically, she added, 'Ryan was right.'

'And this is my son, Steven,' Beth went on.

Though the eye-colour was different, there was no mistaking the family likeness as Steven came forward to shake hands warmly. 'It's very nice to meet you, Miss Adams... Or do you mind if I call you Virginia?'

'I hope you will.' Virginia's smile held both relief and pleasure, and encompassed them all.

With obvious pride, Steven went on, 'May I introduce my wife, Madeline.'

His pride was fully justified. A natural blonde, with a stunning figure and long slender legs, Madeline was one of the most beautiful women Virginia had ever seen.

'Hello, Miss Adams.' The aquamarine eyes surveyed her coolly. 'Are you nicely settled in? I must admit we were all rather stunned when Ryan said he was bringing a woman he'd only just met back with him.'

The words and the accompanying smile were, on the surface, civil enough but, sensing an underlying hint of censure, Virginia said, 'I'm sure you must have been. Everything has happened so quickly that I still feel that way myself.'

'Won't you take off your coat and sit down?'

'What can I get you to drink?'

Steven and his mother spoke simultaneously.

Before Virginia could respond to either, Ryan, who had been standing quietly in the background, said firmly, 'Thanks, but Carlson will have the car waiting. We're dining at Clouds. I booked a table for seven thirty as Virginia will need an early night.'

'I'm quite sure you both will,' Madeline murmured sweetly.

Accompanying them to the door, Beth gave Ryan a little smile and patted his arm, as though in tacit approval.

Then, turning to Virginia, she urged, 'As we're so close, do pop in any time. You'll be very welcome… By the way, I've tried to make sure you have enough supplies to last until you get sorted out, but if there's anything else you need just let me know.'

'Thank you, you're very kind,' Virginia said, and meant it.

'Not too much of an ordeal, was it?' Ryan asked as the elevator carried them downwards.

'Not at all. They couldn't have been nicer.'

'Madeline could,' he said bluntly. 'But then, I should have expected it. She's not one to make friends with other women, particularly beautiful ones.'

Startled, Virginia protested, 'But I'm not beautiful.'

He turned his head to smile at her. 'That's a matter of opinion. I think you are.'

Even if she didn't think so, she found herself walking on air because he thought her so.

Clouds, with its live orchestra and gleaming dance floor, its rich ambience and even richer clientele, was out of this world.

Almost literally.

One of the highest restaurants in Manhattan, it had magical views over the jewel-encrusted city. A city that, like a beautiful woman, only truly came into its own at night.

But for all the wealth of wonder outside, Virginia's eyes were more often on the man who sat opposite her at their small table.

To begin with she made an effort to be practical, to ask about the gallery and the job she would soon be starting, but Ryan shook his head at her.

'This is no time to be talking about work. We're here to relax and enjoy ourselves. Okay?'

'Okay.'

Embracing the here and now, and refusing to allow the future and what kind of problems it might hold, to dim her happiness, she gave herself up to the sheer delight of being with Ryan in such a marvellous venue.

The evening flew as they talked and laughed, drank fine wine, and ate delicious food, which, head-over-heels in love, she scarcely tasted.

Ryan was a charming and stimulating companion who struck sparks off her and made her feel wittier and more glamorous than she knew herself to be.

But as well as the razzle-dazzle there was a sense of harmony between them, a feeling of rightness and content-

ment, as if they were both exactly where they wanted to
be.

By the time the coffee was served, however, beneath the
surface ease was a growing tension, a sexual awareness that
made her unable to meet his eyes, and caused her first to
stumble over words, and then lapse into silence.

'More coffee?' Ryan asked.

'No, thank you.'

'Would you like to stay and dance for a while...?'

Just the thought of being held in his arms made her tremble and turned her insides to jelly.

'Or perhaps you're ready to go?'

Unworldly though she was, she knew he was asking a
great deal more than that simple question, and what she
answered was crucial.

Once she had burnt her bridges, there could be no turning
back. So was it the employer, or the man, who really mattered?

Certainly the man.

But suppose he just wanted a one-night stand? Or, at the
most, a brief fling? Could she live with that? The loss of
pride? The possible humiliation?

The problem was she didn't know him well enough to
be certain what kind of man he was beneath that charming
exterior.

Some men could be cold-blooded and calculating. What
if she proved to be just an embarrassment to him once he'd
got what he wanted?

She could end up with no job, no money, nowhere to
live, and no way of getting home.

The possibilities were dire.

But somehow none of it seemed to matter.

It was as though the whole thing had been preordained.
As though they had been destined to meet and become
lovers...

While the thoughts raced through her mind, he sat quietly watching her face.

Though he showed no outward sign, she sensed his impatience and, her own suddenly matching it, said thickly, 'Yes, I'm ready to go.'

While he paid the bill, her coat was produced, Carlson was alerted, and a minute later they were going down in the elevator, standing carefully apart.

The limousine was waiting, and they drove back in silence, keeping a good foot of space between them, as though afraid to touch in case the conflagration started.

When they reached Falconer's Tower, Ryan said goodnight to Carlson and paused to have a word with the night security guard, his leisurely air belying the need that was driving him.

In the elevator, he took Virginia's hand and, feeling her tremble, said, 'I hadn't meant to rush you, but I find I can't help myself.'

Then with a scrupulousness she could only admire, 'You do want this, don't you?'

'Yes,' she whispered.

'Sure?'

'Quite sure.'

He bent his dark head and kissed her.

During her years at college she had gone out with a number of would-be boyfriends and had been kissed many times.

At worst, they had been hot and wet and faintly nauseating, causing her to break off that particular encounter without delay. At best, they had been pleasant. But even the pleasant ones had never stirred her enough to make her want to repeat the experience.

Ryan's kiss, on the other hand, filled her with a soaring wonder and delight that melted every bone in her body and left her hungry for more.

As the elevator slid to a halt and the doors opened, she

found herself wondering briefly which apartment he would choose to take her to.

Probably hers.

Using his own seemed to *commit* him more. Added to that, he no doubt had a staff of servants to complicate matters.

Still holding her hand, he led her across the lobby to his penthouse.

'What about the servants?' she asked huskily.

'There's only Rawdon, and he's very discreet. He has his own quarters, and stays there unless I buzz for him.'

Opening the door, he swept her into his arms and, using his heel to close the door behind them, carried her through to the bedroom.

Setting her down gently, he slipped off her coat and shoes and, his eyes dark and intent, began to undress her.

Though there was an urgency that wouldn't be denied, his hands were deft as he removed her stockings; and he unfastened her bra without fumbling.

As soon as she was naked, he laid her on the bed and gazed his fill, before stripping off his own clothes.

Broad across the shoulders and narrow-hipped, his limbs perfectly in proportion, he was magnificent, and her breath caught her throat at the sight of him.

He carried not an ounce of surplus weight, and muscles rippled beneath a smooth, tanned skin as he leaned down to kiss her.

Then, a man claiming his mate with a kind of triumphant certainty, he lowered himself into the waiting cradle of her hips.

Poised for an instant, hard male flesh against female softness, he smiled into her eyes while she gazed back at him.

Though she wanted him with every fibre of her being, she gasped at his first strong thrust. But the brief pain was unimportant, swept away in the heat and rapture of their coming together.

The first driving need over, amazed and pleased by the fact that she had been a virgin, he made love to her again.

This time he took it slowly.

As well as using a leisurely and skilful expertise that lifted her to heights of ecstasy she had never even dreamt of, he made love to her with words, telling her how exquisite her breasts were, how flawless her skin was, how much she delighted him.

She was still quivering with pleasure when he lifted himself away and, gathering her close, settled her head on his shoulder.

His hand stroking up and down her arm, he said softly, wonderingly, 'You're such a joy to make love to. Not only are you the most beautiful woman I've ever seen, but you respond with such warmth and passion. I can't understand how you've managed to stay a virgin this long.'

Feeling like an oddity, she said, 'It wasn't intentional. Somehow it just happened…'

Naturally discriminating, she had avoided the more obvious pitfalls of adolescence until maturity had helped her to value herself as a woman.

'I didn't like the idea of casual sex, and I never met a man I cared for enough to sleep with.' Too late she realised how revealing that last sentence was.

'Does that mean you care for me?' he asked tenderly.

Somehow, she answered, 'It means I find you attractive.'

'Is that all?'

'Isn't that enough?'

'I hardly think so. You see, I want to marry you.'

'Marry me?' She sounded as staggered as she felt.

'Marry you,' he repeated firmly.

Convinced that this must be some kind of leg-pull, she said, 'Hadn't you better be careful? I might take you seriously.'

'I *want* you to take me seriously.'

'You can't mean you really *do* want to marry me.'

'It's hardly the kind of thing I'd joke about.'

'But we've only just met.'

'Don't you believe in love at first sight?'

'Yes…' Having lost her heart to him the moment she had set eyes on him, she could hardly deny it.

His hand moved to take her chin and lift her face to his. 'I was rather hoping you did.'

'B-but we're poles apart,' she stammered. 'You're—'

'A man who wants to marry you.' Dropping a kiss on her nose, he added quizzically, 'I must say you're taking an awful lot of convincing.'

'I don't understand why you want to marry me. Most people these days just opt for a relationship.'

'Is that what you want?'

'No,' she admitted.

He kissed her. 'Me neither. I guess I've just got old-fashioned values. Finding my future wife has too, is an unexpected pleasure.'

My future wife…

Much as she wanted to believe it was possible, she was still troubled by their differing backgrounds.

'Another reason for getting married is that in a year or two's time I'd like to have children and I want them with you. Wouldn't you like a family?'

'Yes, I would.'

Watching her face, he asked, 'So what's bothering you?'

'Our lifestyles are so dissimilar.'

'But not incompatible. Don't you think you could get used to being rich?'

'It's not just that. It's the whole thing. You live in a completely different world. Move in a different society…'

'You're living in my world now, and the society I move in would welcome you with open arms. You're beautiful, intelligent, well-educated; you have character and style—'

'And famous parents?'

'Not to mention a chip on your shoulder.'

Knowing he was right, she mumbled, 'I'm sorry, I don't seem to be able to help it.'

'Well, if having famous parents bothers you that much, we'll keep quiet about it and pretend they don't exist...'

'It doesn't bother me, it's just—'

'Though, as I owe them a big debt of gratitude, I would have liked to invite them to the wedding.'

His hand had moved down to her breast and was playing with a pink nipple, sending little shafts of pleasure through her.

He had such power over her it was frightening.

Needing to assert herself a little, she said, 'I haven't said I'll marry you yet.'

'Well, I'm warning you, if you don't say yes, and name a date immediately, I'll make love to you until you do.'

'Mmm...' she murmured. Then, daringly, she added, 'It might be better to refuse then...'

He laughed joyously, and kissed her again. 'So long as I get the right answer in the end, I think I'll do things my way.'

CHAPTER FIVE

THE rest of the night was spent in a much more enjoyable occupation than talking, and they were having breakfast next morning in the penthouse's large sunny kitchen before Ryan once again brought up the subject of marriage.

'So when is the wedding to be?'

Virginia was perched on a stool opposite. Her face was shiny and innocent of make-up, her curly hair still damp from the shower.

She was wearing one of his white towelling bathrobes and it practically buried her, the shoulders halfway down her arms, the sleeves rolled up several times to leave her hands free.

He thought how lovely she was, how completely and utterly irresistible.

She looked up, her eyes, jade green in the bright sunshine, searching his face. 'Are you *certain* you want to marry me?'

'One hundred per cent.'

Watching her frown a little, as she returned to buttering her toast, he asked, 'You're not still having problems with the idea?'

'I keep wondering about your family. What if they object?'

'I'm certain they'll do nothing of the kind.'

'Just suppose they do?'

'As head of the family, I don't need their approval,' he pointed out evenly. 'But I'm sure they'll all be delighted for me. Beth in particular.'

'So to get back to my original question, when is it to be? And don't suggest spring. I don't want to wait that long.'

'When would you like it to be?'

'As soon as possible. The middle of December, say? That gives us about two months to plan everything.'

'Plan everything?' she echoed.

He raised an eyebrow at her. 'Why so surprised? Doesn' it usually take time to organise a wedding?'

'Not if it's a quiet one.'

'But ours isn't going to be a quiet one.'

'Oh, but—'

'If you were thinking of some hole in the corner affair the answer's no. I want to flaunt my bride. I'd like us to get married at St Patrick's and have the kind of wedding that will take New York society by storm...'

Seeing he meant every word he said, she threw in the towel, and agreed dazedly. 'All right, if that's really what you want.'

'And if you have no objections, I'd still like to invite your parents.'

'Of course we'll invite them.'

'That's my girl.'

'I'm sorry to have been so stupid about the whole thing.'

Quietly, he suggested, 'I think your father should have the chance to give you away. Don't you?'

'I suppose so. Though I doubt if he'll want to.' Then realising how ungracious that sounded, she added, 'But we could always ask him.'

Ryan smiled at her and reached across the breakfast bar to take her hand and raise it to his lips.

'Now, with regard to the planning; I'm sure Beth will be only too happy to help... That is, if you'll let her?'

'Of course I'll let her... But are you sure she'll be all right? You said she'd had a heart attack.'

'I'm convinced that kind of excitement will only do her good.'

'In that case I'd be very grateful for her help.'

'Then, as soon as we're both dressed, we'll go down and give her the good news.'

To Virginia's relief, Beth, a romantic at heart, showed every sign of being as delighted as Ryan had forecasted, and if any of the others had any doubts, they kept them to themselves.

Her own parents, who lived in Soho in a handsome cast-iron building embellished with Italianate pillars and curlicues, were given the news the same morning.

Her mother, tall and dark-haired still, with the face of a dreamer, said she was pleased; while her father, grizzled and handsome, offered his congratulations and best wishes.

When Ryan suggested quietly that Brad might like to give his daughter away, to Virginia's surprise, he agreed at once. 'Just let me know the time and place.'

He produced a bottle of champagne and they toasted the engagement, before retreating back into their own little world.

After lunching in Chinatown, Ryan took Virginia to choose an engagement ring.

Dazzled by the vast selection of glittering stones, she finally picked out one that appealed to her.

'It's a sardonyx,' the jeweller explained, 'and a rare and beautiful one. The sardonyx is starting to gain popularity among the more romantically inclined because, in the language of gems, it means conjugal happiness.'

Liking its clear glowing amber colour, the antique setting, and most of all the sentiment attached to it, she glanced at Ryan, seeking his approval.

'Would you like to try it on?'

'Please.'

He slipped it on to her slender finger and, finding it a perfect fit, studied it for a moment before agreeing, 'Yes, it suits your hand.'

'You wouldn't sooner I had a diamond?'

Shaking his head, he said, 'Diamonds are a bit boring for you, my love.'

The endearment was all she needed to make her day perfect.

As though caught up in some magic spell, everything continued to go well. Janice was thrilled when they asked her to be bridesmaid, and accepted eagerly, while Steven declared himself delighted to act as best man.

Only Madeline, though staying coolly polite in front of Ryan, tended to make snide remarks when he wasn't around. Especially about Virginia's engagement ring.

'What exactly is it?' she enquired, looking down her nose at the large oval stone in its heavy gold setting.

'It's a sardonyx,' Virginia said quietly.

'How quaint. Wouldn't a diamond have been a better bet? It would be worth more if Ryan changed his mind and you got to keep it.'

But not even the older woman's spite could spoil Virginia's happiness, and she lived in a rainbow bubble of pure joy. Ryan loved her and they were going to be married; she would be part of a happy family. Her dream was coming true.

Though she spent a lot of her nights in his bed, concerned about what the family might think, she resisted all his urgings to move into the penthouse completely. She even refused to have a key.

When, after taking the first two weeks off to show her New York, Ryan reluctantly returned to work, Virginia, feeling the need to be independent, and unwilling to let him support her before they were married, decided it was time she did the same.

As they were lying in bed that night, pleasurably content after making love, she broached the subject. 'Ryan...'

'Mmm...?' Taking her hand, he separated her fingers, planting a kiss on each.

'I'd like to start my job at the gallery.'

'There's absolutely no need for you to work.'

'But I want to. If I don't, what shall I do with myself all day while you're at the office?'

'My love, there's your trousseau to buy and a wedding to organise… And, speaking of weddings, where would you like to go for our honeymoon?'

'I don't really mind.' Anywhere would be heaven with Ryan.

'Well, we could either find some snow and go skiing, or head for the sun. Do you have a preference?'

'Sun, I think.'

'Mexico? Hawaii? The Caribbean?'

'I've always wanted to go to Hawaii.'

'Then, Hawaii it is.' Gathering her close, he closed his eyes, thick dark lashes lying above his hard cheekbones like fans.

'Don't go to sleep yet,' she said.

He opened one eye. 'Does that mean you're not satisfied? You want more?'

'No, it means I've no intention of being sidetracked with all this talk of honeymoons.'

'Sidetracked? I don't know what you mean,' he said with a pretend innocence.

'You know perfectly well what I mean. I want to start the job you promised me.'

He groaned.

Tilting her face, she began to plant little baby kisses along his firm jaw line.

'Darling are you trying to cajole me?'

'Yes…'

'Well don't stop, I like it.'

'Ryan.'

'What about the wedding?'

'Beth, bless her heart, is doing most of the work, and seems to be having the time of her life.'

'Very well,' he capitulated with a sigh, 'if that's what

you really want. But do take a day off here and there to shop for your trousseau.'

'I will,' she agreed happily, and rewarded him with a kiss that eventually led to other things.

It was quite true that Beth was having the time of her life, and one day she said as much.

After a hectic and enjoyable morning of trousseau shopping, she and Virginia were eating lunch at Blundells and discussing the actual wedding day.

The ceremony had been scheduled for eleven o'clock, and afterwards there was to be a reception for two hundred guests at the Waldorf Astoria.

Her enthusiasm unabated, Beth said, 'I guess the next step will be to work out a seating plan.'

'Well as you know everyone and I don't, perhaps you'll advise me?'

'I'd be glad to.' Her cheeks a little flushed, the older woman admitted, 'I absolutely adore all the excitement of planning weddings. In fact there are times when I wish I was like Mrs Bennet and had five daughters to marry off.'

'Well, you're not far behind,' Virginia said with a smile. 'This is your second wedding and you still have another daughter to go...'

Shaking her head, Beth said, 'It's the first, actually. Madeline felt she wanted to do her own thing without any—'

She stopped speaking abruptly, but Virginia felt sure that the word on the tip of her tongue had been interference.

After a moment Beth went on almost apologetically, 'I know I should have asked sooner if you really minded me poking my nose in, but you were so nice about it that I...' The sentence tailed off.

'Of course I don't mind! And I've never thought of it as poking your nose in. In fact I don't know what I'd do without you.'

Looking relieved, Beth said, 'I did begin to wonder, as you have a mother of your own, if you would have preferred me to keep out of it.'

'Whatever put that idea into your head?' Virginia asked. Then realised that perhaps she should have asked, whoever?

Madeline, she was beginning to know, had an armoury of poisoned darts that she placed to do the most harm.

Giving Beth's hand an impulsive squeeze, she added, 'My own mother isn't the slightest bit interested, so it's lovely to have someone who is…'

As the older woman beamed her pleasure, Virginia added, 'Just promise me you won't overdo it.'

'If you mean my silly old heart, don't worry. Doing something I really enjoy is therapeutic.'

Her confidence fully restored, Beth went back to cheerfully discussing the seating arrangements for the reception.

'One of the first things we'll need to decide is who we put next to the ambassador. He's a charming man, and a good conversationalist…'

Though Virginia loved her job and enjoyed the days spent in the gallery, she always found herself eagerly anticipating the evenings spent in Ryan's company and the nights spent in his arms.

He was a wonderful lover, skilful and passionate, generous and tender, and the days and nights flew past in a whirl of happiness and excitement.

By the first week in December, most of the wedding arrangements had been made, leaving only a few things still to do.

Virginia was seeing less of Ryan now, as he worked late most evenings to tie in all the loose ends before their month in Hawaii.

On the Friday, Virginia took the day off and, accompanied by Beth, went to Claud Fucielle for the final fitting of her wedding gown.

Made of ivory silk, it was beautiful and romantic, with a medieval-type bodice and sleeves, and a full skirt that rustled when she moved.

As they drove back home after yet another afternoon of trousseau shopping, and tea and crumpets in the old-fashioned comfort of Myers, Beth queried, 'Will you be seeing Ryan this evening, or is he planning to work late again?'

'No, he isn't working, but I won't be seeing him. He mentioned having to attend a charity dinner.'

'Ryan's a good man. He gives to a lot of charities both here and abroad. In fact, though he rarely talks about it, he supports some of them practically single-handed...'

Yes, she could believe that, Virginia thought. Ryan was both caring and generous.

'Tell you what,' Beth pursued after a moment, 'if you've no other plans, why don't you have dinner with me? Janice is out, so I'll be on my own.'

The two had become firm friends, and Virginia answered at once, 'Thanks. I'd love to.'

Frowning a little, Beth added, 'I've just remembered that Steven's away on a business trip, so I suppose I ought to invite Madeline as well. Though I very much doubt if she'll want to come...

'Mrs Cluny usually serves dinner at seven-thirty. But don't wait till then, come down as soon as you're ready.'

When Virginia rang the bell at six-thirty, she felt nothing but relief to be told that Madeline had refused the invitation.

Echoing her thoughts, Beth went on, 'I must say I'm rather relieved that she had other plans. Somehow I don't find Madeline all that easy to be with.'

Neither of the women cared much for television so they spent a pleasant evening playing crib and listening to music, while they sprinkled a companionable silence with snippets of conversation, as people do when they're comfortable with each other.

It was almost eleven o'clock before they said their goodnights and Virginia left.

Wondering how late Ryan would be, she began to walk up to the next floor. She had just reached the top of the stairs when she saw that the penthouse door was open and two figures were standing in the doorway, very close together, and facing each other.

Ryan, his legs and feet bare, was wearing a short navy blue bathrobe, and Madeline, a black satin kimono with matching slippers. Her gleaming blonde hair hung round her shoulders.

She was very tall for a woman, and her pale head was almost on a level with his dark one. A long, scarlet-tipped hand resting on his sleeve, she was talking quietly, intimately.

Feeling awkward, Virginia hesitated.

Madeline cast the briefest glance her way; without seeming to notice her presence and, apparently wrapped up in each other, the pair kept talking.

A moment later Madeline put her arms around Ryan's neck and they kissed briefly but, to Virginia's eyes, passionately.

Suddenly chilled, she stood rooted to the spot while Madeline swept past, giving her a glittering glance that was at once inimical and triumphant.

'So where did you spring from?' Crossing the lobby to meet her, Ryan took Virginia's cold hand.

Through stiff lips, she said, 'I've been having dinner with Beth.' Even in her own ears her voice sounded strained and jerky.

Using the hand he was holding, he drew her into his arms and bent to kiss her mouth.

In a purely involuntary reaction, she turned her head away, so that his lips just brushed her cheek.

Straightening, he advised coolly, 'Don't let it throw you. It was just Madeline being...suppose we say...demonstrative...'

Demonstrative was the last thing Virginia would have suspected the ice-cool Madeline of being.

Seeing her troubled face, he tried to make light of it. 'Relatives do kiss you know.'

They were a close-knit family and relatives did kiss. But should sister-in-law and brother-in-law kiss in quite that way?

Drawing her towards the penthouse, he said, 'Come and tell me what kind of day you've had? How did the fitting go?'

As the door closed behind them, making an effort to match his casual tone, she said, 'Fine.'

When he would have gone straight through to the bedroom, she hung back, and with a faint sigh he led the way into the spacious living-room.

Remembering how Madeline had refused Beth's invitation, and wondering if they'd spent the evening together, she asked, 'What happened, did your dinner fall through?'

'No. It finished earlier than I'd expected.'

'Oh.'

'I got back about half an hour ago and rang your bell. When there was no answer, I presumed you were in the shower or something. If I'd realised you were with Beth I would have come down.'

Instead he'd apparently been having a tête-à-tête with Madeline... The thought came unbidden. She tried hard to dismiss it, and failed.

Watching her face, Ryan said briskly, 'Look, I think we'd better clear the air.'

Leading her to the couch, he gently pushed her down and took a seat beside her. 'I don't know what kind of scenario you're coming up with in that head of yours, but let me tell you straight away that Madeline and I had only been talking a couple of minutes. She didn't even come inside.

'I'd just finished taking a shower when I heard the bell. I went to the door fully expecting it to be you…'

While Virginia wanted desperately to believe him, a little demon of doubt pointed out that it was an odd time for a woman to call on her brother-in-law, dressed only in a kimono…

As though answering the thought, he explained, 'She'd popped up on the spur of the moment to ask me to choose between two possible wedding gifts, and to tell me how pleased she was for both of us…'

Reading Virginia's expression, he added, 'Yes, I must admit I took that with a pinch of salt. On the whole Madeline isn't the kind to be pleased for anyone but herself…

'However, I may be misjudging her, she certainly sounded genuine.'

'And that's when you kissed her?'

'I didn't kiss her. She kissed me.'

Then quizzically, he added, 'Now, have you finished giving me a hard time?'

'I'm sorry.' Her misgivings set completely at rest, she went into his arms like going home, and lifted her face for his kiss.

It was Janice who, a few evenings later, innocently put fresh doubts into Virginia's mind.

Not long in from the gallery, she was having a leisurely cup of tea in her kitchen, when the phone rang. She picked up the receiver to find it was her future sister-in-law, sounding excited.

'They've delivered my bridesmaid's dress, and a selection of headdresses. Mom's out, so can you spare a few minutes to come and help me choose which of them looks best.'

'I'll be straight down.'

Clad in her peach silk finery, Janice came flying to meet her. 'There's one or two that are out of this world! Come and take a look.'

The two women were in the midst of assessing the various headdresses when they were interrupted by the doorbell.

'That'll be Mom,' Janice said. Adding indulgently, 'She's always mislaying her key.'

'I'll go,' Virginia offered.

When she opened the door, her heart dropped to find it was Madeline, beautifully dressed as usual, her blonde chignon gleaming.

Brushing past without a word, she went through to the living-room, leaving the younger woman to follow.

'Where's Ryan? I'd like to talk to him.'

'I'm sorry, I'm afraid I don't know,' Virginia answered evenly.

'I felt sure he'd be with you. He's usually dancing attendance.'

The two younger women exchanged glances.

Surveying the expensive-looking bridesmaid dress and the collection of headdresses, Madeline observed, 'The amount this wedding must be costing, it's a blessing the family's a wealthy one.'

'Are you staying?' Janice asked shortly.

'No. Steven's taking me out to dinner. But I wanted a word with Ryan first.'

'Sorry we can't help you.' Janice sounded anything but sorry.

Moving towards the door, Madeline fired her parting shot. 'I presume poor Ryan didn't realise what he would be letting himself in for when he agreed to a big wedding.'

When the door had closed behind her, seeing the expression on Virginia's face, Janice advised sympathetically 'Don't let her get to you.'

'I can't help it,' Virginia said unhappily. 'She makes me feel like a gold-digger.'

'Those cracks about the expense of a big wedding are rich coming from her. She was an aspiring actress who hadn't a cent to her name when she got her claws into Steven, and Mom spent a small fortune on their wedding without a word of thanks from her.

'She might be beautiful, but she's thirty-two, seven years older than Steven, and hard as nails. It's a great pity he ever married her. Ryan had more sense.'

'Ryan?'

Sounding a little awkward, Janice explained, 'Madeline was Ryan's lady friend first.'

Apparently realising that she'd said too much to stop there, she played it down. 'They had a brief fling before she transferred her attention to poor Steven.

'He's been besotted from the word go, a willing slave who worships the ground she walks on. How is it that men can be so blind? So easily dazzled by a beautiful face and figure?'

'Well so long as he's happy...' Virginia began hesitantly.

'I don't see how he *can* be happy,' Janice said gloomily. 'In the few months they've been married, she's made him jump through hoops and, since Ryan brought you back, I'll wager she hasn't been fit to live with.

'My guess is that when it was too late she realised she'd made a bad mistake: it was Ryan she really wanted. That's why she's so jealous of you. In fact, from the way she goes on, I get the impression she still thinks of Ryan as hers...

'But let's forget about her...' Selecting a band of small cream silk rosebuds, she set it on her smooth dark hair and asked, 'What do you think of this?'

The choice of headdresses finally narrowed down to two, so Beth could have a say, Virginia left Janice to it and made her way back to her own apartment.

All the time she had been smiling and attentive, part of

her mind had been trying to cope with the knowledge that Madeline and Ryan had been lovers before she had left him for Steven.

Sinking down onto the settee, staring blindly ahead, Virginia wondered what had made her leave him. While Steven was a lovely man, he hardly measured up as a serious rival to Ryan.

So perhaps Janice was right. Maybe, when it was too late, Madeline had realised that she'd made a bad mistake, and it was really Ryan she wanted.

Virginia went cold.

That kind of situation would almost certainly lead to tragedy, so she could only hope and pray that Janice was wrong.

But was she?

All at once Virginia's mind was filled with images of Madeline and Ryan kissing. If it was her own husband Madeline loved and wanted, would she have been kissing Ryan so passionately?

But even more important, knowing what had once been between them, why had Ryan allowed it to happen?

Or had he just allowed it. What if he'd lied when he'd said *she* had kissed *him*. What if the passion had been mutual?

No, Virginia told herself fiercely, a man like Ryan wouldn't carry on with his stepbrother's wife.

For one thing, if it came out it would destroy the family unity and break Beth's heart and, for another, he would be married himself in a few days' time.

He couldn't still want Madeline, or why would he have asked *her* to marry him? Though theirs had been a whirlwind romance, Ryan was hardly the kind of man to marry on the rebound.

*   *   *

Over the next few days Virginia did her best to push all the doubts and uncertainties away, but they returned time and again to haunt her.

She found herself thinking over every conversation she had had with Ryan, examining everything he had ever said or done.

He wanted her, she was sure of that... But did he *love* her? Though he had called her 'my love' from time to time, and had asked if she believed in love at first sight, he had never actually said the words, I love you.

And it might not even be *her* he wanted. Ryan was a red-blooded man, and if the woman he truly wanted was married to his stepbrother, perhaps any woman would have served the purpose?

Could she risk asking him how he really felt?

No, he would be bound to lie. He couldn't admit the truth and chance splitting the family.

But if he didn't love and want her, why had he chosen to marry her? She would have lived with him without any commitment, and he must have known that. So why had he decided to go the whole hog, to insist on a big society wedding that was sure to hit the headlines?

No, she must be what he wanted.

Still the doubts came creeping back, and Virginia began to sleep badly. Even when she was lying in Ryan's arms, she found herself unable to free her mind and rest.

Anxious to hide it, however, she made a gallant pretence of being her normal self. Which, judging by Ryan's sharp glances, failed to convince him.

When dark smudges like mauve bruises appeared beneath her eyes, he was driven to ask what was wrong.

'N-nothing,' she stammered.

Stroking her hair, he said, 'I'm quite certain there is. I'm beginning to know you, the way you have secret spaces, the way you keep part of yourself hidden, even from me...'

Then coaxingly, he asked, 'Why don't you tell me what's bothering you?'

When she remained silent, he persisted, 'Are you afraid I won't make a good husband?'

She shook her head.

'Scared I'll beat you, or keep you short of money?'

'Of course not.'

'Shall I go on with this guessing game, or are you going to tell me?'

Seeing he had no intention of giving up, she said desperately, 'Surely all brides-to-be have a few last-minute doubts?'

His indigo eyes studied her in a way that was both critical and assessing. 'Do they?'

Seizing the chance, she asked, 'Don't bridegrooms-to-be have any doubts?'

'In my case, none whatsoever,' he said firmly. 'I've never been so certain of anything in my life. I want you for my wife.'

Then, almost fiercely, he said, 'Don't let any doubts plague you. Just remember you're mine, and I'll never want to let you go.'

That night she slept, the sleep of sheer exhaustion, and got up the following morning feeling happier and more confident than she had felt since learning about Madeline and Ryan's 'fling'.

The next few days passed in a whirl of last-minute activity and, before she knew it, it was the eve of her wedding.

She and Ryan breakfasted together that morning and, before he left for his office, he kissed her and whispered huskily, 'I guess the next time I see you will be in St Pat's.'

Beth having said seriously that on their wedding day it was bad luck for Ryan to see his bride before they met in church, they had agreed to sleep apart that night.

Nor were they seeing each other in the evening. Steven had insisted on giving Ryan a stag party, while the women had a girls' night out at Martindales.

Martindales was a fun place with good food and an excellent floor show and, had there been only Beth and Janice, Virginia would have looked forward to it, but Madeline had announced her intention of coming. Which made a difference.

In the event it proved to be a great deal more pleasant than Virginia had anticipated. Not only did Madeline keep her claws sheathed, but she actually went out of her way to be agreeable.

The champagne flowed freely and, by the time the night was over and they reached Falconer's Tower, they were somewhat merry.

When the elevator had carried them upwards, they all got out in the lower foyer and stood for a moment or two talking before they said their goodnights.

As Madeline let herself into her own apartment, Beth said to Virginia, 'Have a good night's sleep, and give us a call in the morning when you're ready for some help getting dressed.'

'Thanks, I will.'

'I'm so pleased you're going to be part of the family.'

'So am I,' Janice added warmly.

The three women exchanged hugs and, as mother and daughter bickered gently over who had the key, Virginia made her way upstairs.

Her dream of being part of a happy family would soon be true, and she walked on air.

She had been in her apartment only long enough to take off her coat, when the doorbell rang.

It was a few minutes before twelve and, hoping it was Ryan calling in to say goodnight, she hurried to open it.

To her surprise, it was Madeline.

Without waiting for an invitation, the blonde walked in. 'I came to tell you how happy I am about the wedding, and bring you this. It will do for something borrowed.'

Opening the small flat box, Virginia found a pretty satin and lace garter.

'Why, thank you, it's lovely. I'll be sure to let you have it back.'

Madeline's beautiful teeth gleamed in a smile. 'Don't worry, I always get back what's mine.'

Puzzled by the other's tone, but deciding to ignore it, Virginia said, 'And I'm glad you're happy about the wedding.'

'Though I knew Ryan was doing it for *us*, I must confess that there have been times when I've felt a little jealous.'

'I don't understand,' Virginia said blankly.

'You mean he didn't tell you why he was marrying you? But perhaps he thought it was best not to. After all, ignorance is bliss, so they say.'

In a voice she scarcely recognised as her own, Virginia said, 'I think I'd sooner know.'

'Well, you see, Ryan and I were lovers before I married Steven—'

'I'm aware of that.'

Just for an instant Madeline looked put out, then she went on, 'We had a red-hot affair, but when passions run high so do tempers.

'He'd been hedging about getting married, and we quarrelled. I started to go out with Steven. I only did it to bring Ryan to heel but, though he's always been mad about me, he can be stubborn.

'I'd learnt my lesson, so I refused to sleep with Steven. When he got desperate enough to propose, I decided I'd be a fool not to accept—'

Breaking off, Madeline said sharply, 'There's no need to look so disgusted. If you're thinking I'm a gold-digger, well, it takes one to know one... And after all, a girl has to look after herself...

'Though I must admit that as soon as we were married,

I regretted it. I knew I'd made a bad mistake, that I'd never got over Ryan...'

So Janice had been right, after all.

'One night when Steven was out, Ryan and I kissed, and all the old passion flared up. We became lovers again, meeting whenever we could, sometimes here, sometimes in town...

'But after a while, Ryan called a halt in case anyone was getting suspicious. He was very concerned about upsetting Beth and the family, or causing a public scandal...'

Her voice as cold as her heart, Virginia asked, 'So what have I to do with it?'

'Ryan decided that if he was safely and publicly married, with all the trimmings and the bride's parents in attendance, it would avoid the risk of any scandal and paint a picture of good, solid respectability.

'In other words, it should make a perfect smokescreen. So long as we're discreet, who's going to suspect a newly married man of playing around with his sister-in-law? No one. Least of all his loving family...'

Virginia felt as if she'd been kicked in the stomach. It was so perfectly logical. It made sense of all the things that had puzzled her: why Ryan had swept her off her feet in the first place; why he'd rushed her into agreeing to marry him; why he had been so keen to tell the family; why he'd opted for a big wedding; why he had never actually said he loved her...

'Which means that we'll all be happy...' Madeline's smile held an almost feline satisfaction.

Her voice hoarse, Virginia exclaimed, 'If you think for one instant that I'll go along with it, you're mad...!'

'I don't see what you've got to lose. You'll still have everything you're marrying him for: jewels, clothes, a wonderful lifestyle, anything that money can buy... And let's face it, Ryan's man enough to keep the both of us happy.'

'Get out!' Virginia cried. 'Take this and get out!' Thrusting the garter into Madeline's hand, she opened the door.

'Suit yourself,' Madeline said. 'But when you've had a chance to think about it, you'll see I'm right.'

Her head feeling as if an iron band was tightening round it, her stomach heaving, Virginia leaned against the closed door.

When the nausea subsided a little, in a voice she didn't recognise as her own, she called a taxi and, her whole being clenched into a knot of anguish, went through to the bedroom to pack.

Ignoring the bags already packed for her honeymoon, she gathered together just the things she had brought with her, and bundled them into her old suitcases.

Then leaving her engagement ring and everything that Ryan had paid for, taking only the money she had earned, dry-eyed and frozen inside, she closed the apartment door behind her and rode the elevator down.

Her dream was over.

As luck would have it, the security booth was empty, the night-security guard out doing his rounds.

Hurrying across the lobby, she put down her cases while she released the dead-bolt. A moment later she had slipped out without being seen and, her cases banging against her legs, was hurrying towards the waiting yellow cab.

Her luggage stowed, the driver asked, 'Where to, lady?'

'The airport, please.'

'JFK?'

'Yes.'

CHAPTER SIX

SHIVERING, feeling all the despair and desolation she had felt at that moment, Virginia came back to the present.

After a moment, his fair face still showing his concern, Charles asked, 'So what did you do then?'

'I sat in the airport until morning, then I managed to get a seat on an early flight to Heathrow. By the time I should have been getting married, I was more than halfway back to England.

'When I got to London I booked in at a cheap hotel, and on Monday morning I started looking for a job... The rest you know.'

Frowning, Charles remarked, 'You haven't mentioned leaving a note or anything.'

'I didn't.'

'You mean you left without a word to anyone?'

'Yes... I suppose I was in a state of shock. I certainly wasn't in any condition to think straight. And what could I have said? What possible reason could I have given for not going through with the wedding? The truth would have torn the family apart, and Beth had a weak heart...'

'You didn't consider tackling Falconer?'

She shook her head. 'I couldn't bear the humiliation. I never wanted to see him again.'

'I take it you continued to feel that way?'

'Yes. That was why I didn't want my parents to know where I was. They might have told him.'

'I see. So you were virtually in hiding, and that's why you'd dropped the Adams, and were calling yourself Virginia Ashley?'

'Yes.' Despairingly, she added, 'I was just beginning to feel safe. It was an awful shock to see him in the gallery.'

Charles squeezed her sympathetically. 'I could tell his presence affected you deeply. In fact I wondered at the time if you were in love with him?'

'I just don't know,' she said, and tried to tell herself it was the truth.

'Taking everything into consideration,' Charles remarked seriously, 'it's just as well Falconer didn't see you.'

She bit her lip. 'I'm afraid he did.'

'How do you know?' he asked sharply.

'I walked home through the park. He'd been waiting in the mews, and he followed me.'

Charles's mouth tightened. 'Did he speak to you?'

'Yes.'

'He didn't touch you, did he? I'll break his damn neck if he did.'

That kind of wild threat was so unlike Charles's usual pragmatic approach that, scared of what might happen if he took on Ryan, she stammered, 'N-no…not really. I mean, he just put his hands over my eyes and said, ''Guess who?'''

'But he scared you?'

'Yes, he scared me. He said…' Her voice shook so much she had to stop and take a steadying breath before she could go on. 'He said he wants me back.'

Charles stiffened. 'Wants you back? After the shabby way he treated you! Why does he want you back?'

'He was furious at the way I'd left him and spoilt all his plans. He said there was a score to settle.'

She folded her arms over her chest, rubbing them as if she were cold. 'I told him I had absolutely no intention of ever going back to him.'

'Falconer doesn't look to me like the kind of man who would take no for an answer.'

'He isn't.' She swallowed hard, then said in a rush,

'That's why I told him we were living together. I hope you don't mind?'

'No, of course I don't mind.' With dry humour, he added, 'Taken one way, it's true. Taken the other, it's flattering.'

After a moment he asked carefully, 'Was that what finally got rid of him?'

'Not exactly...'

'So how did you shake him off?'

'A little boy who was playing with a toy yacht fell in the lake, and while Ryan was pulling him out I made myself scarce and took a taxi home.'

Then, urgently, she said, 'Charles, I don't want to go back to him.'

'I'm very glad to hear it.' He patted her hand. 'There's no need to look so fraught; he can't force you to.'

'No, that's what I keep telling myself.'

After a thoughtful silence, he remarked, 'I presume it was seeing Falconer again that made you change your mind about marrying me?'

'Yes,' she said in a small voice.

'Then I suppose I should be grateful that fate brought him into the gallery, and gave you a chance to realise you no longer loved him...'

Though Virginia felt a strong sense of shame, she let it go.

'Now you've got your feelings sorted out once and for all,' Charles went on, 'you'll be able to put him right out of your mind... And, before too long, he'll be safely back in the States.'

Agitated and guilty because she hadn't told Charles the whole truth by a long chalk, she bit her lip.

His eyes on her face, he said quietly, 'Something's still bothering you. Would you like to tell me what it is?'

'What am I going to do until he *does* go back?' she burst out. 'He could walk into the gallery any time.'

'I'll tell you what you can do, you can take a few days off...'

'Oh but—'

'No buts. Helen and I can manage for a while and, if he does happen to come in, I'll deal with him.'

Seeing the look of doubt on her face, he asked, 'What's wrong? Don't you think I'm capable of dealing with a man like Falconer?'

'I'm sure you are,' she said with a great deal more confidence than she felt. 'And I'm equally sure that, instead of letting things get out of hand, you can do it diplomatically.'

'Then, what's the problem?'

There were more problems than she could shake a stick at. Remembering Ryan's mocking, 'Be seeing you,' she shivered.

But if she stayed in the house and refused to open the door to him, she'd be safe enough. He could hardly break in.

Seeing Charles was waiting for an answer, she managed a smile. 'Maybe I'm just being paranoid.'

'I'm convinced you are, so stop worrying.'

'I'll try,' she promised.

'Now let's forget all about Falconer and get back to a much more pleasant subject. You said you'd be happy with a quiet wedding.'

'Yes.'

'Would you like to be married in church, or at the register office?'

'Church, I think. If that's all right with you?'

He smiled and gave her a little squeeze. 'I'd prefer to be married in church myself. First thing in the morning I'll have a talk with the Reverend Peter Coe, the vicar of St Giles—he's a personal friend of mine—and see how soon it can be arranged. It can't be soon enough for me.' His arms tightening, he added deeply, 'I'll do my utmost to make you happy.'

When he tilted her face and began to kiss her, she willed herself to relax and enjoy it.

After a while his kisses grew more ardent, and she had to quell a little twist of anxiety. What would she do if he wanted to take her to bed?

Throughout her stay in his house, Charles had behaved like a perfect gentleman. But he was a man, after all, a man she had just promised to marry. And now she had told him about her relationship with Ryan, he must feel he had a right to the same privileges.

She had no doubt that he would be a caring and sensitive lover, and once she had made a commitment it would set the seal on their future together. It might even help to drive Ryan from her mind.

But when, his fair face a little flushed, Charles took her hand and began to lead her up the stairs, her steps were oddly reluctant.

Feeling that reluctance, he paused on the landing, his eyes on her face, puzzled, a little pleading. Gritting her teeth, knowing it wouldn't be fair to him to back out now, she turned and led the way into her bedroom.

Drawing her close, his ardour returning, he began to kiss her once more and, putting her arms around his neck, she forced herself to respond.

He was passionate yet tender, the kind of man almost any woman would be pleased to have as a lover, and closing her eyes she tried to concentrate on enjoying his kisses.

His lips brushed the side of her neck and slid to the smoothness of her shoulder. 'You're so beautiful,' he murmured, 'so soft and warm and truly feminine. I've never known a woman who affected me as much as you do.'

She was very conscious of his touch, of every move he was making. Too conscious. If only she could lose herself in the warmth of his lovemaking. Instead, her mind seemed to stand apart, a cool spectator, treating the experience like some ordeal that must be endured, rather than enjoyed.

Suddenly he let her go and drew back, his face impatient baffled. 'What's wrong, Virginia?'

'N-nothing,' she stammered.

'Something must be. It's like trying to make love to the Venus de Milo.'

'I'm sorry, truly I am.' She sought for an excuse. 'It' been such a traumatic day that I...I just...' Her grey-green eyes filled with tears.

His face softened at once. 'I'm an insensitive brute. should have realised you'd still be upset. Forgive me.'

Desperately ashamed of the way she was treating him especially as he was being so sweet about it, but quite un able to remedy matters, she found herself repeating help lessly, 'I'm sorry.'

'It's all right, really it is. I shouldn't have rushed you. He kissed her forehead. 'Now, off you go to bed, and don' worry about a thing.'

At the door he turned to add, 'Once Falconer's gone back and we're married, it will all come right, I promise you.'

The following morning they ate breakfast together as usual before Charles prepared to set off for the gallery at his normal time, but alone.

Her actions unconsciously wifely, Virginia accompanie him into the hall.

At the door he kissed her cheek gently, and said, 'You know where I am if you want me for anything.'

Her beautiful eyes reflecting how lost she suddenly felt she said uncertainly, 'I'm not sure what I'll find to do al day.'

'Why not go into town?'

No, she dared not do that; Ryan might be having he watched.

Well aware that Charles was concerned about her, she said more cheerfully, 'Perhaps I'll just do a spot of spring cleaning.'

'Isn't it a bit late for spring-cleaning? In any case that's the kind of thing I pay Mrs Crabtree for.

'Come on, you haven't had a break since you started at the gallery, so make the best of it, just relax and catch up on some reading... Pretend you're on holiday. If it keeps fine and hot, as it's forecast to, you could make some sangria and sit outside and get tanned.'

At the rear of the house there was a green and pleasant garden that caught the morning and early afternoon sun. It boasted a small paved area, and some comfortable patio furniture.

'How lovely and decadent!' Her spirits lifting a little, she added, 'I might just do that.'

Then only too grateful for his unstinting kindness and caring, she said, 'Tell you what else I'll do, I'll cook you a really nice meal for tonight.'

'Wonderful!' Grinning at her boyishly, he added, 'A man who's hoping to do business with me has insisted on taking me out to lunch, but I'll be sure to have something light.

'Oh, just one thing, can you time dinner for a bit later than usual?'

'Seven-thirty?'

'To be on the safe side, make it eight.'

Her heart sank. 'Fine.'

Knowing it wasn't fine at all, he explained, 'After the gallery's closed, I have a business appointment. A very important one, otherwise I would have cancelled it.'

With unusual animation, he added, 'If all goes well, it should mean a virtual end to my financial problems.'

'Oh, that's marvellous.'

'I'll give you all the details later... Don't worry about a thing, now.' He kissed her, and was gone.

Standing staring at the closed door, she felt a sense of loss. The whole day stretched ahead, flat and empty, with nothing to do but think of Ryan...

Tuesday was one of the days Mrs Crabtree didn't come

in, so Virginia spent the first part of the morning washing the breakfast dishes and doing a spot of housework.

She was just about to look in the freezer, when the phone rang.

This might be him.

No, she really was getting paranoid. Ryan would believe her to be at the gallery. In fact the only person who would expect anyone to be home at this time of day would be Charles.

Going through to the hall she picked up the receiver and said, 'Hello?'

'Not sunbathing yet?'

As she had surmised, it was Charles.

'No, not yet.'

Sounding unusually animated, he went on, 'I've had a talk with Peter and he's suggested going for a special licence. That way we can get married in a few days' time.'

A few days' time.

Rather than being a promise that could be fulfilled at some unspecified future date, it was suddenly on top of her, breathing down her neck.

'Because it's June, and June is the month for weddings apparently, the church is fully booked on Saturday, but we could be married on Monday, if you're in agreement?'

Monday was less than a week away.

Though Virginia was still sure she was doing the right thing, just for a split second, the thought of their wedding being quite so soon threw her.

After a barely perceptible hesitation, she said, 'Yes...'

He picked up that hesitation. 'You don't sound too certain?'

Virginia took a deep breath. 'Yes, I'm quite certain. Monday will be great.'

She heard his sigh of relief.

'The next thing we'll need to discuss is a honeymoon. In the meantime, be thinking where you'd like to go.'

'What about the gallery?'

'If I can't get someone in to help Helen, I'll close it. The start of our married life is much more important than the gallery…'

How could she go wrong with a husband like that? she thought, her heart swelling.

'I'm getting another call coming through, so I'd better go. I'll try not to be too late tonight…'

When they had said their goodbyes, she replaced the receiver and went back to the kitchen to take the chicken portions for their evening meal out of the freezer.

That done, she sliced fresh lemons to make lemonade, before changing her jeans and shirt for old denim shorts and a tank top, and taking her long curly hair up in a ponytail.

Then, having poured herself a glass of lemonade from the covered jug, she picked up a new book she hadn't yet found time to read, and barefoot, carried them both outside into the sunshine.

The garden was high-walled and private, surrounded by neighbouring gardens, so that the only way into it was through the house. She would be quite safe here.

Although the book seemed to be well-written and the story showed every sign of being an exciting one, she was unable to concentrate. Ryan's dark face kept coming between her and the printed page, and she found herself wondering anxiously what his next move would be…

'Good morning. Sleep well?'

As though her thoughts had conjured him up, there he was, lounging in the kitchen doorway, dressed in well-cut trousers and a white silk shirt open at the neck.

The shock was so great that she jumped to her feet, dropping the glass she was holding. It smashed to smithereens on the paving stones, splashing her with sticky lemonade.

He clicked his tongue. 'Dear me, how very careless.

Don't move your feet in case you tread on some broken glass.'

His warning came too late. She gave a little cry as a sharp sliver jabbed into her big toe.

'Sit down, let me take a look.' He pushed her gently back into her seat. Then, crouching on his haunches he lifted her slim foot and eased out the needle-sharp piece of glass.

A spot of bright-red blood welled.

Bending his dark head he put his mouth to the wound and sucked, causing a kick of desire that made her stomach clench and her mouth go dry.

Then, having run his tongue tip over the broken skin to feel for any tiny particles of glass that might have remained, he said cheerfully, 'That's fine.'

Still holding her foot and looking up at her through lashes any female might have envied, he added quizzically, 'You're the only woman I've ever known who has feet beautiful enough to start a foot fetish. Now, stay where you are, otherwise I might have to do that all over again.'

Disappearing into the kitchen, he returned after a moment with a plastic dustpan and brush and swept up the scattered pieces of glass with neat efficiency.

'I see there's more lemonade in the jug, so as soon as I've disposed of the debris I'll pour some for us both, and join you.'

Virginia was still trying to pull herself together when he returned with two glasses and, putting them on the low table, dropped into the lounger alongside her own, handsome as Lucifer and twice as dangerous.

With cool insolence he let his eyes travel slowly over her from head to toe, making her very conscious of her bare legs.

Studying the denim shorts, the tank top, and the ponytail, he mocked, 'Dressed like that you look for all the world like a fifteen-year-old schoolgirl.'

Finding her voice, she said thickly, 'But I'm not. I'm almost twenty-five.'

'Which is just as well. The word I left out of my description was desirable.'

Alarmed by the little flame burning in his eyes, she demanded, 'What are you doing here? What do you want?' Then, in confusion, she asked, 'How did you get in?'

Smiling at her consternation, he answered, 'Through the front door, like any respectable visitor.'

'You would have needed a key.'

'I have one.' With an air of satisfaction, he displayed a key, before slipping it back into his pocket.

'Where did you get that?' she asked sharply.

Unblushingly, he admitted, 'I borrowed it from your purse last night.'

Too late she recalled how the purse she had dropped had been picked up and placed on the hall table, where it still lay.

Seeing the impotent anger in eyes now darkened to the colour of charcoal, he added, 'I was rather hoping you wouldn't miss it. In any operation, the element of surprise is a valuable one, and I've always found it pays to wrong-foot your opponent.'

'Do you have to sound so damn smug?' she burst out furiously.

He shook his head reprovingly. 'Temper.'

Realising that if she kept rising to the bait she was playing right into his hands, she struggled to regain some composure.

When she could trust her voice, she said, 'I don't know what you hope to gain by this. I've no intention of coming back to you.'

'So you said,' he agreed. 'That's one of the reasons I'm here, to try and change your mind.'

'How did you know I'd be at home?'

'First thing this morning I called in at the gallery and had a word with Raynor.'

Her blood ran cold.

'I have to admit I was mistaken about him. He's no wimp.' Ryan sounded as if he was relishing the thought of some stout opposition. 'Though he looks ineffectual, he stood up to me with the kind of backbone I was forced to admire...'

Seeing the look of horror on her face, he smiled with wry amusement. 'To set your mind at rest, I meant verbally rather than physically...'

She breathed a sigh of relief.

But standing up to Ryan, even when the conflict was verbal, was no mean feat. She knew quite well how, without ever raising his voice, he could intimidate all but the strongest of men.

'So you won't need to bind his wounds.'

Ignoring the sarcasm, she demanded anxiously, 'What did you say to him?'

'Considerably less than he said to me.' His voice as brittle as ice, Ryan added, 'It was most interesting and instructive.'

Holding her breath, Virginia waited.

After a moment, Ryan went on, 'Then he called me a swine, and told me straight that if he ever did manage to locate and buy *Wednesday's Child*, he had no intention of letting me have it, so there was no further need to come into the gallery.'

'Is that all?'

'No. According to him, I've upset you enough. I gather the only occasion he actually knows about is our dalliance in the park.'

'Hardly a dalliance,' she said resentfully.

Ignoring the interruption, Ryan continued, 'If he'd been aware that I knew where you were living, and had been to the house last night, he would never have left you at home by yourself...' Then, like a whiplash, he asked, 'Why didn't you tell him about my visit?'

'I—I didn't want to upset him.'

'He'd be a great deal more upset if he knew I was here now,' Ryan observed with satisfaction.

Trying to keep some kind of grip on the situation, she asked, 'Why are you here? Apart from trying to change my mind.'

His blue-violet eyes narrowed against the sun and, gleamed through thick dark lashes as he explained idly, 'I thought I'd take you out to lunch.'

'Then think again! I've no intention of having lunch with you.'

Unruffled, he agreed, 'Just as you like. We don't *have* to go out to lunch. And, on second thoughts, you're quite right. It will be a lot more fun to stay here.'

Virginia bit her lip, recognising belatedly that it would have been much safer to lunch in some public place, rather than be here alone with him.

Her apprehension was compounded when he added, 'It will give us plenty of time to...shall we say...indulge other appetites?'

'No!' Agitation brought her to her feet. 'I'm going to marry Charles. If you lay so much as a finger on me I'll...I'll...'

'You'll what?'

He took a step towards her. She retreated until the wall of the house brought her up short.

Following her, he put a hand each side of her head, flat-palmed against the stucco, trapping her there.

'Tell me, Virginia, did you dream of me after I'd gone last night?'

'No, I didn't.' She spat the words at him. 'I told you there'd be no need to.'

His face grew taut. 'You didn't sleep with Raynor?' he asked sharply.

She wanted to say she had to get back at him but, remembering the uncomfortable little scene in her bedroom,
how she'd treated Charles, somehow she couldn't…

A hand beneath her chin, Ryan lifted her face to scrutin-
ise it. 'Did you?'

'Whether I did or not is nothing to do with you.'

She heard the breath hiss through his teeth before he said,
'From now on I'm going to be the only man who makes
love to you. I've been waiting so long to…' Putting his lips
to her ear, he whispered graphic details of all the things
he'd been waiting to do to her.

The erotic images his words provoked made her stomach
fold in on itself and a shiver run through her. As she struggled to appear unmoved, she heard his soft chuckle.

'You respond so beautifully, my pet. Your body is already reacting to the mere thought of being made love to…'

It was true. Her nipples had grown firm and were plainly
visible through the thin material of her close-fitting tank
top.

'And that's such a turn on…'

He traced them with a fingertip, making pleasure tingle
through her, before querying softly, 'So which is it to be?
Shall we go to bed and see how long you can hold out?
Or would you like to have lunch with me after all?'

'Yes,' she said desperately.

With a slightly crooked smile, he asked, 'Which?'

Her voice hoarse and impeded, she said, 'I'd like to have
lunch with you.'

'Good. Somehow I thought you'd come round to my way
of thinking.'

Holding her upper arms, he kissed her lightly. 'Though
I must admit it might have been more flattering, and a great
deal more fun, if you'd decided to go to bed. Still, I can
wait. I've already waited for well over two years, so a few
more days aren't going to make that much difference.

'Now suppose you go and put on something a shade

more suitable for lunching at Moonrakers. I'll give you fifteen minutes.'

He released her and sat down again.

Marvelling at what lengths he would go to to get what he wanted, she fled into the house and up the stairs.

When she reached her room, her first thought was to barricade herself in, but almost immediately she realised how impractical that idea was. Reluctantly abandoning the idea and afraid that he might come looking for her if she exceeded the fifteen minutes he'd allowed, she showered and dried herself quickly.

Then coiling her hair into a neat chignon, she donned fresh undies and the grey silk suit she usually wore to work. A touch of make-up to boost her morale, and the glasses to hide behind, she was once more a businesswoman rather than the fifteen-year-old schoolgirl he'd called her.

She even had a few minutes to spare.

If she gathered up her purse and went quietly out of the front door, once at the end of the street, she would have a good chance of picking up a cruising taxi before he even realised she was gone.

Holding her breath, she crept down the stairs carefully avoiding the tread that she knew squeaked and, crossing the hall, reached for her purse.

It was no longer there.

Well, she would ask the taxi driver to take her to the gallery, and borrow the fare from Charles, even if it meant telling him the whole truth.

Her hand was on the latch when Ryan's mocking voice asked, 'Trying to sneak off without me?'

She jumped a mile, and spun round to find his big frame filling the living-room doorway.

'It's just as well I was on my guard.'

'Damn you!' she muttered helplessly.

Strolling over, he stood looking down at her suit, the heavy glasses, and the neat coil of hair.

An unholy gleam in his eye, he murmured, 'My, my…how very restrained and businesslike.'

'You said "something a shade more suitable."'

'The only place a get-up like that is suitable for is a place of work. However it can be remedied to some extent… When did you start wearing these awful glasses?'

'Some time ago,' she answered stiffly. 'And I don't think they're awful.'

He lifted the despised glasses off her nose and squinted through them. 'You don't need these, they're plain glass.' Tossing them carelessly onto the hall table, he added, 'It's much too late for disguises.'

Then, before she could protest, his deft fingers were plucking out the pins that held her chignon in place.

'That's a lot better,' he said triumphantly, as her ash-brown hair tumbled around her shoulders. 'Now at least I won't look as if I'm having lunch with some school-marm.'

'Go to hell!' she burst out.

With a plaintive sigh, he protested, 'Now, is that kind?' Then, coaxingly, he said, 'I think, having hurt my feelings, you should kiss me better.'

His eyes crossed, he pursed his lips in readiness.

Caught unawares, she almost laughed. He'd always been totally irresistible when he was clowning.

'Go on,' he urged, 'quickly, because Maxwell and the limousine are waiting outside.'

'I've no intention of kissing you.' But she was seriously tempted, and her voice shook betrayingly.

'Then I'll kiss you.'

'I don't want you to kiss me.'

'Of course you want me to kiss you. You just don't want to admit it.'

A second later his mouth was covering hers. He wasn't holding her, and she could have moved away. Instead she stood as though she was glued to the spot while his lips teased hers, coaxing them to part for him.

When they did, his arms closed around her and he deepened the kiss until her head reeled and nothing in the world existed but Ryan.

She was dimly aware of his heart thudding—or was it her own?—the rapid rise and fall of his chest, and the masculine scent of his aftershave.

Beneath her palms his silk shirt felt cool and fresh, until the heat of his body seeped through...

When he finally released her, he was breathing like a man who had just lost a race, and she was totally dazed, mindless. His for the taking.

If he had just led her upstairs she would have gone, but instead, his voice ragged, he gave her a chance to back out. 'Would you like to change your mind about going out to lunch?'

Somehow, she made herself answer, 'No, I wouldn't.'

'Hoist with my own petard,' he commented ruefully.

But she sensed it was what he'd wanted her to say, as though going out to lunch was part of some bigger, more important plan.

CHAPTER SEVEN

OPENING the door, he escorted her down the steps to where a limousine was waiting by the kerb. The chauffeur, who was lounging in the sun, straightened up at their approach and held open the door.

When Ryan had helped her in, he slid in beside her and picked up a jacket that had been lying on the seat. Taking a tie from the pocket, he put it around his neck and knotted it, remarking ironically, 'Must observe the niceties.'

By the time they reached their destination, a pleasant top-floor restaurant only about half a mile from the gallery, and close to Kenelm Park, Virginia had recovered enough to appear at least outwardly composed.

Though at first glance Moonrakers appeared to be full, and the one unoccupied table near the door bore a reserved notice, Ryan was greeted by name, and a table for two was immediately set up in a secluded corner.

'Don't tell me,' she said tartly, 'you have a stake in the place.'

Once again she felt the almost overwhelming pull of his attraction as, grinning, he denied it. 'Not this time, I'm afraid. The owner happens to be a friend of mine.'

'How fortunate.'

'Isn't it?' His eyes were warm and teasing.

Feeling her spirits lift, she was halfway to enjoying herself when, abruptly recalling the past and what he was trying to do, she was shaken by how close she had been to liking him again.

While they ordered and the meal was served, Ryan made an effort to keep up a light, entertaining conversation.

But retiring into her defensive shell, refusing to come

116

out and play his game, she answered in monosyllables when she was forced to answer at all.

At length he enquired, 'Something wrong?'

'What could possibly be wrong?' she asked sarcastically.

'You seemed to be opening up a little and then suddenly, snap, you're oyster-tight again! Why don't you make an effort to relax, so we can enjoy our lunch together?'

'You might have coerced me into having lunch with you, but it doesn't mean I have to enjoy it.'

With a slight shrug, he let it go and lapsed into silence. But she was conscious that he watched her constantly, as if he was unable to keep his eyes off her.

The food was good but she ate automatically, tasting very little, her mind beset by uneasy questions.

After that searching and passionate kiss in the hallway, he must have known she was his for the taking, so why had he offered her a chance to back out?

She could only be thankful that he had, but the question remained, why? Why had he been so determined to take her out to lunch? Ryan wasn't the kind of man to do anything without a good reason...

She was still pondering that unanswerable why, as they drank their coffee.

'When did you agree to marry Raynor?' Ryan's smooth, casual-sounding query came out of the blue.

Her head came up sharply. 'What?'

'I asked when you agreed to marry Raynor?'

She braced herself. 'Charles told you we were getting married?'

'He told me you were *planning* to.'

Remembering how Ryan had said, 'Over my dead body', she blenched. 'Y-you didn't...?'

'Beat him up? No of course I didn't. I merely warned him what the consequences would be if he didn't back off, and smartly.'

She put a hand to her mouth.

'What did you expect me to do, *congratulate* him?'

When she said nothing, he persisted smoothly, 'So tell me, Virginia, when did you accept Raynor's proposal?'

Ryan never missed a trick, she thought with some bitterness.

Carefully, she said, 'It's a few weeks since he asked me to marry him.'

'And did you say yes straight away?'

'Of course I did. I love him.'

'If I remember rightly, you said, "Passionately."'

'Yes... Passionately.'

Ryan sucked in his breath, and his eyes wickedly amused, charged, 'The lies fairly hop out of you.'

'I told you in the park that Charles and I were going to be married.'

'No you didn't. You said, "He wants to marry me," which is quite a different kettle of fish. Why don't you be honest and admit that when he first asked you you turned him down. You only agreed to marry him after what happened last night.'

'I did no such thing,' she denied stoutly.

'Don't bother with any more lies. Raynor admitted it was only last night that you agreed. Which tells me a great deal... Though he put a somewhat different interpretation on it. You see he's under the impression that you agreed to marry him when you discovered you were finally over me. Would he be quite so happy if he realised that you're only using him as a kind of safeguard?'

'No, it's not like that. I'm very fond of Charles, and I respect him. He'll make a good husband and father.'

'So you've discussed having a family?'

'Yes.'

'How many children did you decide on?'

Though well aware that he was deriding her, she answered, 'Four.'

'So you accepted his proposal, made plans to have children, but you still didn't sleep with him.'

'Did he tell you that too?'

'He didn't need to. Apart from a couple of remarks he made that were dead giveaways, I know a frustrated man when I see one. And he's absolutely mad about you. He may soon start putting you under pressure.'

'As you've done?' she flashed.

'Ah, but there's a difference.'

'A difference?'

'You want to sleep with me,' he said softly. 'You don't want to sleep with him.'

'What makes you so sure?'

'If you had wanted to sleep with Raynor you would have done it before now.'

'I've already told you—'

'Indeed you have, so don't bother telling me yet again how good a lover he is, and how he's not hidebound enough to simply take you to bed. I don't believe you've been sleeping with him. Otherwise you would have done so last night.'

Rattled because he was whang in the gold, she mocked, 'When did you become a psychologist?'

'It doesn't take a psychologist to work that one out, any more than it takes a mathematician to add two and two.'

'What kind of expert would it take to work out that you're wasting your time? That it really doesn't matter whether or not I've already slept with Charles—'

'You know it matters to me. Some children will happily share the same lollipop, but even as a young child I always wanted one that was mine alone.'

Ignoring the interruption, she ploughed on, 'What *does* matter is that I'm going to marry him, and that I'm not coming back to you.'

'That's where you're wrong,' he said with quiet certainty. 'But we'll talk about it later.'

After a glance at his watch, he signalled the waiter and paid the bill. Then, an arm around her waist, he began to lead her towards the door.

Head down, she was trying to think how best to get away from him when he paused and, an odd note in his voice, said softly, 'Virginia…'

As she glanced up, he bent and kissed her full on the lips, and lingeringly.

Ryan wasn't a man to be demonstrative in such a public place and, taken completely by surprise, she stood motionless until he lifted his head and began to walk once more.

Caught up in the circle of his arm, she moved as a sleepwalker might, until the sight of a fair-haired man staring at her as though he couldn't believe his eyes brought her to life with a rude awakening.

Charles was sitting at a table a few feet away. He was accompanied by a man with a red neck and crinkly dark hair thinning drastically on top.

The balding man, who had his back to them, was talking animatedly, hitting the table with the side of his hand to emphasise some point he was making.

As they drew level, his eyes still fixed on them, Charles rose to his feet like an automaton, while his companion stopped talking and glanced up at them.

'Raynor,' Ryan nodded politely.

'Falconer,' Charles acknowledged stiffly.

'As you were otherwise engaged,' Ryan said easily, 'I thought I'd take Virginia out for lunch.'

Turning a stricken, accusing look on his bride-to-be, Charles said, 'I understood you were staying at home.'

'I intended to,' she began, 'but—'

'I can be very…persuasive,' Ryan broke in, giving her a smiling, sidelong glance. A glance that made them conspirators. 'Can't I, my love?'

Watching Charles freeze at the endearment, and knowing

his companion was listening to every word, she stammered, 'I—I...'

Ryan squeezed her arm. 'It took a little time, but when I—'

Terrified he was going to explain exactly what methods of persuasion he had used, she broke in hurriedly, 'Shouldn't we be going?'

'You're quite right, we should,' he said at once. Then addressing the two men, 'My apologies gentlemen, for interrupting your lunch.'

A second or two later, Ryan's proprietorial arm around her waist, she was being swept through the door. Glancing back over her shoulder she saw that Charles was still on his feet, swaying a little like some punch-drunk boxer.

Dazed and incapable of coherent thought, she felt very much the same.

While the lift, containing perhaps half a dozen people, carried them smoothly downwards, she struggled to take in what had happened, all the implications of that awkward little scene, and what had gone before.

The question of why Ryan had pressured her into lunching at Moonrakers, and why he'd kissed her in such a public place, was now answered. Somehow he had known that Charles would be there and, intent on causing trouble, had staged the whole thing.

Brilliantly.

He had manipulated her with consummate skill. Even his timing had been superb, but then, she had always been aware that he was a first-rate tactician, a master of strategy.

Remembering Charles's accusing look, she knew she must have appeared more than willing to be there. Exactly how Ryan had wanted her to appear, she realised bitterly, as she recalled his arm around her waist, his little conspiratorial glance, the way he'd squeezed her arm, his endearment...

As soon as they were out in the sunshine, she turned on

him fiercely. 'You're a rotten, miserable, unscrupulous, bast—'

A finger placed on her lips stopped the outburst.

'Two many people about,' he said calmly, 'If you want to hurl abuse at me we'd better take a walk in the park.'

The limousine was drawn up by the kerb, the chauffeur standing by.

'Drop us at the nearest entrance to Kenelm Park, please, Maxwell,' Ryan instructed, and handed her in.

While they drove the short distance, Virginia sat in tight-lipped silence, furious with Ryan, but equally furious with herself for not having guessed what he was up to, and somehow preventing it.

As they drew up alongside the elaborate Victorian gates that marked the main entrance to the park, Ryan said, 'You can take the rest of the afternoon off, Maxwell. We won't be needing you.'

A broad grin spreading across his face, the man said gratefully, 'Thanks, Mr Falconer.'

Jumping out, Ryan offered Virginia his hand.

Face set, she ignored it.

The intended rebuff was spoilt when she stumbled, and only Ryan's prompt action saved her from falling.

Holding her unnecessarily close, he observed with a smugness that grated on her raw nerves, 'That's what comes of trying to be too independent. It's a good thing I was there to help you.'

Jerking herself free, she headed blindly for the tall black-and-gold wrought iron gates which still incorporated an old-fashioned turnstile.

The park was green and bathed in sunshine and, following the lunch-time invasion, relatively deserted.

Selecting a sun-dappled spot beneath the trees, Ryan turned to face her and invited, 'Okay, let it fly.'

Bristling with barely contained fury, she accused

hoarsely, 'You staged the whole thing just to cause trouble! Don't try and deny it.'

'I wasn't going to. I'm quite pleased by how well it worked.'

Helplessly, she said, 'I don't see how you knew he'd be there...'

'Simple. His companion, who arranged the time and place, was in my pay.'

Ryan's calm admission brought a fresh surge of anger. 'You're loathsome and despicable—'

Looking amused, he said, 'While your choice of adjectives is quite wide, you've forgotten vile and contemptible—'

Virginia, who had never in her life struck a blow in anger, and hadn't thought herself capable of it, saw red. Without conscious volition she swung her hand and smacked his face with enough force to jerk his head sideways.

Palm tingling, suddenly horrified by what she'd done, she stared aghast at the dusky red mark her hand had left on his lean, tanned cheek.

With long fingers, he touched the spot tenderly, and winced.

'You're only trying to make me feel bad,' she said thickly.

'And you don't?'

'Yes, I do,' she admitted miserably and, though she hadn't meant to, found herself apologising. 'I'm sorry...'

'I guess I asked for it. Though I've still no intention of allowing you to slap me and get away with it scot-free.'

As she stepped back, scared by the menacing gleam in his eyes, he added, 'Don't get the wrong idea, I've never struck a woman, and I don't intend to start now. But there are other ways...'

Panic-stricken, she turned to run, but he caught her arm and spun her round. A moment later she found herself amongst the shrubbery, her back against a tree. 'More enjoyable ways,' he finished softly.

Despite her attempts to free herself, one hand behind her head, he plundered her mouth, while his other hand undid the buttons of her blouse and slipped inside to find her breast.

When he began to tease the nipple through the flimsy material of her bra, terrified of where it might be leading, she attempted to bring her knee up, as she had been taught in a self-defence class.

He neatly blocked the move and, in retaliation, nipped her lower lip between his teeth, just hard enough to make her give up any further attempt to fight back and freeze into stillness.

'That's better,' he murmured and, using lips and tongue and experienced fingers, soon had her mindless with wanting.

She was dazed, knocked completely off balance, when he finally called a halt and, having deftly rebuttoned her blouse, drew her clear of the shrubbery and back onto the path, tucking her hand beneath his arm.

The whole thing was effected so smoothly that, by the time a woman walking a white miniature poodle approached, apart from Virginia's hectic flush, they showed no sign of doing anything more unseemly than taking a stroll.

'Fancy a coffee? Or an ice cream?' Ryan asked. He sounded infuriatingly cool and casual, as if nothing at all had happened.

In spite of the adrenalin pumping through her veins, Virginia felt incapable of either fight or flight. 'I'd like a coffee, please.' She tried to emulate his careless tone and failed singularly.

'Then let's carry on to The Hungry Hippo. There's an exciting choice between plastic cups and thick pottery mugs, but the coffee's some of the best I've ever had in London.'

The Hungry Hippo was a small, open-air snack bar on the edge of the park. It boasted a blue awning with a picture of a pink and cavernously yawning hippo, rickety plastic chairs, and tables with wobbly umbrellas, several of which were vacant.

Choosing one slightly apart from the rest, Ryan settled Virginia into a chair and mounted the steps to the wooden hut.

Sitting limply in the sun, she watched him lean his elbows on the counter while he chatted with the woman who appeared to be in charge of the coffee machine.

Though middle-aged and matronly, she was clearly affected by his charm, and kept patting her tightly permed hair into place as she served him.

When he returned he was carrying two blue pottery mugs adorned with pink hippos. Placing one in front of Virginia, he remarked, 'The coffee here is piping hot, and I've discovered through trial and error that the mugs are preferable to getting one's fingers scalded.'

A cautious sip proved the coffee was every bit as good as he'd said. Even so, it was an unlikely place for a multi-millionaire to frequent and, puzzled, she commented, 'You sound as if you come here often.'

'I've been a few times,' he admitted idly. 'I'm staying at the Kenelm Mayfair. Kenelm Park is handy for a spot of morning exercise, and the snack bar opens early for coffee.'

Frowning, she asked, 'How long have you been in London?'

'Ten days or so, this time.'

This time...

Answering that unspoken thought, he said, 'I've been over several times just lately.'

With a sudden unease, she wondered why.

Her voice studiously casual, she asked, 'On business, presumably?'

'Yes… You might even say delicate and confidential business.'

She wished desperately that he would hurry up and finish his business, whatever it was, and go back to New York.

'When do you think you'll be going home?' she asked without a great deal of hope.

'When my business is completed and I've got what I came for.'

On the surface his reply was innocent enough, yet something about the way he smiled, a certain nuance in his tone, increased her feeling of uneasiness.

Convinced it would be unwise to go any further along that track, she lapsed into silence while she finished her coffee.

As she put down her mug, with the suddenness of an ambush, Ryan said, 'You still haven't told me why you thought it necessary to leave me practically at the altar.'

'And you haven't told me why you thought it necessary to marry me in the first place.'

'You don't think it might have been because I fell head over heels in love with you?'

'No, I don't,' she said shortly, and thought, if only it had been.

A knife seemed to twist in her heart.

Unable to bear the pain, she added, 'And I don't want to talk about it. It's all over and done with. Nothing can alter the past.'

'The moving finger, and all that?'

In no mood to be drawn into a philosophical discussion, she said raggedly, 'I must go. I need to get home.'

As she started to rise he put a restraining hand on her arm. 'There's just one thing before you think of leaving. When I spoke to Raynor this morning I could hardly credit his absurd accusations. I need to hear from your own lips why you left me.'

'Because I'd no intention of letting you use me while you played around with Madeline.'

'I'd guessed it was something to do with Madeline. You were never the same after you saw her kiss me that night… But there was nothing between us, I swear.'

'She told me herself that the pair of you had been lovers… And before you bother to deny it, Janice told me the same thing.'

'It's true that Madeline and I had had a brief fling, but that was all in the past. Do you really think I'd have played around with my stepbrother's wife or cheated on you?'

'If you wanted her yourself, and he'd taken her away from you.'

'I didn't want her myself. What little there had been between us was over well before she married Steven.'

Virginia shook her head. 'She told me what your plans were, how you were marrying me so the family wouldn't suspect what was going on.'

He muttered something under his breath that sounded suspiciously like an oath. Then, with a sigh, he said, 'And you believed her.'

It was a statement, rather than a question, but she answered, 'Yes, I did. That's why I'm *never* coming back to you.'

He smiled without mirth. 'Even if you don't know the meaning of the words love and trust, I want you back Virginia, and I'll extract payment for every day you make me wait.'

His certainty sent a chill down her spine, making her shiver.

Jumping up so violently that she sent the rickety plastic chair tumbling backwards, she croaked, 'I must go.'

Rising to his feet with fluid grace, he righted the chair and said, 'I'll walk you back.'

Thrown by his sudden compliance, she found herself wondering agitatedly what he was up to.

But perhaps, satisfied that he had done enough harm for one day, he was prepared to rest on his laurels for the time being?

She could only hope so. There was still Charles to face, and she felt unable to cope with anything further.

Picking up Virginia's hand, Ryan tucked it through his arm. When she made an attempt to withdraw it, he tightened his elbow, and feeling unequal to a fight, she weakly left it where it was.

Though very conscious of the bone and muscle beneath the fine material of his sleeve, and the occasional brush of his thigh against hers as they walked, she tried to appear unaffected.

Neither of them spoke until they turned the corner into Usher Street, then Ryan broke the silence to ask, 'Not having second thoughts?'

She glanced up at him. 'About what?'

'About coming back here. It may not be wise.'

'Wise? I don't understand what you mean.'

'If Raynor turned nasty—'

'Charles hasn't a nasty bone in his body.'

'I wouldn't be too sure of that. He looked pretty upset at lunch-time.'

'He might be shocked and angry, but he would never lift a finger, if that's what you're suggesting.'

'Jealousy is a powerful emotion. It can make even the most placid people do things they would never normally dream of doing.'

Shaking her head, she said with finality, 'Charles would never do anything to harm me.'

'Are you absolutely certain of that? It might be safer to book you into a hotel.'

Knowing now that this had been carefully planned as a two-pronged attack, and Ryan was doing his utmost to care and unsettle her, she said calmly, 'I'm absolutely certain.'

As he escorted her up the steps of number sixteen, he asked, 'What are you intending to tell him?'

'The truth, of course.'

Though it was still sunny, since they had left the park a wind had sprung up, and now it blew a tendril of brown curly hair across her cheek.

Brushing it back, he tucked it behind her ear.

That light but sure touch made her tremble.

Smiling knowingly, Ryan queried, 'The whole truth? Or an edited version of it?'

Remembering the stricken look on Charles's face, she hesitated, then said distractedly, 'I don't know. I don't want to hurt or upset him any more than I have to.'

'He really matters to you?'

'Yes, he does. He's been wonderful to me, and I care about him.'

'I'm beginning to believe you.'

It struck her that Ryan sounded more pleased than bothered.

'Perhaps I'll just tell him you coerced me.'

'Do you think he'll believe it?'

Knowing how damning the little scene must have appeared, she said with rather more confidence than she felt, 'I'm sure he will.'

Then feeling the need to fight back, she added sardonically, 'Though I must admit you engineered the whole thing quite brilliantly, I'm afraid it's been a complete waste of time and effort.'

'Not a complete waste.' A gleam in those indigo eyes, he added, 'There were parts of it I really quite enjoyed.'

'I'm afraid I can't say the same.'

With a slight shrug of his broad shoulders, Ryan queried, 'So when are you planning the wedding for?'

The sudden question took her by surprise and, withou
thinking, she answered, 'Next Monday.'

Only when the words were out did it occur to her that i
would have made more sense to lie. That way the weddin;
might have been a *fait accompli* before he realised.

But now it was too late.

He raised a dark brow. 'As soon as that?'

'We have no reason to wait.'

Drily, he said, 'I can understand why Raynor's in ;
hurry... Or do you still intend to hold out on him?'

Her lips tightening, she said, 'No, I don't.' Then, curtly
she said, 'Now, as you have my key, would you mind let
ting me in?'

'Certainly.' He opened the door then dropping the key
into her hand, said, 'You'd better have this back.'

'Quite sure you wouldn't like to keep it?' she asked caus
tically.

He grinned. 'Thanks, but that won't be necessary.' Bend
ing his dark head he kissed her, before saying with cer
tainty, 'Next time *you'll* come to *me*.'

She was still standing as though made of marble whe
he reached the bottom of the steps and turned. 'By the way
you'll find your purse on the coffee table in the living
room.'

A second later he was striding away down the street, the
rising wind ruffling his dark hair.

Feeling curiously shaky, she went inside and closed the
door behind her. Then grimacing at her own stupidity i
locking the stable door after the horse had bolted, she pu
on the safety chain.

Next time you'll come to me.

If he was trying to rattle her, he'd succeeded. He'
sounded so terrifyingly confident. So sure of himself.

But she mustn't let him get to her, she told herself firml
as she went upstairs to change.

When she was dressed in trousers and a bottle-green top

he went through to the kitchen and began to prepare the
pecial meal she had promised Charles.

While she worked, her mind kept going over and over
he day's events like a video that refused to be switched
off.

Ryan's sudden appearance in the kitchen doorway; the
vay he had removed the sliver of glass from her foot; the
methods he had used to coerce her into having lunch with
him; the accusing look on Charles's face...

She groaned. Though she had tried to make light of it to
Ryan, what Charles had seen that lunch-time might have
done more harm to their relationship than she could ever
repair.

Please, God, it hadn't, but all she could do was wait and
ee what his reaction was when she told him the truth. It
might not be easy to convince him that Ryan had engineered the whole thing...

By half past-seven, with the dining-room table set and
he coq au vin simmering in the sauté pan, unable to settle,
he prowled about, restless as a cat shut in the wrong house.

Staring out of the window she saw that a front had gone
hrough, pushing the good weather before it. A strongish
wind was herding clouds like shaggy grey sheep across the
ky, and it had started to rain.

At twenty-to-eight, she was spooning a creamy sauce
over the prawn starter when there was the sound of a key
n the lock, followed by a metallic rattle and clunk.

Hurrying through to the hall, she called, 'Just a minute.'

After a short struggle, she released the safety chain and
opened the door.

'I'm sorry, I forgot I'd left it on.'

The rain was coming down in earnest now, and though
he car-parking area was just down a side street, Charles's
air hair was darkened by downpour.

His face set, and offering no word of greeting, he closed
he door and hung up his jacket. Then, going into the small

cloakroom, he towelled his hair and ran a comb through it while Virginia hovered helplessly in the hall.

'Charles, I need to talk to you, to explain.'

Still without a word, he followed her across the hall and into the living-room.

Her knees feeling as though they might buckle at any minute, she sank down on the couch while he remained standing.

Knowing that it wasn't going to be easy, she suggested, 'Shall we have a drink before dinner?'

'If that's what you'd like.'

He went over to the sideboard and, filling two glasses with pale dry sherry, handed her one.

She took a nervous sip that was more like a gulp, while his stayed untouched.

'Aren't you going to sit down?' she asked awkwardly when he showed no sign of joining her.

'Perhaps you'd better come straight to the point,' he said tightly. 'I presume you've decided to go back to him?'

'No!' she cried. 'No! I told you I'd *never* go back to him.'

'That wasn't the impression I got at lunch-time.'

She swallowed hard. Convincing him looked like being every bit as difficult as she'd feared.

CHAPTER EIGHT

'IT WAS the wrong impression,' she said earnestly. 'I realise what it must have looked like, but Ryan set the whole thing up to make you think that.'

It was obvious Charles didn't believe her, and her lovely eyes filled with despairing tears.

Immediately his face softened. Sitting down by her side he took her hand. 'Perhaps you'd better tell me the whole story. Why did you go to meet him in the first place?'

'I didn't go to meet him. He came here.'

'He knew where you were living?'

'That first day in the park I told him I was living with you.'

'Surely you didn't give him the exact address?'

'He already knew.'

'The devil he did!' Charles exclaimed. 'How did he know?'

'He'd had detectives looking for me ever since I left him, and somehow they'd managed to find out where I lived and worked.'

'So he came here,' Charles said slowly. 'How did he know you'd be home?'

'He said he'd been into the gallery, so I imagine he found out then.'

Charles muttered, 'Damn... Helen must have told him you weren't there before I arrived on the scene.'

He gave the hand he was holding a squeeze. 'It must have been a nasty shock when he turned up here.'

'It was.'

'Why did you let him in?'

'I wouldn't have done, but he took me by surprise and

133

was inside before I realised.' Her voice shook. 'I asked him what he wanted, and he said he'd come to take me out to lunch.

'At first I refused, but he wouldn't take no for an answer and, at the finish, thinking it would be better to be in a public place rather than here alone with him, I agreed to go.

'What I hadn't realised was that he intended to take me to the same restaurant as you—'

'How could he possibly have known where I'd be lunching? The only people who knew were Andrew Bish, who made the booking, and myself.'

'Andrew Bish, if that's his real name, was in Ryan's pay.' Seeing Charles looked unconvinced, she insisted, 'It's quite true, he admitted it.

'The whole thing was carefully planned and staged. That's why he kissed me; that's why he called me "my love"; he wanted you to see and think the worst.'

Blue eyes looked steadily into greeny-grey. 'Is what you've told me the truth?'

'Yes, it is.'

It was. Though not the whole truth by a long chalk.

'And you don't want to go back to him?'

'I couldn't bear to,' she said shakily.

'What about us?' Once more his nice-looking face was full of tension. 'Have you changed your mind about marrying me?'

'No. I still want to marry you. If you haven't changed your mind,' she added uncertainly.

His answer was to pull her to him and hold her as if he'd never let her go.

It was such a relief to see joy replace that look of strain, to be held and cradled in the warmth of his arms, that it wasn't until a faint smell of burning came drifting in that she recalled the meal waiting on the stove.

'Oh, dear!' Pulling herself free, she scrambled to her feet. 'I forgot all about the coq au vin.'

Following her through to the kitchen, he said, 'Don't worry, if it's spoilt we'll have a meal out. There's plenty to celebrate.'

'I think it's just caught, rather than spoilt. Come and have a taste and see what you think.'

She spooned up a little of the sauce and offered it to him.

'Mmm… Much too good to waste. We'll eat out another night.'

They began their meal in a silence, both relieved and thankful that what might have been a serious breakup had ended with even greater understanding.

After a while, her thoughts straying to the business appointment Charles had described as 'important', and how he'd said with unusual animation, 'If all goes well, it should mean a virtual end to my financial problems', she wondered how it had turned out.

Then recalling his, 'There's plenty to celebrate', and sensing an undercurrent of excitement in her usually phlegmatic companion, she asked hopefully, 'Did everything go well this evening?'

'Very well. I would have told you at once, only the whole thing's been overshadowed by more important issues.'

'Tell me now,' she suggested with a smile.

'I'll give you one guess.'

'You've had a find?' In the art world there was always the possibility of coming across something that would mean big money.

'You could say that. Just over a week ago I received a phone call offering me a Roisser…'

'A *Roisser*?'

'I could hardly believe it either. Still, I agreed to take a look at it. The caller, who identified himself as Mr Smith, insisted on the greatest secrecy, so I made an appointment for him to bring the painting over the following evening when the gallery was closed.'

'And?' Virginia prompted eagerly.

'I was quite certain it was genuine.'

'Was it signed?'

'Only with an elongated R. But that's how Roisser often signed his work. It's as distinctive as his brushwork. His two most famous paintings, *Dragonflies*, and *Midsummer*, that hang in the Louvre, are signed that way.'

'So which one was this?'

'Footprints.'

Her jaw dropped. *Footprints* was recognised as one of Gerard Roisser's masterpieces.

'But surely that went to the States in the early nineteen-seventies and disappeared into the Jefferson family's private art collection?'

'You're absolutely right, it did. However, earlier this year the painting was purchased from a Mr Otis Jefferson of New York.'

With a stirring of unease, she asked, 'But if everything was quite above board, why the need for all the secrecy?'

Not one to be rushed, Charles began the story in his own precise way. 'The young man who wanted to sell it had recently inherited his godfather's estate in Kent.

'He'd borrowed heavily on his expectations, but unfortunately for him there was very little money, only a mouldering pile of a house, and a collection of pictures.

'Because he didn't want his titled family, and his wife in particular, to know he had extensive gambling debts, he was desperate to raise some money without "causing a stink," as he put it.

'None of the family were art lovers and, realising that one picture out of so many was unlikely to be missed, he decided to sell the Roisser. Not only was it the most valuable but, as his godfather had suffered a stroke shortly after its purchase, it had never even been hung.

'Because he needed the money urgently, he was prepared to part with it for considerably less than it was worth. His only stipulation was cash in hand, and the whole thing kept a complete secret.'

'But doesn't a deal of that kind create all sorts of...problems?'

'Yes, it does,' Charles admitted frankly. 'Apart from the fact that it isn't easy to raise a very large amount of ready cash, it means the painting has to be passed on in the same shady way.'

'But you've never countenanced anything like that,' she said desperately. 'And there's the good reputation of the gallery to think about.'

'Yes, I know. That's why, if things hadn't been so difficult, I would have had nothing to do with it.'

Virginia felt her nerves tighten. Charles had always been strictly law-abiding. His financial troubles must be a great deal worse than he had admitted if he would allow himself to be pushed into taking that kind of risk.

Carefully, she said, 'You're talking as if you're planning to go ahead with the deal?'

He grimaced. 'I know exactly what you're thinking. It must sound like utter madness. But it's not as if I'm doing any real harm, and it will solve nearly all my problems.'

Afraid for him, she protested, 'Isn't the whole thing far too risky? Suppose it got out?'

'There's not much chance of that. Mr Smith isn't likely to blab, and I presume I can rely on you to say nothing?'

'Of course you can.'

He patted her hand. 'That's my girl.'

Deciding to try the down-to-earth approach, she objected, 'But if you're already in financial difficulties I don't see how you can hope to raise what you've just admitted is a very large amount of ready cash.'

'I've already solved that. I found a source that will give me a short-term loan using the business as collateral.'

She blanched. 'Are you absolutely certain the painting's genuine? Supposing this is just a clever con?'

'I'd stake my life that it's a genuine Roisser. But to be on the safe side I contacted Otis Jefferson and, though he wouldn't tell me the name of the buyer, he confirmed that last year he'd sold *Footprints* to another collector.'

'But suppose this Mr Smith showed you the genuine Roisser and then—'

'My dear girl,' Charles protested mildly, 'do you take me for a fool? I'm well aware that a last minute switch could be made, that's why I refused to let the painting out of my hands. It's been locked in our strongroom since that first night.'

Virginia played her last card. 'I know there are always some of the more unscrupulous dealers or private collectors who will buy without asking too many questions, but it might take a long time to find one who—'

'I had a buyer, a private collector named Anderson, already lined up.'

'You've already found a buyer?' she echoed stupidly.

'If I hadn't had a buyer waiting, I couldn't have afforded to take the risk.'

That sounded more like Charles the businessman, and she breathed a sigh of relief.

Leaning over the table, he patted her hand reassuringly. 'Don't worry, my dear. Everything has gone through smoothly. Tonight I handed over the picture and got my money back, plus a very handsome profit. We'll be starting our married life nicely solvent, rather than in the red.'

She smiled, wanting to be happy for him, but at the back of her mind was a nagging doubt as to the wisdom of it.

Yet if the transaction had already gone through, and the new owner was happy, what could possibly go wrong?

After the meal, which Charles pronounced excellent, he

helped her wash the dishes and, because of the change in the weather, lit a fire.

At ease together, the rest of the evening was spent in the aura of cosy domesticity that had grown up over the past months.

Only when bedtime approached and they mounted the stairs together, as they had done many times before, did Virginia start to feel uncomfortable. What if Charles wanted her to sleep with him?

If he did, this time she must go ahead and do it. Yet even as she made up her mind, she was aware of a strange feeling of reluctance.

It was all Ryan's fault, she told herself vexedly. Once he had gone back to the States, and she and Charles were married, everything would be fine. But for the moment he had totally unsettled her.

Either reading her mind, or perhaps remembering her coolness of the previous night and losing confidence, Charles said, 'There's nothing I'd like better than to take you to bed, but I know you've had an upsetting time lately, so I won't press you... After all it's less than a week to our wedding day.'

Stooping, he kissed her chastely on the cheek.

She kissed him back, gratefully.

If he had hoped for a different response, he hid it well.

'Good night then. If you want to sleep in tomorrow, I'll try not to disturb you...'

Virginia shook her head, 'I've decided to go into work as usual.'

'Don't let what happened today throw you. Now you're on your guard you could always keep the chain on the door.'

But recalling Ryan's parting words, 'Next time you'll come to me,' she felt convinced that he would come to neither Usher Street nor the gallery.

'No, I'll go into work with you.' Carefully, she added, 'At least we'll be together.'

Charles looked gratified.

For the next two or three days life regained some semblance of peace as she and Charles went back to their ordinary routine.

Each morning they drove to the gallery and passed the day working as usual, before returning home to cook a meal and spend a quiet evening together. And each night they went upstairs and parted to go into their respective rooms with nothing further being said, and no more than a light kiss on the cheek or forehead.

But, in spite of the outward normality, Virginia felt restless and on edge, stuck on hold.

Though there was no sign of Ryan, she couldn't believe he had given up so easily, and waiting for him to make his next move was like waiting for the second shoe to drop.

He couldn't seriously expect her to go to him.

Or could he?

It was the not knowing that got to her. The fear of what he might be planning. A fear that lurked at the back of her mind like a dark shadow during the day, and woke her, palpitating, from sleep in the middle of the night.

The worst part was trying to hide it from Charles. He seemed to be on a high, happy that his mounting debts had been paid off, and confident that Ryan had given up and was going to leave them alone.

But then, of course, she had kept a large part of the truth from him, and he didn't know Ryan as well as she did.

As the wedding day approached, rather than fading away, Virginia's anxiety intensified, until she was practically living on her nerves, only waiting for the whole thing to be over.

Once they were on their honeymoon, she comforted herself repeatedly, she would be safe from Ryan and able to relax.

At Charles's insistence they were closing the gallery for the day on Monday, so that Helen could come to the wedding.

Guessing how the other woman felt about him, Virginia had been doubtful whether she would want to come.

But Helen had accepted the invitation with a smile and, hiding her lovelorn state behind a resolutely cheerful façade, had assured them that as it would be mid-week when they were away, if she just had someone who could sit behind the reception desk, she could easily hold the fort.

Some temporary help had been arranged, and after the ceremony the newly-weds were due to fly to Paris.

'Four days should allow enough time to take my wife trousseau shopping on the Champs Elysées,' Charles remarked, as he sat on the edge of Virginia's desk, 'and we'll have a longer honeymoon later.'

Seeing the shadow hadn't lifted from her face, he squeezed her hand and said seriously, 'Don't you think it's time you stopped worrying about Falconer? If he was planning to try any more tricks he would have already done so. In all probability he's gone back home by now.

'Tell you what, I'll check. I have his hotel phone number in my office.' Charles hurried away.

He was back almost immediately, a smile of satisfaction on his face. 'Just as I thought, he left for the States first thing Wednesday morning.'

'He *did*?'

'The hotel clerk was quite certain.'

Mingled with Virginia's relief was a feeling of incredulity that Ryan had given up so easily.

The following day was Saturday, always the busiest day at the gallery. But because—almost as if she were superstitious—Virginia had so far bought nothing new for the wed-

ding, Charles insisted on her taking as much time off as
she needed.

'Go and buy a nice new outfit, and some pretty undies,
and have a leisurely lunch in Harrods.'

Smiling, she set out to do his bidding but, anxious not
to be too long, she ate an early lunch and, dropping her
purchases at home on the way, took a taxi back to the
gallery.

She was surprised to find that Charles had gone out.

'He wouldn't have left just Moira and me,' Helen explained, 'only it was something that needed his attention
and couldn't wait. He said he'd be back as soon as possible.'

In the event he was absent for the entire afternoon, so
Virginia saw nothing of him until just before it was time
to go home, when he appeared at her office door looking
rushed and harassed.

'I'm afraid I have to go straight out again. Do you mind
locking up for me and making your own way home?'

'Of course not. Is everything all right?'

'Something rather urgent has cropped up. I have to go
to Sussex.'

'Shall I hold dinner for you?'

He shook his head. 'I'll be out for dinner.' Then, with
an attempt at a smile, he added, 'I've no idea what time
I'll get back, so don't wait up for me.'

A moment later he was gone.

Frowning at the closed door, she wondered what could
have happened to throw the usually unflappable Charles out
of his normal, calm routine.

Trying to subdue a sudden rush of foreboding, she told
herself it was probably just something he needed to deal
with before Monday, but the feeling of impending disaster
lingered, refusing to be banished.

When she had taken her duplicate set of keys from her
desk, she went down to make the usual security checks and

ascertain that every member of the public had left the gallery.

Moira, the young art student who came in to help on Saturdays, had already gone, and the only person still there was Helen.

'Charles looked worried to death when he got back,' she said, her nice hazel eyes anxious, 'and he was acting strangely.'

'In what way?' Virginia asked.

'A man who had just bought a Jules Pesaro wanted to ask his advice about a frame, but he virtually brushed him off. Said he had to go straight out again. It's so unlike Charles to be rude to the customers...'

Wanting to reassure the other woman, but unable to, Virginia admitted, 'All he told me was that something urgent had cropped up, and he'd like me to lock the gallery.'

'Do you need any help?'

'No, thanks. I've done all the checks, so you may as well go.'

As Helen was about to pull on her coat, the phone on the reception desk rang. Lifting the receiver, she said, 'The Charles Raynor Gallery. Yes... Yes, she's still here.' Then, to Virginia, she said 'It's for you.'

'Hello?'

Without preamble, Ryan laid it on the line. 'I'll be going back to New York tomorrow and I want you to come with me.'

Watching all the colour drain from the younger woman's face, and concerned for her, Helen pushed the chair closer.

Sinking limply into it, Virginia said, 'I thought you'd already gone home.'

'That was just a flying visit; now I'm back at the Kenelm Mayfair. I'm in the Imperial Suite, and I shall expect you to join me there tonight.'

'Well you'll be disappointed,' she told him hoarsely.

Infuriatingly calm, he disagreed, 'I don't think so. You'll
come if you care about Raynor.'

There was silence while the threat, and it was a threat,
drip-fed itself into her befuddled brain. Then she stammered, 'W-what?'

'I said, you'll come if you care about Raynor... And
don't forget I want you there *tonight*. No matter how late
it is, I'll send a car for you. You'd better write down the
phone number and ring me when you're ready to come.'

With a feeling of inevitability, and knowing Ryan never
made empty threats, she picked up a pen, and her unsteady
fingers hardly able to control it, wrote down the number he
gave her.

'By the way, don't bother to pack more than a few overnight essentials,' he added, 'you can buy everything you
need in New York.'

The line went dead.

For a moment or two she sat staring blindly at the number on the pad until the figures seemed burnt into her brain.
Then, making a great effort to gather herself, she replaced
the receiver.

'Are you all right?' Helen wanted to know. 'You've gone
as white as a sheet.'

'Yes, I'm all right,' Virginia lied through stiff lips. 'It
was just a bit of a shock. I thought he was in the States.'

Her hazel eyes curious, Helen said, 'It was the man
who's been into the gallery a couple of times this last week,
wasn't it? Ryan Falconer. As well as being attractive, his
voice is very distinctive...

'The last time he came in, the day you weren't here,
Charles took him into his office. Though neither of them
raised their voices, my guess is they had a real set to.'

When Virginia made no comment, Helen went on,
'Though he's absolutely gorgeous—those eyes—I should
imagine he can be quite formidable.'

'Yes, he can.'

After hovering for a moment or two, seeing the younger woman wasn't about to elaborate, Helen said, 'Well if there's nothing I can do for you, I'd best be getting off.'

She pulled on her coat and picked up her bag. 'I'll see you at the church on Monday.' Her voice wasn't quite steady.

On an impulse, Virginia asked, 'You love Charles, don't you?'

Flushing, the older woman said defensively, 'Whatever gave you that idea?'

'You do, don't you?' Virginia persisted.

'Yes,' Helen admitted quietly. 'But don't think for a minute that I—'

'I'm not jealous,' Virginia denied quickly. 'I was just asking, because he may need your support...'

'*My* support?'

'And if he does, I'd like him to have it.'

Just for an instant, hazel eyes met grey-green and held. Then Helen nodded and, putting the strap of her bag over her shoulder, made her way to the door.

Virginia followed and, having locked up after her, set the security-alarm system before leaving by the back way.

After a couple of days of cool, unsettled weather, it was once again warm and sunny and, accompanied by a sensation of *déjà vu*, she walked home through the park.

The house, when she reached it, was empty and waiting. The shopping she had dumped on the couch earlier had a forlorn, abandoned air.

Carrying the packages up to her room, Virginia put them on the chest of drawers and, without taking a second look at the contents, went downstairs again.

For the moment she felt oddly calm, suspended in time, like a victim with her head on the block, just waiting for the axe to fall.

She prepared and ate a solitary meal, hoping it would

take away the hollow feeling, then washed the dishes before going through to the living-room.

The house felt oddly empty, and she found herself listening to the silence. Making an effort at normality she switched on the television, but after a while the silence seemed preferable.

Left alone with her thoughts, and beset once more by gnawing worries and unanswerable questions, the evening crawled past on leaden feet.

When Charles had failed to return by nine-thirty, Virginia, who had slept badly the last few nights, went upstairs, weary and emotionally exhausted.

Hoping against hope that Ryan had been bluffing, but convinced all the same that he hadn't, she showered, cleaned her teeth, and prepared for bed.

Leaving the bedroom door open so she would be sure to hear Charles come home, she snuggled down to try to get some sleep.

But once beneath the duvet, she tossed and turned restlessly, unable to settle. Finally giving up the attempt, she switched on the bedside lamp again and picked up a book.

While she forced her eyes to read the print, her brain stubbornly refused to take it in, and she found herself repeatedly rereading the same page.

It was almost eleven when she finally heard the front door open and close. For what seemed an age she sat waiting for Charles to come up to bed.

When he didn't, she pulled on her dressing gown, knotted the sash, and in her bare feet went quietly down the stairs.

The hall and the living-room were in darkness, but there was a rectangle of light spilling from the open doorway of the kitchen.

Moving silently to the threshold, she looked in.

Charles was slumped in a chair by the table, his shoulders bowed, his fair head supported in his hands. He looked prematurely old, as if life had suddenly defeated him.

As she hesitated in the doorway, he glanced up and saw her.

She watched him straighten his shoulders, watched his attempt to return to the quietly confident man she knew, and her heart swelled with sympathy and affection for him.

Sliding into the seat opposite, she reached across and took his hand. It felt icy cold.

'I wondered why you weren't coming to bed.'

'I was thinking of having some cocoa.' Even his voice sounded beaten.

'I'll heat some milk.' She jumped to her feet, glad to have something positive to do.

When she had made two cups of milky cocoa, she put one in front of him, and sat down opposite again.

While, fair head bent, he spooned sugar into his cocoa and stirred it as if his very life depended on it, she jumped in at the deep end.

'I know something's terrible wrong. Won't you please tell me what it is?'

He picked up his cocoa and put it down again untasted. 'The Roisser I bought...'

Backed into a corner by her fears, she waited for what she was now certain was coming.

'It's a worthless copy,' Charles said flatly. 'A brilliant fake. I know Roisser's work and I could have staked my life it was absolutely genuine.'

Her voice commendably steady, she asked, 'How did you discover it wasn't?'

'Anderson rang me up at lunch-time in an absolute frenzy. A chance remark made by someone in the know had convinced him that another collector had the real *Footprints*.

'He made further careful enquiries and discovered that the painting is in Sir Humphrey Post's private collection, and has been ever since he bought it from Otis Jefferson last year.'

'There's no way he could be wrong?' Virginia asked without much hope.

'That was my first thought. So, to be on the safe side, I discreetly approached both Sir Humphrey Post and Otis Jefferson.

'Having obtained Sir Humphrey's permission, Jefferson confirmed that Post was the man he'd sold *Footprints* to.

'Though I hadn't told him the full story by any means, Sir Humphrey, who apparently knows the gallery and its reputation, was very cooperative. He invited me to have dinner at Ferndale Manor, his home in Sussex, and see the painting for myself...

'There's not a shadow of doubt that he has the authentic *Footprints*, with its completed provenance.'

'What about Mr Smith?'

'As you might expect,' Charles said bitterly, 'the telephone number he gave me in case I needed to contact him is no longer in use.'

'And the man you sold the copy to? Anderson?'

'If only I could return his money, the whole thing could be hushed up and my reputation saved. But I can't... And if he doesn't get every penny back by Monday, he's threatening to call in the police.

'I've been the world's worst fool. I'll lose the gallery and everything I own, and it's odds-on I'll end up in prison.'

As Charles's despairing words echoed through her head they were replaced by Ryan's. 'You'll come if you care about Raynor...'

Somehow he had known what was going to happen, and was offering a way out... *So long as she went back to him...*

Icy cold and calm, her thinking swift and lucid, she asked, 'How much money do you need?'

He named a staggering sum.

With a feeling of inevitability, Virginia went through to the hall and rang the number that was branded on her mind.

When Ryan's voice answered, she said stonily, 'I'm ready to come.'

'How much does Raynor need?'

She told him.

Without the slightest hesitation, he said, 'Maxwell will bring a cheque.'

'When will you want the money back?'

'I won't. This is a one-off payment to provide Raynor with a fresh start, and give me what I want.'

Glancing through the kitchen door on her way to the stairs, she saw that Charles was sitting exactly as she'd left him. He didn't appear to have even noticed her absence.

After she had dressed again, she pushed a few essentials into an overnight case, as Ryan had instructed, and fastened it.

Catching sight of the packages abandoned on the chest of drawers, she thought with bitter irony that running away and leaving her wedding things behind was getting to be a habit.

When she had made her way downstairs once more, she put her case and bag in the hall and faced the hardest task of all.

Charles was still sitting staring blindly into space, sunk in a stupor of despair. Standing by his side, she put her hand on his shoulder.

He glanced up. His blue eyes were curiously blank and unfocussed, as if he were looking inward, rather than at her.

'I want to talk to you.'

'Can't it wait 'til morning?' Even his speech was slightly slurred.

'No, it can't.' Afraid for him, she shook his arm.

As though he'd made a great effort, his gaze came into

focus. 'Of course... Don't worry, I'll cancel the wedding. I wouldn't expect any woman to tie herself to a penniless gaolbird.'

'You won't be a penniless gaolbird,' she said firmly. 'Ryan's prepared to cover the amount you need. Tomorrow you'll be able to give Anderson back every penny of his money.'

It took a moment or two to sink in, then Charles shook his head as if to clear his brain. 'What did you say?'

She repeated it.

Sounding dazed, he said, 'When did you ask him?'

'I spoke to him on the phone a few minutes ago. But I didn't ask him. He offered.'

'How soon does he want it back?' Charles queried thickly.

'He doesn't want it back.'

'*That* amount of money? He *must* want it back!'

She shook her head, adding quickly, 'Don't worry, he can afford it. He probably gives a lot more than that to charity.'

'Why would Falconer help me out? It's not as if we're friends...'

It was the question she had been dreading.

CHAPTER NINE

As SHE hesitated, wondering how best to break it to him, he said violently, 'No! You told me you'd never go back to him, and I won't allow you to sell yourself to save me.'

'I'm doing nothing of the kind.'

Then, knowing that somehow she must convince him, otherwise he would refuse Ryan's help, she said, 'Look, I wouldn't dream of going back to him simply for the money, but—'

'But you can't bear the thought of marrying a bankrupt? I don't blame you...'

'Please will you stop interrupting and *listen* to me? If you hadn't a penny, and you did have to go to prison, I'd still marry you if I really loved you...'

Almost matter-of-factly, as if he'd always secretly known it, he said, 'But you don't.'

'Not enough,' she admitted.

'Perhaps I always knew I was living in a fool's paradise, but I didn't want to admit it.'

'I wanted to love you. I tried to love you...'

He sighed deeply. 'It's still Falconer you care about, isn't it?'

'Yes.'

'Though you tried to deny it, I think I've always known it. I've been trying to tell myself I was mistaken, but that day in the restaurant, when he kissed you, it was painfully obvious.'

'I'm sorry.'

'And we were so close to being married.'

'It would have been a mistake,' she said with conviction. 'I'm not saying we couldn't have made it work, but it

151

wouldn't have been fair to you. I would have been short-changing you.

'You should have a wife who loves you with passion, a wife who feels about you the way I feel about Ryan.'

'Are you going back to him?'

'Yes.'

'For good?'

'For as long as he wants me.'

'You said you didn't want to go back.'

'I didn't.' She was unable to repress a shiver. 'But I find I can't help myself.'

Charles was no fool and, after a moment, he stated, 'So when you told him I was in a mess, he offered his help with strings, and that's when you decided to go back to him.'

'No, you're wrong.'

'It's no use,' he said tiredly. 'I know you're only doing it for me.'

Feeling as if she was picking her way through a mine-field, she repeated, 'You're wrong! I'm going back to him because I *want* to.

'I'd already decided before I even knew what kind of a mess you were in... I was waiting to tell you.'

He sat up straighter. 'You say you'd made up your mind *before* you knew about my problems?'

'Yes.'

'So when did you talk to him about it?'

On safer ground now, she answered, 'He's back in London, and he rang me up at the gallery just after you'd gone. He's flying home again tomorrow, and he wants me to go with him.'

Seeing Charles wasn't altogether convinced, Virginia added, 'Ask Helen if you don't believe me. She answered the phone and recognised his voice...'

The doorbell pealed through her words. 'This will be

Ryan's chauffeur. He's bringing a cheque, and taking me back with him.'

She hurried to the door to find Maxwell standing on the step.

Handing her a white envelope, he said, 'Mr Falconer asked me to give you this, and wait for you.'

'Thank you. If you'll be kind enough to put my case in the car I'll be out in just a minute.'

'Certainly, miss.'

She took the envelope back to the kitchen and put it into Charles's hand.

He tore it open and looked at the cheque.

His face showed a strange mixture of awe and relief and anxiety. 'Falconer's actually rounded it up by several hundred thousand. He's either extremely generous, or he rates you very highly.'

Then, urgently, he asked, 'Are you really *sure* you want to go back to him?'

'Quite sure.'

'You said he only wanted you back because there was a score to settle.'

She answered with care. 'That might still be true, but, no matter how tough the going is, I'd sooner live with Ryan than without him.'

'Rather than put you at risk I'm more than willing to tear this cheque up and take my chances.'

Gambling, she said, 'You can if you like, but I shall go back to Ryan anyway.'

Watching him waver, she added, 'Now you know how things stand, unless your pride won't let you keep it, it would be a waste to tear it up...'

'The money isn't important compared to—'

'Oh, but it is,' she broke in. 'Not only does it save you, it also saves me. You see it enables me to leave you without feeling too guilty. If it hadn't been for the money I couldn't have gone back with Ryan and left you to face ruin on your own.'

She touched his cheek with her hand. 'You're one of the nicest people I've ever met, and I'd be very grateful to have you for a friend.'

'But not for a lover.' There was an edge of bitterness to his tone.

'The way I feel about Ryan precludes that. I tried to tell myself that after we were married the sexual side would come right, but I know now it never would have. And it would have been my fault. The passion was missing.'

He managed a wry smile. 'I can only feel sorry about that.'

'You'll make some lucky woman a wonderful lover—someone like Helen, who *does* love you passionately.'

She saw the surprise on his face. Clearly he had had no idea.

Perhaps she shouldn't have said anything. But possibly the knowledge would make him look at the other woman with new eyes, and if he could once see how very attractive she was...

'And speaking of Helen,' Virginia went on casually, 'perhaps she would be kind enough to help you pack up the things I've left, and take them to a charity shop.'

Stooping, she kissed his forehead. 'Thank you for being here for me when I needed you most.'

'Virginia...'

She was at the door when he spoke her name, and she stopped and turned.

'If things don't work out, I still will be here for you, even if it's only as a friend.'

'Thank you.' She smiled and blew him a kiss before gathering up her bag and letting herself quietly out of the house.

The journey through the late-Saturday-night traffic was a slow one, but Virginia scarcely noticed. Drained and empty, she sat staring straight ahead with sightless eyes, like a zombie who could neither think nor feel.

When they reached the Kenelm Mayfair, Maxwell jumped out and, carrying her case, escorted her up to the Imperial Suite.

Ryan opened the door himself, clad only in a short silk robe and, taking the case, said, 'Thank you, Maxwell. Sorry to have kept you up so late.' A generous tip changed hands. 'Goodnight.'

'Thank you, Mr Falconer. Goodnight... Goodnight, miss.'

Once inside, Ryan dropped the case and studied Virginia's pale, drawn face. 'You look absolutely shattered. Straight to bed, I think. We'll leave the talking until morning.'

His dark hair was still damp from the shower, and he was freshly shaved. He'd always been punctilious about shaving at night, aware of what damage stubble could do to a delicate skin.

He led the way through to a bedroom decorated in smoke-grey and misty-blue. There was a large bed, the duvet turned down ready.

All at once she found herself remembering clearly what he'd said in the park. 'Now I've found you, I want you in my bed. I want to make love to you until you're begging for mercy and I'm sated. Then I want to start all over again.'

A shudder ran through her.

She had put so much effort into convincing Charles that it was what she wanted to do, that she hadn't paused to reconsider all the consequences.

But perhaps that was just as well. If she had, she might have got cold feet.

Now here she was, and it was much too late for second thoughts.

If he'd cared about her in the slightest… But he didn't.
He just wanted to make her suffer for leaving him.

And it could only get worse. Once they were back in the
States it would mean additional pain and humiliation. She
would become his whipping boy while Madeline looked on
and enjoyed the spectacle.

But somehow, until his need for revenge had been met
and he tired of her, she would have to cope…

'Let me help you,' Ryan's voice cut through her bleak
and unhappy thoughts. 'You look about out on your feet.'

He began to undress her, neatly and methodically. When
he unfastened her bra, she crossed her arms over her chest
in an age-old gesture of modesty.

'Something wrong?' he asked.

Shivering, she answered, 'I haven't unpacked my nightdress.'

'You won't need it.' A faintly amused look on his face,
he added, 'It isn't cold in here, and I've seen you naked
before.'

But not for a long time. It was like beginning all over
anew on a relationship that this time she could only dread.
Already she was starting to tremble with the thought of
what lay ahead.

While her treacherous body would no doubt respond and
enjoy what was happening, her mind would stand aloof,
hating the enslavement of her senses, but powerless to do
anything about it.

It would have been infinitely preferable if she could have
rejected him with both her mind and body and, because she
had no choice, merely *endured* what was happening to her.

But she knew only too well that that wasn't possible.

If it had been, she saw with sudden insight, Ryan
wouldn't have wanted her on those terms. He wasn't the
kind of man who would be satisfied to make love to a truly
unwilling woman.

Not even because she owed him.

'Hadn't you better jump in?'

His question startled her. She had been unconsciously waiting for him to pick her up and throw her on the bed like some triumphant conqueror.

She climbed in reluctantly and pulled up the duvet.

A moment later he discarded his robe, switched out the light, and slid in beside her.

When he turned and took her in his arms, she made a small, despairing sound in her throat. But all he did was draw her shivering body against the naked warmth of his, and settle her head on the comfortable junction between chest and shoulder.

She was so wound up, that it took her a second or two to appreciate that, because of her obvious exhaustion, Ryan wasn't going to make love to her.

But if she had been thinking straight, she would have realised that Ryan hadn't undressed her like an eager lover, but rather as a parent might undress a tired child.

It seemed strange to be held once again, and at first she lay stiffly, listening to the strong beat of his heart beneath her cheek.

Then gradually she relaxed, and by the time she drifted off, her mind befuddled with sleep, lying in his arms seemed like coming home after a long and desolate journey.

Drifting to the surface, half asleep and half awake, she lay relaxed and refreshed, listening to the muted sounds of London just stirring into life.

After a moment she became aware of a hand cupping her breast the thumb rubbing lightly over the nipple. Opening startled eyes, she saw Ryan, his face only inches away.

By the side of his mouth was a small crescent-shaped scar, a thin, silvery thread that disappeared into a shallow dimple when he smiled, as he was smiling at her now.

'Good morning. You're the only woman I know who wakes up beautiful.'

He himself looked fit and healthy, his tanned skin clear, his blue-violet eyes bright and, making him look very masculine and sexy, the beginnings of a dark stubble.

She could feel his breath, warm and fresh and sweet, on her lips, and she very much wanted him to kiss her.

As though reading her mind, he dipped his head and touched his mouth to hers. Without any urging, her lips parted beneath that light pressure.

With a little murmur of satisfaction, he deepened the kiss, while his hand began to travel over her slender body.

Her heart started to race and her breath quickened with pleasure as those experienced fingers reacquainted themselves with her slim waist, the curve of her hips, her flat stomach, the smooth skin of her inner thighs, and the nest of silky curls.

Feeling the swift leap of response, he broke the kiss and moved to nuzzle his face against the soft firmness of her breasts.

While she gasped and shuddered, he coaxed a dusky pink nipple into life with his tongue, before drawing it into his mouth and suckling sweetly.

By the time he had leisurely, and with great enjoyment, rediscovered each erogenous zone and had explored every inch of naked flesh, she was a quivering mass.

But, while giving her the greatest pleasure, he had skilfully kept her poised on the brink and, ignoring her husky pleas, had teased and tantalised without allowing her the satisfaction she craved.

She had imagined that her mind would stand apart, but when her body finally welcomed the weight of his, she was enslaved, heart and soul and mind. No part of her stood aloof while he took her to a climax of such intensity that she thought she might die.

Afterwards, her head on his shoulder, his body half supporting hers, she lay emotionally drained but completely fulfilled.

After a while, as though needing some final reassurance, Ryan asked quietly, 'Raynor was never your lover, was he?'

Unable to lie, she shook her head.

'But in two-and-a-half years there must have been others?'

'No.'

'No one?'

'No one.'

His sigh of relief was audible, before his arms tightened possessively and he said with soft triumph, 'My very own lollipop.'

Still entangled in a golden web of pleasure, she couldn't even summon up any resentment.

'Why was there no one else?' His sudden question took her by surprise.

Because he was the only man she had ever loved.

When she didn't answer, he persisted. 'You're young and lovely, and a passionate woman, so *why* was there no one else?'

Afraid that he might guess the truth and use it as a weapon against her, she asked, 'Have you never heard the old saying, once bitten, twice shy?'

'You make me sound like the big, bad wolf.' He spoke lightly, but she could have sworn that he was disappointed.

For a little while she lay, his breath stirring her hair, then she yawned, and a moment later, cradled close, she was asleep once more.

A light kiss awoke her. She opened her eyes to find Ryan sitting on the edge of the bed, freshly showered and shaved, and casually dressed.

He smelt pleasantly of shower gel, of male cologne and minty toothpaste.

'I hate having to disturb you when you were sleeping

like a babe, but breakfast will be here in a few minutes, and we really should get moving.'

Touching her cheek with a lean finger, he added, 'Which is a great pity. It would have been nice to have spent the morning in bed.'

His little reminiscent smile brought back vividly what had happened earlier and, recalling how she had begged and pleaded, her own sensual abandon, she blushed hotly.

As he rose to his feet, she stumbled out of bed and high-tailed it for the bathroom, his soft, satisfied laugh following her.

How could she have surrendered control so easily? she asked herself vexedly, as she stripped the Cellophane from a toothbrush and cleaned her teeth with unnecessary vigour. She had been a weak fool! Where was her will-power, her pride?

But what use were self-recriminations? This was how it would always be with Ryan. Love, the emotional counter-part of sex, made her belong to him more than herself. When she had told Charles that it was Ryan she still loved, it had been the truth. She had never stopped loving him, and never would.

Despite the scented steam filling the shower stall, she shivered. It made her so vulnerable. Gave him such power to wound her. Power he would ruthlessly exploit.

Perhaps her only faint chance was to deny that love, to make him believe it was just physical attraction that drew her to him...

She was just finishing drying herself when a light knock at the bathroom door made her clutch the towel to her.

'Breakfast's arrived.'

'I'll only be a minute.' She was aware that she sounded breathless.

As soon as she was satisfied that he'd gone, she hurried into the bedroom and, opening her case, pulled out clean clothes and dressed as quickly as possible.

It was the same kind of neat, off-the-peg silk suit that Ryan had jeered at, but because she rarely went out socially there was little in her wardrobe other than business clothes.

Having made-up lightly, she was about to coil her abundance of ash-brown hair into its usual neat chignon when, recalling what had happened last time, she left it loose.

Ryan was standing by one of the windows in the sunny lounge looking out over the busy street to Kenelm Park. A breakfast trolley was waiting close by.

He turned at her approach and pulled out a chair for her with his customary politeness. When she was seated, he poured orange juice for them both and suggested, 'Bacon and scrambled eggs?'

'No thanks. Just toast and coffee.'

He watched her butter a piece of crisp golden toast before querying, 'So how did Raynor take it? I thought he might object to you selling yourself.'

She bit her lip before saying shortly, 'He did. In fact he was ready to tear up the cheque.'

'I presume you dissuaded him? Otherwise you wouldn't be here. I must say I'm rather relieved that he decided to put his own interests first.'

Hearing the faint hint of contempt in Ryan's voice, she flared. 'It wasn't like that at all. Don't sit there in judgement when you know nothing about it.'

Lifting those broad shoulders in a slight shrug, he asked, 'So how was it?'

'I had to lie through my teeth. I told him I *wanted* to come back to you.'

'And he bought it?'

'Not at first. He was still concerned that I was doing it for him.'

'So how did you manage to convince him otherwise?'

'I told him you had rung me at the gallery—Helen will confirm that—and, because I'd realised that marrying him would be a mistake, I'd agreed to come back to you, before I knew he had any problems.'

'It still sounds a bit thin.'

'In the end I was forced to tell him that I still loved you.'

'And do you?'

'You must be joking!'

His jaw tightened before he said coolly, 'I suppose it doesn't much matter how you feel so long as you're here.'

No, he wouldn't care a jot, she thought bitterly. But the fact that he didn't, still had the power to hurt her.

'Believe me, I wouldn't be here if there'd been any other way, but I couldn't stand by and see Charles totally ruined.'

'You don't think it was his own fault for being too reckless?'

'Charles is never reckless,' she said with certainty.

Ryan scowled, obviously annoyed by the way she was standing up for the other man. 'Well, you must admit that he was taking a serious risk, buying something that couldn't be fully authenticated.

'And, after all, it's unlikely that he's ever seen the genuine painting; and, if he has, he could only have been a child at the time. The painting has been in Otis Jefferson's private collection for the best part of thirty years.'

'Charles knows Roisser's work well, and he was convinced it was genuine. In the same circumstances plenty of men might have been tempted.'

'I wouldn't have thought that many would be so easily led astray.'

'Who are you to judge him? Have your business dealings always been whiter than white?'

She stopped speaking abruptly as a thought struck her. Charles had presumed that it had been *after* he had returned home and told her about *Footprints* being a worthless copy that she had mentioned it to Ryan... She had been right, Ryan must have known all along.

Her voice sharp, she asked, 'How did you find out about

ll this? The whole thing was supposed to be a closely
guarded secret, and you must have known what sort of mess
Charles was going to be in before he did…'

Then, with a growing suspicion, she said, 'No, that isn't
possible, unless—'

'I had second sight?' he suggested.

'But you haven't.'

'No, I haven't,' he agreed.

'So how did you know?' Only three people had been in
on the deal. The seller—and he was hardly likely to have
said anything—Charles himself, and Anderson, the man
who had bought the forgery.

When Ryan hesitated, as if undecided whether or not to
tell her, determined to get an answer, Virginia insisted, 'I
want to know how you knew?'

Looking amused by her vehemence, he raised his hands
in a gesture of surrender. 'Okay, I'll come clean.

'As you're aware, I've been on the lookout for some of
our mother's earlier paintings, and I'd made arrangements
to lunch with a man named Anderson, a collector-cum-
dealer who has found stuff for me in the past.

'Having promised to keep an eye open for what I wanted,
he hinted that if I was interested, so long as the deal was
kept private, *Footprints* might possibly be for sale…

'I was interested, to say the least. You see, I happen to
know the owner of *Footprints* well. Sir Humphrey Post is
not only a friend of mine but he's also Beth's uncle…'

Though Virginia had known Beth was English, she still
felt a shock of surprise, almost disbelief…

But Ryan was going on. 'Sir Humphrey stayed at the
penthouse when he visited New York last year to buy *Footprints*. He said at the time that he'd bought the painting for
his own private collection, and had no intention of ever
parting with it…

'When I mentioned that small point to Anderson, he was
more than a little upset, as he'd paid out for what he now

felt convinced was a forgery... Though he admitted it was
a clever piece of work, and he genuinely believed that
Raynor had been taken in the same as he had...'

Virginia felt a pricking in her thumbs. Though Ryan's
explanation was a perfectly logical one, somehow the
whole thing sounded too pat, too much of a coincidence...

Yet what else could it possibly be?

After a moment, watching her face, Ryan continued casually, 'I presume you didn't see it?'

'No. I knew nothing about it until last night. But, even
if I had, it wouldn't have made any difference. If Charles,
who knows Roisser's work much better than I do, was
fooled, I would have been too.'

'Don't underrate yourself. As well as a good eye, you
have an instinct, a feel for paintings.'

'In this case I doubt if it would have worked. Though
I've always wanted to see *Footprints*, I've only ever seen
a copy.'

'If you'd still like to see the original, I'm quite sure Sir
Humphrey would be happy to show it to you.'

Any other time Virginia would have jumped at the
chance, but in the circumstances... Carefully, she began,
'I'd love to, but—'

'Then I'll ring and make arrangements for us to drop in
at Ferndale Manor on our way to the airport.'

Built of mellow stone, with creeper-clad walls, mullioned
windows, and twisted, barley-sugar chimneys, Ferndale
Manor was a lovely old place.

It had in the past been secluded. But now, besieged by
the present, its surrounding parkland had shrunk to a few
acres, and new estates, both residential and industrial, a
product of the airport, had sprung up around its perimeter.

Added to that, Sir Humphrey explained, after greeting
both Ryan and Virginia warmly, the Manor was too close
to the flight path for comfort.

'Still it makes getting hard of hearing a boon rather than
a handicap.'

He was somewhere in his late seventies, she judged, a
distinguished-looking man of medium height with silver
hair and alert brown eyes.

Remembering Beth, she was struck at once by the family
resemblance.

'I was very much hoping you could stay for lunch,' Sir
Humphrey went on, 'but Ryan tells me you need to be at
the airport before noon, so if you'd like to come this way?'

They crossed the long oak-panelled hall to a modern-
looking door which, when unlocked, opened into a specially built, air-conditioned strongroom.

The walls were thickly lined, and every yard or so there
was a shallow recess in which was hung a carefully lit
painting.

Turning to Virginia, Sir Humphrey said, 'Would you like
to take a quick look at the rest of my collection whilst
you're here, my dear?'

'Please.' It was a chance she couldn't turn down.

The canvases, some by famous painters, others by lesser-
known artists, were first class, she judged, and had been
chosen with care.

'They're all picked from the point of view of personal
liking, rather than as serious investments,' Sir Humphrey
told her.

Then, showing he knew all about her, he asked shrewdly,
'What's your professional opinion?'

'As far as I'm concerned, art should be about enjoyment,
but I imagine that, as serious investments, they're all a
pretty safe bet.'

He nodded, smiling.

'Now for the one you specially wanted to see… Though,
as *Footprints* hasn't yet been rehung, I'm afraid you won't
be seeing it at its best,' he added as he led her to an easel
and removed the cloth covering it.

Looking at the painting, Virginia could immediately see why it was regarded as one of Roisser's masterpieces.

It was both powerful and evocative. Not only was the brushwork brilliant, but the perspective seemed to draw the onlooker into the picture, making them part of it.

A snow scene, it depicted a narrow alleyway between overhanging half-timbered houses, deserted except for a woman clad in ankle-length, voluminous black, holding a small child by the hand. Their different sized footprints, dark against the crisp white layer, followed them along the uneven cobbles.

There was a sombre, almost tragic, feel to it.

In the bottom right-hand corner, black on white, was an elongated R.

'It's wonderful,' she breathed.

Sir Humphrey looked pleased. 'Yes, I've always thought so.'

As, scarcely listening, she continued to gaze at it enthralled, he added, 'It took me years to persuade Jefferson to part with it, and there's not many people who could have talked me into letting it out of my sight...'

Ryan made a sudden movement, breaking the spell. 'It's high time we were on our way, my love. Many thanks, Humphrey.'

When Virginia had added her thanks, the old man accompanied them back to the hall. As they said their goodbyes he took her hand with old-fashioned courtesy before clapping Ryan on the shoulder. 'I'm delighted to hear that congratulations are in order. Don't forget to invite me to the wedding.'

'We won't,' Ryan promised.

Feeling the way Virginia stiffened, he put an arm around her slim waist, and gave her a glinting, sidelong smile. 'We'll let you know the date as soon as we've had a chance to talk it over, won't we darling?'

So he was planning to carry on as if nothing had happened... Well she wouldn't be a party to it...

Sunshine glancing from its polished paintwork, the limousine was waiting on the apron with Maxwell at the wheel.

As soon as Ryan had helped Virginia in and had taken his place by her side, its tyres scrunching on the gravel, the sleek car pulled away.

Standing by the iron-studded oak door, shading his eyes with one hand and smiling genially, Sir Humphrey waved them off.

As they turned down the tree-lined drive, seeing that the glass panel between them and the chauffeur was open, Virginia bit her lip and said nothing, unwilling to go into battle with someone else listening.

Ryan's ironic glance told her he knew perfectly well what was on her mind, but was content to make her bide her time.

The drive to the airport, a comparatively short one, was made in silence. On arrival, Maxwell unloaded their small amount of luggage, and was thanked and tipped handsomely before they went through to a special sector.

As soon as the formalities had been completed, they were welcomed aboard the company jet.

Though full of inner agitation, Virginia had gone through the motions like someone trapped in a bad dream, who made no effort to escape because they knew there was no escape.

When Ryan had seen her settled in the plane's lounge and sipping a glass of fruit juice, he excused himself to go and have a word with the pilot.

After a short wait on the runway the plane took off, and had been airborne for some five minutes before he returned.

As soon as he got back there was a knock, and a white-coated steward wheeled in a luncheon trolley.

The meal was over and the trolley whisked away before

they were left alone and Virginia was able to give vent to her simmering anger.

As the door between the lounge and the galley slid into place, she rounded on Ryan, demanding, 'Why did you tell Sir Humphrey we were going to be married?'

'Did you want to keep it a secret?'

Gritting her teeth, she informed him, 'I've no intention of marrying you.'

'Backing out on the deal already?'

'You didn't say anything about us being married.'

'Surely you didn't think I was planning on just a short-term affair? No, I want what I've always wanted, marriage and on a permanent basis.'

At the back of her mind had been the thought that if things became unbearable she could always run again. But if he was intent on a relationship she had always regarded as binding...

Watching her lose colour, he added sardonically, 'When I pay out that amount of money I expect a great deal in return... Not that merely having you in bed won't be worth every penny... But I happen to want a wife and family.'

A family... How could she agree to have Ryan's children when she knew he didn't love her?

Suddenly, despairingly, she said, 'I don't think I can bear it.'

His face changed. 'Surely it can't be that bad? Once you were happy to marry me.'

'That was when I thought—' she bit off the words, you loved me, and substituted '—you meant it to be a proper marriage.'

'Is there such a thing as an improper marriage?'

Unable to bear his levity, she covered her face with her hands. 'I don't want to marry you. It's bad enough having to go back to New York to face a family who hate me, and a woman who'll enjoy seeing me humiliated...'

He took her wrists and pulled her hands away from her

face, holding them in both of his. 'The family doesn't hate you. I'm sure you'll find that they're only too pleased to have you back...

'And as for Madeline, she's gone for good. Steven divorced her after she ran away with some second-rate film producer... He's been a different man since, so much happier...'

Just for a moment Virginia's spirits lifted, before common sense pointed out that, even if Madeline was no longer on the scene, it would make little difference to her relationship with Ryan.

Too much harm had already been done. If the family didn't hate her, *he* did.

Perhaps, as well as everything else, he blamed her for Madeline's departure, which might not have happened if she hadn't disrupted their plans.

Plans that still aroused a resentment so bitter that she wanted to strike out.

Tearing her hands free, she cried, 'Whether Madeline's here or not, I still couldn't bear to marry you. I don't want to be tied to a man who's capable of cuckolding his own stepbrother—'

Ryan's expression hardened. 'When we get back home I shall expect you to keep accusations like that to yourself, especially in front of Beth.'

Though quietly spoken, it was undoubtedly an order. Before she could attempt to challenge it, he added, 'I refuse to have her upset a second time.'

If only Ryan had cared for her the way he cared for Beth, and Madeline had never existed...

Suddenly feeling unutterably weary and defeated, Virginia sighed.

Picking up on that weariness, he asked in a more gentle tone, 'Tired?'

'A little,' she admitted.

'You didn't get much sleep last night.'

All her nights had been disturbed ones since Ryan had come back into her life, and the lack of proper rest was starting to tell.

'What about a siesta?' he suggested. 'A few hours sleep now will help enormously with the time difference.'

At the rear of the plane there was a bedroom with a luxurious double bed, and her pulse rate quickened as she wondered if he meant he was going too.

Apparently reading her thoughts, he said drily, 'I do mean *sleep*. I have some business to attend to.'

Flushing a little, she rose to her feet, telling herself how relieved she was. But in spite of everything the relief felt more like disappointment.

CHAPTER TEN

INDIGO eyes gleaming, he said, 'You look disappointed. If you are, I'm open to persuasion. Business can wait.'

Wondering how he could walk in and out of her mind as if it were his own penthouse, she said hardily, 'I'm not disappointed.'

'My sweet little liar.' Stepping closer, he rubbed the ball of his thumb across her lips, feeling them quiver beneath that light touch. 'You may not want to marry me, but you do want me...'

It was less than the truth. Despite her disillusionment, despite all her worries about what the future held, she longed for him, yearned for him, ached for him. And it was much more than merely physical. Her whole being was involved.

'And we've a lot of catching up to do.' His lips taking the place of his thumb, he kissed her. A thistledown caress that left her weak-kneed and trembling.

Sliding his hand inside her silk jacket so that it lay just over her heart, he said softly, 'And you can't hide it... I can feel your heart starting to race and your breathing getting faster, and if I touch you here...'

Reacting to his teasing caress, her nipple grew firm.

'Mmm...' he murmured, and began to undo the buttons of her blouse.

'Don't.' She pushed his hand away. 'Someone might come in.'

'Not without knocking. But if the thought bothers you, we could always go to bed.'

Well aware that he was as aroused as she was, Virginia was waiting for him to take her hand and lead her to the bedroom, when he said, 'Or perhaps you'd prefer to go alone, so you can sleep?'

Knowing that he had purposely left the ball in her court and unwilling to let him have the satisfaction of crowing, her voice as dismissive as she could make it, she said, 'Yes, I would.'

'Then, so you shall.'

She should have been warned by his steely smooth tone. Instead, believing she'd won, she turned and headed for the bedroom.

'But first, so you'll be able to sleep...'

He had followed her noiselessly and, before she could begin to guess what he intended, he'd spun her round and backed her up against the dividing wall.

Leaning his body weight forward, so she was pressed against the smoothness of the bulkhead, he used one hand to free her breast from the confines of her bra, while the other slid up her nylon-clad thigh, past the lacy top of her stocking to the edge of her dainty briefs.

'Please,' she begged.

His answer to her plea was a wolfish smile, and a moment later his mouth was at her breast and his long fingers were wreaking havoc. He wasn't satisfied until he'd turned her into a shuddering mass of sensations.

When he finally released her and moved back, eyes still closed, she staggered, and he was forced to steady her.

A hand beneath her elbow, he steered her through the bulkhead door and into the bedroom.

Pulling the blind down over the window, he said, 'Get a good sleep so you'll be nice and fresh when we reach New York.'

His voice was condescending, the mockery blatant.

She adjusted her bra and pulled her gaping blouse together before charging thickly, 'You're a swine.'

He pretended to look hurt. 'I didn't expect to be reviled.

In fact, as I've eased your frustration at the expense of my own, I thought you might want to thank me.'

Knowing perfectly well that Ryan's usual approach was a great deal more subtle and sensitive, and it had been done simply to prove a point, she said furiously, 'Go to hell! You only meant to punish and degrade me. You're cruel and sadistic...'

His mouth tightened as though he were in pain. 'If I am, it's what you've made me—'

A knock cut through his words.

Blocking the bedroom door, Ryan called, 'Yes, what is it?'

A man's voice queried, 'Can you spare just a moment, Mr Falconer?'

'I'll be right there.'

Turning to Virginia, he took her shoulders and stood looking down at her, a strange, bleak expression on his face. Then bending his dark head he gave her a brief but punitive kiss.

A second later he was gone.

Sinking down on the bed she stared blindly after him until, reaction setting in, she began to tremble violently.

What had he meant by, 'If I am it's what you've made me...?' He'd looked so bitter, so wretched, angry with both himself and her...

After a minute or two, making an effort to control her shaking limbs, she took off her suit and blouse and crawled beneath the duvet.

She fell asleep almost as soon as her head touched the pillow, and she only awakened when the plane began its descent and Ryan knocked with a refreshing cup of tea.

If he had seemed himself she might have tried to talk to him, but he looked aloof and unapproachable, and left with just the curt warning. 'We'll be landing in about fifteen minutes.'

When they reached JFK, as though fate was having a

cruel little joke at her expense, the same car and the same
chauffeur as last time were waiting.

She found that New York was hot and sunny and heartbreakingly familiar as they repeated the drive into the city.
The only difference was that this time it was made in silence as Ryan, his dark face sombre, a devil riding on his
shoulder, stared into space.

Remembering the joy of her first visit, and contrasting it
with her feelings now, by the time the car stopped outside
Falconer's Tower, Virginia was a mass of nerves.

With the kind of irony she might have expected, they
were even greeted by the same security man, who beamed
at them, and said, 'Afternoon Mr Falconer. Nice to see you
back, Miss Adams.'

'Thank you, George.' She managed to return his smile.

Ryan led the way to the elevator, and they rode up in
silence, standing apart and avoiding contact, like two wary
strangers.

When they reached the top foyer, to Virginia's surprise,
Ryan opened the door of what had once been her apartment, and ushered her inside.

'I presume that until we get things sorted out you would
prefer to be here rather than the penthouse?'

'Y-yes, thank you,' she stammered.

Sunny and spacious, it was just as she remembered it,
and brought a swift rush of memories that threatened to
engulf her.

Dropping the key into her palm, he said coolly, 'Beth
asked if you would pop down and see her as soon as you're
settled?'

Virginia swallowed hard. 'Of course.'

Sounding a little more human, he told her, 'There's no
need to look so worried. You won't have to face them all.
Janice is in Washington for the weekend, and Steven is on
holiday with his new girlfriend, so Beth is on her own.'

Needing to get it over, Virginia said, 'I'll go down

straight away. There's only one thing… What am I going to tell her?'

He raised a dark brow. 'About what?'

'She's bound to ask why I left so suddenly.'

'And you hesitate to damn me in her eyes?' Then, caustically, he added, 'I'm surprised you care.'

'If I hadn't cared about tearing the family apart, I would have told her *then* exactly what Madeline had told me,' Virginia said quietly.

'It's a great pity you didn't. The whole thing was a tissue of lies, and Beth would have known it.'

As Virginia stared at him, shaken by the unmistakable ring of truth in his voice, he said, 'When you do go down I'd like you to wear this…'

He felt in his pocket and produced a ring, which he slipped onto her engagement finger.

'I had intended to give it to you earlier, but…' With a slight shrug he allowed the words to tail off.

Like someone in a dream she found herself gazing down at the sardonyx. So he had kept it all this time…

As he turned away, tears threatening, she begged, 'Please, Ryan… Won't you come with me?'

'I think this is something you should do alone. Woman to woman, so to speak.'

'But I don't know what to say to her… What to tell her… Suppose she asks *why* I came back to you?'

His chiselled mouth twisted in the semblance of a smile. 'Try the truth. In many ways Beth's a lot tougher than she appears.'

Watching him walk away, and knowing he was going to give her no further help, she hesitated. Then, annoyed by her own cowardice, she squared her shoulders and made her way downstairs.

Beth answered the door and, after one glance at her visitor's face, held out her arms.

Being enfolded in a warm hug of welcome, broke the tension and allowed Virginia's tears to brim over.

After a moment she drew back and, fumbling in her pocket, produced a tissue and blew her nose. 'I'm sorry.'

Her brown eyes suspiciously bright, Beth said, 'You've no need to be sorry for anything.'

Then briskly, she said, 'Now there's someone waiting to see you…' Leading the way to the living-room, she opened the door, adding, 'And so you can speak quite frankly, I'm going to wait in the kitchen.'

Madeline, who had been sitting on the couch, rose to her feet. Beautifully dressed, her blonde hair expertly styled, she looked her usual glamorous self.

Reading Virginia's shocked expression correctly, she said, 'No, this wasn't my idea.'

Then, with more than a touch of venom, she said, 'I need to be on set first thing tomorrow morning, but my ex-mother-in-law insisted on me coming all the way over here.'

All at once icy cool and composed, Virginia said, 'She must have a reason.'

'Oh, she has. She wants me to tell you the truth about what happened between Ryan and myself…'

'I already know,' Virginia told her calmly. 'You had an affair. An affair that ended *before* you married Steven. But because you were jealous, and didn't want Ryan to marry me, you told me a pack of lies.'

'Which you were fool enough to believe.' Madeline's voice held swingeing contempt. 'If it had been *me* Ryan was going to marry, I wouldn't have given up so easily. But then, I *wanted* him. Which you obviously didn't, or you would have fought for him. It's a great pity he's so obsessed with you. You don't deserve him.'

Turning on her heel, she headed for the door. When she reached it, she said over her shoulder, 'If that interfering old bat was expecting me to kowtow and say how sorry I am, she'll be disappointed.'

A second later the door slammed shut behind her.

When she had had a moment to gather herself, Virginia made her way through to the kitchen on legs that weren't quite steady.

Beth looked up from pouring tea. 'I thought I heard her go.' Then, anxiously, she added, 'You look a bit pale. Are you all right?'

'Fine,' Virginia said, with more determination than accuracy. Sitting down at the table, she accepted a cup of tea, and sipped gratefully.

'Perhaps I shouldn't have sprung it on you like that,' Beth admitted. 'But there was so little time and, as she was the one who had caused all the trouble in the first place, I thought it was best if you heard the truth from *her*.'

'How did you persuade her to come…? It was you?'

'Yes, Ryan knows nothing about it… He might be very angry when he finds out. But I felt I must do something. In many ways, he's my favourite son, and he's been so dreadfully unhappy…'

Her eyes filled with tears. Blinking them away, she went on doggedly, 'And "persuade" is hardly the right word. *Coerce* is closer to the truth.'

Smiling now at Virginia's expression, she went on, 'I'd better tell you the whole story. Some time ago I found out, quite by chance, that Madeline was having an affair with a man named Christian Gent, a Hollywood film producer.

'He'd come to New York to try to get backing for his latest film, *Persephone*, but after his last two had been complete flops he was finding it practically impossible.

'It was when I discovered he'd promised Madeline the starring role, which she was dead keen to have, that I decided to take a hand. She'd been making Steven so miserable that I couldn't bear it any longer. I offered to put up a large sum of money in secret if she would consent to leave New York for good and let Steven divorce her.

'As well as giving her the part, apparently Gent wanted to marry her, so she was only too happy to agree. I hope and believe it's been for the best.'

'I'm sure it has,' Virginia reassured her. 'Ryan said how much happier Steven has been since Madeline left.'

Beth smiled her relief. 'I must admit I haven't dared tell either of them. Though I may have to if *Persephone* proves to be a great success and the money starts rolling in…

'Judging by Christian Gent's past record, it's hardly likely, but if I lose every penny I've put into it, it will still have been well worth it.'

After a moment, harking back, Virginia said, 'You were going to tell me how you coerced Madeline into coming here?'

The older woman gave an impish grin. 'Simple. To make sure she toed the line, I'd arranged to have the money paid over in four installments, so all I had to do was threaten to withhold the final one if she didn't do as I asked.'

Virginia was impressed by the martial spirit of a woman she had regarded as too meek and gentle for her own good.

Hesitantly, she began, 'There's one thing I'd like to ask you… How did you know Madeline had caused all the trouble?'

'I didn't know for sure until a couple of days ago when Ryan came home saying he needed to talk to me. He told me everything he'd learnt, and I admitted that, like him, I'd always suspected Madeline of being at the bottom of it.

'He was *livid*. It's just as well she wasn't still here or I don't know what might have happened.'

She sighed. 'I only wish you'd talked to me at the time instead of just running…'

'I wish I had,' Virginia said in a heartfelt voice, 'but I was afraid to in case—' She broke off.

'In case I believed all that rubbish? Oh, my dear, I know

Ryan too well to credit for one instant that he would have
played around with Steven's wife…'

Virginia drew a deep, gasping breath of pain. Beth's absolute certainty was like a dagger through the heart. If only
she had had that kind of faith…

'Apart from anything else,' Beth went on, 'he absolutely
adored you, and I've always known that when Ryan fell in
love he would be a one-woman man.'

On the rack, Virginia whispered, 'None of this would
have happened if I'd trusted him.'

'Perhaps, as events moved so quickly, you didn't know
him well enough. But now…well, you have a lifetime
ahead of you…'

Seeing Virginia's tortured expression, Beth asked with
sudden anxiety, 'It is all right, isn't it? You're wearing his
ring again, and you do still love him, don't you?'

'Yes, I still love him. Even when I believed the worst, I
never stopped loving him.'

'Then, try telling him so.'

'It's too late. He doesn't love me any longer. All he
wants is revenge. He hates me for leaving him the way I
did.'

Beth shook her head. 'Though he was hurt and bitterly
disappointed that you hadn't trusted him, I'm quite certain
he still loves you.

'Off you go now and talk to him. Don't mention that
Madeline was here unless you're forced.'

'I won't,' Virginia promised.

The two women hugged each other briefly.

Virginia had been having a struggle to hold back the
flood of emotion that threatened to engulf her, and before
she reached the stairs she was weeping.

Knowing she couldn't face Ryan until she had herself
under control, she headed for her own door and, blinded
by tears, stumbled inside.

If only she hadn't allowed Madeline to do such mischief...

But what was the use of blaming Madeline? It was her own doing. *She* was the one who, through lack of trust, had caused both Ryan and herself so much pain.

As Beth had said, she hadn't really *known* him, and remembering how, when she'd called him cruel and sadistic, he'd said, 'If I am, it's what you've made me...' she felt as though she were bleeding to death.

Giving way to the anguish that filled her, she sank onto the living-room couch and began to sob, deep wrenching sobs that hurt her throat and took more breath than she'd got.

'For goodness' sake, don't cry like that,' Ryan said harshly.

Startled, she lifted a ravaged face to see him standing in the doorway.

'The door wasn't properly closed, so I walked in. I'll go if you want me to.'

It was too late. She shook her head.

He frowned. 'Surely Beth hasn't...?'

'No, Beth's been wonderful...' But as though the flood gates had opened, the tears were still flowing, pouring down her cheeks in tracks of shiny wetness, the sobs still rising in her throat.

With a sound almost like a groan he moved to the couch and, sitting down by her side, took her in his arms. Cradling her head to his chest, his mouth muffled against her silky hair, he rocked her a little, as though she was a child.

'I'm sorry for the way I've treated you...I've behaved like a swine...'

Full of guilt as she was, his apology only made her cry harder.

Murmuring inarticulate words of comfort, and still cuddling her closely, he let her cry herself out.

When the sobs finally gave way to sniffs and hiccups

he took a handkerchief from his pocket and, holding her away a little, dried her face.

Taking the handkerchief from him, she blew her nose and said with a kind of pathetic dignity, 'I'm sorry. I shouldn't have given way like that. I must look an awful mess.'

Glancing at her pink nose and swollen eyes, her blotched cheeks, he shook his head. 'You look beautiful.'

She made a sound, a cross between a laugh and a sob, and one last tear rolled down her cheek.

He caught it with his thumb and put it in his mouth. 'Don't cry any more. It'll be all right. I promise.'

'Will it?' she asked thickly.

'I shouldn't have tried to make you come back to me when you so obviously hated the idea. You can go home as soon as you like.'

It was the last thing she had expected to hear. Blankly, she said, 'I don't understand.'

He repeated his words.

'What about Charles?'

'Don't worry, I've no intention of demanding my money back.'

'No, we made a deal.'

Sighing, he admitted, 'It wasn't fair.'

'It was more than fair, generous even, and I agreed to it.'

'Being the kind of woman you are, you had little option. But, when I say it wasn't fair, I mean exactly that. What I told you previously was a complete fabrication. I engineered the whole thing.'

As she stared at him open-mouthed, he explained, '"Mr Smith," who turned out to be quite a good actor, was working for me—'

'*You* sold Charles the forgery?'

'No, I sold him the real thing.'

All at once, she recalled Sir Humphrey saying, '*Foot-*

prints hasn't yet been rehung.' Then, though it had scarcely registered at the time, 'There's not many people who could have talked me into letting it out of my sight...'

'You borrowed it from Sir Humphrey!'

'Not exactly. Beth did. And before you condemn her, she did it in the desperate hope that it would bring the two of us together, and everything would be all right.'

But everything wasn't all right...

Pushing away that thought, Virginia said jerkily, 'I don't see how you managed it.'

'"Anderson" was also working for me. Posing as a collector who wasn't over-scrupulous, he had previously contacted Raynor and made his interest in Roisser's works known.

'As soon as Raynor was hooked, confident that he had a buyer, he got in touch with New Finance—one of my financial associates—who had recently offered him a short-term loan on favourable terms. I immediately gave them a cheque to cover that loan.

'Once Anderson had "bought" the painting and Raynor had his money back, plus a handsome profit, if you'd shown any sign of coming back to me, I would have left it at that. But when you were so adamant that you were going to marry him, I was forced to go on.

'The minute Anderson cried forgery, Raynor panicked. As I'd expected, he checked with Jefferson as well as Sir Humphrey.

'After Sir Humphrey had assured him that *he* owned *Footprints* and invited him to go and see the painting, the one thing Raynor failed to do was try to reclaim what he now regarded as a worthless copy.

'By the time he reached Ferndale Manor, the authenticated painting was there for him to see...'

She shivered. Ryan must have wanted revenge very badly to have gone to so much trouble.

Curiously, she asked, 'What would you have done if I'd refused to play ball?'

'I would have told Raynor the truth. But, being the kind of woman you are, I thought it was a pretty safe bet.'

Bleakly, she said, 'All that, just to force me to come back to you.'

'*Force* is the operative word. I should have had the sense to see that it wouldn't work.'

He sighed deeply. 'But I can't bear to see you this unhappy. As soon as you feel ready to travel I'll take you back to London.'

If it had been just revenge he'd wanted, he wouldn't have cared how unhappy she was.

Remembering Beth's certainty that he still loved her, Virginia gathered her courage and said, 'I don't want to go back to London.'

'Well, if you prefer to stay in New York I'll buy you an apartment and—'

'I've got an apartment... Though I'd much prefer to live in a penthouse.'

'You don't have to stay with me just because we made a bargain—'

'I don't *have* to stay with you,' she agreed, 'I happen to *want* to.'

He shook his head. 'I can't bear to see you so utterly wretched...'

'I was only wretched because I'd made such a mess of things.' Then in growing desperation, she said, 'Please, Ryan, I love you. I've never stopped loving you, and I do want to marry you.'

'I've done a lot of thinking in the past few hours, and it wouldn't work. Marriage should be built on *trust* as well as love.'

She bit her lip until she tasted blood. 'Not trusting you is something I bitterly regret... Perhaps, as Beth says, I didn't know you well enough. But what Madeline told me sounded so plausible… And she was so beautiful…'

'She was a first-class bitch,' he said shortly. 'Unfortunately it took me a while to realise it. I knew from the first that she was a gold-digger but as you say, she was beautiful, and I could afford her.

'The trouble started when I quickly grew tired of her and wanted to pay her off. It seems she'd set her sights on marriage, and when I made it plain that I had no intention of marrying her, determined to get a rich husband, she transferred her attention to Steven.

'I tried to warn the poor devil, but he was completely infatuated, and dead set on marrying her. When I persisted, he thought it was just jealousy on my part. Though none of us liked it, for the sake of family harmony, we did our best to accept the situation.

'But hell hath no fury, and all that, and when Madeline saw a chance to get back at me, she took it.' Grimly, he added, 'It's just as well I didn't know at the time or I might have been tempted to throttle her…'

'But Madeline wasn't solely to blame,' Virginia said sadly. 'It was as much my fault for believing her.'

'Why did you?'

She tried to explain. 'Perhaps it wasn't so much lack of trust in you, as lack of faith in myself. No one had ever loved me…'

His hard face softened.

'And right from the start I couldn't imagine why you were bothering with someone as ordinary as me. It didn't make sense that you would go to so much trouble simply to find an assistant curator, and I was half convinced that your interest had something to do with my parents. Even when you proposed, I could hardly credit that you, who could have anyone, would want to marry me…

'And though I'd fallen in love with you at first sight, I

found it almost impossible to believe you had fallen in love with me. It all seemed too sudden…'

'Whereas it wasn't sudden at all. I loved you before we even met.'

Wide eyes on his face, she said, 'But that's not possible.'

'Let me show you something.'

Taking her hand he led her out of the apartment, across the foyer, and into the penthouse.

Hanging in the living-room was a painting she had never seen before.

It was a fairly small oil-on-canvas portrait of a girl with long ash-brown hair curling onto her shoulders. She was sitting on a wooden stool looking through a rain-misted window, drops running down the glass like tears.

Her thin body, clad in a simple pink cotton shift, had a dejected droop, and her lovely face, seen in profile, was melancholy. There was a sense of rejection, of sadness, of inner loneliness.

Yet coupled with that was a feeling of expectancy, as if at any moment a loved one might appear and that wistful young face would smile, the body become eager and welcoming.

As Virginia stared at it speechlessly, Ryan said, 'I first saw *Wednesday's Child* about three years ago when I was putting on an exhibition of your mother's work at the gallery.

'She gave me permission to go into her studio and look through some of her paintings that had never previously been exhibited.

'*Wednesday's Child* had been wrapped in hessian and left behind a stack of old canvases, and I came across it by accident.

'From the word go I was bewitched, enchanted. I couldn't take my eyes off it. If it's possible to fall in love with a picture, then that's what I did.

'I imagined myself as being the one that young girl was

waiting for, the one who would replace her sense of rejection and sadness with warmth and happiness.

'It took a lot of subtle pressure before your mother finally, and with the greatest reluctance, admitted who the girl was.

'When I asked if I could buy the painting, she replied that it wasn't for sale, and she flatly refused to have it exhibited.

'It's my belief that she hadn't been able to destroy something she knew was good, but she'd kept *Wednesday's Child* hidden away because it was too revealing. It showed too clearly how she'd failed as a mother, and maybe she felt ashamed.

'It was several weeks before I could get her to talk about you, but when I finally learnt where you were and what you were doing I couldn't rest until I'd seen for myself what you were really like.

'You were even more beautiful than your portrait, and it was instant enchantment all over again...'

She lifted a glowing face. 'Then, you really *did* fall in love with me?'

'Madly.'

'Beth thinks you still love me.'

'Does she?' he asked drily. 'What do you think?'

Her confidence suddenly shaken, she said, 'I don't know.'

He sighed. 'Tell me what I need to say or do to finally convince you?'

She moved closer and put her hands, flat-palmed, against his chest. 'Say, stay with me... Say, marry me... Then take me to bed.'

'Are you sure that's what you want?'

'I'm sure.'

Taking her hands, he raised them to his lips. 'Stay with me... Marry me... Never leave me again.'

'I won't,' she promised.

Sweeping her into his arms he carried her through to the bedroom.

Their lovemaking was fervent and rapturous, with the added dimension of love not only felt, but declared.

When their hunger for each other was temporarily appeased, and they lay closely entwined, Virginia asked, 'How come you've got *Wednesday's Child*? You said Mother wouldn't part with it.'

'After you ran away, I went to see your parents hoping they might have some idea where you were, but though they were sympathetic, they couldn't help.

'Two days later, *Wednesday's Child* turned up at the penthouse. A gift from your mother.

'So you already had it when you asked Charles if he could get it... In other words, you only mentioned it to rattle me...'

Kissing her ear, he asked, 'Did I succeed?'

'Yes.' She shivered. 'You frightened me half to death with all that talk of revenge.'

'And that's just what it was, talk. I wanted you back, but my pride wouldn't allow me to plead.

'I thought once we were together again and things had settled down I'd tell you the truth. Tell you how much I loved you.'

'Go ahead,' she invited.

He traced her cheek with his finger. 'I've already told you.'

Nestling closer, she said wistfully, 'I wouldn't mind hearing it again.'

'I love you more than words can say and, if you can stand it, I'll tell you so every day for the rest of our lives.'

'Try me.'

His indigo eyes adoring, he laughed, and kissed her. 'I might just do that.'

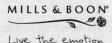

researching the cure

The facts you need to know:

- Breast cancer is the commonest form of cancer in the United Kingdom. **One woman in nine** will develop the disease during her lifetime.

- Each year around **41,000** women and approximately **300** men are diagnosed with breast cancer and around **13,000** women and **90** men will die from the disease.

- 80% of all breast cancers occur in post-menopausal women and approximately 8,200 pre-menopausal women are diagnosed with the disease each year.

- However, survival rates are improving, with on average 77.5% of women diagnosed between 1996 and 1999 still alive five years later, compared to 72.8% for women diagnosed between 1991 and 1996.

Breast Cancer Campaign is the only charity that specialises in funding independent breast cancer research throughout the UK. It aims to find the cure for breast cancer by funding research which looks at improving diagnosis and treatment of breast cancer, better understanding how it develops and ultimately either curing the disease or preventing it.

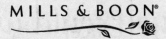

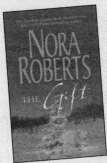

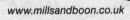